NO MAN'S HEART

JAMIEL JONES

NO MAN'S HEART

Paperback ISBN: 978-1-7330043-5-0
Hardcover ISBN: 978-1-7330043-6-7
E-Book ISBN: 978-1-7330043-4-3

For my characters.

I am you.

You are me.

Thank you for helping me all this time.

CHAPTER I

MIA

Flames gnaw at the edge of my vision, and already I know where I am. Kirk is a cruel man, but this is something I've known ever since I was old enough to understand what true cruelty was. He's said before that his job was never to love me, but to show me how to survive the shit this war-torn world would throw at me. Sometimes I hate him, but as my consciousness syncs with my past and I become the weak seven-year-old girl scrambling through burning streets and crumbling buildings, crying, that sting in my heart bores deeper for those who make Kirk seem like a saint.

Ashes rain from a black sky illuminated by pillars of flames that climb upward. I skid around a corner and flatten myself against a wall, covering my mouth to avoid inhaling more smoke. My lungs burn, but if I cough, he'll find me. And if he finds me, I'm dead again. The screech of metal on concrete makes my innards curl and fear crawls up my spine.

He's not real, Mia, I remind myself.

This is an illusion created by the simulation pod based on my memories. I'm inside pod four-three-one. The same pod I've used for the past ten years, training to kill the Runesians and Savages. This is just a memory, a past trauma I must conquer here and now. I pick up a rock, clenching it in my palm as a Savage, dressed in rags, appears around the corner.

He cackles and raises his serrated blade into the air. "Found you!"

I launch the rock at the Savage's head, dash forward, and pluck the knife from his side. He tries to grab me, but I duck and jam the knife into his stomach. Blood flies, and I veer away, fearing I'll die from disease.

Savage blood is fatal.

But the Savage cinches my wrist, his stomach rumbling with laughter. The knife clatters to the ground, and I see what little damage I've done. Barely a flesh wound. I try to kick him in the groin, but he backhands me, and the taste of iron bursts on my tongue. Why can't I win?

The Savage stomps me, and the sounds of this past world fade with my conviction. Why do I lose to the scum of the earth? Why can't I get my revenge?

He takes hold of my hair, just as I remember, and drags me, kicking and screaming, down the street.

¢

The pod door hisses open, the world around nothing but mush and muted grays. A smug, oak-colored face hangs over me, the faint scent of cinnamon wafting into my nostrils.

Kirk.

"Failure ninety-seven," he says.

I sit up, avoiding his mud-brown eyes that hide behind wire-framed glasses. Kirk snaps his fingers in my face. "What day is it?"

"May 4, 2145."

"Where are you?"

"Compound Marigold."

"Your name?"

"It's Mia. Listen, I'm good." My vision returns to normal, and I swing a leg out of the pod, swaying from dizziness. Kirk moves closer, hands out, and I shove him away. "I'm fine!"

"Doesn't look like it."

"This test is bullshit."

"A soldier knows how to conquer their mind and release their emotions to get the job done. You don't."

"Why does something that happened ten years ago dictate whether or not I can join the RFF? I can shoot just as good as the soldiers here. Run just as fast. I know the battle drills. Come on, Kirk. Please. I'm ready."

He sighs and lies back in the pod next to mine. "We've had this conversation before. You're not ready until I say you are."

The pod door lowers itself, and soon, metal and glass separate me from Kirk. I let the vertigo wash away, then charge out of the room.

Sweat pours off me as I drag myself up the hill toward my apartment building. The heat presses through the bundles of gray clouds looming over Compound Marigold. It would be unbearable if it weren't for the internal temperature mod I have inside of my body, and the barrier, a faint blue film of energy that stretches over and around the Compound. The barrier is supposed to keep most of the heat out, but there must be a leak. I inspect the layer of energy above as I make it to the summit, getting the full view of my prison for the last ten years.

Behind me, the Republic for Freedom's barracks, a wide, fourteen-story, concrete building bases itself at the bottom. The RFF's flag, all blue with four white stars in each corner and one in the middle, flies from the top of each building. The dark walls of Compound Marigold hang in the back, locking us in and keeping everything else out. Near the barracks is what's left of whatever crap, old world town was here before Anomaly Day.

Antique brick and wooden buildings sit squashed together along a few pale, cracked asphalt streets. Streetlights hang from electrical wires, not blinking red, green, or yellow in the past one hundred years. I can imagine what life used to be like.

In this used-to-be small town, vehicles used to stop at the red lights, and a family in a pickup truck would wind down their windows and wave at some middle-aged couple strolling down the street holding hands. Everyone would be smiling because the air was fresh and not laden with the smell of smoke and gunpowder and death. And the people didn't cower inside when it became too hot because the sun's rays didn't scorch their skin. Customers used to flow in and out of the shops below, picking up bouquets, a pie, or coming out with a fresh hairstyle.

I often wonder what happened to those people. Did they die in 2045 like most? Or did they survive and side with the RFF? Maybe they became Savage? Perhaps they fled west and were captured by the Runesians and forced into slavery?

"Mia!" A familiar voice breaks me out of my trance, and I turn.

Barry, a scarecrow of a man who seems to always wear the same overalls and straw-hat, strolls up the hill from our cluster of dark, multi-story apartment buildings, tipping his hat toward me and raising a palm. I meet him up top.

"Hot afternoon, ain't it?" he asks.

"Yeah. What's up with the barrier?"

Barry shrugs and wipes sweat from his dark face with a cloth. "Nothin'. World's still dyin' is all. 'Nother Anomaly Day comin' for us. Where's the old man?"

"Still at the Academy."

"Hard workin' man." Barry sticks a piece of straw from his pocket into his mouth. "Be easy on him, now."

"He makes that almost impossible."

Barry ruffles through my hair as he steps past, waving. "Well, I got some eggs to collect. It's one hunnid and twelve degrees right now, so go head and get out dis heat. Stay cool."

"I'll try." I watch Barry get farther down the hill. When I came to Marigold ten years ago, one of the first things he said to me was about his conspiracy that a second Anomaly Day would be coming. I study the darkening sky above the barrier.

If another Anomaly Day comes like it did one hundred years ago, no one will survive this time.

I take off my shoes and set them near the door of our apartment. It's spotless as Kirk and I left it. We clean every morning. The wooden floors of the common area are swept, and the counters in the kitchen are glossy. The puke-green couch against the wall that Kirk refuses to get rid of vacuumed, and the cushions fluffed. Between the common area and kitchen, a circular wooden table sits with three chairs around it, although one of them has remained empty for the past five years since my older brother, Leon, left. I stare at that chair a bit longer, then head into my room and lean against the door, pulling at my hair. Failure ninety-seven.

"Come on, Mia. What are you doing?" I enter my bathroom, peel the sweaty clothes away from my body, and start the shower.

I tap the mirror over the sink, and a still video of Leon appears. He's in a concrete room, sitting on a crate. A five o'clock shadow wraps around his dark face as he grips the barrel of a rifle that rests against his thigh. The date at the top right corner of the glass reads: June 4, 2143.

Two years ago. The day after Leon told me we might not talk for a while.

Leon scratches his ear, something he does when he's nervous or upset. Every time I repurpose this video of him, I can't help but notice how much darker his eyes have become. When we were children, his pupils were vibrant, like spring before Anomaly Day, blooming with fresh greens out of fertile browns. I want to ask what this war has done to him, but Leon made this video to help me. I slide my hand over the glass, and Leon moves, peering into the camera, smiling. I know it's a fake smile.

"What's going on, brat?" he asks.

I grip the edge of the sink. "I failed. Again. Kirk knows I'm fit enough to be a soldier, but he keeps giving me that stupid test. I just think he's—"

"It's Kirk, isn't it?"

"Yes. Your grandfather's an asshole. I think he wants me to stay trapped here with him forever."

"You know." Leon stands, stretches, and flexes his lean muscles. "Kirk's always going to be an asshole. That won't ever change. Whatever it is he's being stubborn about, show him he's wrong."

"Leon… you've been gone for so long, so you don't know what it's like now. I hope you're still alive. I hope—"

He pokes the camera. "Hey, hey, hey, are you listening to me? Stop crying. I'm not there to help you, so you must help yourself. You can do it. I believe in you." Leon's silent for a moment, and then he pushes his face closer to the camera. "You're the strongest, smartest, most badass little sister

I could ask for. I'm so glad you came into my life, and I know we'll see each other again soon. I gotta go. Me and Liz have a mission. I love you. Bye."

I sigh. That video never lasts long enough. I tap the mirror, and the screen changes to one of the few memories I have of my parents. It's a picture of me when I was around five years old, in between my smiling mother and father. I'm giggling as my father tickles me, my honey-colored pupils, light skin and long, dark hair making me my mother's child. She and I are twins, but I have my father's slim, athletic frame.

I wish I could compare myself to them now, but the Runesians took them away from me. My lips flatline, and I swipe the glass again.

Lucia, Kirk's wife, beams at me. Her eyes and skin remind me of melted caramel. Her wavy hair could be a rapid, churning, white waterfall. I only knew her for a brief time, but she was a light in my world of darkness. The Sickness took her away as it has done millions of others since Anomaly Day.

Lucia's smile vanishes when my mirror blacks out, showing only my shocked reflection. Then the lights overhead flash red.

I cut off the shower and stop breathing, listening. The chaotic screech of the emergency sirens wail outside. I run out of the bathroom and open my bedroom window. Already, soldiers and Marigoldians sprint up the hill toward the Compound's center. I crash out of my bedroom into the common area, where a holographic version of Kirk waits for me in the middle of the room.

"What's going on? Is this another drill?" I ask.

"Get your bag and get to the south gate. Now."

"Are the Runesians attacking?"

The holograph of Kirk flickers. "No. Savages. No more questions. We're running out of time."

CHAPTER 2

MIA

The south gate swells with restlessness. Soldiers stand on the rooftops and around the perimeter with grim but serious expressions. Most of them wear their green and black uniforms under their combat armor, which is the same pattern of camouflage. The combat armor fits their bodies snug and covers their torsos, forearms, and legs. It looks thin, but its durability can stop a few bullets and energy blasts. The back and sides of their helmets showcase one of the five division insignias of the Republic for Freedom.

The soldiers on the roofs and atop the walls sport the crossed red axes of the Ares Division. The ones loading the trucks wear the blue screeching eagle of the Eagle Division. Controlling the crowd are those of the Lion Division, a green roaring lion insignia sewed onto the shoulder portion of their uniforms. Masked up and sprinkled about, scanning the civilians for the Sickness, are those of the Hebi Division. Their insignias show a snake coiling around a sword with a dark, mustard-colored background. Last, there's the Addae Division, staging vehicles. Their half-sun insignia is burnt orange, like dying flames.

Whispers of uncertainty snake through the crowd.

"It's going to be all right," a woman tells her small child.

"Why are they coming here? Why are they inside the Territories?" a man questions his companion, who shrugs.

"Where are you taking us for shelter?" a woman demands from a nearby soldier.

He doesn't respond, and soon a group surges behind the woman, all screaming and demanding answers, their frenzy spiking with the heat. More soldiers come to support their comrade, and one of them, a sunburnt man with sweaty, brown hair that I recognize, holds up his hands, trying to soothe the crowd.

"Listen, everybody. I'm Sergeant Galloway, but most of you know me as Benny. The Compound Commander is linking the generals now." Benny pauses, letting that sentence rest in the air. "We're getting more information, but as many of you have probably heard, about a clan's worth of Savages are heading this way. From our estimates, they'll be here by tonight, which means we need to get all civilians out of here."

"Where will we go?" an older man yells.

"Right now, Compound Talon is the best option. It's southeast of here. We have trucks available for more than half of you. Children under thirteen and the elderly take precedence. Everyone else will travel on foot with me and three of my squads until the trucks can come back and pick you all up."

"What about those with the Sickness?" a woman screams.

"They're quarantined," Benny says. "We can't take them with us. Talon's hospitals are already full."

The tide of the crowd swells with rage.

"My grandmother is in there!"

"I'm not leaving my wife!"

"My baby! You expect me to leave him?"

Benny waves his hands in the air, raising his voice. "I know many of you have family members that are infected, but there's nothing we can do. We can't jeopardize everyone else for those in quarantine. We will protect your loved ones to the best of our ability. If you want to do something useful for your families now, prioritize your safety. Please."

People look between one another, mumbling and nodding, and soon the ripple of dissent ceases. The Marigoldians disperse in different directions as the soldiers scan them for the Sickness and coordinate who goes on which truck.

Kirk appears beside me with his hunting rifle and pack. "Good thing everyone likes Benny. Did you bring extra ammo?"

I nod, watching him as he pushes his wire-framed glasses up onto his nose and scans the rooftops, squinting. I don't understand why he won't get a vision mod like everyone else.

Benny calls for the walkers to gather around him, and I move that way, but Kirk grabs my arm. "You're not walking."

I yank out of his grasp, pointing at the six trucks staged near the south gate. "The trucks are full."

"No, they're not. I just received a link that they have room."

On cue, a soldier yells, "We have room for six more. Let's go! Let's go!"

A few older men, a couple of girls, and a woman rush for the trucks.

"Six just left. It's just walking. I can't mess that up," I say.

"Mia, please."

The argument withdraws from my lips, silence settling between us. Kirk's never begged me for anything. He's only ever barked orders he expected to be followed.

"What's wrong with you?" I ask.

Kirk lunges for me, halting himself when I flinch back.

"Sorry…." Kirk never apologizes. "… I'm just trying to keep you safe."

"Save that spot for someone that needs it. You need to treat me like an adult."

"An adult would understand our situation and listen to the more experienced person."

"What are you so afraid of? You trained me yourself."

"You don't know what it's like. When we get to Talon, you can join the RFF. I'll sign the release waiver."

An RFF soldier shouts, "One more. Let's go!"

"She's coming!" Kirk screams.

I turn away from him and merge with the crowd, heading toward Benny.

"Mia! Mia!" Kirk calls, but I ignore him.

He doesn't think I'm ready for the outside world, that I'll always need him, but I won't. That stops today.

Benny waves at us as I settle among the walkers.

He says, "Hello, everyone. Listen up, here are the rules. Stay inside the perimeter my soldiers create. Those of you without weapons, stay in the middle of the pack, and those of you with weapons, please keep them pointed at the ground unless your life is in danger. Whatever my soldiers or I say is law. Drink your water in moderation. No yelling. No breaking off from the group. When we halt, everyone pushes into the wood line until my soldiers clear the area. Got it?"

Murmurs of agreement and nods.

Benny claps. "All right! Be ready to step in ten!"

The heavens take a snapshot of our ruined world, lightning reaching down to sign the earth. Cold droplets splash onto us, and I stick my tongue out, relishing the coolness against my sticky skin. Kirk finds me but stands near silently. I can't read his expression through the sheets of rain, but when another flash of lightning brightens the world, I see it.

Behind the anger.

Behind the stoic front.

Fear.

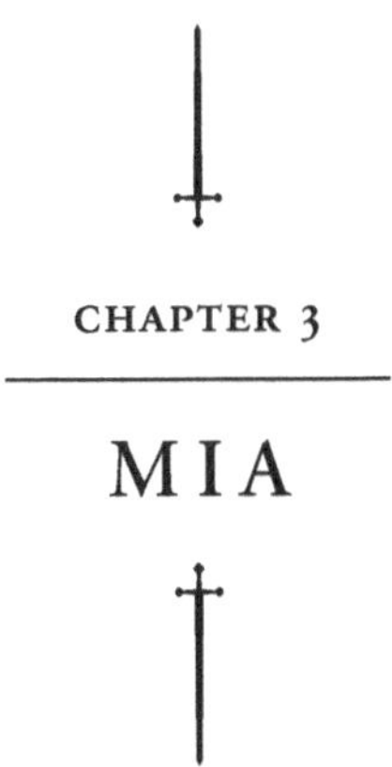

CHAPTER 3

MIA

We leave Compound Marigold behind around 1400 hours. I won't miss it. I understand our circumstances of being outside the walls are less than ideal, but for me, this is the start of my journey. In a couple of months, I can join Leon's side on the front lines, slaying Savages and ridding our land of the Runesians.

I stay beside Benny in the front of our group with my head on a swivel. We travel down a highway where old-world vehicles sit rusted and abandoned. Tufts of brown grass sprout through the asphalt, dying in the heat. When I peer back, Kirk is a few paces behind us, leading the crowd of civilians. My wet clothes dry in the blistering sun as the clouds part and reveal a blue sky. It's been a long time since I've seen the sky without a barrier between us.

Benny laughs at my silly grin. "You're probably the only one in all the Territories excited to be outside Compound walls right now, weirdo."

"Definitely beats being stuck in an apartment with Kirk." I glance back, and again, Kirk's watching me. Why can't he just let me handle myself? The trucks will be here to pick us up in a few hours. "He's suffocating sometimes, I swear."

"Be easy. I'm thankful he's here. Kirk saved my ass once when he was still a soldier in No Man's Land. He saved a lot of people's asses. You know he's a legend, right? The only man to battle the Almighty and live to tell the tale."

"Yeah, yeah, yeah, I know. War hero. Legend. Offered a position among the generals several times but refused. That doesn't mean he's not an asshole."

Benny sighs. "I don't think Leon would appreciate you talking about his grandfather like that…" Benny reacts to the look on my face. "My bad. I forgot. Still haven't heard from him?"

"Nope." I kick a rock. "And Kirk won't tell me what's going on between them. I don't know where he's at, or even if he's alive."

"I'm sure Leon's fine. He's a fighter. Strong and stubborn, just like you. How long has it been again?"

"Two years since we last talked. Five since he left Marigold. Do you know anything?"

Benny shakes his head. "I'm sorry, Mia. That's not my place. Like I said, knowing him, he's thriving under pressure." Benny turns, holding up a fist, and his soldiers push out on each side into the wood line. He pats me on the back. "It's time for a break. Listen, don't dwell on it. Focus on the present. And drink some water. Your cheeks are turning red."

Benny joins one of his soldiers, and they disappear into the forest.

I inspect a car on the side of the road as everyone else from our group follows Benny's orders to push into the wood line. They lean and sit against trees, chugging what little water they have left. Rust clings to the car over every surface except for the passenger door. Blood red letters there read: DEATH TO RUNESIANS, AMEN.

I smile and take a few swigs of water. I'm not the only one the Runesians have hurt. Many lost their families when they landed on the west coast in 2055.

Kirk approaches me from behind. "You should sit while you can."

"I'm fine."

"You're in the open. You know the rules."

I trail a finger along the prayer painted on the door, doubling it with a silent plea of my own, then turn. Kirk's shoulders bundle with irritation. Me being out here has him at his wit's end, I'm sure. I wipe sweat from my brow and head for the shade.

"How much water do you have left?" Kirk asks as I sit against a tree.

"Enough."

"You're being immature."

"You're being annoying."

Although Kirk is old, he has a better body than most men half his age. He grows with his anger. "This is why I didn't want you out here. You're still just a kid trying to act tough. You don't know how dangerous it can get."

"I'm seventeen, Kirk, and I do know. Did you forget my parents were bombed by the Runesians, and the Savages kept me as a slave? I'm not that defenseless seven-year-old you saved anymore."

"It's my job to protect you. That's all I'm trying to do."

I stand. "I don't need your protection."

"Why are you being like this?"

I'm sick of this. Sick of arguing. Sick of Kirk. I've held my thoughts in long enough. "Because you won't tell me where Leon is or what he's doing, and you constantly treat me as a child. You've trained me for the past ten years, yet you're so afraid. I'm not Lucia, and I'm not your son. I'm not even your actual granddaughter. I can take care of myself!"

Disappointment etches itself onto Kirk's face. "Okay, Mia, you got it. You got it." He slings his gun and slips past me, deeper into the forest.

CHAPTER 4

MIA

My sweat sizzles when it drops onto the splintered asphalt. I drag myself forward near the back of the group. Benny said the trucks should be here within the next hour. But after we slug over a hill, and that time passes, worry ignites in my heart. They're late, and we can't walk too much longer. Waves of invisible heat wriggle in my field of vision as each step gets harder and harder to take.

I drink some water, then jog ahead on the outskirts of the group, reaching Benny.

"Hey."

He glances at me, grinning. "You look like shit. Are you gonna make it?"

I jerk a thumb back. "Probably not. We're all going to pass out soon. Where are the trucks?"

Benny doesn't respond. He hits the ground, blood exploding from his skull.

"Benny!"

War cries fill the sky, and Savages erupt from the brush on both sides of the road.

"Run!" a soldier shouts just before an arrow punches through his neck.

I spin, running, but there's nowhere to go. Savages are everywhere, killing and capturing. Bullets and energy beams volley back and forth as the soldiers try to protect us, but the Savages squash their efforts. Smoke envelopes the area, and a burly Savage corners me, raising an axe. I freeze. What's happening? Did I pass out from heat exhaustion? Is this a dream?

"Die!" the Savage yells.

A bullet knocks the Savage off his feet and then Kirk's in my face.

"Come on, this way!" Kirk drags me through the smoke and into the woods, a few others behind us. He pulls me uphill, and soon the sounds of chaos fade. I collapse to the ground, throwing up, and Kirk leans against a tree, panting.

I touch my face, and when I withdraw my hand, my fingertips are speckled red. Whose blood is this? Is it Benny's?

"Mia, did you hear me?" Kirk comes over from his tree, kneels, and places a hand on my back. "Are you hit anywhere?" I shake my head, and he says, "We need to move. The Savages will be hunting us."

"What's the plan, Kirk?" a familiar voice asks, and I glance back at Barry, who slings his shotgun.

"We push through the night," Kirk says. "Barry, you're our rear guard. The rest of you, stay quiet and behind me. Whatever I say, you do. This is how you survive."

Barry tips his straw-hat. "Roger, boss man."

I peer around. Besides Barry, there are two women and a young man I've never seen before. Compound Marigold is the smallest Rear Compound within the Territories. Everyone knows everyone, so these three must be Nomads, travelers who sell and trade goods throughout the region and choose not to be tied down to a Compound.

One woman is thin, with short, blond hair. The other is heavier set, and brown, wearing a brown baseball cap.

The young man is lean with curly brown hair. Somehow, his features are both rugged and smooth, making it hard to place his age. When he catches me staring, he grins, his brown pupils flaring with a sort of whimsicalness only a child would have.

"On me. Let's go." Kirk pushes into the foliage.

It doesn't take long for night to fall. We stay silent and keep moving. Kirk keeps a brisk pace as we travel downhill, then the terrain grows steeper.

Behind me, one woman curses the other. "Dammit, Michelle, come on!"

"I-I can't!" The brown woman hangs onto a tree for support, wheezing. I backtrack toward them and the blond turns to me. "She has asthma."

"Just—Clara! Go!" Michelle's face wrinkles with pain. "I don't want to—" She clutches her chest.

I place my hands on Michelle's shoulders. "We're not leaving you behind. Take a deep breath. Come on, in." I wait, repeating myself, and soon Michelle follows my instructions. "And out. Again. Come on… there you go. Yes, there you go."

"Let's go! Keep up!" Kirk commands.

"Thank you," Michelle says.

"No problem." I turn and jog to catch up to Kirk.

Hours pass. My feet ache. We make it to a clearing and the first signs of light break through the purple clouds. Kirk lets us take a break, so I sit against a tree, clasping my trembling hands together. Benny's dead and Kirk was right. I'm not ready. When that Savage attacked, I froze. Even after all the training I did in the pods, even after losing to my past countless times, it seems I'm all talk. I didn't even notice the ambush. And maybe if I hadn't distracted Benny, he wouldn't have gotten killed. I'm still just as useless as I—

"Mia!" Kirk growls. He stands over me, hand out. "I called you three times."

I take it and he pulls me up. "Sorry."

"Sorry gets you dead. Listen."

I stop breathing, then distant yowls from dogs reach my ears.

"Everybody run!" Kirk pushes me ahead of him. "They've caught our scent!"

Branches grasp at my legs and arms as I propel myself through the wilderness.

"Keep running. Don't look back!" Kirk yells.

Gunfire mixed with guttural inhuman screeches fill the sky as the wild screams from the Savages pierce my ears. I swing my arms and push myself to go faster. If I stop, I'll be a slave again.

Arrows whiz past me. I look back—and the world tilts as I tumble into a thorny bush.

"Help!" Clara cries behind me as I stand.

"Go, Mia. Run! Run!" Kirk hollers.

I take off, slowing to a jog when Clara's pleas reach me again.

"Please! Somebo—"

Am I just going to leave everyone behind? Am I that much of a coward? That useless? What happened to that vengeance I wanted? I turn around, aiming my rifle at a Savage dragging an unconscious Clara away. Before I can pull the trigger, a child jumps in front of me, and swipes the gun out of my hands.

The child sits like a dog, cocking its head to the side with an other-worldly grin. "Milk!"

I pull out my knife, backing away when I realize the child in front of me isn't normal. He wears scraps for clothes and has pale, bruised skin with peeling scabs that ooze pus. His ribs protrude from his torso, and dirt clings to the hair covering his face.

"Milk!" He crawls toward me, his boney spine raised. When I see the shackle around his neck, I remember that I've heard about these people before. These tortured souls who can never return. This child is a Lost One. Taken away from humanity by the Savages' torture and drugs.

He pounces, and I backpedal, running into the arms of someone far stronger than me. They slam me onto the ground. A naked female Lost One mounts me, her fingers cinching around my throat. I stab her wherever I can, but her grip only grows tighter.

"Dresses!" She drools. Her saliva rains onto my face.

The child Lost One claps and dances around us. "Milk! Milk!"

I plunge my blade through the female Lost One's chest, but the vigor in my arm fades when the air making it to my lungs decreases.

"Dresses!" The Lost One raises one claw-like hand and whacks me in the face. My world shakes.

"Mia!" Kirk's voice is distant, dwindling.

The sounds of turmoil cease, a prying, white noise to the other side inviting me to a peaceful slumber.

Then there's nothing but darkness.

CHAPTER 5

LEON

May 4, 2145, 08:48

The distant growl of thunder reverberates through a silver sky, threatening rain. A mass of soldiers crowd the muddy, cratered wasteland that is No Man's Land. Leon keeps his head high as the sharp, irony tang of blood envelops him. He holds back the bile churning at the base of his throat and strides ahead of the four others dressed like him in dark Scout armor.

Slow down. They're praising us, a voice says in Leon's head through his Cerebral Link, and then someone grabs his shoulder. Leon glances back at Zero, who opens his helmet's face shield, his blue-gray eyes ablaze. *We deserve some glory.*

Zero takes off his helmet, and sweaty, brown hair spills from his scalp. He's a tall, ruggedly handsome man with a slim face and a crooked nose. The mass of Republic for Freedom soldiers around them cheer even louder.

Without us, most of these losers would be dead, Zero says.

They're not supposed to know our identities, a female voice says. *Put your helmet back on.*

Unclench, sister. Zero reaches over, grabs Leon's balled fist, and raises it into the air. *Don't be like Liz.*

Shut up. Liz shoves Zero in the back.

Faced with the congregation of appreciation, Leon sees snapshots of his brutality: a blade plunging into flesh; Runesian soldiers, dressed in their black and gray camo, dropping like flies in the mud as his bullets tear through them; a young soldier, no older than sixteen, ripping off his flag and offering it to Leon with tears in his eyes before dying in the muck next to his comrades.

Leon yanks his fist out of Zero's grasp and takes off down the manmade aisle toward their black airship. Liz's face shield opens, her ruby green eyes brimming with concern as she watches Leon run up the ramp.

Leon bursts into the bathroom, slinging his helmet to the ground. He presses his chest plate, deactivating his armor and tearing the pieces off him as if they're on fire. He runs to the sink and vomits into the basin, cleaning the sour taste off his tongue with cool water.

"Are the bodies messing with you, son?"

Leon snaps up. Blood trickles from his left nostril, dripping into the sink, mixing with his dinner from last night. He backpedals and crashes into the door. "Dad?"

A man, broad and average height like Leon with a buzz cut and leathery skin, stands in the mirror. He wears a baggy, gray striped suit, and holds a pistol. Leon's father grins, his lips stretching far too much, his eyes turning blacker than oil. "I've come to warn you that your time is running out." His father raises the gun to his head.

"No!" Leon surges forward, but the bang racks everything, and his father falls wayside.

¢

The doors separate, revealing a dark room, a blue holo-sphere floating in the middle of the opening around a square-shaped table with a glowing white surface. Zero and Liz sit around the table with the Scout commander, One, a woman with graying, shoulder-length brunette hair.

"You're late, Jackson," One says.

There's not an ounce of light coming from her steel gaze. The rigid lines on her pockmarked face grow deeper. Her callous appearance makes Leon stand a little straighter and raise his head higher.

"Sorry, Commander. It seems I'm having stomach issues."

One sets her jaw. "Do I need to scan you?"

"No. Just had a bad dinner last night."

One accepts that and rises as Leon sits, the holo-sphere transforming into a map. She traces her finger over the map of what used to be the United States, a white line trailing it from east to west. "The Republic for Freedom has made progress against the Runesians here, here, here, and now here, thanks to your mission last night. They should gain substantial ground in the northwest in the coming days. Tonight, we have a new objective in the south. Reports from Eagle soldiers say multiple plague camps have popped up along the border, spreading all the way toward South America. Most of these camps are abandoned or have few guards. Drone images confirm these statements." Pictures of tent cities smashed together from afar and above populate the holo-sphere on all sides. "The RFF wants us Scouts to clear these camps to prevent any surprises in their advancement. You three, along with six others of your choosing, will clear the two camps at these coordinates."

Inside Leon's head, the camps' locations download with pictures.

One continues, "Anybody that isn't us dies. No survivors. Make sure your body armor and helmets remain sealed. This could be a trap set by the Runesians to weaken us with the Sickness. Questions?"

Liz, fit and cream-colored with a mane of hair that resembles flames, raises her hand. "What about children?"

"No survivors."

"But the RFF has refugee—"

"Full. I said no survivors. The Republic for Freedom has enough qualms about us as is," One says. "But we're the elite, and they need us to win this war. We do the dirty jobs because they can't. You've done these types of missions before, so what's the hold up now?"

"No holdup. Just curious." Liz gets up.

"Where are you going?"

"To my room until we get to the drop point."

"I didn't dismiss you," One says.

Liz shrugs, waving as she steps through the sliding doors. One's attention snaps toward Zero, who holds up his hands in surrender. "Get your sister under control."

"She's your niece," Zero says.

"Just do something about her." Zero remains in his seat, and a vein almost burst through One's forehead. "Now!"

Zero scrambles out of his chair, chasing after Liz. As the doors seal shut, the room settles into silence.

One sits, interlocking her fingers as she stares ahead. "Ever since their parents died, I've done everything I could to protect them. Despite that, she hates me."

Leon can feel the harshness of One's gaze find him.

"I know she only came back because of you," One says. "I've always been curious as to why someone like you joined the Scouts."

"What do you mean, Commander?"

"I've been watching you for the past five years. You're not cut out for this type of work. I can have you reassigned to a line unit within the RFF. You're more than capable of being a squad leader."

Leon shakes his head. "I'm not a leader."

"And you're not a killer. Killers have no remorse, but you always do."

"I joined the Scouts for a reason. I don't want to leave."

One sighs. "Suit yourself. I'll give you one last chance to prove to me that you belong here. Because right now, you seem to be a long-term liability, and I don't need that in what I'm planning."

"What do you want me to do?"

One's lips curl upward. "Lead tonight's mission without fail. If you do, you can stay here. If not, I'm kicking you out, and you'll never see Liz again. Do you accept, Jackson?"

⚸

Clear!

No enemies.

Clear!

Leon's fellow Scouts send him updates through their link as they cycle through the hundreds of tents filled with nothing but discarded cots, food, and the dead. Leon sloshes through a mud puddle, stepping into an open tent. A single man lies on a cot, arm hanging limp off the edge. Leon lifts his rifle as he approaches. His vision mod shows him the wispy threads of heat circulating through the man's body.

The man's pale, yellow skin is creased with the contours of age. Blood drains from his nostrils, staining his white mustache red. He mumbles something in Runesian as he clings to a picture. He doesn't break his mantra as Leon stands over him, rifle aimed at his head.

A few moments pass, and the man lets the picture float to the floor. He laughs, coughing up blood. "Oh. They've sent a crow to deliver me to the other side. Go on, get it over with. I can't move, and I rather not die choking on my blood."

"How long ago did the Runesians abandon this camp?" Leon asks, lowering his rifle.

"Three weeks ago. They instructed the infected not to follow them. Those that did got shot, of course. Can you believe that I'm one of their doctors, and they even left me here? Bastards!" The old man heaves, laughing and throwing up blood. "I would have killed myself, but they took all the weapons."

"Any others here? Children? People that could survive?"

"I'm not telling you, death bringer, killing those who are already dying. You should be ashamed of yourself."

Leon raises his gun. "I am." He shoots the man in the head.

CHAPTER 6

LEON

A muggy breeze carries the fetor of death as Leon steps into the tent where six other Scouts wait. A blue light illuminates Zero and Liz's faces inside their helmets.

"Anything?" Liz asks.

"A dying Runesian doctor," Leon says. "We have one more area to search. I think there are others here somewhere. The doctor seemed to know something, but he wouldn't tell me anything, so stay sharp."

Zero turns toward the exit. "Let's get this boring mission over with."

Leon and Liz step out behind him, two Scouts deactivating their Cloaks, making themselves visible.

"Forty-Two and Fifty-Three, you're with Zero." Leon turns as the rest of the Scouts emerge from the tent. "Eleven, Twenty-Six, Forty-Nine, and Nineteen, you're together. Liz, on me."

The Scouts disperse into their groups and activate their Cloaks.

Decaying corpses litter the row Leon and Liz move down. Flies and rats swarm the rotting flesh.

I'm glad we have on our Scout armor, Liz links, darting away from Leon to check inside a tent. *Clear.*

She comes back out and nods his way.

Yeah. Leon pushes inside the tent to his right, his modded eyes catching the scurrying heat signatures of vermin running from his presence. *Clear. The smell would probably kill us before the Sickness did.* Leon steps back outside, looking up at a yellow moon. *This area is the worse one so far. This must be where they kept their chronic cases.*

Liz joins him and pats him on the back. They watch a few stars twinkle in the empty blackness, then Leon pushes ahead.

You think the Runesians are planning some type of biological attack? he asks.

Liz trails behind him, kicking a ripped open can. *Maybe. The Sickness is killing humanity on all sides, but if they're able to harness its power and use it to end us faster, I don't think they would hesitate.*

They clear the next two tents together, slipping in and out, flowing like water.

Knowing how fucked they are, they're probably experimenting on their people in the lower classes so they can become like the Savage Princess, Leon says, and checks a shack wedged between two tents. Inside there's nothing but rotting food and sabotaged supplies. *Clear.*

The comm inside Leon's helmet crackles, and Liz's voice filters into his ear. *"You really believe the Savage Princess has clairvoyance?"*

"Yes. Every Savage we've captured has said the same thing. She bleeds out of the nose and has migraines, just like the infected. They can't all be that tweaked out. And remember what that Nomad told us a couple of months ago?"

"About the teleporting assassin killing Runesian generals?" Liz burst into laughter. *"Come on, bro. I mean yeah, some people survive the Sickness, but why would it give them powers?"*

They approach the last tent in the row on the corner of the plague camp. Leon scans outside the barbed wire, checking the shadows for heat signatures. He picks up the movement of several animals, but no humans.

Who knows? Traps? Leon shrugs and positions himself on the other side of the door as Liz shakes her head. *Maybe the Scorpilionitis mutates inside certain people and then they can fly and shoot lasers and shit. Ready?*

You've been reading too many old-world superhero comics, Liz says, nodding.

Leon boots the door and zips inside behind Liz. They both freeze when their guns point toward two children clinging to one another with scrawny arms in the middle of the tent. One boy and one girl.

They're paper-thin, pitiful looking kids, their round, dark eyes sunken into their chalk-colored faces.

What do we do? Liz asks.

Before Leon can answer, a shimmering blue sword slides against the armor around his neck, the hum of energy coursing from it pulsing into his skin.

"You're familiar with ion blades, aren't you, crow?" a girl asks. "So, both of you drop your guns and face the wall."

"We're not going to hurt you—"

"Do what I say, or your head goes flying!" The girl presses the blade into the armor. It sparks.

Leon and Liz drop their rifles and pistols onto the ground and raise their hands above their heads. The girl rummages through Leon's pockets, snagging his energy bar, and then his extra blade sheathed around his ankle. She moves to Liz, and Leon sneaks a peek at her.

The girl's a tan-skinned teenager with short hair hanging just above her shoulders. She wears a black tank top and blue jeans. She smashes one of her boots into the back of Leon's knee, and he buckles. "Eyes forward, crow!"

"We don't want to hurt you. Let us help you," Leon says.

The girl scoffs. "You don't want to help me. I've been watching you guys all night. Save the act."

"Kira!" the children scream, and the girl whirls.

The children squirm, tufts of their hair being pulled by someone the girl can't see, but Leon and Liz can.

Zero deCloaks himself, and shakes the children, grinning. "I can rip off their tiny heads, or you can drop the ion blade."

Kira drops her sword, and the blue glow ceases. She raises her hands. "You can have me. Just let them go. Please!"

Leon and Liz retrieve their guns.

"Zero, thanks. We got this," Liz says.

"Really?" He pulls at the kids' hair, and their faces scrunch up in pain. "Because if you were following One's orders, they would have been dead."

"They're kids."

"They're the enemy! It's us or them, remember?"

"The Runesians left them behind. We can send them to an RFF refugee camp. One doesn't have to know," Leon says.

"No survivors. Plus, look at them. They're infected." Zero slings the girl away and pulls out his energy pistol, placing it to the back of the boy's head. "Let's finish this."

Take care of your brother, Leon says.

I'll meet you at the nearest outpost. Go!

Liz raises her rifle, shooting a blast of energy into Zero's shoulder. He spasms, freezes, and drops his pistol.

Leon picks up the boy. "Follow me. Come on!"

He runs out of the tent. Kira takes Zero's energy pistol, then the girl's hand, and follows Leon.

He leads them toward the barbed wire, setting the boy down and stepping on it, so they can cross. "Go on. Into the forest."

Leon peers behind him, catching the heat signatures of Forty-Two and Fifty-Three running toward them. He shoots, splattering bullets in their direction, and they dive behind cover, shooting back. Leon throws an oblong device on the ground. It stretches out, and a rectangular blue energy wall zaps up, blocking the volley of rounds hungry for him. He pops a smoke grenade and sprints after the children into the shadows of the night.

A pink sky filters through wimpy trees, and Leon glances back, checking for pursuers. He cuts his Cerebral Link on. *Liz, it's Leon. I'm safe and headed toward the RFF outpost.* Leon checks the map inside his head. *Outpost seven-one-one. If you're safe, link me back.*

"I'm hungry," the boy cries, shuffling through dead leaves ahead of Kira. "And it's hot."

"It's always hot and you're always hungry, so Max, shut up," Kira says.

"You're such a crybaby," the girl teases.

Max scowls back at her. "Shu—"

"Max. Mercury. Behave, please," Kira orders, stopping and looking back at Leon. "Do you have any more water?"

Leon gives Kira his flask and his energy bar. "You all can have the rest. We're almost there."

"Thank you," she says. She splits the bar into three pieces.

Leon pushes past them, linking Liz again, and again she doesn't answer, so he cuts his link off. The morning sun cuts through the haze that snakes through the forest as Leon leads them downhill.

Another hour passes and Kira pushes up beside Leon, who ignores her presence.

"Soooo. What should I call you besides crow?" she asks.

"Leon."

"Okay. Where are you from, Leon?"

"Compound Marigold."

"Don't know anything about the east. Any siblings?"

"Yeah." Leon looks at Kira. "She's around your age. Seventeen."

"I'm fifteen. Max and Mercury are six. They're fraternal…."

Leon picks up the pace, but Kira matches him. "You don't have to be a dick. I'm just trying to pass the time."

Leon stops, faces Kira, searching her walnut-colored eyes. "You're trying to distract yourself from the inevitable. Better to just face it now. How long do they have?"

Kira hangs her head. "That doctor said a few months. What am I supposed to do after that?"

"You keep going."

"They're all I have. Our parents died from the same thing three years ago."

"Then you fight for them. Fight to stop this war. Fight to figure out what the Sickness is. Fight for a better world."

"Love the optimism." Kira smiles, studying Leon a bit longer, and notices he's helmetless. "You're not afraid of getting infected?"

He walks ahead. "You ask a lot of questions."

Kira smirks, opening her mouth, but Mercury's scream slams it shut.

The girl hacks up blood. "Kira! Something's happeni—"

Leon and Kira run back toward them. Max lies on the ground, shaking and foaming out of the mouth. Mercury drops beside him and clutches her temples. Blood drains from their nostrils as they squirm in pain.

"No, no, no, no!" Kira drops to her knees near them, trying to soothe them with water. "It's supposed to be a few more months!"

Leon takes the water from her. She lunges for it, tears burning down her cheeks. "Give it back!"

Leon shakes his head. "It's time."

The veins in the twins' faces are black. The first sign in some that they only have a few minutes left to live. Leon unslings his rifle. "Kira, keep walking. I'll do it."

Kira ignores him and pulls Zero's energy pistol from her waistband. "They're my family. I'll do it myself. Give us a moment."

Leon turns and walks a few paces, staring up into the trees to see a flock of the Scout's epithet waiting for the death to come. Their beady, dark eyes focused and hungry. Two minutes go by, and then Leon hears the first zap of energy, followed quickly by a second.

A crow caws, and Leon turns to see Kira with the gun to her head.

"Kira, don't!"

"There's nothing left for me here!" She squeezes the trigger, burning a hole through her skull.

�

Leon places Kira's arms around Max and Mercury, then places rocks around them and covers the three with leaves. He finds some dead wood and throws that on top of the pile, adding as much weight over the makeshift grave as he can. When he's finished, he links Liz. *They're dead, Liz. All three. I'm heading—*

An unrecognized link signal pings, and Leon accepts the transmission.

Leon Jackson, this is General Wilde of the Lion Division. I've been trying to reach you. Where are you?

It doesn't matter. Leon starts counting. It'll take One seven seconds to track his exact location. *Why are you linking me?*

I understand the Scouts' secrecy, but this is urgent. Wherever you're at, you need to get home now. Compound Marigold was attacked last night by the Savages, and just an hour ago, Kirk's link went offline.

What about my sister? Leon asks.

She evacuated with him. Both are missing and not among those confirmed dead.

Can you evac?

General Wilde asks a question of her own. *Why can't you take an airship?*

It's complicated. I can explain later. This is where I'll be.

Leon sends General Wilde the coordinates and ends the link. The back of his neck tingles and he spins, aiming his rifle into the brush. A shadow peeks at him from behind a tree.

"Come on out!" Leon yells.

The right side of Leon's head explodes with pain. He sways as blood runs from his nose, then falls, everything within him becoming cold and numb. Leaves crunch as a slim, womanly shadow stands over him.

It kneels and grabs Leon's chin, its touch making him nauseous. The shadow doesn't have a face, but Leon can hear its voice. It's a piercing and cruel whisper. "What will you be worth before you die?"

KIRK

September 3, 2135

Kirk peers through the doorway into a spare bedroom. A young, tawny-skinned girl with dark hair sleeps, her thin arms wrapped around herself. He knows he should wake her. She can't stay here with them—he already has one hungry little mouth to feed.

A hand tugs on the back of his shirt, and he turns.

"Lucia." He slides his hands around her waist. "Why are you up? You should be resting."

Lucia scrunches up her face. "I may be ill, but I should at least be able to greet my husband when he comes home from saving lives." She peeks around him. "Especially when he brings a guest back with him. She's a cute little girl."

"I'm getting rid of her tomorrow morning, so don't get attached." Kirk kisses Lucia on the forehead and walks into the kitchen. He holds his hands under the stream of water in the sink. "The Runesians bombed that town near here. Somehow, their Cloaked ship slipped across our border. When we got there, everything was ruined, but there were signs of survivors and Savages. It took us three days to track them down. We managed to save her, and a few others, but some of them got away with the other children."

"That's awful. She should stay with us for a while."

Kirk scrubs his hands. The dried blood won't come off. "She's traumatized. When I found her, the Savages had her cutting into a dead man. She can go to Talon with the other orphans."

Lucia glances back at the girl, then glides forth as if on air, resting a palm on Kirk's face. "Find some kindness in your heart."

"I'm only kind to you."

"And why is that?"

"Because you're the best thing that ever happened to me."

The two share a kiss, but Kirk pulls away first. "Did you get medicine from the doctor? I can feel the heat coming off you."

"Why should I get medicine if others don't? I'm infected, Kirk. The medicine doesn't work anyway. You know there's nothing we can do but wait." She reads Kirk's expression and hugs him. "I'll be fine. Don't you worry."

Kirk holds his wife tight, breathing in the smell of honey that wafts off her. "I love you."

"I know you do." Lucia buries her head into his chest.

¢

Kirk wipes sweat from Lucia's brow as she lies in bed. Her brown skin glistens with sweat. She blinks. It's long and deliberate, as if even that action is too much for her body to handle.

"Have you taken Mia to the doctor yet?" Lucia asks. "I want to make sure she is healthy."

"She doesn't need a doctor."

"Will you please just take her to the doctor? I want to be sure—" She breaks into a fit of coughing.

Kirk grabs a glass of water from the nightstand. "Here." He holds the cup for her.

"I want to be sure I didn't infect her," she says after Kirk removes the glass from her lips and sets it aside.

"I've taken her to get scanned every day with me and Leon. She's fine.

Why do you care so much about her in your condition? She's a little orphan girl. What can we do for her? Why do you want another responsibility?"

"My condition has no relevance here. It is nothing! Think about Leon. The boy's parents—" Another fit of coughing. "They can help each other. An orphanage will do Mia no justice. They'll just send her to war when she's of age."

"You need to calm down. Your fever will rise," Kirk says. "Lucia?"

He reaches for her, but she flips away from him. "Don't tell me to calm down. Take Mia to the doctor. Get a full evaluation completed on her."

"I don't want to leave you like this."

"I am not a child. Go. I can take care of myself!"

Kirk sighs and leaves. He goes into Leon's room.

The lean and dark twelve-year-old is behind Mia, helping her hold a gun. "... and then you click this lever." He stops when Mia raises her head.

Leon hides the gun behind himself, green-brown eyes wide with alarm. "Sorry! I just thought—"

Kirk holds up a hand. "It's fine." He motions toward Mia. "You. Come."

Mia shuffles forward, looking back at Leon.

"Come on!" Kirk snatches Mia's arm. "We don't have all day! Leon, make sure you check on your grandmother. Refill her glass of water every fifteen minutes."

The boy straightens his back. "Yes, sir!"

The doctor turns toward Kirk after giving Mia candy. He opens the door, and the two of them step out into the hall.

"So, is she healthy?" Kirk asks.

"Perfect for a seven-year-old. There are a few Scorpilioniti rogues in her system, but they're inactive and showing no signs of compromising of her health. She's asymptomatic, like most of the population."

"When can she leave?"

"Excuse me, sir?" The doctor pushes his glasses onto his face and looks at his holo-board.

"She's not my granddaughter," Kirk says. "I want to send her to the orphanage in Talon."

"Oh. Apologies. Well, the next transport won't be here for another few days. I can link you when it's on the way."

"Sure."

"Will there be a problem with her staying with you in the meantime? I can make arrangements."

Kirk contemplates, then Mia peeks out into the hall. He sighs. "My wife's taken a liking to her so she can stay with us until then."

When his apartment door slides open, Kirk's gut twists. The faucet in the kitchen runs.

"Leon?" He pulls Mia inside. The stillness in the air siphons strength from his body. Then, with sudden dread, Kirk rushes for his bedroom. "Lucia!"

Leon presses on the unmoving Lucia's chest. "Come on, grandma! Come on, wake up! Please. Please!"

Kirk pushes him out of the way. "Move!"

Tears run down the boy's cheeks. "She said she didn't need more water. I'm sorry, grandpa. I'm sorry, I should have—"

"Lucia!" Kirk compresses her chest. He opens her mouth and blows. More compressions. "Lucia! Wake up, baby. Come on!"

"Lucia!" Kirk's voice cracks. He checks her pulse. Nothing. He keeps trying to resuscitate her, but she doesn't move. He stops, sweat runs from his armpits, staining his shirt. He turns toward Mia and Leon, his lips curled back, and his teeth clenched. Kirk swings a hand through the air. "Get out of here!"

"But grandpa—" Leon begins.

"GET OUT!"

Leon pulls Mia out of the bedroom, and Kirk slams the door shut. He sits on the bed, cradling Lucia's head.

"No, no, no, no, no." His sorrow drips onto her. "Please come back. Please!" Lucia does not answer. Kirk rocks back and forth. "Please, Lucia! Please don't leave me…."

Ȼ

Kirk stands in the room alone, looking at Lucia's picture on the wall above his headrest.

"I'm sorry, Lucia," he says. "I know you wanted to keep Mia, but I can't do it. After Danston… and with Leon, I just can't. I'm taking her to the airship today. She'll be better off in Talon."

Kirk pats his pockets. They're all empty. He looks up at Lucia's picture, grinning. "Did you hide my glasses again? I haven't seen them in days."

He searches through the bedroom. When he looks under the bed, he finds a wooden jewelry box he's never seen before. He sets it on the bed and opens the lid. Inside are his glasses resting on top of a folded letter.

He puts the glasses on and unfurls the paper.

To My Grumpy Husband,

You can see now. I fixed your glasses again. I don't foresee you ever getting vision mods, but one can hope. I hope you treat the children better when I'm gone. You can be tough and love them all the same. But enough of that. I wanted to tell you that despite your attitude, I love you. You are the best thing that happened to me as well. I am sorry I must say goodbye this way, but I am tired. I am better at hiding pain than you, this, you know. I figure you'll be distraught, but don't be because we'll see each other again, and then we'll be together forever. Until then, write to me whenever you feel alone or sad or afraid. I will always listen. I will always be there. I love you, Kirk Jackson. You are a good man despite what you believe. Stop being so hard on yourself.

My final mission for you is that you take care of Mia. Teach her how to protect herself, but also how to have a heart. She's outspoken, so have patience. And for Leon. Be easy on him, please. The boy's been through enough. Let them both grow into who they're supposed to be. I must stop now. I think it is time. My hand is aching! Take care, my beloved. Until we meet again.

Love, Lucia.

Kirk clutches his chest when his heart pangs, the ache eddying through his being until he can't stand anymore. He collapses onto the bed. In the pit of his stomach, a black hole tears through his existence. Hot tears blister down his cheeks as he grieves, hugging himself. The cold misery drowns him. He sinks farther into it until a warmth envelopes him. He looks up, and Mia and Leon wrap around him.

"Thank you." Kirk sniffles, seeing the small bag on the floor in his doorway. "You can unpack that."

"I'm not leaving?" Mia asks.

"No. I need a granddaughter, and Leon needs a sister."

Mia smiles and cries too.

CHAPTER 7

MIA

May 5, 2145

Two Savages stand silently on either side of us, holding spears. Black kill dots line their skin, marking how many lives they've claimed in battle. Their armor is made from scraps of metal, leather, and wood. What are they waiting for? We've been tied to these trees since this morning. Kirk and the young man with curly brown hair are to the right of me, and Michelle and Clara are to my left.

Barry was killed in the ambush.

One of the Savages shifts their weight and stands straighter. "Heads up."

They both kneel as a stocky Savage with unkept, dirty blond hair approaches. He wears a circular, silver emblem on a strap that crosses his bare chest. It's a sickle-shaped C with a sword that pierces through it diagonally. The symbol is also scorched into the tan skin above the Savage's right eyebrow. He stops in front of the two Savages, blue eyes like the depths of an ocean, drowning them. "Why are you two still standing here? Get out of my sight before I kill you."

They scramble to their feet, running down the hill.

He watches them, then focuses on us. "I'm Glare." He kneels in front of Kirk and sniffs him. "Nice to meet you, Kirk Jackson."

"I've never heard of you," Kirk says, "but it's a pleasure."

Glare raps a knuckle against his emblem. "I'm War Hand of Calamity Clan. Maybe I'll be the one to tear off your head." He taps Kirk in the face when he doesn't reply, rises, and peers at me, his gaze freezing the blood flowing beneath my skin. "What's your name?"

I don't answer, so he starts toward me.

"Her name is Mia," Kirk says.

Glare takes a handful of my hair. "Well, Mia, are you a mute or something?" When I don't answer, he shakes me. "I hate you Compounders." Glare pushes my head against the tree, rubbing it into the bark. "If it was up to me, I'd have your heads on spikes by now."

He pushes off me and leaves. I watch him swagger away, his tomahawk glinting in the harsh sunlight as he tosses it up and catches it.

"Don't provoke them!" Kirk hisses.

"I'm not," I say.

"You are. Comply. Answer. Survive."

"Shouldn't we be discussing how to escape instead of how we comply with Savages?"

Kirk sighs. "No, we shouldn't be because we're not. I'm a high value target. They won't blunder someone like me. That War Hand doesn't have the final say in killing me it seems, but with you, that might not apply. Just promise me, Mia, you'll do everything in your power to survive, no matter what happens to me."

I study Kirk's expression and again, I find that same fear from before. "I promise I'll survive."

"Good."

Red stretches over the sky as a white sun dips into the horizon. Torches crackle in the clearing below, and soon the Savages surround us, eyes red and wide from whatever roots or mushrooms they've shoved down their throats.

Glare steps in front of the crowd. "Cal's late. Grab them and put them in the arena." The Savages cut our bindings and push us down the slope into a ring of torches. "On your knees! All of you!"

None of us move, so a few Savages encroach upon us.

"Let them go," Kirk says. "You can have me."

"How is that fair?" Glare asks. "You alone killed five of our people. Another two dead from that other old shit."

"It's fair because I'll give you the chance to kill me in a duel in exchange for their safety. You win your glory."

Glare laughs, raising his tomahawk. "Pass."

"He's mine!" a voice booms from the shadows of the trees uphill.

Glare freezes mid-swing, the crazed smile on his face disappears, and his body deflates as the surrounding Savages kneel. A group of three Savages proceed down the hill.

The one in the lead is shirtless, wearing a bear headpiece and dark jeans. The flames that flicker against his bronze skin make him almost appear golden. He steps past us, slapping a hand on Glare's back. "Greedy as always."

"You're late. I was just following your orders."

"I know," the Savage says. "We ran into some trouble."

"Where's my sister?" Glare asks.

"She's already headed back to her territory. She told me to tell you to come home sometime. Scar and Moth miss you."

"Yeah. Right. Let me kill Kirk."

The Savage removes his hand from Glare's back, finally taking us in with amber eyes. "You know I can't do that," he says, unsheathing a curved sword with strands of hair tied around the hilt. He places the tip against Kirk's throat and raises his voice, speaking to everyone. "This man has been on the Glory List for years. He's a legendary warrior. A man even our War General, Calamity the Almighty, could not finish off in battle. Tonight, I, Cal, Chief of Calamity Clan, will finish what the Almighty couldn't in a deathmatch against Kirk Jackson!"

The Savages erupt in a choir of depravity, singing for Kirk's death. Cal removes his headpiece, placing it on the ground. Dark hair falls just past his ears and a gruesome scar runs down the right side of his face from his forehead to chin.

He moves in front of the young man with curly hair, Michelle, and Clara. "But first come these three."

Michelle and Clara cling to one another. The young man glowers defiantly up at Cal, who places the sharp edge of his sword against his neck.

"What's your name?" Cal asks.

"Daniel," the young man answers.

"I like the look in your eyes. Who are these Compounders to you?"

"They're nothing. I don't know them."

Cal takes a step back and flips his sword around, offering it to Daniel. "Kill these two women, and I'll offer you a spot in my clan."

Daniel reaches for the hilt, and I hope he'll shove the blade through Cal's chest. It would be a simple kill. But when he grabs the sword and stands, his face is blank, wiped of emotion. Daniel takes his position over Michelle and Clara. They beg him for mercy, but it's like he doesn't hear them. He lifts the sword and thrusts it through Clara's chest without hesitation.

"No!" Michelle jumps on Daniel before he can pull the sword out, trying to save her friend.

I should help her. Kirk must read my thoughts.

"Don't move," he says.

Daniel gets the sword out, slick with blood, and swings it through Michelle's neck. A red geyser erupts from her headless body and splatters onto Daniel's face.

Cal takes his sword and raises Daniel's bloody, shaking fist into the air. "Welcome Daniel!"

The Savages explode with cheers. "DANIEL! DANIEL! DANIEL!"

Cal shoves Daniel into the crowd, and they batter him with slaps on the back, but I know he doesn't feel them. He just murdered two innocent women to survive and there will never be any coming back from that.

Cal spreads his arms out. "And now for the finale!"

Two Savages come from behind, lifting me off the ground. "No!" I struggle, kicking out and digging in. "No! Let me go!"

A blade pokes into my back, and one of them says, "Shaddup!"

Someone throws Kirk a sword. After he picks it up, he stands, facing Cal. "I offered your War Hand a duel in exchange for their safety, but now I want to change the conditions."

"I'm a man of honor. Go on," Cal says.

"That girl, Mia. No harm of any kind will come to her. If I give you the chance to kill me, I want to ensure she's safe."

"Deal. I wasn't planning on harming her anyway. She's too pretty. But what if you kill me?"

"Then me and her walk out of here unharmed."

Cal grins, takes a knife from his side, and slits his palm. He raises it and shows his clan. "See this, Calamity! I accept the conditions of this deathmatch with a blood oath. If I should fall, Kirk and Mia will leave this place unharmed!"

Nods of acknowledgement come from Calamity Clan. Glare crosses his arms and spits on the ground.

Kirk backs away, giving himself some distance. I know how strong he is. He trained me in the pods for ten years, and I've never beaten him in a sparring match. Kirk won't lose.

He's the man that forged the path to victory hundreds of times for the Republic for Freedom. He's the man everyone calls a war hero. The man everyone looks up to and cherishes. He's the man that saved me from a life of slavery. If I owe him anything right now, it's my unwavering belief that he'll win and save us.

Kirk and Cal settle, gauging one another. Cal bends his knees slightly, raising his sword high above his head and behind him to the right. Kirk squats lower, right leg forward. He holds his sword upside down, butt of the hilt to the sky. I've seen this position many times before. Not once have I ever managed to defend against the entire attacking sequence.

I clasp my hands together as silence falls over the clearing. I don't think I've ever prayed, but now, I do. There's this crackle in the air. It's like lightning is riding my shoulders, and I must force myself to breathe.

Kirk lunges forth, slicing up—the Savages rage, cheering on their chief.

Cal meets him in the middle, slashing down. Their swords clash, and the clang of metal rings in my ears. Kirk's arm shakes, but he continues the sequence, spinning, going for Cal's side. But the Savage blocks the strike, and counters with a thrust. Kirk weaves, and Cal lashes out with his foot, slamming it into the knee that supports most of Kirk's weight, causing him to falter. Cal's like a snake with his sword. He pushes Kirk on the defensive.

Kirk blocks the first strike, and parries the second, but he's still trying to recover his footing, and Cal advances. His leg axes through the air, aiming for Kirk's face, and he raises his arms to defend. Cal doesn't stop. He whirls with a reverse roundhouse kick, knocking Kirk back. Cal leaps into the air with a scream, his sword high over his head, thirsty for blood and bone. Kirk settles into a guard, but the force of the blow smashes through, and the tip of Cal's blade rips down Kirk's chest. Cal lands one final strike. His foot barrels into Kirk's jaw, dropping him to the ground.

The Savage chief grins, resting his sword on his shoulder. "Come on. This isn't the man the Almighty gave so much praise."

"I'm just getting warmed up, boy." Kirk pushes himself up, wipes a dribble of blood from his lips, and cracks his neck with a sly grin. "Do you know how many of your kind I've killed over the years?"

With a war cry, Cal charges, and Kirk feints a thrust, forcing Cal to sidestep right into his real attack. A slash—Kirk's sword skims the skin under Cal's pectorals, white meat filling with red. Cal backpedals, but Kirk matches his pace, hacking, and slashing, not giving him a moment to counter. Sparks fly as metal screams against metal.

Kirk acts as if he's going for a wide strike on Cal's left, and when the chief goes to defend, Kirk slips in, his fist mighty, a hammer, bulldozing up into the Savage's chin. Cal crumbles, red spilling from his mouth as his amber gaze scalds Kirk, who stands over him.

"Bite your tongue?" Kirk raises his sword.

Yes. Yes. Yes! Kill him! I smile.

Kirk brings his blade down over Cal's head, but where he strikes, there's nothing but air. The Savage chief has slipped to Kirk's side, and now his arms wrap around Kirk's waist as he tackles him, not wasting any time sinking his teeth into Kirk's throat.

Cal comes up, mouth full of Kirk's flesh. He spits it out, smiling. "No. Just you."

He wallops Kirk in the face with a fist. Then another. A scarlet tooth flies, and then Cal leaves him, retrieving his sword. The chief approaches Kirk, who rises, unarmed, hand over his neck wound. "I commend you, Kirk Jackson. Thank you for giving me this opportunity. I swear on my mother, I'll take good care of Mia."

Kirk stumbles forward and Cal reaches out, catching him. "Die mighty. On your fe—"

Metal slips into Cal's side. Kirk rips out a knife and curls an arm around the chief's neck, locking him in place as he pokes him again and again and again. Cal screams out, grabs the scruff of Kirk's shirt, and pulls him into his blade.

The blade slides through Kirk's abdomen, out of his back. Kirk stabs Cal once more, and the chief angles his sword up, digging into the attack. I surge forward, but the Savages yank me back, and Cal steps back, towing his sword from Kirk's flesh.

Kirk sways, his arms hanging limp. Blood, like rain, plummets from his body.

Cal holds his side, then takes his knife from Kirk's hand and sheathes it. He motions me forward. "Come say goodbye, Mia."

The Savages push me forward. My heart teeters in my chest. With each step, I feel like I'm on a sliver of earth, tight-roping my way across a bottomless chasm. The Savage chief backs away, and I wrap around Kirk, supporting him.

"Please don't go." I place my forehead against his.

His brown face grows gray, and his knees cave, but he wraps around my neck. "Don't cry. Not in front of your enemies. Remember… what you promised?"

"Yes." I kneel, help Kirk to the ground, and cradle his head in my lap.

"Stop crying. Be strong." Kirk smiles, his bloody palm squeezes mine.

How does he smile at a time like this? He saved me during the ambush. I've been nothing but dead weight. Maybe if I had gotten on that truck back at Marigold, he wouldn't have had to worry about me. He could have escaped on his own. Kirk coughs, droplets of his life kissing my skin. An empty feeling expands in my chest, just like it did when I wandered the streets searching for my parents. Like the day Kirk found me carving through the dead. He saved me from that hell, but what can I do for him now? What have I done for him but been a nuisance? A brat who never appreciated all the knowledge and tough love he bestowed upon me.

Kirk's smile widens. "Survive, Mia."

I clench my teeth. "I will!"

"Tell Leon. I'm… sorry. I love you… both." Kirk peers into the scarlet sky, brown gaze softening. He utters a final word. A name. "Lucia."

CHAPTER 8

LEON

May 5, 2145, 21:00

Flies swarm three headless bodies. Between two torches, a sharp stick stands erect, a cruel totem of heads staring at the RFF soldiers in the moon's silver light. Three soldiers search the clearing for landmines, their scanners hovering over the ground.

"Clear!" A soldier calls back.

Leon rushes into the field, and together they take down the totem. He crashes to his knees, clutching Kirk's head. "I'm sorry, grandpa."

Leon glances around the apartment. The same wooden table with three chairs around it sits in the middle of the room under a dim light. The same ugly green couch hides in the shadows of the common area facing a holo-screen. The apartment smells the same. Like honey, cinnamon, and bleach.

Leon goes into the bathroom and sees a picture of himself, Kirk, and Mia hanging on the wall. There's a mustache on his top lip, the dark curls on his head shining in the light. Leon frowns at his younger self. He can't remember the last time he smiled like that. He wishes he could be that boy with so many dreams again. He wishes he could be excited about tomorrow again. Back then, things were so simple. Leon just had to keep up with

Kirk's routine and be the best big brother he could be to Mia. He rinses his face in the sink. When he looks into the mirror, his forest-brown eyes are on fire. Leon grips the edge of the sink until a shower of tears douses those flames.

Kirk's bedroom is neat. A twin bed rests against the back wall, his grandmother's photo still reigning supreme in the middle of the wall to his left. Right beside the door, a desk sits with a leather-bound journal on it. Leon lowers himself into the chair, opening the journal. He knows if Kirk were here, he'd be subject to physical assault for going through his things.

"But you can't hit me when you're dead, can you, Kirk?" Leon glances up with a grin.

He opens the journal and lets the pages cruise under his thumb. A third of the book is full. Leon reads the first page: To My Love, Lucia.

He reads through some of the entries but finishes none of them. He closes the book, deciding that being inside Kirk's mind for too long might break him. Leon sets the journal on the table and rises. He pauses, peers back at the journal, and returns to it. He goes to the last entry and begins reading.

Dear Lucia,

Good morning, beautiful. It's 05/04/2145. Mia's still asleep. I don't sleep much. Too many dreams of you and of all the… dirty things I've had to do to survive. I've been worrying lately. I hope Mia can't tell. I don't want her to follow in Leon's footsteps because he's still with the Scouts against my wishes, and she looks up to him far too much. If she found out what Leon was doing, she'd be mortified. It's not only the work they do, but who leads them. That damned Katherine should not be trusted. She's too power-hungry for anyone's good. I fear for Leon. I worry about the things he's done and will have to do. I hope I've made him strong enough. I love that boy. I love him and Mia so much. That's why I've been so hard on them despite your wishes.

I hope you can forgive me. I'll be with you soon, my love. I can feel it. Everything is distant and gradually slipping away. Every word. Every person. Tastes. Smells. Feelings. Is this how you felt when you were writing to me that day? Please watch over Mia and Leon. I hope I've left them prepared. I love you for all eternity, and when we meet again, I'll hug and kiss you relentlessly.

Love, Kirk

P.S. I still have the glasses. Mia gets annoyed like you did, and I find that funny.

A knock comes at the front door, and Leon closes the journal. He rises and moves into the common area. "Who is it?"

"Pizza guy!" a muffled voice on the other side answers.

Leon grins, opens the door, and Liz plows into him. She lifts him off the ground with a bear hug.

"What happened to you?" he asks once she lets him go. "You weren't answering my links."

"I almost escaped, but the other Scouts backed Zero and detained me. One came out to the plague camp, but then there was an ambush by a platoon of Runesians. Nineteen came to move me and I convinced him to let me go so I could help fight. When he did, I ran." Liz turns around, pointing at the back of her neck. A two-inch vertical cut scabs over. "Tore out my link to ensure One couldn't track me. Heard what happened and figured you would be here, so I hitched a ride when the RFF rotated outpost commands."

"One's having an aneurysm right now."

"Hopefully. Screw my psycho aunt. After you showed me what she said to you after I left our brief, I knew I couldn't stay any longer. I'm glad we did what we did. Are those kids in a refugee camp?"

Leon shakes his head. "They died. The Sickness killed the little ones, and the older one killed herself. I couldn't stop her." Leon's voice trembles. "I—Kirk. You know…."

Silence fills the space between the two and Liz moves closer, pulling Leon into her. "You don't have to be strong around me. Cry. I'm here. I'll always be right here."

Leon sobs into Liz's shoulder, his tears soaking her red hair.

Leon and Liz stand together in the first rank of the formation, both wearing the Lion's insignia on the shoulders of their dress uniforms.

General Wilde, a stout woman with cornrows and a scar on the left side of her full lips, stands in front of the formation of soldiers on a podium above Kirk's casket. She looks up into the sky and then down at her feet, her cape billowing behind her. There's this pressure constricting around Leon, blocking the air from his lungs.

General Wilde speaks. "Kirk was my first and only squad leader when I joined the RFF. He's the reason I'm a general today. He was always encouraging, brave, and resilient. Everything I know, I learned from him. I owe Kirk everything because he saved me and the rest of the squad countless times. So, today we mourn a legend. A man of honor and bravery. A man many have the utmost respect for. We grieve for a hero and a leader. We send Kirk Jackson off with immeasurable sadness. He gave his life for his people, so I want those of you here with me today to show Kirk that his fight continues with us. He was a Lion, and he deserves to go off mighty. Roar, soldiers! Roar until your voices break! Roar until your teeth shatter! Roar until your ears bleed! Roar for Kirk Jackson!"

General Wilde yells up, and soon, everyone around Leon screams and wails. They roar for his grandfather.

"Come on," Liz says, tilting her head back. "KIRKKKKKKKKKKK-KKK!"

The pressure around Leon bursts, and more air fills his lungs. He roars, but something snares it, and he can't stop the pain. His knees buckle, but General Wilde is suddenly there.

She hugs him. "Roar, Leon." General Wilde puts her lips next to his ear. "Kirk wants to see you still have some fight!"

Leon roars into the sky, his soul bleeding for Kirk. He lets it all out in one breathless vocalization of love.

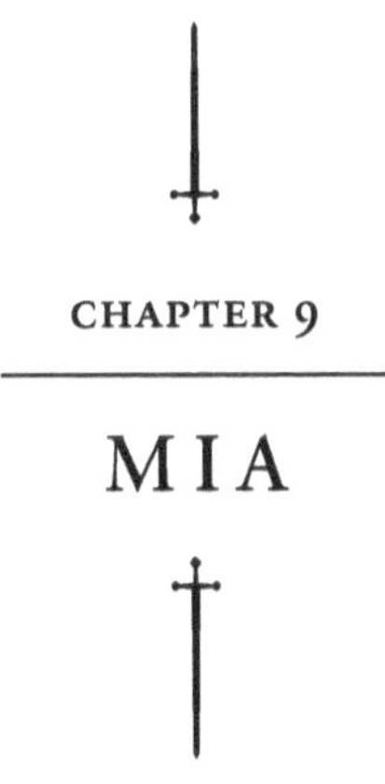

CHAPTER 9

MIA

May 6, 2145, 14:34

The metal of the truck grumbles when one of the prisoners back here with me shifts their position. It's a domino effect, and soon everyone squirms and cracks. We've been crammed back here in the darkness for hours, our anxious breaths mixing, making the body odor and mugginess unbearable. I pull my shirt away from my collarbone and fan myself with a hand. It doesn't help. Only blows the smell of shit up my nostrils. I don't know where the Savages are taking us, but it seems the old woman beside me does. She's been praying all night.

Her boney elbow jams into my side when she fastens her hands together. "We are the damned. On this black earth, we have been forsaken. This is Hell. God has cursed us and left us at Satan's mercy. And he is not the merciful one. He sends his Savages to torment us. To test our might. Ohhhh, God! If you can hear my prayers, bless light on us. Bless light and give us mercy. Give us strength. I beg of you! Take me from this despicable place, for I am your child! You are my glory and my everything!"

I'm still skeptical about God. Kirk always said we could only count on ourselves and look where that got us. Well, me. But if there is a God, this old lady is right about one thing: God certainly has cursed us.

The trailer door opens to a blinding sun, but my vision mod adjusts to the sharpness of the light. A mutant Savage aims his gun inside. His left eye is bigger than his right. He's short and thin with mud-colored skin. "Move back against the wall. All of you!" he shouts.

"God!" the old lady jumps up and charges the open door. The Savage shoots her, and she flies back, dead. The people scream and cower.

Another Savage, small and blond with missing teeth, crawls inside. She shoves the weird-eyed Savage to the side. "Lero, you idiot! Chief doesn't want anybody dead!"

He shrugs. "Relax, Tabby. Finger slipped. What's one old bitch? She wouldn't have been a good slave anyway."

"It's Tabatha!" The Savage woman growls, then scans us and points at me. "You! Come over here!"

I get up and Tabatha snatches my arm, squeezes tight, and pulls me close. When she talks, her spit flies in my face. "Don't go thinkin' your special cuz the chief likes you." She pushes me toward the ledge, and I hop down.

We're stopped in front of a dilapidated grocery store. Savages come from the building with empty hands. There are two other semi-trucks behind the one I jumped out of, and together they make a crescent shape. Around them are a slew of smaller cars and trucks with turrets mounted on them. I glance into the sky, hoping to see an RFF drone, but there isn't any such hope. The RFF should have our position by now. It's been an entire night.

Lero pokes his gun's barrel into my back. "Up front."

I move. I can only wait for an opportunity to escape. The Savage takes me to the passenger side of the truck. I climb inside, crawling to the other side to peer out of the window. There, another Savage stands guard. I sit back in the passenger's seat and cross my arms until Cal comes, hopping in on the driver's side and starting the truck. All the injuries he received from Kirk are covered with bandages.

"Put your seatbelt on," he says.

I ignore him, and he reaches over and pulls the seatbelt over my chest. A Savage worrying about seatbelts? Weird. He honks the horn and pulls off. In the side mirror, I see the rest of the Savages clambering into their vehicles, their wheels kicking up dust.

"We have about an hour's drive left."

I stare out the window. Can I make the jump and survive? What if I break a leg or my arm? What if I get a concussion? Cal is saying something.

I turn to him, and he asks, "I was asking if you were related to Kirk? You two didn't look alike."

I frown. Why is he acting so familiar? Why does he say Kirk's name as if he wasn't the one who killed him?

Cal doesn't let up. "I know you're angry, but—"

"Shut up! Don't you dare act like there's any justifiable reason for what you did! You're a murderer! I want nothing to do with you or this clan of animals!" I want to puke. Being so close to this Savage makes me sick.

"Harsh," Cal says.

The gray landscape blurs. I wish I had a Cerebral Link. I could tell Leon that I was in trouble, and we could fight Calamity Clan together. The truck slows.

"Entering auto-pilot mode," it says.

I can feel Cal's eyes. I want to claw them out. Cal's touch stabs into my shoulder, and I snap. "Do not touch me!"

His hand recoils, and he hangs his head. When he gazes at me with sympathy, it makes me angrier. I wish I had my machete—I'd lodge it in his skull.

"You're right. There's no excuse for what I did," he says. "I did it for selfish reasons to reach my father. You have every right to feel the way you feel."

What is wrong with this Savage?

Cal continues. "I will show you that me and my clan are different from what you believe. This doesn't mean anything to you right now, but I know that you're the one the Wise One told me about. I can feel it."

I scoff as I turn toward the window. A typhoon of grief swirls in my gut, and I grind my teeth together. I won't cry here. Not in front of this Savage. I won't give him anymore power over me.

We go as far into the forest as the trees allow, and Cal gets out first. He opens my door, and I climb down, standing beside him. Some of Calamity

Clan stands around us, and I wrinkle my nose. The Savages smell like rot and death.

"Calamity!" Cal calls out, gathering his people's attention as they dismount the vehicles and unload their loot. "Tonight, we feast. Make sure the prisoners are put away and divided. Lost Soul will be here to claim her portion in a week. Spread the word to our clanspeople of our triumphs against the Republic for Freedom!"

Lero cups his hands around his mouth. "You mean of how you skewered Kirk Jackson?"

The Savages swell around us, cheering Cal's name. "CAL! CAL! CAL! CAL! CAL!"

I lean back against the truck. They can make fun of Kirk's death all they want. I'll pay them back tenfold. Calamity Clan dances around Cal. They're distracted. I slip around the front of the truck and break for the woods. Direction doesn't matter. I just need to get as far away from these animals as possible. I run and run and run, not stopping when my chest burns—not stopping when the lactic acid builds in my legs, and they become heavy.

I swat branches out of the way and leap over fallen logs. A grin slashes across my face. That's Savages for yo—

Electrical currents frenzy through me, and I'm knocked back onto the ground. My limbs spasm. It feels like someone is shoving a rod of lightning into my spine. Why is there a barrier here? Savages don't use sophisticated technology like this. It goes against their belief that humanity's constant innovation caused Anomaly Day. Who here is smart enough to even keep the barrier operational? I squint in dismay as the faint film of blue energy becomes more visible. Then someone grabs me.

"I thought you Compounders were smarter than that." Glare picks me up and forces me to walk in front of him. I don't have the strength to fight back. "I know your eyes are modded. Are you stupid or blind?"

He shoves me again. We walk a bit farther, and he pushes me against a tree. "Where did you think you were going, princess?" Glare licks the back of my neck. The sensation makes everything inside of me wriggle with aversion, and I jerk away. Glare throws me to the ground and climbs on top of me.

"Get off…."

"Make me!" Glare begins to lift my shirt.

I spit into his face, and he smacks me, his fingers curling around my neck. My temples feel like they might explode. I claw into his face, but he doesn't let up. My vision grows darker and darker. Just when I think it's over, someone rips him off me.

Cal kneels next to me, cradling my head. "You're going to be okay." Then he gently places me down and stands. He whirls on Glare and hammers a fist into his jaw. "What were you doing?"

Glare turns back, spitting out blood with a scowl.

"Answer me!" Cal's voice shakes the trees. Birds take flight, but Glare does not.

"I was just trying to apprehend her," Glare says, "but she fought back."

"Go." Cal points back toward the trucks. "Help unload the trailers."

Glare turns to leave, but Cal grabs his shoulder. I'm still catching my breath, but I feel it. The tenacity in both these men.

"Never touch her again. She's mine," Cal says.

Glare swipes Cal's hand away and disappears into the greenery. Cal kneels beside me again, putting his water pouch to my lips. "I'm sorry, Mia."

I hate myself in this moment because for a split second, I believe him.

CHAPTER 10

MIA

Cal leads me to the shore of a murky lake where Savages fish and bath. In the middle of the water from wobbling canoes, Savages cast nets into the water, then hoist them back up with scores of fish. Their scales shimmer in the sunlight as they wriggle to their deaths. Savage women scrub their bodies, and their children's bodies with green spongy objects and cloths. The children wave and smile at me while most of the women lips curl with scorn. The shore is a mix of sand and mud, twigs, rocks, and shells.

Cal pauses near the edge of the lake, and I stop a bit away from him. Trees surround this area on all sides, their reflection, along with mine, upside down. My entire world has been flipped on its head.

"No more hot showers," Cal says with a laugh. He waits for me to say something, but I hug myself as an empty coldness grips my insides. He turns toward the foliage. "Come on. There's something I want to show you."

I follow Cal through the brush, passing two Savages with fishing buckets and spears. We move through clusters of colorful tents and a few rickety wooden buildings. Cal kneels and grabs a fistful of grass and mushy dirt. "It's very soft here. Sometimes, this area becomes swampy, so most of our buildings are up there."

Cal points, and I tilt my head back. Circular-shaped buildings are suspended in the air, some built around the shafts of trees, others held up by wooden platforms and beams. Savage children sprint across bridges, playing tag. A boy leaps into the air, latches onto one of the many ropes that hang from sturdy branches, and swings to another platform.

"Pretty cool, huh?" Cal steps onto a walkway that curls around the trunk of a tree.

"It's different," I say.

We travel across a few bridges until we reach an area where Calamity Clan's flag reigns supreme, the sickle-shaped white C with the sword through it on a burgundy background crinkling in the breeze. A young Savage stands motionless beside it.

"This is the middle of our village. If you ever get lost, come toward the flag to reorient yourself," Cal tells me. He takes me into a crowded restaurant and bar where Savages cheer on a wrestling match between two of their clansmen.

The bar area takes up the entire back portion of the space. On the floor there are multiple wooden tables and chairs pushed to the sides so the two Savages fighting can have some room. A few shoddy booths with fur for comfort sit nestled to the right, groups of Savages laughing together. Red, blue, and green neon lights snake around the ceiling and up some of the walls that hold several wooden dart boards.

We approach the bar, and the Savages there offer us their stools, but Cal shakes his head, leaning against the counter until an autumn-haired woman in a green plaid shirt and blue jeans slides in front of us. "And our chief in shining armor has returned. Want a drink?"

"No." Cal motions toward me, then to the woman in plaid, who cleans a wooden cup. "Mia, this is Dana, Calamity Clan's quartermaster, project manager, and technology wizard. Without her, we wouldn't have this village."

Dana spits in her hand and holds it out for me to take. I hesitate.

"Don't be shy," she says. "We're both outsiders."

I take her palm, holding back the disgust. "Nice to meet you."

Dana smirks. "Heard you had a run-in with my barrier. What did you think?"

So, she's the one responsible for the barrier. That makes sense. There's no way a born Savage could build and operate such technology. They're too stupid.

"It hurt."

"Good." Dana looks proud of herself.

"I always knew you were a sadist," Cal says.

"Only sometimes."

A Savage barrels into the bar and knocks over a stool.

"Kill him!" someone shouts.

"Hey!" Dana screams. "Just because the Sickness has my dad down today doesn't mean y'all can trash the place!"

Cal ushers me away as another Savage pounces on top of the one that knocked over the stool, punching him in the face. "We'll be seeing you."

Dana waves. "Let's chat sometime, Mia!"

We go back outside.

"Break that stool, and I'll fry you!" I hear Dana holler.

Cal takes me to a market area where Savages barter and trade items at different stalls. The sugary scent of desserts and the savory char of fire-roasted meats fill the air. We head to a school where Savage children sit huddled together as two Savages each show them a handful of berries.

One of the teachers is light-skinned with curly hair. A tattooed line runs down the right side of his face. The other is the color of chalk with russet-colored hair spilling to his shoulders. They notice us at the same time and come over. The children follow, their eyes lighting up. Soon, there's a crowd around us.

"Chief Cal, you're back!" a Savage girl cries.

"Did you kill any bad guys?" a Savage boy asks.

"Is this your girlfriend?" an older Savage girl demands, then sniffs me. "She smells nice. I think she's pretty."

"Hey kids," the light-skinned Savage says. "That's not how you greet our chief."

A few of the children gasp and kneel. The others quickly copy their peers.

"Now, go sit down and wait for us to return," the chalk-colored Savage says, and the children scurry away, peeking back with curious expressions. He turns back toward us. "I'm Phoenix, by the way."

"And I'm Marco," the other adds.

I remember them now. They were with Cal when he showed up at the clearing. Marco and Phoenix offer me their hands, and we shake.

"Welcome," Marco says.

"You two make sure you have a few drinks," Cal says, and opens the curtain.

"We will as long as you're there." Phoenix holds the curtain for us as we step out.

"I will be." Cal leads me across a bridge. "There's one last place I need to show you."

We travel through the village back toward the center. Moss grows on the sides of the buildings and stretches along the ropes of the bridges. Nets travel up and down from the ground level with supplies. An advance pulley system carries arrows, water, food, and other miscellaneous objects over my head in buckets through the village, Savages dipping their hands inside to take what they need. Back at the flag, four different bridges intersect this location. One of them leads to a single building with a tree sprouting out of it. I trail Cal across the bridge, and he opens the door.

A tree trunk is in the center of a large room. Most of the bark has been scraped off. Many weapons lie strewn about on the floor. A sword. A bow and arrows. A machine gun and an energy spear. To the right, there's a king-sized bed with furs covering it. Above it, a rectangular window lets in the sunlight. There's nothing on the left side but shade.

"Come over here." Cal leads me to the back of the room, showing me a throne made of wood and bones with fur draped over the seat. He grabs my shoulders, and I tense. "Relax. I'm not going to hurt you." He gently pushes me into the seat. "This can all be yours."

I could send my knee into his jaw. I could fight him with these weapons and raze this village to the ground. But I don't do any of that. When I was younger, Kirk told me a beautiful woman can get almost anything she wants if she wants it bad enough and plays to the fantasy of men. I don't think I'm that beautiful, but it's clear this Savage likes me, so I should use that to my advantage.

"I want you to Unify with—" Cal begins, but a rapid knocking at the door interrupts him. He turns. "Come in. What is it?"

A Savage burst inside. "It's Glare. You gotta come. He's killing the new guy!"

Cal and I make it back to the ground. There's a pack of Savages gathered cheering. Cal clears the way for us. Glare sits on top of Daniel, punching him.

"Glare!" Cal pulls him off. "What's your problem? We're supposed to be celebrating."

"I'm disciplining a slave."

"He proved himself in front of everybody. You saw!"

"Ah!" Glare sticks his arms out and backs away from Cal. "So, now, in Calamity, we have Savages as pathetic as this? He's weak. He shouldn't be one of us!"

"He earned his spot."

"You don't get to make that decision on your own. You can't just bring people here and make them Savage. They haven't been tested. How is that fair to those of us who spent our entire childhoods training to be recognized?" Glare points at Daniel, and then at me, his gaze making the hairs on my neck and arms stiffen. "Don't you agree, Calamity?"

Calamity Clan agrees with cheers and fists raised into the air.

Glare sneers at Cal. "So, Chief. Let's see how your princess here holds up in a fight to the death."

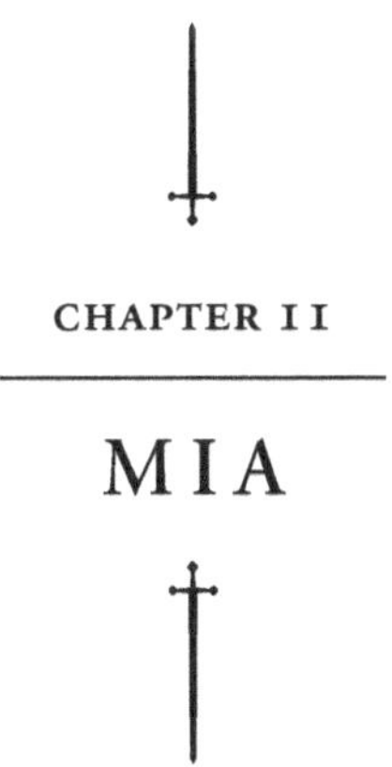

CHAPTER 11

MIA

This place brings back violent memories. Cal pushes a ladder into the darkness. "I'm sorry, Mia."

I begin my descent, ignoring him.

"You'll only be here until tomorrow night," he says, as if a twenty-foot hole in the ground is a justifiable place to keep a person.

My feet sink into cool sludge when I reach the bottom. I turn, and my heart shatters.

Two children huddle together against the earth across from me, one boy and one girl, both no older than twelve. The girl has her arms wrapped around the boy. They stare at me wide-eyed, trembling. How does doing something like this to children cross any human being's mind? I remind myself that the Savages lost their humanity long ago. This type of logic doesn't apply to them.

The fading sunlight lets me see the girl's big, hazelnut-colored eyes under her bushy eyebrows. She stands, and her dark hair tumbles over her brown face.

The boy is pulled to his feet by the girl. He's shorter than her, his pale skin black with muck. I'm sure his hair would be golden if it weren't for the mud, and his cheeks round if it weren't for being starved.

I step forward and stop, the boy's eyes halt me. They are bluer than the ocean and sky combined, but the hostility there is a warning. Something's wrong.

I hold my hands in the air. "It's okay. My name's Mia. I'm not here to hurt you."

Streaks of sunlight uncover the bruises and scars on the children's arms, legs, and faces.

"I'm not one of them." I step forward. "I prom—"

The girl's hand is a blur, then a rock hits me in the head. I'm stunned for a moment, but I see the girl coming at me with a sharpened stick, and I kick at her. She tumbles backward, and the boy jumps onto my back, his grubby fingers trying to dig into my eyes.

I spin around to get him off. "Stop! Stop! Please! I'm not one of them!"

The boy yanks my hair, and the girl kicks me in the shin. I buckle, fall, and curl into the fetal position as their feet and fists batter me. An agonizing minute or two goes by, and the children stop attacking. I sit up, my head throbs, and a new gash stings on my forehead. The children watch me. They must think I'm angry, and to an extent, I am, but not with them. They attacked me for a reason. They don't trust me because the Savages have abused them.

"I'm not Savage," I say.

"Liar! Did we pass? We can be Savages," the girl says.

"We won't disappoint you anymore," the boy adds.

These poor children. I stick my hands into the air and stand, pushing toward them again. I know better than anybody how they feel. I know exactly what they need.

"I won't hurt you. Please believe me," I say.

There's nowhere for them to run. I brace myself for another attack, but they don't move. When I reach them, I tug at their mud-sodden shirts, pulling them into my arms. I squeeze tight, and their small bodies shiver against mine.

I learn a lot about the children within a couple hours of talking. The girl's name is Jade, and she's eleven. The boy's name is Sannvi, and he's ten. They were a part of the same Nomad caravan. Calamity Clan attacked them, and they were taken in as slaves a few of months ago. Jade lost her older sister, and Sannvi, his parents.

Jade is the one talking. She tells me they weren't aggressive enough, and that's why they were sent to the pit field. Different Savages beat them or tricked them into failing so they would be prisoners longer. They've survived off bugs and rainwater for a month.

"You both are very strong," I say, and hold them close as the coldness of the earth creeps under my skin. "I promise I'll get you both out of here tomorrow."

"Really?" Sannvi clutches my shirt.

I can't let these children live like this. I want to show Jade and Sannvi that there is good in this fucked up world. "Really."

CHAPTER 12

LEON

May 7, 2145, 09:56

Two up-armored vehicles stop outside of a rusty, run-down charge station. Leon and Liz jump out, and General Wilde meets them near their vehicle.

"Well, what do you think?" General Wilde asks. "This is as close as we can get to Calamity Clan. Our drones have been tracking these Savages for years, so we know how far out they normally patrol. I've linked the known routes of their typical movement patterns."

Leon inspects the charge station. "It can work. We'll make it work."

The morning is hot and spiteful—gnats and mosquitoes swarm them already. The two soldiers assigned to Leon get out of the back and open the trunk of the truck.

"Let's go check it out," General Wilde says, leading Leon and Liz toward the charge station. "You'll be out here for a few weeks. I'll have an experienced team from Talon on rotation with you. If there's any need for reinforcements, the next closest outpost is Outpost Zion."

"How long do you think it'll take to get Talon ready to assault Calamity Clan?" Leon asks, as he follows the general into the charge station.

"A month. Maybe two." General Wilde picks up a dented soda can, inspects the nutritional information on the back and frowns. "Many of them are inexperienced, so I must make sure they are ready for battle within the pods. The Calamity Clan Savages haven't posed a serious threat in years, so we've left them alone to focus on the Runesians, but that seems to be changing."

Old magazines and ripped cardboard boxes litter the charge station's floors. Dust filaments float through the air and fall onto bare shelves. Leon walks behind a counter, and the smell of decaying flesh hits him in full force. He covers his nose and pushes through plastic stringers into the back, to the source in a filthy bathroom. A dead woman with gray skin and sunken eyes. Flies and roaches crawl over her. Leon rushes out into the front of the building. "Corpse. Bathroom."

"I'll get my guys on it," General Wilde says.

Leon steps outside and inhales the fresh air.

"You gonna be okay, man?" Liz asks, stepping out behind him. "That wasn't your first dead body."

"My stomach's just a little messed up, but I'm fine. I just need to save Mia. So, let's set this place up, and do what we came out here to do, alright?"

Liz watches him for a moment, then turns back toward the door. "Okay. I'll move some shelves around inside."

She disappears into the charge station, and Leon goes for the truck.

Allie, a plump woman with blond hair, struggles toward the building with two of the six capsules they'll need to place this outpost and some of the surrounding area under a Cloak and EMP barrier. She juggles each, trying to keep them balanced on her arms.

Leon rushes to her aid, taking one. "Let me help."

"Bit off more than I could chew." She lets him take one, and they place them inside. "Thank you, Sergeant."

The two go back outside and head for the truck. Leon says, "Just call me Leon."

"Gotcha."

Leon swipes pests away from his face. "So why are you a problem child?"

Allie smirks. "Is that why the general reassigned me under you?"

"Kind of. But you seem fine to me."

"I am fine. My other leaders were the problem. You know men, they don't like when a female's plan is better than theirs."

Leon chuckles as they stop near the trunk. "Well, you're safe here to speak out if you ever think my plan has holes or could be better."

Allie smiles. The freckles on her pink cheeks flare as she grabs another capsule. "That's what my other three squad leaders said too. But I'll keep that in mind."

She carries the other capsule away, and the other soldier, Julio, a dark-haired man with a scruffy beard, and red-brown skin, comes from the driver's side. He has a short torso, but his arms and legs are long, making him seem taller. He shoulders past Leon, grabbing his sleeping gear.

Leon pulls a capsule toward himself. "Hey, Rodriguez. I want us to be a team, alright? Whatever happened in the past, let it stay there."

Julio stops, not looking back. "So, you read my profile?"

"Yeah, and trust me, I understand how you fe—"

Julio whirls and shoves Leon in the chest. "You don't understand shit about me, crow!"

Leon holds his hands in the air. "I got you, man. No need to get hostile."

"You can stand there and put on that show, but you're just a crow, and that's all you'll ever be."

"I'm not a Scout anymore. I'm out here for my sister."

"I read your profile too. It was blank, aside from your date of rank. The general just handed you the position of sergeant. But I know the dirty work you've done. I bet your sister doesn't, does she?"

Leon's silence is enough of an answer for Julio.

"That's what I thought. I'm out here for my own reasons." Julio turns and walks toward the charge station. "Stay outta my way, and I'll stay outta yours."

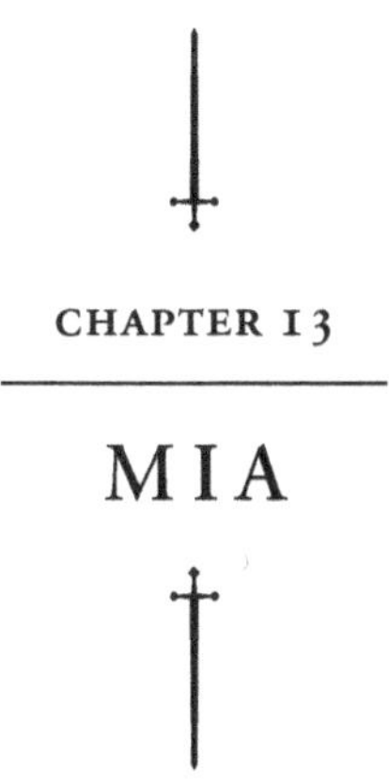

CHAPTER 13

MIA

May 7, 2145, 20:00

A ladder drops into the pit, and Jade and Sannvi cling to me.

"I'll get you out of here like I said. Just wait here."

They nod and let me go. I take to the ladder. An older woman the color of coffee with crimson pupils and long silver hair waits for me in a patch of moonlight. She wears a dark gown that matches the black cat tails dangling from her earlobes. When she smiles my way, it's warm and bright, but something tells me this is a powerful woman. One I shouldn't cross.

"You're just as beautiful as Cal told me," she says. "I'm Rhena, the Scarlet Witch, one of the elders of Calamity Clan."

A witch. Great.

"Mia. Thank you."

"Come." Rhena places a hand on the small of my back and leads me into the woods. "Daniel is already at the arena. I'm here to give you this." She holds out her palm, and in it is a dark feather, the thin white quill sharp. "It's laced with poison. Use it quickly. The Ogor has killed five today."

"Why are you helping me?" I shove the feather it into my pocket.

"Cal asked me to."

A few moments later, we step out of the brush and into a clearing full of Savages. They cheer, weapons and fists raised. Rhena leads me into the chaos. The plethora of golden bangles jangling on her wrists reflects the sharp flames.

"KILL HIM! KILL HIM! KILL HIM!" the Savages chant.

When we make it to the front where Cal, Glare, and Daniel stand, all their eyes are glued to the carnage inside the ring of torches. A pot-bellied, ginger-bearded giant towers over a man shielding himself with a trashcan lid.

The man begs. "Please…"

There's a dead woman lying near them, the dirt beneath her stained red from her cracked skull.

"Bash his head in!"

"Rip him apart!"

The Savages sing for iniquity, and the Ogor tears the trashcan lid from the man's grasp and slams a foot into his face. Blood bursts from the man's nose, and the Ogor lifts him by the scruff of his shirt.

Glare cups his hands around his mouth. "Make this one interesting!"

The Ogor raises a bloody hammer and nails the man in the face. I hear the bone underneath his skin crunch and splinter.

"OGOR! OGOR! OGOR!" the Savages cheer.

The Ogor cracks the man another time, and his ears bleed.

And again. His limbs go limp.

And a final time. His neck breaks, his dented head falls forward, spilling blood down the Ogor's arm.

The Ogor drops his victim and roars. He looks demonic, his tomato-colored face and orange beard speckled red. Glare goes into the arena, raises the Ogor's arm, and the Savages go wild.

Daniel turns to me. "How are we supposed to beat a monster like him?"

I look across at the Ogor, who chomps on a chicken leg. Glare is in his ear, pointing my way. The Ogor smirks at me and licks his lips. Did I lie to Jade and Sannvi?

Cal whispers in my ear, "Use that feather the first chance you get. Don't give him a chance."

The Ogor stands, belching. Savages slap him on the back. Kirk taught me how to handle myself, but he also taught me not to fight if I know I'll lose. The Ogor is an enormous man, if I can even call him that. He doesn't look human. The closer I inspect, the less human he appears. His pointy ears aren't where they're supposed to be, yet, farther up on the sides of his bald, oval-shaped head, which is uneven, as if someone forced the middle of it down and it remained that way. The Ogor watches me, and his lightless eyes resemble the same non-humanness of Lost Ones.

I've come across people like him before. Everyone calls them mutants. People with genetic mutations because of the Scorpilionitis bacteria that lives inside of everyone. The Ogor is a mutant like that weird-eyed Savage, Lero, but his mutations are more noticeable. In Compound Marigold, I came across a Nomad with seven fingers, and one woman gave birth to a child with an eye in the middle of his face. There was a boy with fangs. An older woman with four eyes. Leon joked once that if he were born with a mutation, he'd want it to be something useful, like having retractable claws tougher than anything like that old-world superhero, the Wolverine. I wish I had something to help me now against the Ogor.

"Mia," Cal says, and I turn to him, shocked by his expression. Fear. Why is he afraid? Why does this Savage care if I live or die? We just met. "Don't die. Please."

Rhena stands in the clearing between us and the Ogor. "This will be the final fight this evening," she says. "Will our champion slave prevail against the newcomers Mia and Daniel, or will they show their grit and earn their place within our clan? I ask now that our challengers choose a weapon."

Daniel grabs a knife from the ground, and I pick up a fork. There's a tire iron lying on the other side of the arena, and the trash can lid is between us and the Ogor.

"May you all show courage in the face of death. Begin!" Rhena leaves the arena.

The Ogor doesn't move. His eyes flick between me and Daniel, but when he slides a foot forward, it's in my direction. Like a bull, he charges. I dart close to the arena's edge, and turn, then try to stab the Ogor with my fork. He dodges and swipes the back of his hand across my face.

White noise. I wipe the blood from my lips, and go at him again, but the Ogor catches my wrist and slings me to the ground.

The Savages chant for my death. "KILL HER! KILL HER! KILL HER!"

The Ogor towers over me with a foot raised. I try to push myself off the ground, but a wave of pain ripples down my arm, and I collapse. My right shoulder's dislocated—the Ogor slams his foot into my chest. His weight crushes me.

I feel my ribs crack. When I suck in a breath, pain explodes in my chest, and tiny black bubbles burst in my field of vison. Kirk's voice sings to me. *Survive, Mia.*

I pull the crow's feather from my pocket and stab the Ogor in the ankle. He laughs and brings his hammer down. He misses, bashing the ground next to my head, and then he roars and whirls. A knife sticks between his shoulder blades.

"Come on, ugly." Daniel dances back, hiding behind the trash can lid. "Did you forget about me?"

The Ogor snarls, attacking Daniel, and I sit up, taking a shallow breath. A few ribs must be broken. Pain spikes through my chest. I need to move. Jade and Sannvi are waiting for me. Daniel saved me. Despite him killing two innocent women to survive, if I don't help him, we'll both be killed.

I groan when I stand. My right arm hangs limp. I can't move it. The Ogor hammers the trash can lid that separates him from Daniel. The giant drips sweat, and I can tell he's already getting slower with each strike. I go for the tire iron.

"Mia!" Daniel screams.

The Ogor busts through Daniel's defense, and the trash can lid goes flying. Daniel ducks under the Ogor's wild swing but can't dodge his vise grip.

I run toward them—the Ogor slams Daniel into the ground. I beat the giant in the back with the tire iron before he can slam Daniel again. The Ogor whirls, tries to grab me, but Daniel crashes into him, rips the knife out, and frantically stabs him wherever he can. I join the attack, battering the Ogor from the front.

The Ogor grunts, crashing to a knee when Daniel shanks him in the side. Daniel goes to pull out the knife, but the Ogor clobbers him in the head, and he falls back. I swing the tire iron at the Ogor's face, but he catches it, tears it away from me and smashes his hammer into my side. I keel over, holding my ribs, and the Ogor steps toward me. He swings at me. I throw my hands up, but the blow still connects, knocking me across the ground.

Darkness eddies in the corners of my vision and blood trails from my forehead. I try to stand, but the world tilts. Everything hurts—the Ogor latches onto my ankle and pulls me toward him. I kick back, but his strength overwhelms me. He climbs onto me, flips me over, and places his hands around my neck. I claw at his arms.

"Fight, Mia!" someone yells. "Us outsiders ain't weak!"

Oh, Dana. She's here to watch me die. Nothing works, and less air makes it to my lungs. The Ogor's face blurs above me, and cheers for my death fade.

I'm sorry, Jade and Sannvi. I lied. This is not a fight I can win.

CHAPTER 14

LEON

May 8, 2145, 10:45

Leon leads his team down a cracked asphalt highway surrounded by trees on both sides. They keep a staggered column, with Liz in the rear.

This is boring, Liz links.

Julio kicks a rock past Leon. *Agree.*

Allie, see anything? Leon asks, glancing into the sky at the drone that hovers above them.

Nothing, Allie confirms.

Leon holds up a fist, and the group stops. The world is too still. No birds sing. No squirrels scurry up trees. No deer crash through the foliage. Silence rings in Leon's ears. It's like a constant, pestering, high-pitched frequency that rattles his brain. He scans the trees, trying to ignore the sensation of ants crawling all over him.

His father, Danston, in the same baggy, gray suit appears before him. "Can't believe my old man's dead. Maybe us Jacksons are cursed or something." Danston walks circles around Leon. "I would write an elegy, but he made me quit writing when I was a boy. Said it was a waste of time. Do you know what else is a waste of time, Leon?"

Leon winces, unable to answer. His head is on fire, but when his father pushes the cool barrel into the middle of his forehead, everything within him turns to ice.

Danston says, "You searching for that girl. You know she's hanging from a rope by now!"

The pistol kicks as his father shoots—someone tackles Leon to the ground, and he comes back to reality. It's Julio.

Leon crawls after him into the wood line. "What's going on?"

"Savages. Fuck, man. Why are you spacing out, crow?"

Allie confirms. *Savages. They've split up. Four. Four hundred meters. Two o'clock. Four. Three hundred meters. Ten o'clock. The last two are driving down the road in a truck with the back covered.*

Yaps rise into the sky.

We stand our ground. Allie, provide aerial support, don't shoot unless necessary, Leon says.

Copy.

"Finally, something interesting," Julio says.

"Liz. Take out the four to the ten. Leave one alive. Julio, on me. Keep up." Leon scrambles to his feet. "Let's go."

Leon lies prone, Cloaked. A mangy, black dog with demon eyes and two tails barrels out of the brush toward them.

Rodriguez, kill the dog, Leon links.

An energy beam knocks it down with a sharp and high-pitched yelp. Smoke trickles from its body, the fetor of burnt fur and blood fill the air. Leon searches through his scope, but still can't see the Savages.

Allie. I need eyes.

They've spread out in a wide semi-circle, two hundred meters, she says.

He waits, the silence daunting. Then he hears it—the crunch of a branch to his right.

Rodriguez, take the one on the far left, Leon commands. *Keep them alive.*

Leon levels his breathing and focuses his sight on the Savage near him. He squeezes the trigger, knocking the Savage back with a bullet to the head. He repositions himself, and searches for the second one, but must tuck into cover when a hail of bullets pelt the earth near his hiding spot.

"Where are you, coward?" the Savage calls out.

Leon throws his gun out, distracting the Savage, and tackles him from his blind spot. He hammers a fist into the Savage's face, then reaches for his sidearm, but a sting of electricity paralyzes him. Leon's Cloak deactivates as he falls to the side, and the Savage rises, blue sparks coming from his gloved hand.

"Die!" the Savage jumps on top of Leon, pulls out a knife, and stabs Leon through the palm.

Leon spasms, the currents of electricity still jolting through him as the Savage forces the blade toward his face. It's millimeters from his eye. Leon thrusts his hips, unbalancing the Savage, and then he jumps up, and rips the knife from his hand. Before the Savage can stand, Leon plunges the blade through his neck, pushing him to the ground.

"Bastard!" A third Savage charges Leon with an axe.

Leon raises his arms to defend himself, but a zing of energy zips by him, and the Savage drops.

Julio deCloaks himself, smiling. Leon picks up his gun. "Thanks." He turns, raising his gun. "Behind you!"

The last Savage tackles Julio from behind. The two wrestle on the ground, and Leon rushes forward to get a clear shot. Julio claws the Savage in the face, flips him over and gets on top, but the Savage throws him off, and whips out a blade. He takes a handful of Julio's hair and is about to slash his throat, but Leon taps his trigger twice. One bullet tears through the Savage's neck. The other rampages through his skull, and he keels over.

Leon helps Julio up, then inspects his injured left hand. It stings more than a normal stab wound should. Poison. He doesn't have much time. Leon wraps a bandage around his palm and points at the Savage Julio shot earlier. "Wake him up."

They stand over the last Savage, who grunts and curses in anguish as he fingers his charred stump of a leg. Leon kneels in front of him, tapping him on the cheek. "Hey-hey-hey, focus, focus. I can save your life if you give me some information."

"Go fuck yourself!" the Savage screams.

"I need information about a girl named Mia. Is she in your camp?"

The Savage spits into Leon's face, and he stabs his blade through the wild man's hands, pinning them to the stump. The Savage roars in agony.

Leon twists the blade. "The girl. Mia. Answer."

"Fuck! Fuck! Fuck you! Kill me, you asshole!" he yells.

"I think I'll keep you alive instead. Give him some adrenaline."

Julio crouches near the Savage with a needle out of his first aid kit.

Leon links Liz. *Liz, update?*

One fled, she says. *The rest look pretty dead to me*, she says.

Allie's voice cuts through. *The Savages in the truck just stopped in the middle of the road. They're letting Lost Ones out of the back! Liz, five of them are headed to your location. Another two are coming toward you, Leon.*

"Julio, go help Liz!" Leon orders, and Julio races off. Leon connects back to Allie. *Get out here now!*

Already in the truck! ETA: five minutes.

Guttural cries frenzy through the forest, and Leon kneels, aiming toward the road. Here they come.

CHAPTER 15

LEON

Sweat trails down Leon's face as he scans the trees, keeping his gun level and ready. His hand throbs, and a numbness rides up his arm. Branches snap and leaves rustle. He swings his gun to the left.

"Fish!"

Leon whirls. A male Lost One strides out of the brush, leaping side to side. Leon shoots, grazes its shoulder. It twists and lowers itself to all fours, and lunges toward him. Leon shoots again, this time hitting it in the chest. It flies back, and he lines up a third shot between its eyes, but another Lost One pounces on him, scratching and beating at him.

The Lost One sinks its teeth into Leon's neck, and they fall to the ground. Leon stabs the Lost One in the flank until it lets go, and he jumps up, kicking it in the head. Before it can recover, Leon sends a bullet through its skull, and looks for the first one, but it's gone. A trail of blood leads off deeper into the forest.

Tracking a runaway. It's injured, Leon links his team.

Let it go, Liz replies. *Allie's here and taking fire on the road from the last two Savages.*

That thing used to be human. Allie will be fine if she stays in the truck. You and Julio capture them. I'll be there.

Leon tracks the Lost One to a swamp. He can hear it splashing in the marsh ahead.

"Fish! Fish! Fish! Fish!" it sings.

Leon slides against a tree, watching the Lost One. Its back is coarse with lean muscle and scars. He places his sights on the Lost One's head and steadies his breathing as he toys with the trigger, gradually squeezing it.

The Lost One holds two frogs. It stuffs one into his mouth and swallows it whole. "Fish!"

Leon freezes, holding the tension. There's a tattoo over the Lost One's heart. It's a ribbon with writing on it, reading: Amor Bianca, My Beloved.

A flash of cold grips Leon's spine and that shadowy figure appears, leaning against the tree adjacent to him with its arms crossed. "Watch your back. He's going to kill you."

Leon turns just in time to redirect a blade. He grabs a Scout's arm, and tries to break it, but the Scout kicks back, and they tumble to the ground, rolling away from each other.

"You must be new," Leon says, unsheathing his ion blade. It burns blue.

"How'd you know?" The Scout copies Leon, a glowing white ion blade cutting through the darkness of the marsh.

"Every Scout learns to stab deserters in the back. But that's only hypothetical because rarely will you ever get close enough to one to do it. Only newbies try, and without a Cloak at that. Should have shot me in the head."

"I wanted my first desertion kill to be proper, and you ruined it." The Scout lunges forth.

Leon meets him in the middle and tries to lop off his head, but the Scout ducks, and Leon sidesteps, raising his foot for a kick but the Scout tackles him, his ion blade plunging into Leon's kidney.

The blade digs deeper. It burns through Leon's organ as the Scout moves it up. Leon screams and stabs the Scout in the side.

"Too slow!" The Scout yanks his ion blade out and goes for Leon's head.

Leon reaches up, grabs the Scout's wrist, and sends his attack into the dirt. Then he curls around the Scout, sliding behind him, choking him. "This is how you do it."

Leon takes his ion blade from the Scout's side and buries it into his back, straight through the heart. The Scout slumps, and Leon falls to the side, putting as much pressure as he can on his wound. He pulls out a shot of adrenaline and sticks himself in the thigh.

Liz, I need help. I'm bleeding out…., he links.

The sky churns above him, the leaves whisper in the hot wind. Leon's father and the shadow appear together, their arms wrapped around one another.

"He never amounted to much," the shadow says.

"He's just following in our footsteps, dear." Leon's father raises the pistol. "We're such a tragic family."

The world goes silent and the gun kicks. For a moment, everything's cold and gray. Leon feels as if his body levitates into the air. He goes up and up and up until the scents of cinnamon and honey grab him, tugging him back down. He opens his eyes, and Kirk and Lucia kneel around him.

"Show some grit, boy," Kirk says.

Lucia places a palm on his cheek. "You still have so much to do."

"Grandpa… grandma…."

Dizziness overwhelms Leon, and he faints into a void of black.

MIA

August 31, 2135

"Stand up against that tree!" a fat Savage with tattooed lines down his white belly and an X burned onto his left cheek points.

My left foot is heavy because there's a metal bracelet connected to a metal rope around it. It hurts. Last night the Savages made us walk for a long time, and now we're some place in the woods. The Savages have a bunch of tents where they sleep. Wires crisscross between the trees, and cans, metal plates, and other items hang from them.

The fat Savage's stomach pokes me in the face before he smacks me to the ground, looking back at another Savage, who has an X just like the fat one in the middle of his forehead.

"What's wrong with her?" the fat Savage asks.

"You probably stink."

The fat Savage yanks me off the ground and puts a knife to my neck. "Do I stink, you little bitch?"

I wriggle in his grasp, crying.

"Do I fucking stink or not?"

"No!" I cry.

He shoves me toward the tree. "Go stand near that tree and don't move or I'll kill ya."

I do as the Savage says.

He holds a bow, an arrow drawn back on the string. "Watch me get it right above her head!" He lets the arrow loose and I close my eyes, hoping it doesn't hit me.

There are nine other kids here with me. They make us sleep in a deep hole. Bugs crawl over me and my stomach growls. I can't remember the last time I ate. This girl beside me, she cries. I don't think I can cry anymore. My head dips again, but I jerk awake. If I fall asleep, will I get in trouble? Will the Savages be mad at me again?

"Hey," a boy whispers. He stands in the middle of our hole with a stick in his hand. The moon reveals the freckles dancing across his cheeks. He raises the stick into the air. "My dad said Savages are stupid. We can trick them and run away. I'll beat them with this stick!"

"They have swords and guns," I say.

"Scaredy cat."

"Leave me alone."

Morning comes, and a ladder drops into our hole. "Come on up!" a Savage yells. "We got work for y'all to do!"

The boy from last night goes first with a stupid grin on his face. When we're all up top, the sun hurts my eyes, so I cover them with an arm.

"What's this?" a Savage asks.

It's the boy, pointing his stick at the Savage. It's sharp at the end. Maybe he really will beat them.

"It's a stick, dummy." He spits at the Savage's feet. "My dad said that's how your people show disrespect to each other. You can burn in hell for killing him!" The boy tries to stab the Savage, but the Savage snatches the stick and punches him to the ground, stomping on him. "Eh, Wally, we got us a rebel."

That Savage with the dark lines down his stomach comes over. He has a sledgehammer over his shoulder. The other Savage points to the boy under his foot. "This one tried to shank me."

Wally stands over the boy. "You think you're a big man, don't you, little guy?"

The boy sits up, holding his jaw. "I'm sorry. I won't do it again!"

"You got your one chance when we saved you from that town, and now you want another one?"

"Yes! I'll be the best worker. I promise."

"I don't care about your promises." Wally flips the sledgehammer off his shoulder and crushes the boy's hand. His scream drills into my ears, and Wally kicks him in the face, sneering and turning to us. "All of you are our slaves. That means you do what we say when we say. You have no rights. You're nothing. You work and you survive. Simple. Let this one here serve as an example of what will happen if any of you ever disobey us or try to go against our rule."

He raises the sledgehammer over the boy and brings it down right on top of his head.

It rains, and in the hole, we sink in the sludge. What did I do to deserve this? My stomach feels like it's flipping in on itself. My mom would never let me be this hungry. Lightning streaks across the dark sky, and thunder growls, just like my stomach. How many days has it been? I think two.

The same girl from the other night, she cries again. The other kids must be sleeping.

"Why do you keep crying?" I ask.

The girl sniffles. I can't see her face because it's dark, but I know she's there, looking my way.

She asks her own question. "How old are you?"

"Seven."

The girl sighs. "Basically brainless, then."

"What?"

"Nothing. I'm nine. My name's Jocelyn. What's yours?"

"Mia."

"Well, Mia. I'm crying because I understand that we're going to die here. Maybe you're too young to understand what death is, but that's what happened to our parents, and that's what's going to happen to us with these Savages."

"They're going to make us die? Like go away forever?"

"Yes. Maybe. Maybe not," Jocelyn says. "But I think the sooner we're dead, the better. This will only get worse."

The next day is hot, and we wear those metal bracelets attached to the metal ropes near a pile of bodies. Flies buzz around us and the dead. I know they're dead because they don't move, and the older kids whisper it. I throw up from the smell.

Wally waddles into our group, that hammer he used on the boy still stained red. "The nine of you are gonna de-bone these bodies. We want the ribs, the leg bones, and arm bones. Which one of you is the oldest?"

No one answers and Wally smashes the ground with his sledgehammer, making dirt fly. A dark and skinny boy with a phoenix tattooed on the back of his right shoulder, steps forward.

"Name and age."

"Ronan. I'm ten."

"Okay, Ronan, you're in charge. You know where all the bones I want are, don't you?"

"Yeah."

Wally claps. "Good boy. Get it done and you'll be rewarded."

They give us knives and hammers, and Ronan shows us where to cut, and where to pound to break the bone. I don't know how much times passes, but soon, the smell goes away. I am too weak to beat out a bone, so Ronan comes around, doing most of the hammering, while the rest of us cut. Jocelyn works beside me, her face starch white. She's a pretty girl, I think. Brown hair and tan skin. She's tall, but that's just because she's nine. Our pile of bones grows as the heat steals the sweat from our bodies, and soon Jocelyn starts her crying again.

Ronan tries to comfort her before the Savages hear, but it's too late. She jumps up, arms covered in red. "AHHHHHHHHHHH!"

"Get back to work!" Ronan hisses. "You'll get us in trouble."

"I don't want to be here! I don't want to be a slave!" Ronan tries to force her arms down, but Jocelyn shoves him away and holds up her knife. "Stay away from me!"

I look back, and the Savages watch, snickering. Why don't they stop her? What if she hurts Ronan?

"We have to do this," Ronan says. "We have to survive."

"I can't." Jocelyn holds the knife to her throat.

Ronan reaches for her, but Jocelyn's faster. I close my eyes but I hear her body hit the ground.

CHAPTER 16

MIA

May 8, 2145, 13:00

Birdsong lifts me out of unconsciousness. A blue jay sits in the window above me, the turquoise feathers on its chest vibrating as it sings. I watch the bird fly into the room and land on a throne made of wood and bones. My next heartbeat fills my body with ice. I lay in Cal's bed, body covered with a fur blanket. I sit up, a jolt of pain erupting in my chest. It feels like microscopic blades are piercing my lungs. I stand and lift the thin, white gown I'm wearing to see bandages wrapped around my torso.

At least I'm alive. I thought for sure I had died. Now, I must focus on escape, but there are many things I must consider. The barrier. I'll have to steal breaker gloves to open a hole in the electrical field. I'm sure Dana will have some. Then there's Jade and Sannvi. It will be tough to travel with two children. They'll slow me down, but I can't leave them here. What about Glare? He tried to have the Ogor kill me. If I run, he'll be the first one volunteering to hunt me down. I don't know how far Talon is, let alone where it's located from this Savage village. It could be twenty, fifty, or one hundred miles away. Walking would get us captured, so I must steal a vehicle. This escape plan will take some time. I must ensure I build positive relationships with these Savages, especially Cal. I'll need him to fall for me. That way, he'll be easier to manipulate.

The door opens, and Cal enters, an ear-to-ear smile plastered on his face. Tucked under each of his arms are Jade and Sannvi. They crash into me, and I wince as their skinny arms wrap around me.

"I told you," I say, squeezing them. Sannvi's stomach rumbles, and I look up at Cal. "We need some food."

He moves past us to his throne. "Don't worry. It's coming. More importantly, you and I need to discuss a few things."

I let go of the children, and stumble as a sharp pain spikes across my ribcage. Cal rushes off his throne to assist me, but I hold out my hand. "I'm fine. I don't need your help."

"Are you sure?"

"I'm walking, aren't I?"

Cal lowers himself back onto his throne. "I got those kids out, so now it's time for you to hold up your end of the deal."

"Which is?"

Cal grins. "You'll become Savage."

"I thought if I won, I would be granted the Savage title?"

"You've been accepted into the clan, but you're not a full-fledged Savage yet. That requires months, sometimes years, of training. But there's a quicker way."

"What about Jade and Sannvi? And Daniel? Is he alive?"

"He's alive. They'll be granted the title of Savage after their training. I have absolved your titles as prisoners and failures."

The door opens, and Cal gets up, grabs my hand, pulling me forward with him.

Rhena comes in, followed by four Savages, each carrying wooden trays full of food. There's a roasted chicken, cuts of beef, fruits and vegetables, a mound of rice, and tall, wooden cups. Rhena places a large blanket on the floor near the foot of Cal's bed. Today, instead of cat tails, squirrel tails hang from her ears, the ends drape past her shoulders. The Savages place the food down and leave.

"How are your ribs?" Rhena asks.

"I think they're okay."

"I'll bring some more medicine later. You should heal within a few days. The fractures weren't that severe." Rhena looks at Cal. "And about tomorrow. Everything will be ready. Mia will be breathtaking."

"Thank you. I don't know what I would do without you," Cal says.

"Enjoy the food." Rhena bows her head and leaves.

"What was she talking about?" I pull my hand out of Cal's.

He lowers himself and grabs a chicken leg. He motions toward Jade and Sannvi, and they plop down, Jade snatching a wing, and Sannvi, the other leg.

Cal takes a bite. "It's your end of our deal."

"I thought me becoming Savage was the deal?"

"It is. But this is what I meant earlier when I mentioned a quicker way. You will Unify with me to become Savage."

"What does that mean?"

Cal beams up at me, his lips and cheeks shiny with grease. His next words cement themselves into my gut, and I sink. "It means you will be mine. My partner, for life."

CHAPTER 17

MIA

May 9, 2145

The sounds of guitars, drums, and ukuleles fill the forest. Rhena taps her foot to the music as she stands over me, raising my chin. It's just her, Jade, and me, in Cal's home. Jade wears boots, a velvet-colored skirt, and Savage light armor made of leather, with a dark T shirt under it. Her face is painted half white and half black. Just like every other Savage today.

"Mia, you will be all white, and Cal will be all black," Rhena says as she slathers more white paint upon my face.

I clench my teeth. This is something I must deal with until I can turn this beautiful village into ashes. Cal needs to trust me for my escape to be successful. But I can't help the hate that flows through my veins. I will be Cal's property. He said I wouldn't be a prisoner anymore, but with this Unification, what's the difference?

"You two will merge tonight into one and be bonded for eternity." Rhena's wet fingers glide over my lips.

My leg shakes. *Bite your tongue, Mia. Bite it. Don't let ruin slip from your lips.* But I don't. I can't.

"So I'll be his prisoner forever?" I ask. "Some bond. I don't want to be with hi—"

Rhena takes my chin, forcing me to look at her. "Quiet! How dare you disregard my chief's compassion. Be grateful. Cal is a great man. He's saving your life."

"He's stealing it!"

Rhena dabs her fingers in the bowl of paint and traces a line down the bridge of my nose. "Your situation is delicate. You must trust that Cal has your best interests in mind. He's trying to protect you from Glare. In our culture, you are not Savage unless you complete training or prove your worth to the clan. By Unifying with Cal, your worth is solidified. Training will take too long."

"But isn't Cal the leader of Calamity Clan?" I ask. "His say should be final."

Rhena looks at Jade. "Let's get her arms, child. Mia, yes, Cal is our chief, but some clans have set things in place, so the chief doesn't abuse their power. Ours is one such clan. Cal is a fair leader, so Glare has just as much influence as him, even though he's second in command."

They rub cold paint down my arms, and I ask, "Why would he do that?"

"I cannot say. I should not speak about such a thing."

"But how does being Cal's property through Unification stop Glare?"

"You misunderstand, child. Unification is the bondage of two souls. There is no hierarchy. You will be Cal's equal."

"But we hardly know each other. I don't understand his reasoning."

Rhena places her palm on my cheek. Her red pupils are full of wisdom, bright. "You don't have to. Just know that he sees something in you. You best not disappoint, girl."

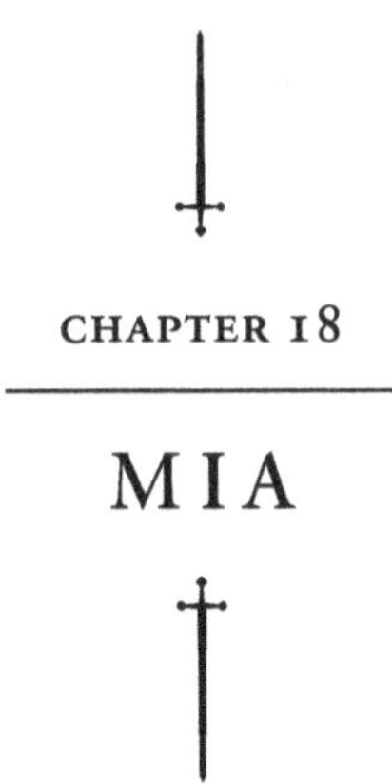

CHAPTER 18

MIA

I'm naked.

Stars play a woeful symphony in the sky, twinkling and dimming under the glow of the moon as I wait behind Calamity Clan. They surround a clearing that entraps a nude Cal. His skin is painted black. Someone squeezes my left palm, and I ground myself, looking at Jade. When she smiles at me, her warmth resonates with my soul. Does she understand what's happening? I'm about to be shackled to a Savage.

"My dear, are you ready?" It's Rhena, coming from behind us, placing a palm on my back. I shake my head. "Do not cry, girl. Look who's watching."

Jade's lips lie flat as she sees the bleakness inside me.

"Don't ruin your pretty face. It took us a lot of time to paint it perfectly, right, Jade?" Rhena takes my other hand, and Jade nods.

It feels like chains are coiling around my limbs, but I keep my tears at bay, focusing on Cal. My future with him is waiting, whether I want it or not. I can't deviate from my best chance at survival or put Jade's and Sannvi's lives in jeopardy. I remind myself that this is only temporary. Soon enough, I'll have a blade to Cal's throat, and he will beg for his life, but I'll show no mercy.

A Savage wearing a cloak joins Cal, blowing into a bull's horn. Calamity Clan kneels, and Rhena speaks as we walk down an aisle alit with torches on both sides toward the Unification circle made with various animals' blood. "Tonight, Calamity, we witness the Unification of Chief Cal to a woman he's waited most of his life for. A woman that the universe and our ancestors gifted him. Mia. She will go through a change, and when she wakes tomorrow beside Cal, she will be Savage!"

The Savages roar as they rise to their feet, and I look at Cal, who watches me. We don't break eye contact with each other until Rhena places me next to him. Jade leaves my side, disappearing into the sea of painted faces. My stomach hurts, so I turn back to Cal. He's frozen in place. Is he nervous?

Rhena drops her cloak before Cal, showing her mature, naked body painted half white and half black. The Savage who blew the horn steps in front of me. He's an older man, short, muscular, and bald. On one of his arms, I see many kill dots where the paint is thin.

He reveals himself painted just like Rhena. "I am Basco, Rhena's partner." He holds out a hand, and I take it, trying to distract myself from his nudity. "Good luck."

I flash him a quick smile and he turns away. Two Savage kids run up, one handing Rhena and Basco wooden bowls containing purple berries. The other gives them knives. Rhena takes Cal's left hand and slices his palm, squeezing his blood over the berries.

Basco skims his blade across my flesh. It stings, but I don't flinch. He drapes his hand over the back of mine and squeezes. My blood drips onto the berries, and then Basco places the bowl on the ground and wraps my hand.

Rhena stoops, mashing and mixing the berries and blood. Basco kneels and mirrors her. When they rise, the two switch bowls, and Rhena chants in a low tone. "With this joining of souls, Cal and Mia shall be bound for eternity. Mia will be Cal's sun, and Cal will be Mia's moon. Forever they are destined to love. Forever they are destined to be until death." Rhena places the bowl to Cal's lips, and Basco pushes my bowl toward me. "Drink each other's life force. Drink each other's essence and be bonded through life and into the next."

What? No. Savage blood will kill me. It'll rot my insides, and I'll die.

I take a step back, but Basco's hand finds my wrist. He keeps me rooted in place. "What are you afraid of, girl?"

"His blood is poison."

Basco breaks into a quiet fit of laughter. "That is a myth. We are human, just like you. You must start before he finishes."

I glance at Cal. He holds the bowl to his face, slurping the berries and my blood. I'll survive this. I'll survive. I'm doing this for Kirk, and for Jade and Sannvi. Cal's blood will not kill me.

"Ready?"

I nod, and Basco tips the bowl. I part my lips, the berry juice and blood flow into my mouth. I don't taste. I just swallow until Basco throws the bowl to the side. The aftertaste is sweet and then bitter. I wait for my body to give me a sign that the Savage's blood has corrupted my system so I can throw it up, but nothing happens. My skin does not burn. My hair does not fall out. I still have feeling in my limbs, and I don't feel sick. There's no rash. How can this be?

Rhena throws her hands into the air. "Let the Unification begin!" She looks between us and frowns as the Savages clamor with excitement. "Kiss. May tonight prove that the pain you'll both endure is worth it."

Cal reaches for me.

I hate this.

His arm wraps around my waist.

I hate Savages.

He presses his warm body against my cold one.

I hate this feeling in my heart.

He leans down, and I meet him halfway. Calamity Clan shakes the forest with their voices as our lips join. Cal is rough but passionate, holding onto me as if I will blow away. He kisses me as if he's searching for something he's lost, and then he rips himself away.

"You're the one I've been waiting for," he says. "I know it."

I'm stuck in a trance. A star floats down from the night sky, hanging above us. I hate Cal. He thinks he's in control of everything. But he's wrong. I survive by making this Savage fall in love with me. I grab his face and pull it toward mine until our lips connect again. This kiss seems to last a lifetime. But when we break apart, there's a darkness swirling around Cal. I step back. Savages are demons.

A light-headedness makes me sway, and Cal grabs my shoulders. "Mia, you need to focus."

Here it comes. I knew it. I'm dying and hallucinating because of Cal's blood.

"I won't die," I say. "I'll do anything to make it out of here."

Cal doesn't say a thing. No one does because there is no noise in the world. I'm trapped in a bubble of silence. But Cal's darkness bares its fangs at me. It towers over him and consumes me.

My body burns, and I wake trapped in a dark void. It tangles my legs and presses me down into something soft, and I scream, "Help! Help! Somebody, help me!"

The darkness vanishes. Cal stands at the foot of a bed. "Mia, you need to calm your mind."

"What's going on? Where are we?"

Cal tosses thin, white garments onto the bed, and turns his back to me. "You're safe. We're in my place. Put those on. What you're feeling is the ritual. The berries and blood. Tonight, we suffer through our worst hallucinations. We must help each other through them."

I get dressed. The contour of Cal's back is detailed and scarred from years of training and his harsh Savage life. Blood drips onto the top of his head, and I look up to see a floating decapitation hovering in the air.

Kirk's head rains blood onto the floor, and I gasp, falling back.

"What do you see?" Cal turns toward me.

"My grandfather."

"It's okay—"

I shoulder past Cal. "You did this!" I hear myself talking, but I can't stop it. "You killed Kirk."

"Yes. Because he was dangerous. If I kept him alive, he'd threaten everything I've worked so hard for."

"What have you worked for?" I turn back toward him. "All you Savages do is kill and raid and fight. You're a bunch of lunatic murderers. You're not trying to restore civilization. You're trying to break it."

"You disrespect yourself!"

"I'm not one of you. I never will be."

"We're not all what you think."

"History proves otherwise."

Cal crosses his arms. "Oh yeah, and what do you know about Savage history?"

I scoff. "In 2045, right before America's government collapsed, billionaire Damascus McCarthy ordered his followers to decapitate those protesting his views. They called your people savages, and he liked it so much that he officially adopted the name. In 2054, at the end of the year, two RFF generals approached McCarthy, aka Damascus the Great, for peace, and he killed them both and kept the fighting going. Should I continue?"

Cal gets in my face. "I'm not the Great! You know what your problem is?"

"I don't have a prob—"

He pokes me in the chest. "You think you're better than us because you come from some fancy Compound. Because you can recite your history from those bullshit RFF data books. You think we're all evil because of the stories you've heard, what you've seen on your holo-screen. But I know many that have seen their brothers and sisters and mothers and fathers brutalized by the RFF. You're so smart but can't even think for yourself."

"The Runesians killed my parents, and your people came after to take what was left. They used me as target practice, beat me, and made me pluck the bones from the dead so they could make weapons. So, excuse me for the way I feel about your people!"

I storm away from Cal to the darker side of his home and slide down to the floor, pulling my knees to my chest. I don't care what he says. He killed Kirk, attacked my people, and butchered many on that highway. The Savages are devils. They always have been. If Kirk hadn't saved me as a child, I would still be a slave or dead. Those are the facts. I bury my head in my arms. I can't do this.

Survive, Mia.

I can't, Kirk. Not here. Not with these monsters. But what other choices do I have? I've taken responsibility for Jade and Sannvi. And if give up, I can't avenge Kirk. He would tell me to put my emotions aside and to do whatever I needed to do for the best outcome. I'm in control here. Cal is my puppet.

I go back around and place myself before Cal, who sits on his throne. "I'm sorry for what I said. All of this is just a lot for me. What you said. You were right. This is war, and all sides have horror stories about the others." I pause, searching Cal's eyes. He gives nothing away. I'm so stupid. If I blow this with him, my chances of escaping are ruined. "We can make this work. I can try. Rhena told me you wanted to get Unified to keep me safe from Glare, so… thank you."

Cal rises, passes me, and picks up his sword. "I didn't save you just because of Glare."

A chill overtakes me, and I see it when I turn, wispy threads of darkness combining into human form.

"I saved you because the Wise One told me about you long ago."

"The Wise One? The Savage your people say can see the future?"

"Yes. Princess Raia. The Savage King's granddaughter. She's Gifted. She sees things no one else can."

I'll go along with this for now. I don't believe in superstitions, but there are so many rumors that sometimes I catch myself wondering if a person like that actually exist.

"What did she tell you?" I ask.

"She said that we change all the bad things."

"What bad things?"

"I've been wondering about that. Maybe you can help me figure it out, but first, there's something I must do."

The darkness grows taller, and I step back. Everything inside of me tells me to run.

Cal points his sword at the apparition and spits at its feet. "Mia. Meet my father, Calamity the Almighty. The man I must kill."

CHAPTER 19

MIA

A foul stench, like decaying flesh, fills my nostrils, and I cover my nose with my shirt. There are stories about the Almighty, which many believe to be true. The soldiers in Compound Marigold said that bullets bounce off his steel skin. Cal slashes through his father, harming nothing. He swings through the phantom again and again and again. I don't know how long I watch him try to slay this perversion. But when it dissipates, Cal drops his sword, drags himself over to his bed, and falls onto it. He screams into a pillow, his body trembling.

I stand over him. "Cal?" He doesn't answer. I climb onto the bed beside him. "Look at me."

After a few moments, Cal flips over. "Every time I look at you, Mia. I see my mom. You remind me of her. Your hair. Your skin. Even the way you smile sometimes."

"I'm not her."

"I know who you are. You're strong and passionate and beautiful, despite everything you've endured. And I see a resemblance is all."

I reach for Cal's hand, cling to it with both of mine, and pull it toward my chest so he can feel the drum of my heart. This is my chance.

"What happened to her?" I ask.

Cal looks away. "The Almighty killed her when I was fifteen—five years ago."

"Why?"

Cal's nails dig into my palm. "He hated her. He beat my mom for something every night. He always said she was disrespectful, disobedient, and useless. Whenever I tried to defend her, he beat me so badly I couldn't move the next day. He slept with other women in our clan and would force my mom and me to watch sometimes. He would scream, 'Cal, this is what a man does. This is how a man becomes powerful!' My mom tried to shield my eyes once, and he broke three of her fingers. She was a good woman, Mia, and my father despised that light inside of her. When I was a little older and well into my training, my mom tried to teach me how to cook, forage, and make clothes, but my father would drag me away and throw her in the pit field for weeks!"

His hand balls into a fist inside of mine. I squeeze it. "Cal, we're here. Right now, right here. It's just me and you."

"That bastard would leave my mom in the pit field for so long that when they dragged her out, she was skin and bones. And still, in secret, she showed me books and taught me things. I asked her to run away, and she always refused, saying she couldn't leave me. On my thirteenth birthday, I challenged the Almighty to a duel. If I won, he'd let my mom go. If he won, he'd make sure I never interact with her again. I was a fool, Mia. I gave him exactly what he wanted...."

Cal's gaze is full of melancholy, and then the lines in his face deepen and darken. His amber pupils are balls of fire as he points to the scar on the right side of his face. "That's the day my father gave me this scar. After I lost, he threw my mom in the pit field. Four months. She still holds that record. When he finally let her come out, I thought she was dead. He told me if I tried to contact her in any way, he'd kill her. He kept telling me to be a man. He said my mom was weak, and that she was going to make me weak, too. For two years, I didn't speak to her. Didn't even glance her way. I waited and got stronger. I had an escape plan for both of us. One night, the Almighty was away, so I went to my mom. She cried and told me to get away from her. She feared what the Almighty would do to us if we failed, but I didn't care. I took her, damn near dragged her, and we ran. When we were captured, my father didn't hesitate … H-h-e—for an entire month—he carried her head around on a stick, gloating to the clan. He said, 'This is weakness. This is disobedience. And this is an example of what happens to people who defy me!' A year passed, and the Savage King invited the Almighty to be the War General of Savages. That same night, I killed all his loyal men in single combat. I killed all the women who slept with him for benefits. And then I became Calamity Clan's chief. The Almighty's the only one left I must kill. For my mom."

I don't know if it's the berries and blood, but there's wetness on my face. I see Cal, Chief of Calamity Clan, for who he really is. I hate to admit this, but he's like me—stuck in past and thirsting for vengeance against someone who wronged him.

Cal cups a hand around my face, wiping a tear with his thumb. "You're not supposed to be the one crying."

His touch is electric. It buzzes and tingles under my skin, and then Cal takes my hand, the electricity sliding through him and into me. His dark hair sways in the calm wind that blows through the window. His strong shoulders rise and fall as he leans closer. His veins bulge in his hands and arms as his fingers entangle more and more with mine, and then we move as if we're magnets, our lips pulled together.

Heat.

Cal grips the back of my head, pushes me down onto the bed, and slips off his shirt. The moonlight gleams off his bronze skin, revealing a thin strip of black hair that branches out over his abdomen and broad chest. He caresses my face, kissing me. I moan. I don't think I've ever felt this way before. I don't even know if I understand what this feeling is. Our lips try to solve more of each other. Our bodies intertwine… start to become one.…

I open my eyes and place a hand on Cal's chest. "Stop, please." No, what am I doing? Cal falls to the side. I'm an idiot, and I've ruined this moment.

"Can you tell me something?" he asks. "Do you remember which clan those Savages you told me about were from?"

"If they had markings, they were covered. They all had X's branded somewhere on their bodies."

"Then they weren't from any of the seven clans. They were exiles, banished for some crime."

"That doesn't make it any better."

"I know," he says. "Just thought you should know. If any of them are still alive, I'll find them and kill them. You don't ever have to forgive me, but I'll protect you. Always."

Does he mean that? I turn over, and Cal scoots closer to me, wrapping an arm around my body. He buries his face into my hair and slides one of his legs between mine.

"You smell good," he whispers.

A tingling sensation whirs throughout my body, then disgust pours over me. Despite everything in Cal's arms, I feel a sense of security. I can't tell how much time has passed. I don't think I sleep. Do the berries and blood ever wear off? I want my mind back. A bird chirps from somewhere, and I stir, coming out of a fog. Sunlight pours into Cal's room. He wakes and I get up, staring out of the window. The blue jay sits on a branch outside, its beak open in song.

"We made it," Cal says. He stands, grabs my hands, and places his forehead against mine. "We're Unified."

He comes in for a kiss, and I let him. I want to make up for last night. He breathes me in, stealing my breath, stealing my steel. He hugs me, and a warmness encompasses my chest. There is no ache there from my fractured ribs.

What is wrong with me? I should despise him more. His sob story could have been a lie. I can't let something like that make me have sympathy for a murderer. But maybe I can't help it. Rhena is the Scarlet Witch, after all. Maybe my mind has been permanently poisoned by her Savage witchcraft.

"You look sad?" Cal lifts my chin.

I pull away. "Just tired."

"I'll go get us some water."

Cal leaves, and I sit on the bed. I won't forget who I am. I won't forget what these Savages did to my people. Did to me. Cal killed Kirk. They can drug me all they want, but I'll never be one of them. I'll deceive them and use them for my goals. By the time the Savages understand what has hit them, it will be far too late.

I made myself a promise, and I intend to keep it.

CHAPTER 20

LEON

May 11, 2145

Sunlight shines through giant windows, reflecting the golden light off the shimmering towers of the Inner Ring of Talon. Leon winces, and turns toward Liz, who sits in a chair at the foot of his bed. "And you're sure they didn't scan me?"

Liz stops filing her nails and jams a finger under one of her eyes. "Don't you see these bags? I've been with you for the past four days. Stop asking. Why didn't you tell me you were infected? You know I don't care about the Sickness. We all have it."

"I'm symptomatic. You're not. And my symptoms aren't normal."

Liz sits up in her chair. "What do you mean?"

"Abilities. Like the Savage princess and that teleporting Runesian assassin."

"Bullshit. Those are just stories."

"No, Liz. I'm being serious. You just showed me the log of the Savages we captured confirming the princess's clairvoyance."

"They'll say anything to get a fix. It's not confirmed."

Leon places a hand on his chest. "I'm confirming it. I have these episodes, and everything disappears. Then my father shows up, or this shadowy figure. Back in the forest, the shadow warned me about the Scout attacking. And then after that, I was dying, but Kirk and my grandma saved me. I'm not crazy. You have to believe me."

Liz's silence worries Leon, but when she smiles, his doubt dissipates.

"I believe you," she says. "So, what now?"

"This stays between us. I can't control it, and I don't want the RFF finding out because they'll lock me away, and I'll be someone's lab rat."

"Gotcha." Liz stands, stretching. "Get dressed! General Wilde will be here soon."

"Why do generals always want to do meetings so early in the morning?"

Liz shrugs. "I have no clue, but she did say not to be late." Liz claps. "So, chop chop."

A white car with tinted windows rolls to a stop in front of Leon and Liz and the doors rise. General Wilde sits inside. She wears a crisp Republic for Freedom green-and-black dress uniform. Her golden shoulder lapels stop just above her Division's insignia, a roaring green lion.

"Get in," she says.

They get into the car and sit opposite of General Wilde on tan leather seats. The car speaks, *"Destination: General Assembly Tower. May I proceed?"*

"Yes." General Wilde pulls the end of her white general's cape off the floor, placing it on the seat as the car pulls into the street. "How are your injuries, Jackson?"

"The nanobots repaired my kidney. I'm fine. Thank you."

"You're lucky Liz was able to do some first aid, and that we managed to get there in time." General Wilde glances out the window, then back to Leon and Liz. "Well, I guess I should explain. One's here, and she wants Rodgers back. She's already admitted to being responsible for sending her Scout after you and has said she'll do it again unless Rodgers returns."

Leon shakes his head. "Liz isn't—"

General Wilde holds up a hand and taps the lion stitched on her shoulder. "Rodgers is a Lion now. You both are, so trust me with this. We want to use this opportunity to corner One, but for that, we need both of you to cooperate. What do you say?"

Leon and Liz share a glance, and then Liz's ruby greens light up. "I say we send her to hell where she belongs."

CHAPTER 21

LEON

They are the last ones to arrive. In the middle of the room, around a glowing, blue holo-sphere, is a dark, U-shaped table with neon blue lights zig-zagging through it. The five generals of the Republic for Freedom sit around it with One, who has a Scout standing behind her. General Wilde leads Leon and Liz to the right and takes her seat next to General Asaju of the Addae Division. The built, obsidian man with black and gray hair nods their way as they take their places behind General Wilde.

General Freed of the Eagle Division, a man with pockmarked skin and watery blue eyes clasps his weathered hands together. "Good. Shall we begin, Katherine?"

"Of course. Thank you all for attending my summons," One says. "My request is simple. I want Scout Eighty-Five, Elizabeth Rodgers, back. I am willing to pardon Leon's actions if she returns."

"What exactly were Leon's crimes?" General Wilde asks.

"You read the report. But I'll reiterate. During our mission to clear the plague camps, he acted on his own and saved infected Runesians instead of disposing of them. Not only that, but he also fired rounds at his comrades. Scout Code 7-A1.9 states, 'Any Scout who deserts the organization before they complete their contract is subject to death.' And as you all know, any persons who shoots at friendlies is instantly considered an enemy."

General Campos of the Hebi Division, a Japanese-Latina woman with a mole on her left cheek and flowing, dark hair, raises her hand. "But in this situation, shouldn't Rodgers be held accountable as well? It doesn't make sense that only Leon is punished for the crime of desertion when she deserted too, as the report states. I can't support Liz's return or Leon's execution."

"I don't think that's fair. Liz is my blood," One says. "I raised her. Is it wrong for me to want her to be with family?"

"Family has nothing to do with blood." General Asaju pats his heart with a fist. "It's about who understands you here, has your back, and loves you for you. I'm out as well."

"Then that makes three," General Wilde states. "Jackson and Rodgers are Lions."

The Scout behind One lowers their face shield, his dull, blue pupils flashing with rage. Zero's lips curl up and his crooked nose crinkles. "How can you stand there and just turn your back on us? One raised us the best she could. Mom and Dad wanted us to be with—"

"You don't get to talk about them!" Liz's fists curl. "And I don't care what anyone here says, but I'm never rejoining the Scouts."

One's gaze spills venom. "You will. You know the rules."

"What rules? Those are Scout rules never mandated by the Republic for Freedom. You're here, meaning you are an entity a part of the RFF, whether you want to admit that or not. And if that's the case, then you violated the Republic for Freedom's law because you ordered us to kill children, which is strictly prohibited and punishable by prison or death. It doesn't matter if they were infected or not. We were acting in benefit of the RFF. Your rule about death for desertion doesn't hold up, and no division within the RFF practices such methods. I'm not coming back."

"Then Leon will die. I won't stop hunting him."

Liz's smile drips with danger. "And if he does, you'll be in my sights next."

One shoots out of her chair. "You ungrateful child!"

"Enough!" General Freed garners everyone's attention. "We will continue this amicably."

General Wilde raises her hand. "Liz brought up some interesting points. Why are you here, One? You're not a general within the RFF. You don't have a division. You've claimed for years that your Scouts are not RFF personnel, so you could go off into No Man's Land and be unaccountable. If I were to ask Leon and Liz how many missions they went on that you misconstrued, I bet most of the orders you gave them could sentence you to death."

One glares at General Wilde. "I've done all I could for the Republic for Freedom for years. I'm the reason you haven't lost this war. Do you wish to lose my services? Ask yourselves that?"

"This is why we can't trust you, Katherine," General Freed says. "Any person saying what you just did doesn't want this war to end."

"I do! It would be over if you agreed to the plan I proposed years ago."

"We're not nuking the west coast." General Campos massages her temples. "That's too violent and would set the environment back by two hundred years. This planet is already dying."

One turns for the door. "Then there's nothing left for us to talk about. I won't be working with the Republic for Freedom any longer, and Leon will always be a target for assassination. I have no reason to be among people who don't trust me. Let's go, Zero."

General Flower of the Ares Division stands in their way. He's a sturdy, tan man with large, tattooed tiger stripes stacked down his arms and legs. He doesn't wear his military uniform or cape like the other generals, opting for a more comfortable cutoff shirt and shorts with sandals. The sclerae of his eyes are amber, his pupils jet-black as he challenges One with feline predation. "But we're not finished talking. Sit."

"Move," One says.

General Flower smirks, fangs sliding from underneath his lips. "Make me."

Zero steps in front of One. He locks eyes with General Flower.

"Katherine," General Freed calls out. "We have reason to believe you've been keeping us in the dark about your affiliations. There's a rumor you've worked with the Runesians and that you're currently working with the Canadians. That Scout armor isn't made anywhere within the Territories."

"That's ludicrous. Scout Eighty-Five will say anything to spite me. I've never worked with the Runesians. We're leaving." One goes to step around General Flower, but he holds out an arm.

"A person who has nothing to hide doesn't run," he says.

Zero grabs General Flower's arm, and General Flower slides a foot between Zero's legs, and trips him while simultaneously grabbing his throat and slamming him on the ground.

One draws her pistol. "What do you think you're doing?"

General Flower presses a sharp nail against Zero's throat. "Tell us the truth, or I'll rip your nephew's throat out."

The other generals stand, drawing their guns, aiming at One.

General Campos presses her barrel into One's back. "Last chance, One."

After a long moment, One holsters her pistol and holds up her hands. "Fine."

"We want an in-person meeting with the Canadians," General Wilde says. She holsters her weapon. "You're not permitted to leave the Compound until we have one confirmed. Is that understood?"

"Give me two days." One makes her way out of the room.

General Flower lets Zero up, and he follows One out of the room. All the generals except for General Flower sit back down, and General Asaju looks between Leon and Liz, asking, "Can we trust her?"

They both answer. "No."

"We should remain cautious when we meet the Canadians. We don't know what intel she's fed to them about us," General Freed says.

General Campos sips a drink from a thermos. "We need leverage. Something we can offer them that One can't."

"I agree. But we don't know what One has established with them."

"We can guess," General Asaju says. "I'm willing to bet One has offered them land."

General Wilde shakes her head. "No. There's something else going on here. There's something both One and the Canadians want jointly. The Canadians have known of our struggle for the past century, and I'm sure they know who we are, but they only associate with One? It doesn't make sense, especially since we've tried for years to gain contact with them."

"I agree with Dianna. Katherine came up with Kirk and I, and she's the ambitious sort. She's always sought to do things her way. Whatever it is she wants, it takes priority over ending this war," General Freed says.

General Flower plops down into his seat. "I say we just kill her."

"Pasco, everything can't be solved by killing." General Campos sighs in exasperation, focusing on Liz. "Any more details either of you can give would be a great help."

Liz shrugs. "She's a control freak. And a liar. She has worked for the Runesians before, by the way. She made my brother kill a Runesian deserter when were kids."

Silence. Something clicks inside Leon's brain. He's worked for One for five years and what Liz said was true. One's word was law to them for so long. Kirk's last entry in his journal replays in Leon's mind.

That damned Katherine should not be trusted. She's too power-hungry for anyone's good.

"She wants more power," Leon whispers to himself.

"What was that?" General Wilde asks.

"One likes to be in control. She wants power." Leon glances around the room, making sure his words stick with each general. "And the easiest way for her to obtain that is if you guys are all gone."

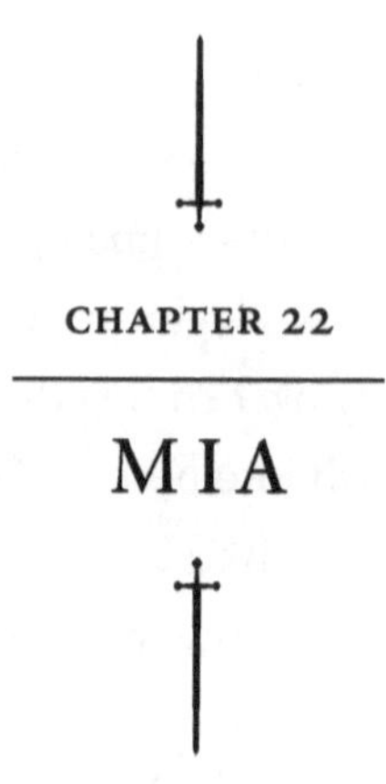

MIA

May 11, 2145, 18:30

I can't stop grinning as I watch Cal gather his battle gear. The celebration for our Unification ended early because a single Calamity Savage returned earlier with news that the rest of his patrol was killed by the Republic for Freedom a few days ago, and that two of them were taken prisoner.

Cal sheathes his sword and holsters his pistol. "You seem pleased about this."

I sit on the bed as he slides a brown leather tank top on. I can't miss this opportunity. "No. It's sad. I'd like to go with you. Maybe I can help get your people back peacefully."

Cal tightens his boots, then looks up at me. "Why, so you can run away?"

"I'd never leave Jade and Sannvi behind. I'm with you. We made it through the Unification ritual together."

"And because of that, I know your heart. You hate me. Besides, you're not ready. What if everything goes south, and the RFF kills all of us?"

He's not stupid, and he's not wrong.

"That's why you need me," I say. "My brother's in the RFF. I name drop him or Kirk and give you guys a way in. This doesn't have to end with more bloodshed."

"That's what Daniel is for. I'm not letting you be a sacrificial pawn."

"Daniel won't pull it off. They won't believe him."

"And they'll believe you?"

"Yes. I'm more convincing than Daniel. I know more about the RFF than anyone else here. It would be a mistake not to take me."

"What are you after, Mia?"

"I want to prove my loyalty to Calamity Clan," I say. "To you."

Cal comes closer and pulls me from the bed. "If I let you come, what's in it for me?"

And there it is. Another exchange. Nothing is free here. I must pay a price. Maybe this way, I can get him to let his guard down. No. I must be rational and bide my time. Kirk told me how these things are. I must act and create an opening for myself. I can be strategic here if Cal isn't greedy. I move closer to him, and our lips tickle one another's, playing a dangerous game. His grip on me gets tighter.

"What do you want?" I ask.

"More of you."

"I can do that." Can he feel my heart galloping in my chest?

"You sure?" Cal asks.

I'm lost in this Savage's energy. I want to touch the scar on his face because I know it'll make him shudder. Make him weak. I want to control him and crush him. This is what I must do to survive and escape from this hell. This act will allow me to continue protecting Jade and Sannvi. I will shove Cal's head on a stick along with Glare's and make a tribute to Kirk.

I nod and Cal smiles because he believes one day I will love him. He trusts his stupid Savage ritual.

Stealing a heart is easy. Crushing it is the fun part.

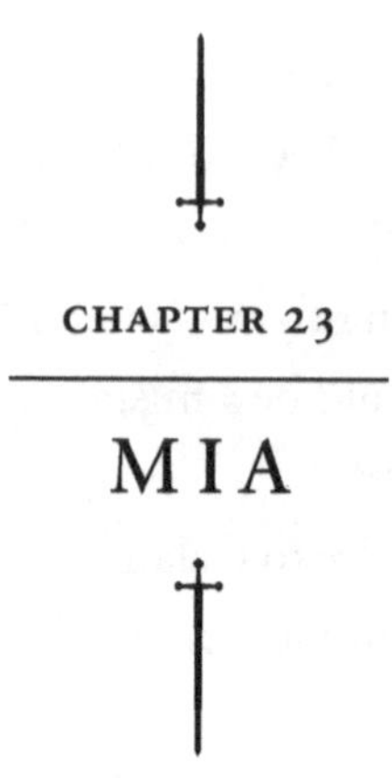

CHAPTER 23

MIA

If this plan of mine doesn't work, Glare will have more reason to want me gone. I need this to work. There's also the matter of me and Cal's agreement. If he means what I think, I may have—I shake my head. None of that matters now. I can contact Leon at the outpost, and things should become clearer for me. Maybe I can escape and come back for Jade and Sannvi later?

"You're the prettiest warrior there ever was." Rhena walks up behind me. "Basco said you picked up a few basic sword techniques."

"Took me all day." I laugh, unsheathing and holding up a gleaming katana. "Cal said I needed a weapon to look more official."

"You watch your back out there," Rhena says.

Cal steps up beside me wearing his bear headpiece. "Good, you're Savage."

I look down at myself. I wear a stained, dark, armored, short-sleeved shirt and dark pants with my boots. I slide my sword into its sheath and raise my arms. "It stinks."

"You're the one that picked it out of the pile," Cal says, then turns to his clanspeople. "Are you ready, Calamity?"

Glare starts the roaring, the whites of his eyes bulge. He looks far more demonic than usual with the all-black war paint on his face. The Savages bounce and scream and beat their chests. They shove berries and roots and mushrooms and flower petals into their mouths. Glare and that weird-eyed Savage Lero crowd Daniel, pulling berries and flower petals from their pockets. Lero takes a bite out of a root and Glare, a mushroom, chewing as they watch Daniel until he gets the hint and partakes in the drugs offered to him.

Glare coils around Daniel and cheers. He then grabs the back of Daniel's head, forcing their foreheads together and whispering in his ear. When they look at me, Daniel's face twists with perturbation, while Glare's expression stays malevolent.

What did he say to him? Rhena steals my hand from behind, leaving something in it. "There. That will help with the nerves. It's a small dose. It shouldn't do much but calm the jitters."

"Rhena," I face her. "If anything happens to me, please watch over Jade and Sannvi."

Rhena bows her head and lets go of my hand. "I will do everything in my power, but remember, those two need you."

"Let's move!" Cal commands.

The Savages march off. I follow them and look back. Rhena has her head down, chanting, sending us off with a prayer.

We wait until nightfall, a few miles away from the outpost. With night vision binoculars, Cal surveys a brick high school fortified with laser fences, barbed wired, and barricades. "There must be at least one hundred of them in there."

"We can take them," Glare says. "As long as princess does her job."

"You really think it will work?" Daniel asks.

"I have a better chance of not getting shot than you." I stand. "Cal, tie me up. It has to look like I escaped."

Cal takes my sword and restrains my wrists with rope. "I'm trusting you."

An explosion brightens the black sky to the east, shaking the world. Our signal. I step out of the trees into the street. Cal and Daniel nod at me while Glare slides his pointer finger across his throat.

"You better come back, princess," he says. "You don't want something terrible to happen to those children of yours."

I don't acknowledge him because I don't want him to see the despair his words ignited. I can't escape knowing Jade's and Sannvi's lives will be in danger. I should stick to my original plan, but I can't let these RFF soldiers be killed. I run off. The lives of so many are on my shoulders, and I have no idea if I'll be able to save them all. I don't stop running until I must maneuver around barricades and barbed wire.

"Help!" I scream out. "Please. Somebody. Help!" Soon I stop in front of a laser fence. The RFF's flag ripples in the breeze behind it. "Help!"

Two soldiers emerge from a wooden shack on the other side of the fence.

"What's the problem?" A short, rugged-looking black man asks.

"I escaped from the Savages. I'm Mia Jackson, Kirk Jackson's grand-daughter."

"It's okay. We need you to calm down and listen to us." A tall and beefy man with short, blond hair lowers his weapon. "Where are the Savages now?"

"I don't know. I'm from Marigold! There are others with me in the woods back there."

"Prisoners?"

"Yes, one of them is injured. We couldn't move him!"

"How many?"

"Six of us."

The short one cuts in, suspicious. "Why didn't you bring the mobile ones with you?"

"Please, sir. My brother's in the RFF! Leon Jackson. We just want asylum from the Savages."

"Why are you dressed like one?" he asks.

"They made me. Please, just let me speak to a commander or whoever's in charge."

He's about to question me more when the bigger one intervenes, placing a hand on his partner's shoulder. The lasers disappear. "I linked our commander. He agrees to speak with you. I hope your friends can wait a bit."

I hold my bound hands out. "Thank you so much. You just saved our lives!"

The two soldiers glance at one another, and the big one cuts the rope from around my wrists. "My name's Evan, and that's Elijah. You're going to be okay."

Commander Finkley, an older, brown-haired man with a hard, weather-torn face, puffs a cigar behind a large oak desk. White smoke curls into the air. "So, you're Mia Jackson?"

"Yes. You don't believe me?"

"No. I do. A picture of you has been floating around the Link Space. We were told to keep a lookout. Your brother's in Talon right now, actually."

For a moment, I consider telling Commander Finkley everything, but thoughts of Jade and Sannvi being harmed keep me level-headed.

"Can you help us?" I ask.

"Of course. But first, can you tell me a few things?" He rubs the lit end of his cigar onto the desk. "That explosion about ten minutes ago—you wouldn't know anything about it, would you?"

"I think the Savages were blowing up old vehicles to set up an ambush."

"Where? And how many of them held you captive?"

"I don't know where, sir. I was in their makeshift camp. I only know about the ambush because I heard them talking. But there's fifteen of them."

"All right. I'll send the word up. Tell me where your friends are located from the gate."

"They're a half-mile to the right in the woods. I'd like to go with you if you don't mind. They won't trust you guys unless I'm there."

Commander Finkley's eyes narrow. "Why? We're the Republic for Freedom."

I should just tell him. He's skeptical. No, I can't. If I blow this, Glare will kill Jade and Sannvi. What would Kirk do? Would he sacrifice two children? I can be the reason the Calamity Clan Chief and his War Hand perish, a massive blow to the Savages. If we take out the Savages here, I should have time to save Jade and Sannvi before the rest of Calamity Clan gets word of what happened.

"There's...." I trail off. Glare's face flashes in my mind. He seemed sure about what he said. He may have a Savage on orders to kill Jade and Sannvi if something goes awry here. There are too many unknowns. I can't act off my emotions.

Stick to the plan, Mia, I tell myself.

"There's a lot you don't know about being a Savage prisoner," I say. "We became close and escaped because we stuck together. We promised each other we wouldn't let anyone ruin that. If I'm not there, they'll run away."

Commander Finkley watches me. He's not going to believe that. Soon, he scratches through his hair with a sigh and pushes himself out of his chair. "All right. I understand. Let's go."

"Wait, Commander Finkley?" He stops at the door. "Can you make sure my brother knows I'm here?"

"I got you. You're all right now. We'll keep you safe."

I follow him out of the door with my fists clenched.

Keep it together, Mia. Ball it up. Seal it away. Survive.

CHAPTER 24

MIA

My heart feels like it might punch through my chest before I reach where Cal and the others are waiting to ambush these soldiers behind me. Is this the only way? I glance back at the squad leader. He gives me a curt nod, oblivious that he and his squad are being led to their deaths. I shouldn't have looked at him. Now, his face will be stuck inside my head. His death will forever be a sin I must carry. A speed limit sign comes into view, and I stop. It's over for these soldiers once I step past that and lead them into the woods.

"Something wrong?" the squad leader asks.

"No. My people are just past this sign," I say, take a deep breath and push into the forest.

Two soldiers stay back to watch down the road. I swallow the lump in my throat. If I try to save these soldiers, I'll be risking Jade's and Sannvi's lives. I can keep more people alive by cooperating.

"Guys! It's me," I call out. "Mia. The RFF agreed to help us."

Nothing.

"Where are they?" the squad leader's irises light up when he switches on his modded eyes, but it's already too late.

"We're right here!"

I turn, and the squad leader swings his gun toward Glare's voice. A second later, a tomahawk cartwheels out of the shadows and into his forehead. Blood splatters onto my face as the Savages erupt from the night, stabbing and tearing through the squad of soldiers in seconds. What have I done? Dead bodies litter the ground around me, and I close my eyes until someone places a hand on my shoulder. I jerk.

"It's just me," Daniel says, his eyes wide with adrenaline as red rivulets of someone's life snake down his face.

I push him away. "What are you doing?"

"Surviving. Like you," Daniel says. "Come on. Cal's on the road. He should have the hostages."

I pull myself together. There's nothing I can do now. I stop Daniel, grabbing his wrist. "What did Glare say to you earlier?"

"He just threatened you. And me. And Jade and Sannvi. It's Glare. He hates us. We're the outsiders, so we must work hard to warm up to him. Come on." Daniel runs off.

I follow him to the road where Cal and another Savage hold two RFF soldiers. Glare curls an arm around Cal's neck, grinning at me. "Holy shit, she actually did it!"

Cal sheathes his sword. "Tie them up. Let's start phase two."

Cal and Glare walk side by side in front of me, leading us toward the high school. When I glance back at one of the soldiers we hold captive, his hate for me is apparent.

"Traitor." He spits at my face but misses.

Lero clobbers the soldier in the ear. "Quiet!"

An alarm wails as we make our way through the obstacles. Commander Finkley, Evan, and Elijah stand on the other side of the fence, weapons raised. They won't shoot, not with their comrades captive. I fall into the back, hiding.

"Where's the girl?" Commander Finkley asks.

"Don't worry about her. I'm in charge," Cal says. "Turn off the alarm."

"You can't win this fight," Commander Finkley says. "No! What are you doing?"

Glare throws one of the soldiers to the ground, stomps on the man's chest. "Listen to our chief!" He swings his tomahawk down and splits the soldier's skull.

I'll never be able to come back from this. The RFF will put a bounty on my head. Commander Finkley holds Evan and Elijah at bay, their faces taut with indignation and disbelief.

"What do you want?" Commander Finkley asks.

Cal steps up to the laser gate. "Open this gate, or we kill your last man and the girl."

"Show me her first, and I will."

"Mia!" Cal shouts.

I bottle up my regret and push through the Savages to stand with Cal. He pulls me in front of him and puts his sword to my throat.

"Drop your weapons and cooperate," Commander Finkley orders.

"But sir—" Elijah starts.

"Goddammit, Elijah, I'm trying to save lives!"

Evan and Elijah place their rifles on the ground. The laser gate opens, and Cal steps inside. He takes Commander Finkley's revolver from him. "Good. Now, let's get down to business."

Glare shoves Commander Finkley against a locker.

"I've cooperated. What more do you want?" the commander asks.

"Two of our men were taken. Since they aren't here, they must be in Talon. We want them back in exchange for all your lives," Cal says.

Good. No one else will die if they cooperate. I still saved lives. I'm still a good person. Commander Finkley nods, then pauses. I wish I could hear what he's saying through his link. I just hope he's not stupid.

"They want to know your name and status," Commander Finkley states.

"Tell them I am Chief of Calamity Clan, Cal. All I ask is that you bring my people here."

"They said they'll be here tomorrow by sunset."

Cal nods, tapping Commander Finkley on the cheek, and we move away. Glare punches the commander in the face.

"Why are you guys so violent? They're cooperating," I say as we enter a gymnasium.

Eighty-seven soldiers sit, bound, and gagged across a basketball court. Savages mill through them, kicking some of them, while others sleep on the bleachers.

"It's our culture," Cal says. "We're not killing anyone else unless it's necessary."

I stop, listening to the metal out in the hall rattle as Glare beats Commander Finkley. I give Cal a look, and he sighs.

"Glare!" Cal calls.

Soon Glare follows us inside. He pulls a limp-bodied Commander Finkley in behind him by the legs. "Can't a man have some fun?"

"We've had enough. We should rest until the RFF comes," Cal says. "They may choose to fight us instead of saving their people."

Glare drops Commander Finkley's legs and shoulders past Cal. "Whatever."

Cal grabs onto him. "Is there a problem?"

Glare swipes his hand away. "You're going soft for her. That's the problem. It's disgusting."

"We can't kill all the time."

Glare's face scrunches up as if those words are foreign to him. He storms into a group of prisoners and kicks one of them to the floor. "Don't look at me!"

"Come on, Mia." Cal goes over to Commander Finkley and helps him to his feet. "I'll deal with Glare later. He'll get over it."

I stand there, watching Glare lean against a wall. When he notices me surveilling him, his blue eyes obliterate me. Under his scrutiny, I feel like prey, like something he wants to tear limb from limb until there's nothing left.

CHAPTER 25

LEON

May 13, 2145, 19:18

The airship lands in the school parking lot. Leon told the generals he didn't need such a large force, but they insisted because of the Marigold incident. Liz comes into the cockpit and steps beside Leon. They watch the sky. Layers of blue, purple, and pink mesh as an orange sun sinks behind the horizon.

"Ready?" Liz asks.

"Yep."

"It's been a while since you've seen her. Are you nervous?"

Leon shakes his head. "Not at all. I just want her safe."

Boots trample the metal floor behind them. They both look back. It's one of the squad leaders. "Sir, we're ready to disembark. Everything's ready!"

Leon and Liz walk forth, Julio and four others behind them with the Savage hostages between them. Mia with five Savages, and two soldiers wait for them past the barricades. Leon's group stops about fifty feet from the Savages. A shirtless Savage wearing a bear headpiece closes the distance between them. Leon meets him halfway. They stop in front of each other, and the Savage holds out his hand.

Leon takes ahold of the man's hand. "Commander Jackson, but just call me Leon. I'm Mia's brother."

"Cal. Chief of Calamity Clan. I'll look past the RFF's massacre of my people if you give me back those two."

"Massacre? Hardly. They attacked us. I was there."

"Then you crossed into my lands."

Leon holds out his arms. "All of this is considered the Territories, which the RFF controls. We've been kind enough to your clan for the past several years and look at how you've repaid us. Attacked a Compound. Taken prisoners. Killed our people. What you've done here calls for us to storm your village and end our coexistence, but in exchange for Mia, Commander Finkley, and the two with you, we'll release your people."

"Mia stays with me. I'll release the commander a few miles outside of our village. Just release my men and you'll have yours."

"You came this far for a reason."

Cal grins. "So did you."

"You're outnumbered and surrounded."

"And your sister will be caught in the crossfire."

Leon tells Liz through their link to release the Savages. Once Cal sees his men walking toward him, he raises a hand, releasing the two RFF soldiers. Each duo passes the two leaders on their way back to their respective sides.

Leon looks past Cal to Mia. "Let me speak to her. Alone."

Amusement spreads across Cal's face. "She's mine."

Leon doesn't bite. He keeps a straight face. "I have supplies for you."

"What kind of supplies?"

"Weapons."

"Ah. Deal. But you're still not getting Mia back. We're Unified."

"You're getting a cache of weapons. That has to be more than—"

Cal walks away.

"Cal, wait!"

He stops.

"Please. We're siblings." He unholsters his energy pistol, holding it out. "And you can have this. Gen 54. Shoots burst, rapid, and needle streams. My pops left it for me."

A long moment passes. Leon can see the desperation sprawling over Mia's face in the distance. Finally, Cal turns back and grabs the pistol. "Deal. Bring the weapons. Then, I send her over. But she's not staying."

CHAPTER 26

MIA

Two RFF soldiers place a case of weapons down in front of us. Glare orders Daniel and two other Savages to take it away. They complain but lug the case into the tree line.

"Two minutes," Cal says.

I jog past the soldiers, letting my emotions loose as Leon gets closer and closer. His smile fills my lungs with air. He looks just as I remember him, only stockier. The peach-colored glow of the sun illuminates his dark face, his brown-green eyes resemble the beauty of the forest we used sneak out to when we were younger. I slam into him. He wraps around me and grabs the back of my head as I cry into his shoulder.

"You're a Savage now!" he says.

I sniffle. "It's what I always wanted to be."

We both laugh, trying to make the situation lighter, but it doesn't work.

"Mia." Leon cups my face in his hands and wipes my tears with his thumbs. I notice the stubble wrapping around his chin and face, and the unruly hair atop his head. "Let me save you."

"What about Commander Finkley?"

I see it in his expression. Leon doesn't care. To him, Commander Finkley's life is an acceptable loss for mine. I pull out of his grasp. "I can't leave."

"Why?"

"There are children there. I have a responsibility to them."

"They're not your responsibility."

"They are."

Leon takes my arm. "Liz and the others will cover. Let's—"

A tomahawk splinters the asphalt near our feet. I glance back, and Cal and Glare grin.

"Remember Jade and Sannvi, Mia!" Glare shouts.

Leon releases me, shoving his hand into his pockets.

I say, "We can't do this right now. If I leave, that one will kill the kids I'm looking after."

Leon places both his hands on my shoulders. From under his sleeve comes a small beetle drone. It crawls over his fingers and into my shirt. "We're attacking Calamity Clan soon if the Canadians decide to help us with this war."

"Communication drone?"

"His name is Spug. He'll help you when we attack. One of my soldiers monitors him when I'm not. Do you still have your vision mod?"

I nod, and Leon lets me go. "Good. Spug will be highlighted. What does Unified mean?"

"Me and Cal are together..." Heat rises in my cheeks. "Like, I guess married or something."

"What? Did he force you?"

"No. Not really. He did it to save me."

"To save you? Don't trust him. You know what Savages are like. Has he—"

"No! I'm not stupid. It's too much to explain. Just promise me you won't attack until I'm ready."

"Time's up!" Cal yells.

I wish I could stay with Leon. I wish I could go with him.

"I can't make any guarantees. But one more thing?" Leon asks. "Which one killed Kirk? Was it Cal?"

I freeze. It was. But these words do not come from my lips. I don't think I owe a Savage anything, but Glare's the most dangerous out of everyone in

Calamity Clan. Although Cal is the one who killed Kirk, Glare is the one I hate more. Cal's… different. I'll consider this my repayment to him for saving me. I'll never forgive him, but right now isn't the time to get revenge.

"Mia!" Glare coos. "Grab my tomahawk, will you, princess?"

I look back at Glare's ugly face, then at Leon. And I lie. "The one who threw the tomahawk. He's Calamity Clan's War Hand. Glare."

Leon nods and his irises glow. I know he just zoomed in on Glare and took a picture. He embraces me one last time. "I'll kill him when I come. I promise. I love you."

"I love you too," I say, and Leon pushes me away.

I bury my emotions deep, and don't look back. I can't. If I do, I'll fall apart.

CHAPTER 27

LEON

May 15, 2145

Lights flash from the crowd as reporters and civilians alike snap photos of the Canadian Prime Minister and her brother stepping out of the limousine. The Prime Minister is a slender woman with brunette hair done up in triple buns. She wears a light blue gown that wraps her gangly figure and glittery blue heels that match her sky blue-dusted eyelashes. She waves, and the plethora of silver bracelets jangle on her wrist. When a camera man kneels in front of her, she poses, her rosy cheeks bunched up in a ubiquitous smile.

Her brother, dark-haired and dark-eyed with a square-shaped face, ignores the reporters and cameras trying to gain his attention. He's broad-chested with a well-groomed beard, and he wears a simple suit, slacks, and a ring on his marriage finger. The two follow Leon and Liz down a red carpet, four Canadians soldiers, dressed in white-and-gray uniforms and combat armor mirroring the Scouts' dark wear, tail them.

A reporter shoves a microphone into the Prime Minister's face. "Prime Minister, how do you like Compound Talon so far?"

She stops, the dizzying array of flashes catch in her glossy eyes. "It's absolutely miraculous. Tropical. The people are warm and carefree, and I've had a wonderful time here today."

Leon and Liz usher her forth, but the reporter jams his microphone through. "Do you think we'll enter an alliance with your country? There were rumors of a private meeting you had with the generals this morning."

The Prime Minister's brother steps in front of her, grabs the handle of the microphone, and pulls it toward him. "You'll find out tonight."

"General Oswald." Another reporter pushes her microphone across the distance. "Apologies, sir. How is the Sickness in Canada? Will an alliance affect those of us here in the Republic for Freedom Territories? Does a different strand reside in your country?"

"No comment."

Leon signals the Canadian soldiers to move as more of the crowd tries to encroach upon them, breaking through the walls of the Republic for Freedom soldiers. They form a shield around the two leaders of Canada and soon they're away from the masses, climbing steps to the entrance of a grand hall.

All five of the Republic for Freedom generals wait for them in their dress uniforms. General Freed shakes hands with the Prime Minister's brother. "Sorry about that. You two are a breath of fresh air here."

The Prime Minister laughs out obnoxiously. "Ivan being a breath of fresh air? He's stuffy and too serious. You must be a comic, general?"

General Freed smiles, places a hand on the small of the Prime Minister's back, and leads her toward the entrance. "I did want to try stand up as a kid."

The Prime Minister's cackles.

A flicker of annoyance blazes across Ivan's face, and then he asks, "Is One inside?"

"She is," General Campos answers, following General Freed and the Prime Minister.

Leon, Liz, and General Wilde hang back as everyone else enters the building.

"Learn anything?" General Wilde asks.

"Not much. Ivan was quiet for most of the day after the meeting. Siggy was like a child in a candy store. I don't think the two of them get along well. They didn't argue, but they didn't communicate, either, unless they had to," Leon says.

"Good work. Keep an eye on them tonight. There are many high-profile individuals here. Let's go." General Wilde walks away.

An extravagant banquet hall with a velvet carpet expands out before Leon as he leans against a wall. Multiple chandeliers hang from the ceiling, and many round tables covered with dark cloth dot the room. Leon keeps his focus on Ivan, who clinks his glass of champagne with different individuals of prominence within the Territories. Henry Ming, the current president of the social network Link Space. Francesca Cage, the CEO of ArmorTech and daughter of the creator of the mechas the RFF use in battle, the Juggernauts. Lindsay David Ackerman, the man who controls all the news footage within the Territories. And then finally, One.

Leon swipes a glass of wine off a server's tray and watches the two converse. One wears a black dress and flat dress shoes. Her hair's put up in a tight, simple bun, and a mundane golden necklace hangs around her neck.

Leon links Allie. *Put a drone near One and Ivan. Link the audio.*

Roger, Commander.

One and Ivan sit in the corner, smiling and laughing. One points to different individuals, and then their voices filter into Leon's ears.

"…she's impressive. Strong. Beautiful. I want her in," Ivan's saying.

One shakes her head. *"She's loyal to the RFF. Her father was a soldier."*

"When they crumble, she'll have a change of heart. Everyone here loves their comfy life. They're complacent and use to the war and making the best of it. When that life is threatened, and the chaos is brimming at their doorsteps, that's when they'll have no choice but to go with the side that will get them their frivolous lifestyles back."

"You may have a point." One's crow's feet crinkle with her fake smile when she waves to someone passing by. *"We should speak somewhere more private. Before the announcements. I want to ask you something."*

The two rise, and Leon downs his glass of wine, and pushes into the crowd.

Liz, he links. *The generals were right. One and Ivan are conspiring. I'm tracking them now. Linking over audio data.*

Copy, Liz says. *Siggy's in the bathroom throwing up. Her guard's in there with her. I'm having so much fun.*

Hey, we might be stopping a coup. What's more fun than that?

You're right. Seeing One behind bars would be fun. Keep me posted.

Leon follows One and Ivan out of the banquet hall into a dim corridor, and then his audio from the drone cuts. The two disappear around a corner soon after, and Leon picks up his pace.

Leon, I think One turned on jammer, Allie links.

Yeah, probably. I'm tracking them. He turns the corner, but they've vanished. Someone chuckles behind Leon, and he turns around, right into a cold barrel.

Zero presses his pistol harder into Leon's forehead. "Stalking the woman that wants you dead is a bright idea."

"Pull the trigger. Ruin this banquet and our chances of ever winning this war."

Zero grins and retracts his weapon, shrugging. "I don't care who wins this war. I just want my sister to be safe, and she isn't when she's with you."

"Liz can make her own choices."

Zero steps closer to Leon. "I'm the one that protects her, not you."

"She doesn't need protection. Don't let One—"

"Shut up. One gave us everything. Everything. She taught us how to survive and made us strong. If it wasn't for her, we'd be meat shields and dead by now in No Man's Land." Zero pokes Leon in the chest. "After tonight, you tell Liz you can never see her again and disappear."

"Or what?"

The two men are face to face, inches apart. Zero's grin widens, his pale blue eyes lightless. "I'll end you, Leon. I don't care what anybody says. Anyone or anything that comes between my job as Liz's older brother is a threat. Don't say I didn't warn you."

Zero walks away and disappears around the corner.

CHAPTER 28

LEON

The crowd buzzes as they wait. Glasses clink and people laugh. Leon and Liz stand next to one another, far enough away from Siggy and Ivan to not disturb them, but close enough to get to them with ease. As General Asaju takes to the podium, One moves closer to Ivan, their heads bowed together.

"Do you think she's playing him?" Liz asks.

"Maybe. It's One. She always wants more than she says."

"This alliance is the only thing saving her from a cold cell."

General Asaju's face appears on multiple holo-screens throughout the room. He smiles, wholesome and bright. "Good evening to you all. I hope tonight has been fun, and I pray that everyone is safe and well. I would like to take a moment of silence for those who have died today before we get into the big news. The death toll on our side today was 1,632. The Runesians continue to press our borders, and we need all the prayers we can get. So please, bow your heads. Pray for those of us who fight to keep our independence, who fight for our people enslaved by Runesians. For those who fight so that we can be here now drinking and eating. For those who tirelessly toil in the blood and guts of others. Pray, my people, because without faith in one another, for one another, we will forsake ourselves to failure."

General Asaju bows his head, and the room grows silent. Leon sees vivid images of Kirk and Lucia inside his head, and thanks them for saving his life. He clenches his fists and prays for the courage to face whatever comes his way.

"Thank you." General Asaju lifts his head. "No matter whether you're a soldier, a factory worker, a technician, armorer, or in school, you matter, and each one of you does an important job that has helped us persist these past one hundred years. But we cannot fight forever, my friends. Fighting gets old. It makes us crazy. Inhuman. And that is why the five generals of the Republic for Freedom have a question for the Prime Minister of Canada, Siggy Oswald, and her brother, the general of the Canadian Armed Forces, Ivan Oswald. After experiencing our Compound and our people. After seeing the threat the Runesians pose. After being with us in solace and gratitude. Will you align yourselves with us to end the Runesians's tyranny? So that we can all gain the peace we haven't known since before Anomaly Day."

All eyes find Siggy and Ivan, and they step toward the podium together, joining General Asaju on the small stage. Siggy grabs General Asaju and pecks him on the cheek. "That was a wonderful speech. Yes, we will join you. Yes! Yes!"

The crowd erupts with cheers. Ivan punches the air. "We fight together as one!"

The other four generals join them on the stage. They shake hands and pose for pictures that will be added to history books. Liz dips into the surging mass of partiers and comes back with two shot glasses, handing one to Leon.

"What's this?" he asks.

"Tequila." Liz smiles, raising her glass. "This is the perfect time for shots."

Leon clanks his glass against hers, and the two throw the liquor into the back of their throats. The party goes on for a couple of hours. Siggy dances with General Flower, who twirls her around. Ivan, General Freed, and General Wilde chat at one of the tables. Leon helps one soldier remove an unconscious man from the hall, and when he comes back, One's at the podium, tapping a spoon against her empty champagne glass.

The music stops playing, and One's voice comes from the speakers. "Hello everyone. Sorry to interrupt, but I have some news to share. Some of you may know me, others may not, but I'm Katherine Rodgers, also known as One, the commander of the Scouts. I've diligently served the Territories behind the scenes for over fifteen years, and before that, I was a Republic for Freedom soldier fighting in No Man's Land. Now that we have friends in the Canadians, I'm sure we can beat the Runesians and Savages by some time next year. With that being said, I want to officially announce my resignation as commander of the Scouts, and the immediate disbandment of the organization. I'm gifting my personnel who wish to continue to serve to the Republic for Freedom. Thank you for your time and may we all be blessed with peace soon."

Applause rages throughout the banquet hall. When Leon finds the faces of the generals throughout the room, they all wear the same emotion.

Dread.

"We need to go out there and arrest her now!" General Flower points to the floor.

General Campos shakes her head, crossing her arms. "We can't. Ivan might call off the alliance. We should have seen something like this coming."

"How could we?" General Wilde sits defeated. "Nobody expects anyone to sacrifice their queen. She's given up her authority and manpower, but for what?"

"We already know what. We have Jackson's audio data. We have Rodger's testimony and clear evidence of her treason for years. We arrest her," General Flower says. "If we let her go now, we can't stop her when she comes back."

"Our hands are tied, Pasco." General Freed gets up from his seat. "We can't risk losing the Canadian's support. But there is one thing we may have. Leon, where is Rodgers? Tell her to bring Siggy here."

"Excuse me, general, but won't Ivan and One find that suspicious?" Leon asks.

"We don't have the luxury of smoke and mirrors right now. They're not pulling any punches, and neither will we. Link them here. Now."

Leon looks at the door. "They're outside, actually."

General Asaju opens the door and pokes his head out. Liz, Siggy, and her personal guard step inside.

"Your team are watching Ivan and One, right, Commander Jackson?" General Asaju asks.

"Yes. They're talking with reporters. Hold up. Link interview." Leon taps the dark bracelet on his wrist and a holo-screen activates.

One nods on the screen, and then a reporter asks, *"So, what do you plan to do in your retirement?"*

"Oh. Well, me and General Oswald are great friends. He's given me permission to live in Canada. I love the cold, and it'd be a great place for my Huskies."

Leon turns off the holo-screen, and Siggy crumples into one of the chairs and places her face into her hands, crying. Her guard, a brown woman with short, curly hair, crouches near her. "Prime Minister?"

"I'm fine, Charlena." Siggy sniffles and looks up. "She just keeps coming with the surprises. Ivan thinks I'm an oblivious drunk, but One's announcements confirmed my suspicions."

"What suspicions, Siggy?" General Wilde asks.

"I absolutely hate to think that he, of all people, would ever betray me, but since One came into the picture, he's been more distant than usual. When we first came here, I wanted to tell you all that One's been in contact with us longer than she claimed, but I didn't know if that was the right move. Ivan's kept me in the dark with most things regarding the two of them. Charlena's been at my side almost constantly for the past several months. I haven't been sleeping. Sometimes I can't eat. I'm relieved to be among you all right now because I feel safe."

"We're in this together now, Prime Minister. You can confide in us. Tell us what's wrong," General Asaju says.

Siggy stands, blue eyeliner bleeding down her cheeks with tears. "To be blunt, I need people I can I trust with my life."

CHAPTER 29

LEON

May 21, 2145

A knock comes at Leon's door as he folds a shirt and places it in his duffel bag. "It's open."

Julio enters. "Just came to tell you good luck up there." He holds out his hand. "And thank you."

Leon pulls Julio into a brief hug. "Appreciate it. But thank you for what?"

"Back in the forest, you saved my ass. It's been so busy these past few weeks, I never got a chance to say it."

"You don't have to thank me for that. It's what we're supposed to do for one another. You saved my ass too." Julio lingers, not saying anything, so Leon folds another shirt, saying, "If you're just going to stand there, grab some of these shirts and help me pack."

Julio silently places himself beside Leon and rolls a long-sleeved shirt into a perfect cylinder. "I came to…." Julio takes a breath. "To apologize for how I treated you initially. I was a dick."

"You were," Leon says. "Apology accepted. No hard feelings. I hope you'll get along with the rest of our platoon while Liz and I are gone. Most of them used to be Scouts. I still haven't decided yet who I'm leaving in charge."

"I don't want the responsibility." Julio rolls another shirt.

"Why not? You're just as capable as any of them. You used to be squad leader, and you're clearly exceptional at ranger rolling clothes."

Julio smiles but doesn't laugh. He says, "You read my file. So, you know that my entire squad died five years ago. Every single one of them except for me—the squad leader."

Leon crosses his arms. "Your file doesn't do the story justice. I want to hear what happened from your lips."

Julio moves into the corner of Leon's room and sits in a wooden chair. He focuses on the floor ahead of him. "We were tasked with taking a building pivotal to the Runies defense. This building would allow us to break a four-week stalemate. The crows oversaw recon. They gave us a go, but their intel was dead wrong, and we were forced into a defensive retreat. Of course, by the time the crows came to help, my squad was gone. They finished the job after using us as decoys, and our company finally managed to outmaneuver the Runies and push them back, but at what cost? I reported the incident to my lieutenant, Neuman, and he said, 'It's our job to die. That's what you, me, and they signed up for.' I kept pushing the issue to get those crows reprimanded, and Neuman kept blowing me off. I think he was in on it, or they paid him off to keep quiet because after that, I was moved to a different division for insubordination. My rank of sergeant was stripped, and fucking Neuman became a commander because of that win on the battlefield. I took the loss there, but I didn't stop. I kept pushing for those crows to be punished, and I guess somehow, they caught wind of it. Last year, three of them jumped me outside a bar here in Talon. One of them said, 'Keep your fucking mouth shut, or we'll make sure you're buried without one.' So, I stopped, because there's a more pressing reason for me to live now."

"Is it about your wife and daughter?"

Julio looks up at Leon. "My ex-wife's not dead like the report says. She ran away and became a Savage after what she did." He leans back in the chair, and tilts his head back, watching the blades of the ceiling fan spin and spin. "I've often wondered if I'm cursed or something. Tragedy after tragedy after tragedy. I don't even have time to focus on one before another one happens."

"Where is she?"

Julio brings his head forth, coal-colored eyes burning with festered rage. "She's with Calamity Clan. When you come back in a few months, I'll find her, and make her remember our daughter."

"I got you. I'm so—"

"Don't be. I have a favor to ask, actually." Leon nods, and Julio asks, "Can I come with you and Liz to Canada?"

"Why?"

"There's nothing I can learn from the crows in our platoon that you and Liz can't do better. I respect you, and having an extra pair of eyes on your back around One and Ivan will do more good than harm."

"Okay." Leon grins. "On the condition you let me help you get justice for your squad."

"There's nothing you can do that I haven't already tried. It's my word versus Neuman's. And the Scouts had their identities hidden. I don't even know what they looked like."

"You didn't record anything from your time in No Man's Land or last year?"

Julio half-laughs. "This is why I know Neuman was in on it, so he could get a promotion. He told us to go dark before entry. Said something about how the Runies were hacking links, but I investigated that afterward, and no one else was talking about that being possible. And last year, they attacked me so fast, I couldn't get a clear glimpse of their faces, but I do have the audio data of when they threatened me."

Leon smirks. "Link me what you have of that night."

✿

The heat scorches the tarmac that Leon, Liz, and Julio stroll across. Beads of sweat trickle down their faces as they approach General Wilde and General Asaju, who wait for them near a white and gray airship.

"You three be careful. Ivan is not happy," General Wilde says. "He didn't expect Rodriguez to be coming. Adds an anomaly to the mix. It's enough Leon and Liz are going."

"I still think this is too dangerous. One wants Leon dead, and then there's that mysterious terrorist organization they have over there, the Foundation. We're sending them into the lion's den," General Asaju says.

General Wilde rests a hand on General Asaju's shoulder and smiles at Leon. "They're Lions, so they'll be right at home. I wouldn't trust anybody more."

General Asaju steps forth, hugging the three of them. "Siggy asked for our help, and you two specifically. But don't push your luck. If it feels too dangerous, link us immediately and we'll get you out of there. Stay vigilant."

They break apart, and General Wilde shakes hands with Liz and Julio, and they walk onto the ramp. The general grips Leon's hand firmly. "Kirk left everything in you, so I'm counting on you to come back alive."

"I will," Leon says, looking ahead at Liz, then Julio. "We all will. Keep an eye out for Mia while I'm away."

General Wilde salutes Leon, then pulls him into a hug. After he breaks away, he joins Liz and Julio on the ramp, and salutes her back.

Siggy waves from the hangar as the ramp retracts into the airship. "See you later, friends! I will take the best care of them."

The hangar door rises, shutting the group in darkness only for a moment. Fluorescent lights flicker on overhead, and Ivan comes through the hangar door, dark eyes boiling. "Welcome aboard. Hope you three like the cold."

CHAPTER 30

MIA

June 8, 2145

Cal and I lie in a hammock watching the stars. This is what he meant when he said he wanted more of me. This I am fine with because it's a step closer into his heart. I've been teaching him different things for the past month since Leon left.

"So the sun's a star?" he asks.

I nod. "Yep!"

"It's just like the little ones, though?"

"They're not really that little. Did you know the sun's gonna explode and kill us all one day?"

Cal facepalms himself. "With this heat, I can believe that."

We fall into silence and listen to the chirping crickets and hooting owls. He turns to me. "Do you think any of this will ever change?"

"What do you mean?"

"The fighting. This war. It's been one hundred years."

"You want the fighting to end?"

"We can't keep killing each other forever."

"I never thought I'd hear a Savage advocating for peace," I say.

"There are many like me, Mia. I'll show you."

"I believe you."

"Really?" Cal rubs a hand down my side.

"Yes."

He kisses me, and I don't reject him. It doesn't feel wrong or muddy—it just feels right. So, I kiss him back, and his heart hammers against my chest. I'm only doing this to survive. If he trusts me, then everything goes according to my plan. When we break apart, he grins, and we drift to sleep, wrapped in each other's arms.

I don't sleep long. There's too much on my mind. I slide out of Cal's grasp and climb out of the hammock onto the platform. He does not wake. I travel around a tree, across a bridge, and into Cal's room. Sannvi's snoring is ostentatious, and Jade is knocked out next to him. They've both been training daily under the Savages. Jade took a liking to daggers and throwing knives while Sannvi's been practicing with an energy spear and short sword. I've been training with Basco, learning the basics of what he calls the katana. Every day with Basco is brutal, but I refuse to be helpless against Glare or any Savage again.

I grab my sword from the bed and make my way back outside. It's quiet, and no one is around. Now is a good time.

"Spug! Spug!" I call, and the beetle drone lands on my right shoulder. "So, how's Canada?"

Leon's voice comes from the drone. *"Same as the last time we chatted, cold. Shouldn't you be sleeping?"*

"I slept."

"No, seriously. Mia, you're taking a risk right now. Only call out to Spug if you have information that we'll need when we attack. Other than that, I'll contact you."

I grin. "Fine, Kirk."

"Shut up. He would scold you too. Love you, talk to you later."

Spug disappears into the trees, and I grip the rope railing, peering into the stars. I wish Leon, Kirk, and I could run around Compound Marigold one more time. I wish I could hold Jade's and Sannvi's hands as we explore a Rear Compound. I wish Cal and I would have never met because he confuses me. Why does my heart skip a beat when he smiles?

Why does my skin tingle when he touches me? I shake my head, trying to clear away my thoughts of him. I don't have time to ponder on trivial things. Survival comes first.

I walk the grounds for a bit, and practice my one-handed sword strike through the darkness, not paying attention to where I'm going. There's no point in trying to sleep with all this anticipation in my chest. Soon, the village above will fall and be nothing but a burnt pile of wood. All the Savages I've met here will die. I wonder if any of them would accept a pardon? Rhena and Basco have done so much for me. I don't want to see them dead.

CLING!

I look up. My sword has clashed with another. Basco pulls a burner out of his mouth and rubs it out under his foot. "Watch where you're swinging that thing. It's dangerous."

Our blades reflect the white moonlight cutting through the foliage. I place my sword in its sheath. "Sorry. What are you doing up this late?"

"Well, it's June. I'm nocturnal in the June besides when I train you. Too hot during the day. What about you? Tomorrow's going to be grueling."

"Just couldn't sleep."

"Because something's bothering you."

I walk ahead, and Basco falls into step beside me, his sword in his left hand. He strikes the air over and over.

"Something like that. Can you teach me how to do that?" I ask.

"Sure."

I unsheathe my katana, and Basco talks me through the steps of achieving a near perfect single hand overhead strike until we end up near a creek. Moon-kissed water tumbles over flat rocks as it travels downhill.

Basco climbs onto a large rock, raising his blade above his head. "Throw me a small rock. I'm going to slash it in two. This is what you will be capable of with a lifetime of practice."

I step into the creek. My feet relish the coolness as I pick a random rock from the stream. I've seen Basco shirtless plenty of times now, but as he waits above me, the hundreds of kill dots splaying down his torso catch me off guard. I can't imagine a man like him killing that many people. So many Savages here adore him, and the children love his jokes. He's taught me so much about the Savage culture and the differences between the seven clans. I'll never say this aloud, but he reminds me of Kirk sometimes. No. What am I thinking? Basco is a Savage, I must not forget. He may be kind to me now, but if he ever finds out my plan to do away with his people, I'm sure he wouldn't mind another kill dot.

I toss the rock at Basco. He slices through it, and the halves splash into the water. He sheathes his blade with a grin. He sits, patting beside him. "What's bothering you, princess?"

"Please, don't call me that," I say, climbing onto the rock Basco sits on.

Glare mocks me with that title every chance he gets. He tries to demean my strength and persistence, but when Leon arrives, I'll be the one laughing when I place his head on a spike.

"Apologies. Rhena says I joke too much," Basco says when I lower myself next to him.

"You do."

"There's not much else to do. All of you are too serious. My advice, enjoy the wise cracks and small moments because you never know when your time will come. This world is such an unfriendly place."

"Okay, Wise One."

Basco nudges me in the shoulder playfully. "I would never steal our princess's esteem! Although I probably am wiser than her."

"You've been around long enough."

"Too long, I think, sometimes. Lucky, I guess."

Basco's kill dots wrap around his arms, snake up his shoulders, and spill over onto his back until they disappear into the shadows. He may have thousands on his body. I will ask. That way, the conversation will be about him, and not me. The less I share, the better.

"How many people have you killed?" I ask.

Basco tilts his head back to take in the moon. "Eight hundred and ninety-seven. I might be off a kill or two, but a lot of their faces have mixed in my dreams. Some of them have no faces."

"Were you with Calamity Clan before Cal became chief?"

"I trained the boy when he was a child often. I was the Almighty's War Hand." Basco stares at me, his old features dragging with remorsefulness. "We killed so much. Too much. Sometimes just because. The Almighty is a fearsome man. I am glad he left the clan or else I would not be here."

"Why do you say that?"

"He would have killed me sooner or later. That man senses weakness and snips it. The only thing that kept me going was Rhena."

"I know the guilt hurts."

"It kills me. But such is life. I try to atone now by doing good, and I renounced being a warrior long ago, but no matter how many charities I perform, these marks on my skin tell the truth of what type of man I am."

I place my hand over Basco's, and when he glances my way, I see he's on the verge of tears. "You're brave, Basco. Strong. Everyone here loves you."

He pulls his hand away. "Those are kind words, but I am a coward. I never had the courage to stand up for what I believed. Never had the guts to look for a way out of murdering all those people. I just did what the Almighty expected of his War Hand, and in turn, I kept myself and Rhena alive."

"You're not a coward. You did what needed to be done. No one can fault you for that."

Basco watches me for a long moment. I can't tell what he's thinking, but then he rises and takes out his blade. "You will be my last student, Mia, so I want to make sure you don't make the same mistakes I did." He slips the sharp edge across his palm and holds it out toward me. I take his wrist, and he pulls me up. He flips my palm over and slices through it. Basco kneels, sets his sword down, and then grabs my bloody hand. "This is a blood oath. You must adhere to it for the rest of your life. You will stay true to the feelings of your heart. Listen to it. Believe in it. And follow it."

"What happens if I don't?"

Basco tightens his grip around my palm. "In Savage culture, if you break a blood oath, you are unreliable. And if I should die, my soul will suffer unrest because you failed to keep your oath. If this were before

Cal, the Savage King, or Princess Raia, then you would even be subject to punishment or death for breaking it." I nod and Basco releases me and clenches his fist until droplets of his blood drip onto the rock. "Mix yours with mine."

I ball my fist, my blood splatting into Basco's.

⚔

I make it back to Cal's house with my hand wrapped. Cal must still be asleep in the hammock because he's not here. I lie on the bed, unable to sleep, and soon Cal creeps in behind me, wrapping his body around mine. The anxiousness, pain, and depression I was experiencing vanishes. His soft breath sends shivers from the base of my neck to the tip of my toes. Everywhere his body touches mine, warmth blooms. I don't know what it is about this Savage. Some days, I want to kill him, and others, I don't know what I feel. Basco wants me to follow my heart, but how can I if my heart is confused? I squeeze my eyes shut. These thoughts are dangerous.

My heart wants justice. This I know. I vowed to kill Cal, but it's nights like these when I wouldn't want to be anywhere else. I know I shouldn't think like this because Cal is my enemy. He's here so I can use him. The deeper in love Cal falls with me, the easier it'll be for me to escape with Jade and Sannvi. I'll get out of here. I keep repeating these convictions to myself even as I count the number of times Cal's heart drums against my back, the rhythmic thump of it falling aligned with mine.

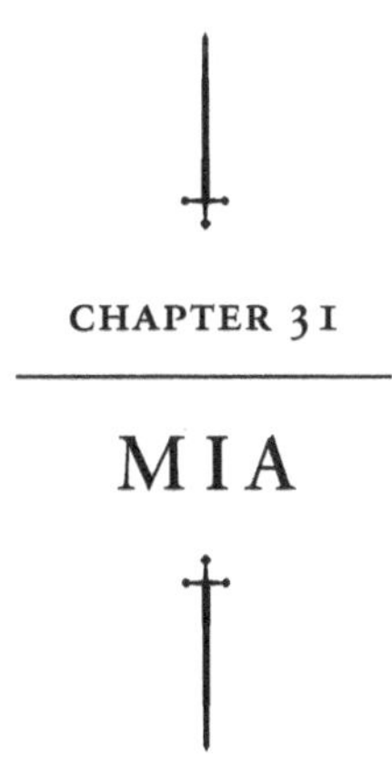

CHAPTER 31

MIA

July 31, 2145

An arc of flames bursts into the air as seven masked fire dancers daringly perform. Their masks are wooden and painted in a variety of colors: green, white, blue, red, orange, black, brown, and yellow. There's a fox, a bear, a lion, a vulture, a snake, a monkey, and a bull. They toss a burning stick between them, catch it with their bare palms, and twirl it through the air. All around the clearing, other Savages join them, their bodies like water, fluid and graceful as they shimmy and gyrate to the bellowing drums and growling stringed instruments.

Stella, a slim and dark-haired woman wearing a white dress, approaches me with Tabatha, the unruly blond I met when the Savages first captured me. Tabatha wears a light blue dress. When she locks eyes with me, she blushes.

Stella holds out a crown made from flowers and sticks. "We made this for you."

"Happy eighteenth birthday," the two say in unison.

"Thank you!"

Stella places it on my head. "Let's dance. This celebration is for you." Stella gasps. "I love your dress!"

I wear a dark satin, one-shoulder strap dress with embroidered lines of gold dust snaking down it. Cal gifted it to me this morning and said the best seamstresses of Calamity Clan spent days crafting it for me. Stella and Tabatha drag me out of my seat, and together, we move our bodies to fit the rhythm of the music. A smile creeps onto my dark lips as Stella and Tabatha twirl around me, and then the music stops. The fire dancers kneel before me. The bull Savage rises in the front, spitting flames into the air. His mask is the only one painted a solid color. Red.

Is this a part of the performance? I look for Stella and Tabatha, but they've vanished. Everyone around the clearing has disappeared too.

"Are you scared?" the bull Savage asks. The odor of rust emanates off him in waves. That's not paint on his mask.

"Whose blood is that?" I ask.

The bull Savage flips his mask up, and the raw detestation from Glare's gaze impales me.

"Yours, traitor!" Glare cleaves into my chest with his tomahawk, and I fall back. The sound of his cackling sinks me. Blood spurts from my insides as Glare crawls over me, licking my cheek, relishing the flavor of my death, his tongue a gross violation of my sanity.

It's cold.

Colder.

And the world slips away.

¢

I awake, rigid as a board. Glare knows. Why else would I have that dream?

"Where are you going, birthday girl?" Cal sits up next to me.

"I need some air. It's hot."

I step outside. The sun hasn't risen yet, but the moisture in the air pulls sweat from my skin as I make my way across the bridge. That was a nightmare. I move through the village, checking back to make sure Glare isn't somewhere lurking in the shadows. Soon, I find myself entering the bar that Dana and her father own. A Savage is passed out in the corner, drooling on a wooden table with a fly crawling over his cheek.

Dana sets a wooden cup down and raises her hands in the air. "I promise I didn't kill him."

I chuckle. Dana's been a great friend to me throughout my time here. "Busy night?" I slide onto a stool in front of her.

"Pretty chill. My dad is knocked out in the back. He can't work like he used to because of the Sickness. Why are you up so early?"

"Couldn't sleep. What about you?"

"I always clean the bar in the morning."

Dana turns her back to me and fills two cups with her homemade brew. She slides me a cup, and I put it to my lips, taking in the cool, foamy liquid. It bites at my throat. There's a sweet aftertaste of apples and honey.

"So, what's going on?" Dana comes from behind the counter and sits next to me.

I haven't spoken to anyone about Glare. Dana's like me, an outsider, so I wonder if she has faced the same problems.

"It's Glare," I say. "I think he wants to kill me."

"Shit." Dana takes a long drink from her cup. "I thought the same thing. He gives everyone a hard time."

"No. This is different. I can tell. It's like he's… jealous or something."

Dana's eyebrows raise. "Of you and Cal?"

"Yes. Sometimes I catch him watching us together. I don't know what it is, but he hates that I'm with Cal. He's just waiting for me to mess up so he can get rid of me. I know it." I chug my drink.

"Have you told Cal?"

"No. Things are good right now between us."

Dana places a palm on my shoulder. "If Glare tries anything, you have me. And I'm sure Cal wouldn't let him harm you. You're not alone here."

I look back at the Savage. He mumbles something in his drunken stupor and slaps himself in the face, killing the fly.

"Thank you. Maybe I'm just being paranoid." I finish my drink. "You never told me how you ended up here."

"Oh." Dana rises, taking both our cups and refilling them. A warm buzz fills my stomach as she leans across the counter, her cheeks already pink. "Cal raided me and my dad a few years back as we were traveling between Compounds. He took everything from us. That same night, just when we thought we were going to die in the pit field, he let me out and started asking me about all the tech we were carrying around. We struck up a deal in exchange for our lives and joined Calamity Clan."

"How do you know so much about modern tech?"

"My mom was an RFF technician before she died in No Man's Land. It's why my dad dragged us from our Compound. He blamed the RFF for her death. We couldn't even bury her."

"I give my condolences."

"No need. We gotta expect death in a world like this. Everyone dies from one thing or another." Dana drinks and smirks my way. "My turn." She glances at the sleeping Savage, then focuses on me. "Do you still hate us?"

I consider this question. I don't see Dana as a Savage, but she is, and she's loyal to Cal, that much is certain. "No, I don't. Before, I thought Savages were the most atrocious people to exist, but after living among you all, I realize I was wrong. It's tough trying to prove myself to everyone, though."

Dana burst into laughter and smacks the counter. "Damn, you're good. No wonder Cal's head over heels for you." She leans closer, irises glowing. "You may have everyone else fooled, but I see you. I've seen that little drone and heard your conversations with your brother. That isn't something you really want to do, is it?"

I sip my drink and keep my eyes level with Dana's. I can't overreact here. Dana's smart. She has a vision mod and intel. If she's known this entire time, then she could have told Cal, but I must assume she hasn't since she's confronting me. This means Dana wants something, and I need to make things sweet for her after the extermination. There's no way she wants to live with Savages for the rest of her life in the wild.

"What do you want?" I ask.

Dana reaches across the counter and pulls me toward her by the scruff of my shirt, and my drink spills.

"I want you to realize that what you're doing is a mistake," she says. "These people are more than Savages. You know that. You've seen that. Cal will forgive you if you tell him. I'll even vouch for you."

I grip her wrist. "He killed my grandfather. Attacked my home. And ruined my life. The Savages kept me as a slave when I was a kid. One of them smashed a boy's head in. How can you align yourself with people like that?"

Dana lets me go. "You're wrong, Mia. I'm sorry that happened to you but those of Calamity aren't the ones from your past. The RFF will kill all the adults. Rhena. Stella. Marco. Phoenix. Basco. Me. My dad. You don't care about any of us, do you?"

"If you're with them, then I can't protect you."

"Calamity Clan is my family. You can sit there and act like you don't care, but I know you're a good person. If you don't tell Cal, I will. I'll give you until the end of the day." Dana takes our cups and turns her back to me. "Happy birthday. Get out of my bar."

I rise and leave. The faint scar on my palm from my blood oath with Basco throbs.

The fire dancers perform, but none of them wear a red bull mask. I wear what I had on in my dream. I tear at the hem of the dress. I can't tell Cal about the RFF's attack. So, what are my other options? One; escape with Jade and Sannvi before Dana tells Cal. Two; kill Dana. I rip my dress more. Both of those plans are shit. I can't escape with all these eyes on me today, and I wouldn't make it far. Not without a vehicle.

Killing Dana is my best bet, but there are many things that could go wrong. She's strong, I can tell. She always keeps at least one electro glove on her, and I'm positive she's tweaked it to make the zap sting more. Doesn't she want more than this? Is there anything I can offer her?

Someone taps me on the shoulder, and I tense, fingers tightening around the hilt of my blade. I glance back at Jade and Sannvi and let out a breath. Jade holds a sheathed blade in her palms and Sannvi a necklace with a blue gem hanging from the end.

"Happy birthday!" they cheer.

I take the blade first, pulling it out. It's a smooth dagger made from stone. Around the hilt are strands of hair.

"You made this?" She nods, and I hug her. "Thank you, Jade. I love it."

"You're welcome. Cal said since I tied my hair around the hilt, I'll always be able to protect you."

I place our foreheads together. "I'm the one that protects you, got it?" Jade nods with a smile. Then I look at Sannvi. "What's this?"

"I bargained for it!" Sannvi cries. "That old witch lady said it glows in the moonlight, and that it'll bring you good luck and protect you from evil!"

I bow my head and Sannvi places it around my neck. I stand, posing. "So, how do I look?"

"Beautiful," Jade says.

Sannvi jumps, clapping. "Amazing! Amazing!"

I wrap my arms around them, and we finish watching the fire dancers perform.

There's a lunchtime feast. Cal, Rhena, Sannvi, Jade, Dana, Basco, and Daniel sit in a circle on the ground with me. Dana acts as if everything is normal, joking and being her usual self.

Daniel asks, "So, Mia. Have you gotten everything you wanted so far?"

I need to talk to Leon. I don't know what I should do about Dana. I can't kill her. "Well, there is one more thing I want."

Basco doesn't notice me watching him. He's sticks a piece of meat into his mouth. Rhena elbows him, and he looks up.

"I want to spar. Today's the day I win."

Basco stands, belches, and rubs his stomach. "Then I must oblige. I won't go easy on because it's your birthday."

Basco's katana gleams in the sunlight as he waits, ready for my strike. I take a breath, and lunge forth, bringing my sword down, but he parries, side-steps, and then draws back, ready to jab at me. I steady myself and go low, slashing at his ankles, but Basco stabs his katana into the dirt, blocks my attack, and then his foot crashes into my chin.

He helps me up. "You are becoming more unpredictable, but you're still a bit slow. And angry. Your attacks were sloppy. If I were going full-speed, I could have killed you."

I rub my chin, massaging the pain away. "Sorry. I'll do better next time."

"Why are you angry? It's your day."

"I'm fine." I swoosh the blood around in my mouth and spit it out.

Basco chuckles. "I've been around enough women to know that's a lie."

"Really, I'm fine. How do I get faster with my strikes?"

"First, never wield a sword when you don't have control over your emotions. Second, time and patience. Practice. Third, courage. You are still afraid of the blade. If you hadn't taken that moment to look away when you went low to make sure you weren't at risk of cutting yourself, your attack would've been faster. Your blood and sweat have wept over that sword. It loves you; love it back."

"I don't think I can form a romantic relationship with a weapon."

Basco grins at me. "But you must if you wish to use it to its full potential. Practice your strikes. I shall return."

He takes off into the woods. Basco always uses the bathroom if we spar around this time. Perfect for me because I send my brother updates.

"Spug!" I whisper.

The beetle drone lands on the back of my right shoulder, but then a branch snaps behind me, and Spug crawls into my shirt. I turn, and Glare walks out of the brush.

"Looks like I'm just in time." Glare whips out a knife. "Who's Spug?"

"I don't know what you're talking about. What are you doing here?"

Glare grabs my blade and grips it until red flows down the steel. "I want you to leave this clan. You don't belong here."

"I'm sorry, Glare. Me leaving won't change your situation."

Glare rushes me, and we tumble to the ground, his blade to my throat as he lies on top of me. "You don't know what you're talking about! I want to kill you so bad."

"Then do it."

He jeers. "Cal will when he finds out you're a traitor."

I draw blood from the side of Glare's neck, and he notices the dagger that Jade gave me.

He laughs. "What are you gonna do when I snap those kids' necks right in front of you? What are you gonna do when Cal finds out his princess is a lying bitch?"

Did Dana tell him? No, she wouldn't do that. Why is he so sure then?

"You don't have any proof."

"Sure, I don't, but you'll give me some," he says, and pushes off me. A cruel sneer rips across his face. "I'll torture those kids of yours until you do."

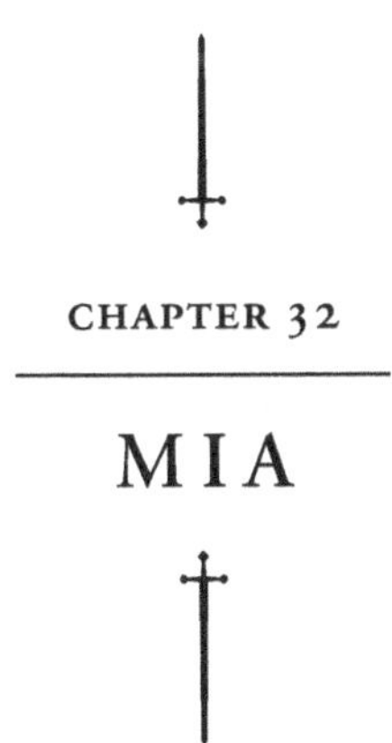

CHAPTER 32

MIA

I must stop Glare before he ruins everything. Basco comes back into the clearing, and I run to him. "I need your help. Please!"

"What happened?"

"Glare assaulted me, and now he's going to convince Cal that I'm a traitor."

"Do not worry, child. Let's go."

We sprint through the forest, catching up to Glare.

"Glare. Stop this," I say.

"Maybe I should just kill you now and save everyone the trouble." Basco steps in front of me, drawing his sword, and Glare laughs. "She's a traitor, you old shit. I'm the War Hand, and you're a Calamity Savage!"

"I've seen men like you before. You are a monster, Glare," Basco says. "Mia is a kind girl, and my student. Why did you attack her?"

Glare unsheathes his tomahawks. His veins bulge in his arms. "I just told you, but I guess you want to die early."

"Go, Mia! Get Cal. I'll hold him here." Basco zips forward, clashing with Glare.

I take off. Basco is risking his life for me, even though Glare is right. I rush through the trees, smacking branches and leaves out of the way, until I make it to the village.

"Cal! Cal!" I run up the pathway. Some of the Savages sense something is wrong and draw their weapons. "Cal!"

"Mia!" Cal comes from the bar with Rhena and Dana on his heels. "What's wrong? Where's Basco?"

"He's fighting Glare."

"Where?"

"Near where we train. Glare attacked me."

Rhena covers her mouth and runs past us. Dana frowns at me, her brow lowered, then takes off after Rhena. Cal takes my hand, and we chase after them. When we make it to where all the Savages are gathering near the trees, Glare is there. A gash runs down his left cheek, and a few slashes run across his arms and chest, but nothing fatal.

Rhena bawls when Glare holds up Basco's head, blood dripping from the decapitation. "Calamity! Basco challenged me, and this was the result! He challenged me to protect Mia, a tr—"

"Glare!" Cal's voice shakes the world.

Glare tosses Basco's head as if it's nothing. It rolls across the ground, and Rhena crashes to her knees, cradling it. I want to puke. This is my fault.

"You went too far," Cal says and approaches Glare.

Glare shrugs. "You went too soft."

"You killed Basco in cold blood. There was no deathmatch sanctioned!"

"I was saving our clan, unlike you."

Cal gets in his face. "What?"

"Kill Mia and those brats! She was talking to the RFF! I know it!"

Rhena sobs. Her grief grows louder and louder in my ears. Cal turns toward the clan, pauses, and looks at me. In that moment, I see it in it his expression. He believes Glare.

Cal glances down, then at Glare. He slips Calamity Clan's emblem off Glare's chest strap. "You are no longer War Hand of Calamity Clan. I want you gone by tonight."

"What? Nonsense!" Glare reaches up, squeezing his chest strap where the emblem was. His face crinkles with rage. "She's a traitor. She was speaking to som—"

Cal shoves Glare away. "You're banished. Leave." He turns and snatches my hand. "Let's go."

"Chief!" someone calls out.

Cal pushes me to the ground and raises his left arm to block Glare's attack. The bottom of the tomahawk hooks into Cal's arm, and blood travels down his arm, dripping to the end of his elbow. With his free hand, Cal threatens Glare's stomach with his sword.

"Give it back!" Glare begs. His face twists into a different emotion I've never seen from him before. Desperation. "Just let me kill her so we can go ba—"

Cal shoves his blade through Glare's gut, kicks him away, and yanks his blade out. "I warned you about what would happen if you ever tried to hurt Mia again."

Cal helps me up, and Glare screams behind us on his knees, holding his wound as blood spills through his fingers. His rage rattles my bones. I hope he dies. That would make me feel better about what I've done.

The sounds of sorrow coming from Rhena slip deeper than any guilt I've felt before.

I killed her partner.

My mentor.

Basco is dead because of me.

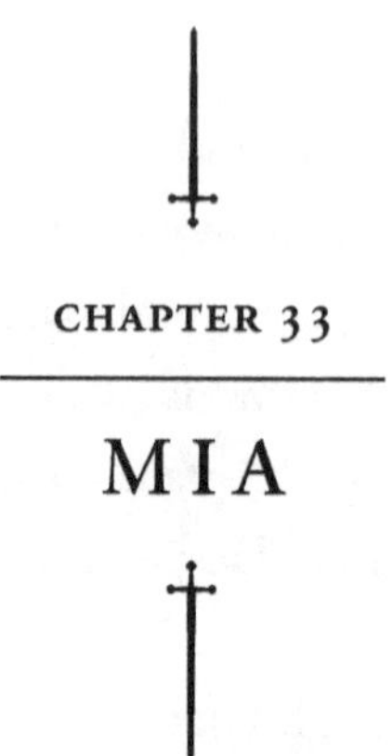

CHAPTER 33

MIA

Cal stands in front of me, shoulders bunched together. "Was he telling the truth?"

"Cal—"

"I saw the look on your face. Was Glare telling the truth?"

Cal deserves to die for his crimes. I don't owe a Savage anything. But my answer betrays my thoughts. "Yes."

"How long have you known?"

"Since Outpost Zion."

"I trusted you. I was starting to believe that things would work out between us."

"Cal, I—"

"Now I look like a fool!"

"I'm sorry. I didn't think this would happen."

Cal pokes me in the chest. "Well, it did. And now I've banished my War Hand, and Basco is dead. This is on you." Cal spits at my feet and storms out of his home.

Why do I feel like this? Why do I feel guilty for trying to survive?

Basco sits on a wooden throne, his head stitched onto his body. The Savages burn their dead. I stand beside Cal, feeling small as I cling to Jade's and Sannvi's shoulders. Glare made sure to tell everyone I was a traitor before he left. A wound like that should have killed him, but his loyal Savages forced Dana to cauterize the wound before he bled out. I don't know what will happen since Glare's still alive. He will not forget what happened here. He'll come back for vengeance upon me.

The trust I worked so hard to gain doesn't exist anymore. If it weren't for Cal, I'd be dead. He's been lying to his clan for me, even though he knows the truth. I still don't understand why he's good to me. I've ruined his reputation and broken his clan apart.

Rhena is with Basco, holding his hand as tears bleed from her red eyes. Cal walks toward her and whispers something I cannot hear. She nods, then kisses Basco on the forehead and hand before joining us. I wonder if she has a blade ready for me under her clothes.

A Savage brings Cal a torch, and he raises it in the air. "Tonight, we send off one of Calamity's best warriors. He was a great teacher to me. Rhena's partner. And a silent father figure to many. Basco died in battle. He died with honor, and tonight, we pay him the proper respect!"

The Savages roar. They mourn a death I caused.

I jump when my name is called. Cal's gaze drills into me. "Mia! She will send Basco off because she was his last student. Come forth!"

My stiff body doesn't want to move in front of everyone with Cal, but I force myself to take the first step. I'm expecting a spear to fly through my back. The animosity pouring off the Savages crushes me, but I make it to Cal and grab the torch. He doesn't let go. "Remember, Mia. This is on you."

Cal's right. He merges back into the crowd, and Daniel and I lock eyes. He'll keep Jade and Sannvi safe. These Savages might kill me for what I'm about to say. I should hate them, but as I stare around, I find faces I know and have pleasant memories with. I know their stories, their likes and dislikes, and their dreams. Marco and Phoenix grew up with Cal and see him as an older brother. Stella loves to cook and teach children. Lero's a comedian. He tells some of the funniest jokes and wishes he could do standup for a large audience. Tabatha loves doing hair.

I hold up the torch and turn to Basco as the corrosion of regret eats at me. For Basco, a Savage. My enemy. His life has stained me, and I don't know if I'll ever be able to wash off this guilt. He taught me how to use a katana. He taught me more about Savage history, which Kirk never mentioned. Basco was my ear to complain in and a record of wise comments.

Shame drips from my soul and the torch shakes in my hand. Who will teach me to become a better fighter now? I wish I felt nothing, but I do, and I guess that means something. More than I'm willing to admit. I place the torch on Basco's lap and watch the jagged flames consume him. The Savages roar, beat their chests, and stomp the ground.

If I owe them anything, it's the truth.

"Calamity!" I shout.

Cal shakes his head, but I ignore his effort to stop me. I must do this. Dana was right. I am wrong about these Savages. These people. Until this point, I've been using them as tools, just like my sword. They've been stepping stones in my plan to escape. I can't keep rationalizing that all Savages are like the exiles that kept me as a slave. The way Savages live is different, but they still have hearts. They still cry for the ones they lose to the angel of death.

Maybe Cal's idea for us to be one is possible down the line. He's a visionary. He's shown me time and time again that he is different. I have not forgiven Cal, but I can acknowledge that he's not horrible. He's not the monster I want him to be, and I hate that.

"Calamity!" I call out again, and they quiet down. I reach into my pocket and hold up Spug. "I've been lying to all of you since I got here. I've hated you and wished for your deaths every night. I thought you were all like the monsters from my past, and because of that belief, I've been using this RFF drone to spy on the clan. In a few weeks, the RFF will be here to exterminate every Savage in this village. I just wanted…."

A few Savages lunge forward, weapons raised, but Cal stops them. "Let her finish!"

I throw Spug into the fire behind me. "I just wanted everyone to know how sorry I am all this happened. People like Basco deserve to be here among us. His heart was pure, and I used that because I knew I could. It's unforgiv—"

"Burn her!"

"Throw her in the pit field!"

"Banish her!"

Cal glances around at his people, seeing the same thing I do. They want to kill me. No, they will kill me as soon as he isn't looking. I don't blame them.

Cal places a hand on the hilt of his sword and steps forward. Calamity Clan's protests sizzle into silence. He draws his blade. "I, Cal, Chief of Calamity Clan, challenge you, Mia, traitor, liar, to a deathmatch!" He places himself several feet away from me. "If you win, you'll have avenged your grandfather, and you can leave with Jade and Sannvi. If I win, you die."

MIA

This is my chance. I can avenge Kirk. I can save Jade and Sannvi. So why are my hands shaking? I try to steady my blade, but the trembling won't stop. Cal's bigger, stronger, and faster than me. All I have is a reach advantage with my katana compared to his curved sword.

He taunts me as he advances. "Come on, what was all that talk about avenging Kirk?" He swings—I deflect the blow. He keeps swinging. "Don't you hate me? Isn't this what you wanted? Here I am, giving you a chance to get everything you want… attack!"

I back away, and Cal leaps forward with a thrust. I sidestep and go in for an overhead strike—he moves and claws into my side, throwing me off balance. I try to block his next blow, but he kicks me so hard in the chest that I flip through the dirt.

Before I can get up, Cal drives his foot into my stomach. I curl into a ball, but Cal pushes me onto my back. "Catch your breath. Get—"

I slash at his ankles, he leaps away, and I get up, charging at him with a snarl. I aim for his left shoulder, doing what Basco and Kirk taught me. He leans to the right, dodges, and I kick his right knee, buckling him. Before he can recover, I smash the hilt of my sword into the back of his head, then knee him in the face. Blood flies from his nose as he falls backward.

I gloat over him, sword pointed at his chest. "This is for Kir—"

Cal spits in my face, and then his legs snare mine and I fall toward him. He clamps a hand around my throat, flipping me over as he slams me to the ground. Cal mounts me, rips my sword away, and tosses it behind him. He punches me in the face.

"This!" Cal punches me again. "This isn't anger, Mia—" Another punch. His tears rain upon me. "This is what I'm willing to do to kill my father!"

He doesn't stop. The world blinks. Darkness, then light. Jade and Sannvi watch me. Daniel tightens his arms around them. Sannvi's crying and Jade fingers her daggers. They need me. But compared to Cal, I'm nothing. He will kill me if that keeps him in charge of Calamity Clan. He needs their respect to reach his father. Killing the Almighty matters most to Cal. I'm just the girl who lied to him, to his clan, and plotted to get him and his people killed.

"Don't look at them!" Cal screams. All I can taste is iron. "You thought you were so smart. Deceiving us. Belittling us. Taking advantage of me and my people!" He gets off me and raises his arms. "Calamity, let no one forget this moment. This pain. I will not be lied to. I will not be betrayed. By my partner or by Glare! I will strike down anyone who stands in my way!"

But he forgets I have things I care about too. Cal is Kirk's murderer. If this is where it ends, then so be it. But I'll take him with me. I force myself up as Cal retrieves my sword.

"Good. You're not dead. I'll kill you with your own sw—"

I throw dirt into Cal's face and duck under his blind swing, shooting forward and slashing across his chest with my stone dagger. He tries to grab me, but I tackle him and place the dagger to his throat. I start to cut across but stop.

"Go on, Mia," Cal says. "Get your revenge."

Calamity Clan will never let me leave after killing Cal, but I press the blade deeper into his skin.

"Deeper. Do it!" Cal yells. "You hate us, remember! We're just filthy, lunatic Savages to you, so just kill me!"

I bite my tongue and press harder. Cal killed Kirk, then ordered his Savages to put his head on a stick. I want him and this clan to feel what

I felt. I want to take something from them. How is it fair that I'm always the one getting taken from? I slip the tip of the blade deeper, and more of Cal's blood bubbles to the surface.

"There you go. Go on," Cal urges.

This is what Kirk would do, right? No. No. What do I want to do? If I kill Cal, I won't survive after this. Jade and Sannvi will be in danger too. But I'll never get another chance like this. I stop. Why is he letting me do this? I shouldn't have been able to win this fight. I've seen Cal spar several times, and I'm nowhere near his level of expertise with melee weapons. Doesn't he want to avenge his mother by killing the Almighty? Isn't that more important than my life?

Cal's death will bring me nothing but more chaos. My mission is to survive. I push myself off Cal. "Mercy."

He sits up and pounds the ground. "Why? You embarrass me!"

I sheath my dagger. "I won't do it. That makes me no better than you or Glare."

Cal stands, grabs his sword, and presses the tip against my heart. "I killed your grandfather."

"He wants me to survive. I can't do that if I kill you." I look at Calamity Clan, then back at Cal. "They'll kill me no matter what you say. I fail. Nothing changes."

Cal sheathes his blade and turns. "Leave. Get your things and go. Don't ever come back. If I see you again, I'll kill you."

¢

Marco and Phoenix stand guard silently as me, Jade, and Sannvi pack the few belongings we have. When they escort us through the village, many of the clanspeople spit at my feet. They take us to a car outside of the forest already on the road, then leave.

I turn and open my mouth, but close it. There's nothing to say. I'm not Savage. I don't belong here with them. They hate me.

"Well, you're leaving. It's a dream come true. Why do you look so sad?" I turn back around and Daniel smiles, just as he always does from the passenger's seat, and for a moment that makes me feel better.

I throw all our things into the trunk, and Jade and Sannvi get into the car.

Daniel gets out and pats the roof. "Fully charged. I programmed the directions to Talon already. You can put it on auto pilot."

"How do you know where Talon is? Does Cal know you're here?"

"I've been there before. A couple of times with my dad. And yeah, he's the one who sent me."

I hug Daniel. "Thank you." My voice trembles. "I wish you could come."

"You know I can't. I killed those soldiers at Zion, Mia." Daniel pulls away. "The RFF would lock me up or execute me on the spot. It's safer here."

I hold on to Daniel's arms. For some reason, I don't want to let him go. "Do you hate me?"

Daniel shakes his head and leads me around to the driver's side. He pauses, staring at me for a long moment before he opens the door. His eyes glisten in the white light of the full moon. "I could never hate you. I want you to be happy. Don't worry about me or anyone here. Go live. Be with your brother. Take a shower. And if we ever meet on the battlefield, promise me you won't kill me."

I smile and hug Daniel again. "I won't kill you, but you know the RFF is going to come, right? Probably sooner since I'm going back."

We break apart. "I know." Daniel steps away and I get into the car. "Forget about us." He salutes me with that whimsical grin on his face. "Goodbye, Mia."

Tears well in my eyes, but I nod and pull off into the night. I watch Daniel on the road through the rearview mirror. He waves, and I let my tears run freely. I'll miss him, and everyone else too. But this is it. This is goodbye. The next time I see anyone from Calamity Clan, we'll be enemies. True enemies. My grip on the steering wheel tightens as a curd of uneasiness forms in my gut because I know what's coming. I know that'll it'll hurt, and that it might even kill me, but what's done is done. There's no going back.

CHAPTER 35

LEON

August 1, 2145

The beeps of the different machines keeping Jace, a frail man with shoulder-length dark hair, alive, drone out the constant rampaging of Leon's heart as he sits near, holding on to the other man's hand.

"It just keeps getting worse," Jace says, voice low. Sweat beads on his forehead. "Every time. Everything hurts more."

Leon takes a cooling towel and places it on Jace's forehead. "That doctor will be here soon."

Jace hacks up blood, and Leon dabs at his lips with a cloth. The world grumbles outside, and Leon glances out of the frosted windows to see the same gray clouds he saw when he first arrived a few months ago. He focuses back on Jace, realizing how much color has drained out of his tawny-colored skin. It reminds Leon of his grandmother, and that same feeling of helplessness, barbed and knotted, rests deep inside him.

"Can you watch over Jenna for me?" Jace asks. "I don't want her going back—"

"Stop talking like you're going to die!"

"I've been fighting the Sickness for years, Leon," Jace says. "I'm in pain. You don't know what it's like. I'm sorry. I should have never gotten close to you like this."

"Jace, I—"

The door to the hospital room slides open, and a man with a silver briefcase, wearing a lab coat over a green-and-blue flannel with khaki pants and loafers, enters. He's stocky with peanut-colored skin and a squared-shape face that holds a salt and pepper beard.

Leon pulls up his mask and stands. "Are you the specialist?"

The man approaches Jace's bedside, holding out his hand for Leon to shake. "I'm Dr. Barnes. But Barnes is just fine. And yes, I'm *the* specialist. The only one worth a damn on this floating graveyard."

Leon takes his palm, surprised by the older man's grip. "Leon."

"I know who you are. The generals filled me in on what's going on here." Barnes pushes his glasses up onto his nose and finally acknowledges Jace. "And you must be the first of Siggy's adopted children, Jace. The dying one."

"Hey, man—"

Barnes holds up his hand, silencing Leon. "I'm only stating facts. Instead of getting angry on his behalf, why don't you sit in that chair so I can take some of your blood. You and your boyfriend here are the same type."

"I don't see how that would help."

Barnes sets his briefcase on the end of the bed and opens it. Inside are medical tools and various gadgets.

"Shroud, activate," Barnes whispers, looking up at the two. "Our conversation can't be heard now by any prying ears or spying devices. You can speak freely."

Leon shakes his head. "What are you talking about? Just run your tests and save Jace's life. He's been suffering for the past two weeks, waiting on you to get here."

"I don't care. I came here for you more than him. If you help me, I'm sure I can make sure he lives longer." Barnes glares at Jace. "Don't bother linking any guards or your mother. Shroud blocks every signal inside and out. Now, Leon, sit. And tell me… how does it feel to be Gifted?"

CHAPTER 36

LEON

August 3, 2145

Barnes plucks a vial full of blood and places it inside another briefcase full of many just like it. He smiles, glancing briefly at Leon and Jace, who lie on the hospital bed together. Leon has an arm around Jace, who's still under a white blanket.

Barnes hums a tune and closes his briefcase. "Don't feel bad about being my guinea pigs for a few days. I saved your life, like I said, while making new discoveries."

A sliver of sunlight casts into the room, highlighting the prominent cheekbones that are now full of vigor on Jace's face. He sits up. "Thank you, doctor. I feel ten thousand times better than I ever have in years."

"Leon's blood should tame your infection. You shouldn't experience the symptoms as severely as you were previously."

"How'd you know I was infected?" Leon asks.

"Gifted. That's the term the Savages use. And I knew, one, because you hadn't been logged by a scanner in the past five months, which is unusual, and two, because of Lucia, your grandmother. You likely caught the Sickness from her when you were a boy and were asymptomatic until recently. You probably don't remember me, but I'm her younger brother. When I found out she was infected, I quit being a medic and fully invested my energy into trying to find a cure for the Sickness. I still have her blood samples, and from them I garnered much." Barnes taps the dark bracelet on his wrist, activating a holo-screen. "You see those bacilli—the rod-shaped bacteria with the tendrils on the end? It has claws, like a scorpion's, hence the name."

"We see them. They're not moving. Are they dead?" Leon asks.

"No. They're hibernating, it seems. I've inferred that these bacteria can live for years without nutrients of any kind. Eventually, they'll perish because they can't enter any organism since they're trapped inside Lucia's blood. But these here are the exact same type you and Jace have inside your bodies. The only difference is the ones within you, Leon, have mutated, which is why I hypothesize that those who suffer from the Sickness and experience the Scorpilionitis mutation and survive gain abilities."

"Wait?" Jace looks at Leon, then back at Barnes. "If you gave me some of Leon's blood, that means the mutated bacteria are inside me, too. Will I be able to do what Leon does with the dead?"

"I can't say for sure. Hopefully not. It may be different from person to person. Over the years, and with the data I have now, I can confidently say there are three types of people living in our world currently: the asymptomatic, the symptomatic, and the Gifted. The most common are those who experience no symptoms of the Sickness. They aren't infected with the aggressive strands of Scorpilionitis in the second group of people, the symptomatic. The people like Jace, Lucia, and those filling our hospitals. Technically, everyone has the Sickness, but not everyone is infected with the aggressive Scorpilionitis that causes death in those whose bodies can't keep up with the evolution of the bacteria. Which brings me to the third, and most rare group—the Gifted. So far, there's only Leon, the Savage Princess, and the rumor of a teleporter on the Runesian's side. All of you have survived the evolution that's taken place inside your bodies, which is why you have abilities."

"But how is that possible? Shouldn't more people have powers since the Scorpilionitis is in our food and water?" Jace asks. "The percentage of people who survive the mutation just doesn't add up. It should be more."

"I agree. But that's a question I can't answer yet. If I knew where the Scorpilionitis came from, I could speculate. But that's a mission for another day. Look at this." On the holo-screen, in a microscopic world, billions of bacteria swim and drift through a space. A red circle appears, tracking three swimming Scorpilioniti. Barnes's eyes widen, and when he speaks, spittle flies from his lips. "This is what's taking place inside Leon's body at a slow rate. Look there, they're like a pack of lions taking down their prey! See how they swarm that cocci!"

The Scorpilionitis sink their claws into a large spherical-shaped bacterium, keeping it in place, and then one of each of their tendrils pokes into the cocci's membrane.

"Not only does this pathogen evolve, but it also assimilates others." The Scorpilionitis detach from the cocci, and it trembles. The cocci grows a tail and elongates, larger than the three bacteria that assaulted it. It sprouts claws, and its greenish tint turns to a darker blue. The tendrils of the three Scorpilionitis attach to the newest of the species, and they swim off together. "And they communicate. They transduced that cocci into one of their own, thus spreading the Sickness throughout your body. Inside those who are symptomatic but not Gifted, this happens at a much faster rate and often fails, and because of this, the Scorpilionitis kill off all other bacteria, making the immune system extremely vulnerable to any new bacteria or illness, even if previously exposed which is why infected people die so quickly. It's bacteria, but also a parasite, and when its host is weak, it does away with them and moves onto the next."

"So, how are you going to make a cure? What does this solve?" Leon asks. "You said my blood only strengthened Jace's immune system because it exposed him to the mutated version of the Scorpilionitis. But that was a gamble, and you can't give my blood to everyone, and even if you could, we'd all still be sick."

"It solves nothing but gives us many options moving forward." Barnes digs into his pocket, pulling out two pill capsules. He holds them out in front of Leon and Jace. "Inside are nanobots that will constantly track you both and monitor the Scorpilionitis. Take them."

"We're not taking those." Leon stands. "You got a bunch of our blood. Isn't that enough?"

"No. You two could help with a cure. You could save humanity. If you're concerned about others finding out, I'll have you know, my research is top secret. I won't tell the generals you're Gifted." Barnes steps closer to the two. "Please. I don't want to be harsh. I want us to trust each other."

Leon and Jace share a glance, then Jace takes one of the pills, pops it into his mouth, and shrugs. "If it'll help everyone, I'll continue being your lab rat." Leon doesn't bite, so Jace nudges him. "Come on. We've both seen enough people die from the Sickness."

Leon stares at the pill, then takes it out of Barnes's hand. "If anything starts feeling weird, I'll come find you. I don't care if you're my grandma's brother. I don't know you and still don't trust you." Leon pops the pill into his mouth.

Barnes smiles, saying, "Thank you."

A knock comes at the door and Jace unlocks it with his link. Liz, and a slim, angel-faced woman with platinum blond hair, step inside, waving.

"Jenna!" Jace flips the covers off himself and runs to hug the woman.

She squeezes him tight. "I thought you were really going to die this time."

The two break a part as Barnes steps past them, near the door.

"Wait," Jenna says. "The Prime Minister wants you to come to Jace's dinner party tonight. She wants to thank you for saving his life."

"I can't stay. Tell her I appreciate the offer, but I have much work to do back in the Territories." Barnes nods toward Leon and Jace. "You both be well. I'll be in touch."

Barnes exits, and Liz steps close to Leon while Jenna horses around with Jace.

"General Wilde linked," Liz says. "She said Mia's adjusting well to the Wolves platoon. She also said her investigation team matched the voice in Julio's audio data from his attack in Talon."

"That's great. Have you told him who it was?"

Liz shakes her head. "I wanted to run it by you first."

"Why? He deserves to —"

"Leon, it was Zero."

CHAPTER 37

LEON

White lightning flashes outside the wall-to-ceiling windows of Penelope Hall as servers move around eight occupied round tables, placing plates of food down. Leon, Jace, Liz, Jenna, Siggy, and Ivan sit at the table nearest to Siggy's throne chair, which is embedded into a stone wall. The other tables consist of One, Zero, CAF officers, a few notable people within Canada, and some of Jace's and Jenna's friends. Above the group, on an arched ceiling, there's a mural of the twelve Olympian Greek gods and goddesses, half-naked, enjoying supper on a slab of gold.

The servers finish their last table, then disappear into the corners of the room, where they wait along the walls near the soldiers who stand guard. Siggy rises with a glass of red wine already stained with red lipstick. She wears a silver, glittery gown, and her usual plethora of silver bracelets on her wrists.

She raises her glass. "Hello, everyone. I hope you can hear me well. The storm outside is absolutely atrocious. First, I want to thank you all for taking time out of your busy schedules to attend this event. This means much more to me than it does to Jace. To have him back in good health after years of searching for an end to his suffering is something I prayed for…."

Jenna leans forward. "She's going to cry."

Leon and Liz grin as a tear rolls down Siggy's cheek.

Siggy continues, "I found Jace when he was only five years old, abandoned on our hollow, icy streets. When I saw him trying to stay warm near a trashcan fire among those of us who have given up on life, I had no choice but to take him under my care. I didn't care that he was infected. I only wanted him to have a decent childhood. All those sleepless nights in the hospital. All those doctors and failed remedies to the Sickness. All the worrying and regret, because why did I pick this boy up off the street if I could not save him?" Siggy holds out her glass. "So, everyone, look at that absolutely handsome young man sitting there smiling. Look at him. Because he's come far, and it's a miracle that's he's alive after everything he's endured. So, cheers, Jace. I love you."

Everyone raises their glasses. "Cheers!"

And they drink. Jace gets up, joins Siggy, and hugs her. He motions for Jenna to join them up front.

Jenna sighs and pushes herself up. "Here we go."

"I'll keep this brief so we can get to good stuff," Jace says. "I am extremely honored by everyone's presence. But really, what I want to do is honor my mother here, the Prime Minister of Canada, Siggy Oswald. She didn't have to cut into her chaotic life to raise not only me, but…." Jace wraps an arm around Jenna's neck. "This knucklehead, right here. Some people forget that the Prime Minister adopted us both because our parents found fault in us. Mine didn't want me because I was infected. But the Prime Minister did. I say this to say that going forward, realize that this woman here is kind and virtuous. She's the best chance Canada's people have at thriving, so don't forget that when times get tough because I can promise you, she's always thinking about everyone else before herself. So, let's do another cheers to Siggy Oswald!"

Leon raises his glass, drinking and watching Ivan not drink. Ivan twists his golden ring around his finger and stares at Siggy with venom in his eyes.

The room settles into the scraping of forks and spoons and the chatter of conversation.

Ivan tilts his glass toward Jace, Siggy, and Jenna when they sit back down. "Nice play, there. Did you three plan that?"

"What was there to plan, Ivan? Can we not show appreciation for one another?" Siggy asks.

"You know the Foundation is going to get wind of this. I'm giving you three compliments, that's all. It's a good preemptive strike against that bastard, Worrell."

"It wasn't planned. Everyone's not always cold and calculating like you."

Ivan's eyebrows rise. "I'm the cold one, Sigs? Funny."

"What's that supposed to mean?"

"Mom…." Jenna interjects, but Ivan burst out of his seat.

He chugs his drink and steps in front of the room, twisting that ring around his finger. "I have an announcement. Well, more of a story to tell. About my dear sister. I think she deserves it!"

Siggy claws at the tablecloth. "Ivan, sit down!"

He grins and continues. "Siggy is indeed a great woman. Our father used to say she was perfect for politics because behind that charming smile was a badger ready to strike. I love my sister, and I respect her, which is why I must say to you all now, she's not the woman I believed her to be. On top of being a drunk, she's also the person who sent thirty-two of our people on suicide missions to space."

Siggy's drink spills as she stands. "Ivan! This is not the place—"

"It's exactly the place!"

Siggy points. "Arrest him!"

Leon places a hand on his pistol when none of the soldiers move. Liz nods at Charlena, Siggy's personal guard, who grabs the Prime Minister, and begins ushering her away. Zero pops up, gun raised, and then Charlena's head matter splatters over Siggy.

Jace and Jenna run to their mother, pulling her away, while Leon and Liz cover them from the sides. They don't make it very far because One and Zero stand in their way, a group of soldiers behind them. The guests gasp and rise from their seats, but when the soldiers encroach upon the cluster of tables, they sit, faces pale and taut.

"Allow me to finish my story," Ivan says. "Siggy's a classic case of a person who's had everything she wanted her entire life. She's a control freak and a narcissist. So, when she lost her control over me due to my fiancé, Isabelle, she got rid of her. Some of you may remember her. She was a brilliant woman. The head scientist in Canada and Siggy convinced her to go to space, knowing she wouldn't come back. Knowing that the past six Optimus missions failed. So what good would a seventh do? Do you have an answer, Sigs?"

"Isabelle wanted to be of service, and I let her." Siggy's pupils tremble. "She wanted to get away from you!"

"You sent her away because you were jealous someone else was more important to me than you. You're conniving and selfish. Someone like you doesn't deserve to lead our people."

"How dare you?"

Ivan's lips furl with contempt. "I'm the new Prime Minister of Canada. Right here, right now."

Jenna aims her gun at Ivan, but one of the soldiers shocks her with a baton, and she crumples.

"Jenna!" Jace attacks the soldier but is subdued moments later when another jams their baton into his back. Jace spasms to the ground beside his sister.

Leon and Liz holster their guns and raise their hands in the air as Zero and three other soldiers circle them.

"Smart choice," Zero says. He places electro-cuffs around their wrists.

"You're making the wrong choice, Zeke," Liz says.

"No, you are. But I'm going to let you learn the hard way."

Leon grins. "Some dogs are just bad, Liz. No need trying to talk sense into him."

Zero punches Leon in the face. "I'm saving my sister. What did you do for yours? I heard she showed up at the gates of Talon bloody from all the Savage di—"

Leon spits blood into Zero's face and headbutts him in his already crooked nose, and the man veers back. One of the soldiers stabs Leon with a shock baton and he jerks uncontrollably to the floor.

Zero looms over him, holding an arm to his nose. "I hope you freeze to death out there!"

"I'm sorr—" A jolt journeys through Leon and he winces. "I don't speak dog!"

The last thing Leon sees is Zero's boot coming for his face.

CHAPTER 38

JULIO

August 3, 2145, 19:00

Yellow streetlights burn through the snow flurries that dust the bare Toronto streets. Julio's footfalls crunch as he moves past shoddy brick buildings and closed ma-and-pa shops. He pulls his beanie tighter around his head and pauses at the entrance of an alleyway. He glances around, then dips into the alley.

A man wearing just jeans and boots staggers toward him, mumbling. As the man gets closer and louder, the words sputtering from his cracked lips become audible. "Every day is Anomaly Day. Every day is Anomaly Day." The man lunges for Julio's arm. "It's upon us! Bet they ain't tell you that, boy! But I see it! And it'll ruin us all! Do you have some points to spare?"

The man's gray pupils melt into the whites of his eyes. His boney chest and face are pink, beard frosted from age and the cold.

"Piss off!" Julio shoves the man away. He glances back at the man, who falls against the wall, and throws a tantrum, his legs flailing in a dirty pile of snow.

"Every day is Anomaly Day! Every day is Anomaly Day!" the man cries.

Julio stops at a dead end. He says to a brick wall, "The one who pulls the shackles from the cat's mouth is the foundation."

The brick wall in front of him swings open. He descends a flight of stairs toward a rusty steel door and knocks ten times. A shutter slides open, red smoke drifting out. Someone on the other side coughs.

"Been a while, foreigner. Where you been?" a man asks.

Julio waves a hand in front of his face. "Dealing with your resident hobo outside. Let me in. I'm already late."

"Jim speaks the truth, unlike you."

Julio sighs. "Your Retainer gave me clearance."

"Our Retainer is dead. And I don't trust you, so fuck off!"

The shutter slams shut. An arm reaches over Julio's shoulder, and he looks back toward a woman wearing a white hoodie and black jeans. The hoodie hides most of her face.

"I'm Rose. Lieutenant Rose of the Foundation." She knocks. The shutter opens. "Lucey, stop being a dick and let me and…." Rose glances at Julio.

"Julio," Julio says.

"… Julio in," Rose finishes.

The steel door groans as it's opened by Lucey, a skinny man with spiky, dark hair wearing a golden necklace and a stained, white tank top. He shoves his left fist in Julio's face, his knuckles reading: F A K E. "You ain't one of us. You're no better than Siggy and that bastard, Ivan. You don't care about our problems, rat!"

Rose places a palm on Lucey's shoulder. "Calm down. You're killing the vibe."

Lucey bristles, and Rose slips past him. Julio sees the dark lines of tattoos branching over Rose's face but can't distinguish them in the gloom. When she smiles back at the two men, one of her eyes glows green, while the other burns blue.

"You boys play nice now." Rose dives into the crowd where hundreds of people wait under blinking strobe lights. As she walks through the throng of people, they split, creating a path for her. Murmurs swim through the mass of Foundation members when a blue light shines onto a concrete wall where a platform descends. Rose steps onto it and rises high above the crowd. She pulls her hood back, revealing bleached blond hair.

Rose comes out of her hoodie and lets it drift down into the ranks of

Foundation members scrambling to catch it. She wears a shirt with the word P E A C E rippling across her chest. She grins at the people beneath her as the blue light turns green, and she clears her throat, her voice booming out of speakers. "For those of you who don't know, I'm Lieutenant Rose. I came here to lead the riot during the Prime Minister's speech in a few days. As I understand it, the Retainer who led this section is dead. Killed by Ivan's men in a raid recently. You need a new leader. If any of you want to volunteer now, come up to the platform."

Julio slides into the crowd, but Lucey grabs him. "You're not leading us, foreigner!"

Julio yanks out of Lucey's grasp. "Touch me again, and I'll break your arm." He maneuvers through the Foundation members until he's at the front, where he takes a hover-pad up.

"Why do you want to be a Retainer?" Rose asks as Julio steps onto the platform.

"I don't. But me and you need to talk. It's urgent."

"About wh—"

Two more people arrive on hover-pads. One is Lucey, and the other is a mutant man with a bald head, no eyebrows, and a tail.

Delight spreads across Rose's face. "We'll have to save that chat for later. Right now, you're a candidate." Rose steps forward. "Foundation! We have three volunteers for the Retainer position, and I have a question for them!" Rose grins at the three men. "Are you willing to bet your blood on it?"

Julio stands in a triangle with Lucey and the mutant. Lucey shows Julio his right fist. D E A T H is tattooed on his knuckles. "You don't belong here. This ain't your fight."

Lucey shoves both hands into his pockets. When he raises his fists, he's wearing brass knuckles.

"I haven't eaten yet, so make this quick!" Rose hollers from above them.

A bat rolls out near the mutant's feet. He picks it up—Julio hears the rebels chanting the man's name. Don, who wastes no time, swinging at Lucey's head.

Lucey ducks and backpedals. "Hey man, what the fuck are you doing? We should gas the foreigner first!"

Don raises the bat.

"Fuckin' muty!" Lucey lashes out at him.

Julio enters the fight and tackles Lucey from the side. He snaps the Lucey's arm backward, and the man cries out in pain.

"Move!" Julio hears and rolls to his feet.

Don beats Lucey with the bat. "That's for messing with my sister. You think—" Wham! "—that you can—" Wham! "—just fuck with us mutants—" Wham! "—and get away with it!" Wham! "Motherfucker!" Wham! "Stay the away from Chloe!" Wham!

After a few more strikes, Don lets the bat clatter to the ground, and rejoins the crowd. A group of Foundation members drag Lucey away. A red spotlight casts down upon Julio, and then Rose starts the applause.

CHAPTER 39

JULIO

Julio reads the blinking neon sign. 24 HOURS OF HAPPY! COME ON IN!

The bell jingles as Julio and Rose enter. A waitress stops sweeping, looks up at them, and takes old-world earbuds out of her ears. "Welcome to Happies. Sit wherever you like, and I'll be right with you!"

"Best eats in all of Toronto. They still wait on you instead of having a bot do it," Rose says, plopping down into a booth. "I love the aesthetic here."

The diner is full of old-world junk. Antique things from the nineties and early two thousands: iPods, so many cell phones, radios, roller skates, CDs, and even Neopets hang on the walls.

"Like, what's a Neopet? How do you even use a CD?" Rose asks.

Julio shrugs. "We've come far."

In the diner's light, he has a clear view of Rose's tattoos. Sprouting from her chest, up and around her neck, are spider webs that stop below her ears. On her left cheek, there's a tiny smiley face.

"You don't talk much, do you?" Rose asks.

"I'm not here to talk about things that don't matter. My people are in trouble, and so are yours."

"So you need the Foundation's help?" Rose grins. "That's cute."

The waitress comes over, all smiles. "What can I get you two this evenin'?"

"Can I get a large cheeseburger with jalapenos and cheese fries and a ginger beer?" Rose gestures toward Julio. "And he'll have the same thing."

"Sure. I'll have that right out for you!" The waitress scurries off.

Rose watches her disappear in the back, then faces Julio, her lips flatlining. "Our affairs are in order. Whatever's going on with you few Republic for Freedom soldiers here is none of our business as long as you stay out of our way."

"It should be."

"Enlighten me."

"Ivan's taken complete control of Canada. He's going to announce his ascension to prime minister during the speech in a few days."

"Lies. We would hear if something like that happened."

"Open your link. I'll send you what my commander sent me. This happened earlier at the Odysseus." Julio sends Rose his visual data, and she replays Ivan's treason in her mind. "My commander checks on me every hour on the hour when I'm undercover. He's been unresponsive for the past two, and so have my squad leader and Siggy's children. They must have been captured, and I'm sure Ivan will be after me next."

"So, you need a place to hide?" Rose asks.

"Yes, and the Foundation's cooperation. Whatever Ivan's planning, you guys can't beat it alone."

"We're prepared."

"Really?" Julio digs into his pocket and pulls out a small black sphere. He presses it, and a holographic map of Toronto shines in Rose's face. On it, forty-seven red dots pulse around the city. "That's every Foundation hideout here. Ivan even has your other locations outside of Toronto. The only reason he hasn't wiped you guys out yet is because of Siggy. You want a say in what happens in this country, help me save them, and Siggy will hear what Desmond has to say without Ivan's interference."

"You must think I'm—"

The bell jingles as two men rush inside with rifles aimed at Julio and Rose.

"Shit!" Rose ducks.

Julio darts out of the booth, jumping over the counter as energy beams volley toward him. He returns fire with his pistol, and the men take cover near the door.

Rose clears the counter, joining him. She checks her gun for an energy cartridge. "Those are convincing actors!"

Julio fires over the counter. "Tell me about it!"

A black cylinder stabs into the shelf over their heads, and Julio covers his ears as the end opens, producing a violent shockwave that rattles his bones and shatters all the glass in the building.

When the disorientation settles, one man is over him. Julio redirects the boot flying toward his face and tackles the guy over the counter. He rolls to his feet, swipes a saltshaker off a table, and hurls it at the man's head. The man stumbles back as salt explodes over the floor.

Julio turns, catching the second man's kick under his arm. He punches the man once in the nose, and then a second time in the temple, crumpling him. The first man pulls out a knife behind Julio, but Rose grabs the back of the man's neck, shocking him with her electro glove until he collapses.

"They certainly were dedicated to their roles," Rose says.

Julio kneels and checks the attacker's pockets. "They weren't actors." He rises, opens his palm, and a holographic image of him appears. At first, in red letters at the top of the haze, it says: CAPTURE. But then it changes to: ELIMINATE. "Ivan wants me dead."

Julio watches a recap of a hockey match on Rose's holo-screen that's jammed between two ceiling-high bookshelves stacked with books and random trinkets. Various pieces of art hang on the walls around the living room. There are a few portraits, but most are just paint splatters.

The first shows a woman sitting in a chair, smiling as she looks out of a window. She looks peaceful, as if nothing in the world could disturb her. Julio wonders if it is Rose, since the woman bears a resemblance. He rises and inspects the portrait, reading the small inscription in the lower left-hand corner of the work. It reads: RIP Lilia. Smile On.

The muffled voices from Rose's spare bedroom get louder, and Julio creeps closer, placing an ear to the door.

"Come on, Desmond, please," Rose begs. "Julio said he can get us close. We can capture Ivan and have him answer for his crimes."

"No. That will only increase the strife between us and the Oswalds. I forbid you. Revenge won't make you feel better. You don't even have all the answers to your sister's death. You're just looking for someone to lash out at."

"Ivan was there! He knows what happened, so he's responsible. You told me you would help make things right!"

"And I will, but not like this," Desmond says.

"You're just like them."

"Rose!"

Julio backs away from the door as it flies opens. "Congratulation," Rose says. "You charmed Desmond. He's agreed to working with you further." A gray-and-white tabby curls around Julio's ankle, purring. "Seems Benjamin likes you too." Rose turns into her kitchen, Benjamin follows. "You want anything to drink?"

"I'll take some water." Julio glances at the painting of the woman again. "Did you paint that?"

Glasses clink. Water runs.

"Yes." Rose moves back into the living room and offers Julio a glass of brandy. "Do you like it?"

"Sure. They're nice. Who was Lilia?"

"My little sister." Rose swirls the dark liquor around in her glass. "Cheers, Lilia!" She finishes her drink in one gulp.

Julio sips from his glass, face twisting from the potency. "Ivan killed her?"

"Eavesdrop much? And basically, yes. My sister was a CAF soldier. Brand new. Excited. And lucky for her, she got put on rotation to escort the most heinous criminals to die in the Land of Ice. Ivan was on the airship when it happened. A prisoner took Lilia hostage and jumped out. Ivan never gave me and my mom more than that and never recovered the bodies. So, I want answers."

"How long ago was that?"

Rose moves away, reaches under the couch, and pulls out a bottle. "Four years ago." She pours vodka into her cup and stares into it. "Am I crazy for holding on to the grief? Am I crazy for wanting some solace in my sister's death?"

"No." Julio shakes his head and moves in front of her. "You're human. Wanting answers is normal. Whoever's responsible should pay."

"Then you'll help me?"

"Sure, but saving my people comes first." Julio raises his glass, and Rose pushes hers forward. The two clink cups and drink.

CHAPTER 40

MIA

August 5, 2145

"Go on," Spike says. "Shoot him in the head."

Sweat trickles down my face, and I exhale, squeezing the trigger of the rifle. The four-hundred-meter target drops and cheers erupt behind me. I switch my weapon to safe, set it down, and turn. The soldiers of Leon's Wolves platoon crowd around me, slapping my shoulder and fist-bumping me. Most of them are leftover Scouts who wanted to keep serving the RFF after One disbanded the organization.

I'm still a bit surprised Leon was a Scout. The platoon told me what kind of missions they went on under One, and now I understand why Leon always seemed so dejected on our links. Now, the fake smiles and the vagueness make sense.

Spike, a six-foot-two woman with skin the color of sand and the sides of her head shaven, holds out her hand once everyone else finishes showering me with praise.

"Welcome to the club," she says. "You got a perfect score. Fifty out of fifty. You're officially a Wolf."

We shake, and I shrug. "That's only the second time."

"No. This course is harder than what the Republic for Freedom requires its soldiers to pass. This is a Scout course."

"Ah. So, I'm Scout material."

"You think you are. I can run the test for you. It'll take three days, but we have enough time before we go pack Calamity Clan up."

"No, thank you." I pick up my rifle and press the touchpad, deactivating the shooting range. The green field display cuts off and is replaced with its white floors and walls. The Wolves leave the range room, but Spike waits for me at the entrance.

"Hey," she says, as I approach. "We're all meeting up later for dinner and drinks. You should come."

We move into the hall, the door sliding shut behind us.

"Sure, thing. I'll see you then," I say.

We go our separate ways and soon I'm stepping out of the building into the modest urban sprawl of the Middle Ring. The muggy heat hits me first, then the odor of smoke, and I look into the sky, seeing pillars of it towering from the factories in the distance.

"Watch out, lady!"

I jump back as three boys zoom by on hoverboards and trip over someone. I turn, and a man wearing a holey shirt and ripped sweatpants jumps up from his cardboard bed.

"Sorry!" I say.

He points at me with a curved, yellow fingernail caked with dirt. "You owe me some points for disturbing my sleep."

"I don't have any."

"Bullshit!" he slurs, coming closer, and I brace myself.

But someone comes from behind me and shoves the man away. The man's eyes widen. He spins away, picks up his cardboard bed, and disappears around a corner. I turn, and Wisse, a lanky mutant man with purple skin and jet-black hair tied back in ponytail grins at me. He wears sunglasses atop his oval-shaped head, a baggy light blue shirt, and baggy cargo pants with sandals.

"I hate these Talonians bums." He holsters his pistol under his shirt. "This is the only Rear Compound that allows people to freeload. This would never fly in Buffalo. Don't they see giving everyone a monthly stipend just makes them lazy or, like that guy, a drug addict?"

"Thank you. I still don't understand it. Back in Marigold, we never had points. There was really nothing we had to buy."

"That's because it was in the boonies." Wisse smirks, his purple tail with white and black stripes flicking behind him with his amusement. "Leon told me. So, where are you headed?"

I point across the street toward the rail station. "Back to the Inner Ring."

"Roger that. Have you decided which squad you're going to join yet?" Wisse clasps his hands together and bats his pretty blue eyes at me. "Hopefully mine."

"I don't know. I think Spike wants me to join hers."

Wisse blows a raspberry and waves off my words. "Screw her." Wisse pulls his sunglasses down over his eyes. "But we'll decide tonight with a friendly drinking competition. You're joining my squad."

Wisse steps past me, waving back as he continues his journey. He slips through the crowd of Talonians, vanishing.

The awning over the rail station provides some comfort from the heat, but the putrid odor rising from the overflowing garbage cans almost makes me sick, so I move closer to the edge. Graffiti litters the brick wall across the track where a group of young men hang out smoking burners and laughing. A balled-up piece of paper cartwheels by and a rat scurries across the gum-stained, lumpy concrete back to its hiding spot behind another full trash bin. A woman adds another piece of garbage to the mountain of trash and it avalanches down. I check the holo-screen to see how long the wait is, then a robotic female voice comes over the intercom.

"Inbound train arriving in five minutes. Destination: Inner Ring. Outbound train arriving in ten minutes. Destination: Outer Ring. Thank you for your patience and remember to keep our station clean by throwing your trash into the trash bins."

The inbound train, covered with dead mosquitoes, flies, and gnats, squeals to a halt, the doors hissing open. A few people step onboard ahead of me, then I enter and take my favorite seat, in the back, to the right, near the window. The train pulls out of the station and in a minute we're on the outskirts of the Middle Ring, where rows and rows of identical houses sit squashed together for miles around the bend. I imagine the houses loop all the way around until they reach the small city area in the center of the Middle Ring.

Two kids play with a frisbee on their sliver of a front lawn, a small dog zipping back and forth, trying to catch it. Talonians pour from the factories, covered in sweat and grime. The Middle Ring is where most Talonians live in their cut-and-paste Republic for Freedom provided houses. It's the second largest Ring next to the Outer Ring, which holds nothing but dilapidated, old-world buildings and a couple of barracks for when the soldiers are out on patrol duty or training.

The RFF prohibits civilians from entering or living in the Outer Ring because of the training the RFF does, but if someone wants to leave the Compound, they're allowed to. Everyone inside of Compound Talon is link-registered, so if an intruder enters, the RFF will immediately know.

Soon the wall that separates the Middle Ring from the Inner Ring comes into view on the holo-screen. Lined up near the wall are the multi-story RFF barracks. Either way I look, the barracks go on for miles around the bend. Each building is marked with white numbers and the RFF flag. The train stops at a station and a group of soldiers, dressed in civilian clothes board. They laugh and shove each other as they take their seats in front of me.

The train pulls out, and through the wall we go—a moment of darkness, and then we're in the Inner Ring. Spherical robots patrol the skies where floating neon billboard showcase new brands of hoverboards, virtual reality games, recruitment advertisements for the RFF, and a new link that's coming soon. Shimmering glass towers sprout from the ground and automated cars wait at the streetlights with passengers inside drinking champagne or jamming to music. The train travels up into the sky and I get a glimpse of a rooftop bar where Talonians mingle and clink their glasses together. The soldiers onboard scream obnoxiously as the train descends as if they're on a roller coaster. Then we're at the station, and the doors slide open.

I take a moment to take in the neon lights and futurism around me. The Inner Ring is where the Republic for Freedom's doctors, researchers, tech innovators, and affluent business owners like Francesca Cage and Henry Ming live. It's also where buildings such as the hospital and the General Assembly Tower are located. I don't understand why General Wilde gave me an apartment here. I would have been fine with a room and bathroom in the barracks. Maybe because I'm Jade and Sannvi's guardian, or maybe because it's easier for her to monitor me.

I enter my apartment on the seventeenth floor and Jade and Sannvi are sitting on the couch with their hands in their laps, backs straight. They don't even look my way, and I sigh.

"What happened?"

I step in front of them. Sannvi has a bruise on the left side of his face, and Jade, a small cut on her forehead. The sliding door to my balcony opens, and General Wilde enters, her cape settling behind her.

She gives me a warm smile. "Sorry. I brought them back home early. I was at the school giving the students a speech when a fight interrupted in the hall." She looks at Jade and Sannvi. "Will you two explain what happened?"

I cross my arms. "Go on."

"They started it," Sannvi mumbles, hanging his head. "They called Jade a monkey."

"And Jade, what did you do?" I ask.

"I ignored them," Jade says, "but then they shoved Sannvi in the back, so I told them to stop, and they said we should go back to being wild people."

"And then?" I tap my foot, looking at Sannvi.

"I spat at their feet and told them to back off," he says. "They were bigger than us. There were four of them, Mia!"

"Why didn't you two walk away? Everyone knows spitting at the feet is something only Savages do, now you two are going to have targets on your backs. Now, they know for sure you two *were* Savages."

Jade stands, fist balled. "They started it! Why should we let them make fun of us? It's not fair."

"You must learn to be the better person. They don't understand all that you've been through," I say. "You don't want your life at school to be hard."

"Then they should just shut their mouths," Sannvi grumbles and stands too. "Why do we have to go to school? All that stuff we're learning is useless. It doesn't help us survive."

"It's not useless." I massage my temples. "Just go to your rooms for now. We'll talk later."

Sannvi storms off down the hall. Jade stands by a little longer, then raises her head and says, "You keep acting like you're fine, but you hate it here just like we do. It's not what you said it would be."

I point. "Jade, go!"

She stomps off and then I collapse onto the couch, looking out at the Talon skyline where the orange sun slides beneath the horizon.

General Wilde lowers herself next to me. She says nothing, so I sit up.

"Are the parents angry? Do they want to talk or something? I don't really know how this works."

General Wilde shakes her head. "I sent an explanation to the parents. Those children will be reprimanded for bullying, but this can't happen again. Jade and Sannvi would have seriously hurt those four if I hadn't stepped in. They have fighting capabilities the children around here do not. Especially Jade."

"I'm sorry. I'll talk to them again. Thank you for everything."

"Are you okay? Is it true what Jade said? Do you hate it here?"

"No! I'm so happy I'm back among my people. I cannot wait until the attack."

General Wilde smiles. "That's good to hear." But then it disappears. "There's something I must tell you. Leon won't be back next week."

"Is the mission getting extended?"

I have enough experience with less-than-ideal news that I already know by the expression on General Wilde's face that something terrible has happened.

"Leon was detained by Ivan and One four days ago. They led a coup in Canada and took control of the country. Right now, Leon's whereabouts are unknown, but we are in contact with the remaining free member of his team, and we're making plans to save him. I just thought it would be appropriate to tell you. Please, keep this a secret. The rest of the platoon don't need to know. I'll tell them soon that his mission is extending."

Leon will be fine. Me and him always find a way to survive. We made it through Kirk's training so we can make it through anything. I won't worry about him.

"Thank you. Got it." I rise and head into the kitchen. "Do you want some water or anything?"

General Wilde stands. "No, thank you. Please, if there's anything I can do for you, let me know. We need you level-headed for the attack."

"I'm fine. Leon will come back." I pour myself a glass of water.

"I'm sure he will. Kirk taught you both how to keep going, no matter what." General Wilde moves toward the front door. "Mia, one more thing."

I drink, then focus on her.

"Will you be able to fight Calamity Clan with a clear conscience? I read Leon's report and watched the recording of your interaction with him. It's okay if you stay back."

I set my glass down. "No. You guys need me out there. I know their village better than anyone. Kirk told me that a soldier knows how to put their emotions aside to get the job done."

My front door slides open, but General Wilde doesn't leave. She looks back at me. "I think a soldier with no emotion is nothing more than a monster, and although we've only known each other for a short time, Mia, I don't think you're the monster you're trying so hard to be."

General Wilde leaves and I flip my hand over, staring at the scar from my blood oath with Basco. When a tear droplet splashes into my palm, I pound the counter.

CHAPTER 41

IVAN

August 6, 2145

Ivan steps out of the limousine, fixing his coat's collar as he checks the gray sky. He pats a nearby soldier on the shoulder. "Another beautiful day."

The clouds rumble over Nathan Phillips Square, full of citizens awaiting a speech.

"We're clear, Prime Minister," the soldier says.

Ivan nods, and four soldiers form a diamond around him and lead him across the street toward the podium. Already, he can hear the citizens whispering. He grins as he climbs the stairs. Today is his day. This is how it always should have been.

Ivan puts on his most humble smile as he looks out at the mass of Canadians. "My people, as you know, I am Ivan Oswald. Today, I am here to announce my official ascension to Prime Minister. My sister, Siggy, is not the right fit to lead this country. She convinced many of your loved ones to journey to space in search of life. And as most of you know, many of them never returned. I combated her decisions every step of the way, but she insisted on acting rashly. For that I am sorry, and still to this day, I visit the memorials of those who sacrificed themselves for our sake. My fiancé, Isabelle, was one of those courageous souls who got sucked into

Siggy's selfish ambitions. Every day, I mourn her. So, I feel it's my duty to make things right by doing what I should have done from the start. If you all will accept me, I will make sure our people never experience such lost again, and if sometime in the distant future, the opportunity presents itself for us to search for our missing loved ones, I'll be first to board that shi—"

"That's bullshit, and you know it!" A rioter yells.

"They're all dead because of you Oswalds!" Another adds.

"You're no better than your sister!" Someone throws a rock, but it bounces off the barrier around the podium.

Ivan frowns, his dark eyes flash with indignation as more rocks batter the barrier. Soldiers push through the throngs of people to subdue the dissent. Somewhere in the chorus, a chant begins for the Foundation. The group grows more volatile, and more soldiers join the fray to calm them.

Ivan clears his throat. "This is why I am here. To end whatever brainwashing the Foundation has placed in your minds and assure you I am doing the right thing. I wish to protect you, and with the Republic for Freedom by our side, that is even more possi—"

"FOUNDATION! FOUNDATION! FOUNDATION!" The rioters chant.

"Liar!" A woman screams.

"Desmond for prime minister!" A rioter hollers.

Ivan keeps his composure, looking back as someone barrels up the steps behind him—one of his soldiers. "Sir, we should leave. It seems most of the people here are Foundation support—"

An explosion erupts from the ice rink in the middle of the square, the three arches over it crumble. The crowd disperses with screams.

"Sir!" Ivan turns, his eyes widening. Another soldier joins the first and opens his jacket, revealing a bomb vest strapped to his chest. "For the Foundation!"

Ivan scrambles and dives off the platform. The explosion slams into his back, and he sails through the air.

CHAPTER 42

JULIO

August 9, 2145

Rose finishes setting up the third holographic array system on her spare bedroom's floor and rises, dusting off her hands. "That should do it. Invite your people, and I'll link Desmond."

The two wait a few moments, and Desmond's hologram appears first. He's a tall man with a hawk nose and receding hairline. He tilts his head toward Julio. Then, General Wilde and General Freed's holograms appear together.

"Any news on Leon and the others?" General Wilde asks.

"They're being moved tomorrow to the airfield. That's what my contacts within the Odysseus said," Desmond says, then peers at Julio. "I think if you want to rescue your friends, your best shot is when they're on the road."

"I agree. We can't do much from our end because of the alliance. We need the Canadians to help hold the northern front within No Man's Land," General Wilde says.

"Don't fret, generals. I can assist with the rescue," Desmond says. "I'll get the route tonight. Rose can put a small team together, and we can move to free Siggy after that."

Julio and Rose both nod.

"We are in your debt." General Wilde's hologram flickers in and out, then steadies. "Have you heard anything about Ivan's status? Does anyone have any updates on who tried to kill him? It's been a couple days of silence since the bombing."

"Unfortunately, no. One isn't letting anyone near him during recovery," Desmond says. "She's even started a mass retaliation against the Foundation. Siggy and Ivan supporters are calling for me to be jailed. I've made a statement that the Foundation does not do suicide bombing. I would never harm Siggy or Ivan, much less have someone kill themselves to hurt them. They're more useful to me alive than dead. I think One is trying to set me up."

General Freed sighs. "This is serious. We should prepare for the worse."

"And what's that?" Desmond asks.

"One rules Canada and destroys everything."

¢

Sheets of rain crash against the windshield, and Rose leans forward, glancing at the side mirror as she slows the truck. "Here they come."

Julio stands in the back, surrounded by four Foundation members. He charges the handle of a sniper rifle. It's a black and silver rifle with a rectangle-shaped receiver and a thin, flute-like barrel. "As soon as I melt the tires, secure the perimeter."

The transport truck rolls by them, and Rose maneuvers their vehicle behind it.

The speakers crackle. *"This is Frostbite Seven. We weren't aware of an escort vehicle joining us. Please state your business."*

"This is Snowfalls Four," Rose answers. "One told us to join here to reinforce transport."

"State mission identification code, over."

Rose looks back at Julio, shrugging, and he mouths the numbers to her and holds up his fingers.

"It's uh… hold up… three, four, seven, eight, one."

"Identification confirmed. ETA to airfield seven minutes, over and out."

Julio pops the hatch of the truck and Cloaks himself, magnetizing the gun to the vehicle's roof. He gets comfortable and peers through the scope.

Rose, get closer, he links.

They speed up, and Julio steadies his breathing, takes aim, and squeezes the trigger twice. Two bursts of energy stab into the back tires, and the transport truck swerves. Rose rams into it and smashes it into a wall.

"Hell yeah!" Rose pulls over and jumps into the back, rallying the Foundation members. "Let's go."

Julio watches them run across the highway toward the transport truck. He climbs onto the roof, looks around, then jumps down. The patter of rain against the asphalt is all he can hear. Where's the traffic? Not a single vehicle is here besides them and the transport truck.

Rose…. Julio starts a slow jog across the road.

Rose checks the front. *Whoa, there's no driver. It was on auto-pilot. Weird they left it up to AI to transport a prisoner.*

A Foundation member opens the truck's back door. Empty.

Julio stops. *Get away from there! It's a tra—*

A fireball shoots into the sky, shaking the world and consuming Rose and the others. The flames don't reach Julio, but the force of the blast throws him off his feet against the truck and knocks him unconscious.

Someone taps Julio in the face. He goes for his sidearm, but a boot crushes his arm.

"Slow down there, bud. You're injured," that someone says.

A sharp pain prods into Julio's side, and he groans, opening his eyes. Dark smoke towers into the sky from the smoldering truck.

"Remember me?" Zero kneels in front of Julio and grabs the shrapnel sticking out of his belly. "Didn't I warn you before about nosing around in other's business?"

Julio's lips tremble, his pupils overflow with hatred. He groans when Zero twists the metal deeper into his flesh.

Zero places his pistol under Julio's chin. "Don't look at me like that. This is your fault, hero. You should have stayed back in the Territories. Now, you have to die and give up searching for that bitch ex-wife of yours.

Shame. Your daughter deserves redemption, but you can't even give her that."

Julio tries to scream, but only coughs up blood.

Zero laughs. "Look on the bright side. At least you can join your squad. Bet they'll be happy to see you. The man who survived when they all died."

"You're…." Julio hacks up more red. "Nothing but a dog!"

"And you're a deadman."

"Fuck you." Julio grins. "Woof. Woo—"

CHAPTER 43

LEON

August 10, 2145

Turbulence rattles the airship as Leon shivers on the hard, thin mattress of his cell. He curls into the fetal position, trying to hold his body heat inside of him, but the metal floors and walls siphon his warmth. It's so cold inside the cell Leon doesn't feel his nose bleeding, but the migraine that racks his skull pulls a groan out of him.

Julio appears on the edge of his bed, feeling his face and neck. "Leon? What am I doing here?"

Leon's lips part as he unfurls himself, but no words come out.

"Everything went black. I tried to save you, but they tricked us. Then Zero came…." Julio clutches his chest. "He shot me. So, how am I here?"

"I told you if anything ever happened to me or Liz, you evade and get back to the Territories." Leon sits up beside his dead friend. "Why did you stay?"

"Because I owed you. None of it matters now. I'm sure I died. I didn't just imagine that, so what's going on?"

"I'm infected. I can see and communicate with the dead."

"So, you're like the Savage Princess? So, the rumors about her are true?"

Leon's shoulders sag. "I don't know. I'm sorry. I should have left you back—"

"I failed because of Zero and One. Don't go beating yourself up over me."

"What about your ex-wife?"

Julio grins. "I'm sure karma will find her. Besides, I can be with my daughter now. Thank you, Leon. For everything. I hope we can see each other again."

Leon's cell door slides open, and three soldiers surround him. He looks over for Julio, but he's gone. The soldiers hoist him off the bed.

"Where are you taking me?" he asks.

The soldier in the middle holds out electro cuffs. "To say goodbye to your friends."

Leon enters the hangar, which might as well be a freezer. Icy mist hangs in the air, frosting the windows of the four drop pods. Only the fourth one on the end remains open. The other three are closed, holding Liz, Jace, and Jenna inside.

"Just in time," Ivan says, smiling, looking back at the pod to the right. "We're almost at the first drop point."

Leon scowls.

"I'm sorry that little stunt your friend pulled with the Foundation didn't kill me. I'm sure everyone thought I was dead, but my suit was reinforced."

"I don't know what you're talking about."

"Of course, you don't." Ivan gets in Leon's face. "But I think you're under the wrong impression. I'm not the bad guy here."

Ivan backs away and someone else enters, and grabs Leon's shoulder, their breath making the hairs on the back of his neck rise.

"Hello, Jackson," One says. "I was going to have you killed, but I've changed my mind. It seems you're a special one, so I think you'll be useful in the future."

Leon shrugs her off. "I'll never work for you again."

One slides in front of him. "Life would be so much easier if you just fell in line. You could go home to your sister instead of freeze in the Land of Ice. This war would be over by now, but you and the generals insist on fighting me. I'll make sure you use your Gift in the best possible way."

"I'm not Gifted."

One smiles. "If you're wondering how I know, let's just say a gun to a man's head will get them talking. Your life is mine."

"My life is my own."

"Let's see if you still have that resolve once you're broken." One raises a hand, and soldiers make sure Liz and Jace's pod doors are secured. "Now it's up to you."

"You choose who drops first," Ivan says. "This is the most dangerous part of the Land of Ice. Jace or Liz?"

Leon looks at the pods again and the windows defrost so he can see Jenna and Liz screaming unheard obscenities. Jace's eyes brighten at the sight of Leon, and he smiles.

"Choose." Ivan crosses his arms. "You have five seconds."

Jace holds his head high, and Liz closes her eyes. Leon charges forth, but his electro cuffs shock him to the ground.

One stomps on his back. "Three seconds. Liz or Jace?"

"Let them go!" Leon struggles under her weight.

Ivan claps. "Time's up! Bye, Jace. Looks like your boyfriend doesn't love you as much as you thought!"

Leon locks eyes with Jace, watching his lips move. Then the floor opens underneath the pod, and Jace is sucked out into cold oblivion. Leon replays the movement of Jace's lips in his mind. He's sure of what Jace said and wishes he could have said it back.

I love you.

MIA

August 14, 2145, 22:00

The luminescent glow of the Inner Ring should be beautiful, but right now the sight of the iridescent city disgusts me. A warm breeze lifts my hair and I glance up at the moon, frowning. It resembles Calamity Clan's symbol, a sickle-shaped C. Tomorrow night I get to gain my revenge on the Savages just like I've always wanted. I've trained years for this. Cried and bled for this. So why don't I feel more alive? Why aren't I smiling right now? The Savages ruined my life, not once, but twice. They murder children, burn towns, and torture people until they lose their minds. Cal killed Kirk right in front of me and then forced me to be his. I hate him. I should have killed him when I had the chance.

The only thing that would make the attack tomorrow better is if Glare were there. I would love to bury an ion blade into his chest. My grip on the balcony rail grows tighter. Most of the misfortune I experienced while living among the Savages was because of him. It saddens me he will not experience my wrath. I sigh, take another look into the sky where gray clouds drift past, and turn into the apartment. Tomorrow, I cut all ties with Calamity Clan. I'll erase them from history, one by one.

The smell hits me first. A putrid stench of rotting meat, fried blood, and charred bone brings bile up my throat.

Wisse pats me on the back after I finish vomiting and flashes me a smile. "You'll get used to it. Soon it won't even bother you. Savages and plague camps always smell the worst."

He carries a dead Savage over his shoulder. A woman with silver hair and blue feathers dangling from her ears. I glance around, watching soldiers line dead Savages side by side or throw them on top of one another. The rows just keep growing and growing and the mounds rise into the sky where the sun sits, smoldering, baking the deceased flesh. A serene peace takes hold of my heart as I walk through the forest, smiling at the smoke trickling from the Savages' burnt homes and the cries of the Savage children grieving over their parents who lie still. Now they know what it feels like to lose. To hurt.

Soon, the rancidness of the dead doesn't bother me. The faces I laugh at. The names, I forget. This is what the Savages deserve. I climb into Calamity Clan's village, where dead Savages scatter the bridges and walkways. Some of them still hold weapons in their hands, and the soldiers remove them, checking their pockets and taking their keepsakes from their ancestors.

"Let me go, bastards! Compounder scum!" I glance to my right and two soldiers are fighting to calm Dana down.

"Come down, miss. We want to help you," one of them says.

"I'm Savage!" Dana screams. "Kill me like you did the rest."

"Hey." I move over toward them. "Dana. It's me. Mia. Just let them help you."

She spits at my feet, each crevice in her face laden with fury. "You're the worse one of all. You laughed with us. Cried with us. Ate with us. And then you left and came back and killed us. How could you, Mia?" Tears roll down her cheeks. "Was it that easy for you to forget?"

I'm about to answer, but then the faces and names return. Rhena. Stella. Marco. Phoenix. Tabatha. Lero. Daniel.

All of them are dead now. I saw their faces. I look around at the flies hovering and crawling over the bodies, and the time I first saw Calamity

Clan's village returns with whiplash. I saw these Savages going about their daily lives with smiles on their faces. A girl cries over Stella near the school, and I remember. That's her little sister. An older man sits with Marco's head cradled in his lap, tears splashing down onto him. That's his father. I step back, shaking my head.

"You remember, don't you?" Dana asks.

"I don't care." My proclamation comes out as a whisper. What's this pain in my chest?

"You killed them. You took them away."

"Shut up. What do you know?"

The fury on Dana's face morphs into pity. "I know that this will eat at you for the rest of your life, and you'll keep trying to forget, but you'll never be able to. You'll always remember what being a monster is like, and you'll hate yourself."

"Shut up!" I turn my back to Dana and walk away.

Dana can't understand how I feel. She let herself be brainwashed by the Savages. I tear through the village. Blackness eats the blue above as I run through the market area and burst into Cal's home. Torches burn beside him as he sits on his throne, head slumped forward. Something in my chest pulls and I rush toward him. Blood drips down his arms, from his fingertips, and pools underneath his feet. Multiple stab wounds crater his torso and a bullet hole, his shoulder. I lift his head and he stares right at me, amber pupils cloudy.

"Finish me." His voice is barely a whisper.

The wood behind me creaks and I turn. The dead block the exit. Rhena, Stella, Marco, Phoenix, Tabatha, Lero, Daniel, and Basco stumble toward me.

Basco holds up his palm and my hand with the scar on it from my blood oath with him burns. I look down and fire engulfs my hand. It travels up my arm and I scream and wave it around. I run forward, but Cal grabs me from behind and the fire jumps onto him.

"Let go!" I try to push him away, but he wraps around me.

"We burn together."

The dead circle us as Cal and I cook in the flames. The stench of my burning flesh clears and the pain dissipates as Cal's embrace grows tighter and tighter.

"Why?" I ask.

"You know why," he says and steps away, taking my fire with him.

"Cal!"

"Goodbye, Mia." Cal drops to the floor and burns away into nothing but ashes.

That feeling in my chest bursts open. I want to go with him. I want—

The dead latch onto me.

"No!"

A hand covers my mouth. Another pulls my hair. One of them stabs me in the back. Then the burning floor breaks opens, and we plummet through the night.

¢

I sit up with a gasp in my bed and clutch my rampant heart. I slip from underneath the covers, grab my bag, and run into the hall, knocking on Jade's and Sannvi's doors. They come out rubbing their eyes.

"Mia?" Jade yawns. "What's going on?"

"Pack some things. We're leaving."

Vigor replaces the sleepiness in their eyes.

"Where are we going?" Sannvi asks.

I smile. "Back to where we belong."

¢

I hold Jade and Sannvi close as we wait for the train, which should be here in five minutes.

"It still hurts," Sannvi complains, rubbing his nape where I cut out his link.

"Get over it," Jade says. "We don't want the RFF tracking us." She glances to her left. "Mia, someone's coming."

Already? I place my hand over the pistol tucked under my shirt inside my waist holster. A person wearing a trench coat and baseball cap approaches. I turn toward them, push Jade and Sannvi behind me, and draw on them. "Stop."

They do and raise their head and hands. "It's just me."

General Wilde smiles at me and lowers her hands. I look around. Does she already have us surrounded?

"Don't worry. I came alone. I'm not here to stop you. I shut off all the surveillance devices in this station because I wanted to speak with you privately," General Wilde explains.

"You knew I was going to leave?"

"It was a potential outcome in my calculations. When I got the notification that your link was offline, I came here immediately."

I lower my aim. "What do you want?"

"I want to know why you're going back."

"Because I've done things I regret, and I don't want more blood on my hands."

"That's commendable. So, you want to save the Savages?"

I nod. "Yes."

"That will make you an enemy of the Republic for Freedom. You're going to be marked as a criminal. You'll become a target for elimination. Leon won't be pleased."

I drop the pistol to my side and hang my head. "I know." I bring my gaze level with General Wilde's. "But I can't just let them die. They're not as bad as everyone thinks. They're just like us. They cry and laugh and love. This might sound crazy, but I think one day, we all might be able to stop fighting and live at peace, or at the very least, we can be allies instead of enemies."

The train pulls into the station, hissing to a stop, and the doors slide open. Jade and Sannvi go inside, and General Wilde comes closer and holds out her hand.

When I take it, she says, "I believe in you, Mia Jackson. I hope one day that we can meet again as allies."

"Me too." She lets go and turns away. "General, wait?" She stops, facing me. "Please save Leon."

She nods. "I will. We'll be attacking tomorrow around 2100, so hopefully you can convince Calamity Clan to evacuate before then. Good luck out there."

"Thank you, general. For everything."

General Wilde smiles. "No, thank you."

I board the train, the doors slide shut, separating me from General Wilde. She waves and then we zoom away.

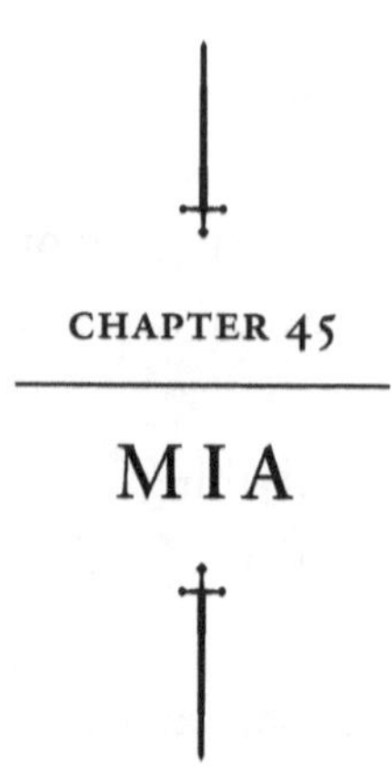

CHAPTER 45

MIA

silver moon casts its glow, illuminating everything except the thick shadows of the forest ahead. I get out, and Jade and Sannvi take off their seatbelts, but I stop them.

"You two should wait here. If I don't come back, go back to Talon."

Cal told me he'd kill me if I return. I know Calamity Clan can see me. I know someone is running to Cal now to report to him. I hold my hands in the air and walk toward the wood line. The car's doors shut behind me, and I look back. Jade and Sannvi join me.

"Fine. But you two stay behind me."

Cal may stay true to his words, but he wouldn't harm Jade or Sannvi. There's a whisper in leaves and although I can't see them yet, I know a squad of them are there, watching, waiting.

"I'm not here to fight," I say. "I've come with a warning. Please let me speak to Cal."

A spear shoots from the foliage, landing in front of me.

"Please! I'm trying to save you guys."

Five Calamity Savages slink out of the shadows, spears held high, arrows nocked back on taut bowstrings. They circle us, keeping us in place. We wait for what feels like an hour.

"Is he coming?" I ask.

One of them smacks me in the calf with the butt of their spear. "You don't ask the questions!"

A few more moments pass, and the glow of a torch appears at the edge of the forest. One of the Savages binds my hands together with rope and pushes me toward the wood line. Jade and Sannvi try to follow, but the others hold them back.

"I'll be alright," I tell them. "Don't worry."

But as I get closer to the forest, and the torch lights up the face of the person holding it, my confidence wanes. Rhena's scarlet gaze burns brighter than the flames, scorching me. I almost dig my heels in and try to turn back, but it's too late. I'm already here and Rhena is before me, her wise features cracked with grief. She looks years older, with dark bags under eyes and deep lines in her face.

Rhena doesn't speak, only turns away and steps off deeper into the forest. The Savages shove me forward. Rhena whirls, snapping, "Leave her! She can follow me on her own. I'm more than capable of killing her how she is now."

The Savages back off and Rhena continues forth, merging with the shadows. "Come on, girl. Don't tell me you're afraid of death now?"

Rhena leads me to a clearing kissed by the moon's glow and pulls down her hood. She doesn't face me. Did she bring me here to kill me? I've never seen Rhena fight, but Basco told me once she used to be an exceptional fighter.

"Rhena, I—"

"Do you love him?" she asks. "Is that why you came back?"

"I-I—what are we talking about? Don't you hate me?"

"If I hated you, child, I would have told Cal to kill you. Instead, he sent me to confirm your intentions."

"But what about Basco? Don't you miss him?"

"Of course, I miss him. Every moment I remember that I can't be in his arms at the end of each day hurts more than I imagined it would, but he's gone," Rhena says.

"He's with our ancestors now, watching over us. He believed in you and that's all that matters. He died protecting you because he knew you were a good person. I won't hold hate for the person my partner died for. Now, answer my question. Do you love Cal? Is that why you came back?"

"I came back to save everyone from the RFF. They're coming tomorrow night. Everyone needs to evacuate."

Rhena steps closer and places a hand on my chest. "Do you love him?"

"How can I? He killed my grandfather. That would be wrong."

"It feels wrong because you see it as a problem you have to fix, instead of just letting it be."

"It is a problem."

Rhena shakes her head and squeezes as if she's trying to rip out my heart. "No, Mia. It is not. The problem with you, me, and all of us is the problem with our hearts. My father taught me that. He was a good man, and my mother often took advantage of his kindness. She claimed she loved him but would always sleep with other men. Not once did he ever ridicule her. Not once did he ever go out to do as she did. I asked him one day why he stayed with her all those years and how could he love a woman who treated him in such a way, and do you know what that foolish man said to me?"

I shake my head.

"My father said, 'No man's heart can win the war against love.' And you, dear child, are no different. Let yourself love Cal. If you continue to fight it, it'll rip you to shreds."

"He killed Kirk," I say.

"Then why did you not avenge him when you had the chance?" Rhena lets go of me.

"Because me, Jade, and Sannvi would have been killed."

"You think that poorly of us?"

I glance down. "Not you. Not everyone."

"Then tell me. Why did you not kill Cal?"

Bile churns in my gut. What is this feeling? Rhena's eyes consume me, washing me over in red. I replay all the moments I've had with Cal in my mind. All the times he's held me in the middle of the night. All the times he's defended me from Glare. All the times I caught him admiring me. And then I remember his face when he told me to leave the clan. He looked sick. Like his entire world was in upheaval and all he could do was hang on for dear life.

I can't deny Cal's feelings for me. He held back in our fight. If he wanted to kill me, he could have. Instead, he was willing to let me gain vengeance and gave up killing his father. Cal's always had my best interests in mind.

I ask a question of my own. "How can I forgive him?"

"Time. He loves you. He's shown you time and time again. I know you feel something for him as well. I'm not saying this will be easy. But you must let go and know that for some reason that's beyond us all, you're exactly where you're supposed to be. That's the thing about our hearts, Mia. We have no control over them at all. They control us, and so we cannot help who we love or why."

The wind lifts our hair and leaves twirl around us. I grab my thumping heart. I know what this feeling is now. This tightness in my throat that makes my mouth dry and my tongue heavy.

"Were you ever afraid when you were with Basco?" I ask.

Rhena smiles, tucks her hair behind her ears, and looks up at the moon. "Yes. I've been in your position before. Confused as to why I loved someone I should not. Basco was the Almighty's War Hand. He took countless lives and often the desolation in his gaze would frighten me. Would he leave me one day? Would he die on some battlefield? Would he point his sword at me? Would it hurt? Would his love fade? Am I good enough? Will I be strong enough? Will the Almighty kill me to snip all the warmth from Basco's life? Everyone has different fears, but what's important is to face them head on, no matter what they are." Crystal tear droplets spill from Rhena's eyes when she stares at me. "Cal is your moon, Mia. Did you forget? Go. Go see for yourself before it's too late."

I find Cal in his home, sitting on his throne. When he sees me, he rises, and fire sparks behind his amber pupils. The closer I get, the hotter my body becomes. My heart hurtles behind this wall of flesh and bone. "Cal, I'm—"

Before I can finish my sentence, he wraps around me, and I melt into his embrace.

"I'm sorry," I say.

"I know. I know." He holds my face in his hands. Tears of joy well in his eyes.

"Why did you let me win? I thought you wanted to avenge your mother?"

"Because I love—"

I kiss Cal.

It's a long, confusing engagement, but I find all my answers there. I break away from him and place a palm on his chest. His heart might torpedo through his ribcage. I remember Rhena's father's words.

No man's heart can win the war against love.

Despite my past with the Savages. Despite everything I've witnessed here in Calamity Clan's village. Despite Kirk's death, I think I've fallen madly in love with Cal. A Savage. A man I'm supposed to despise. A person a part of the faction I promised to end.

"I love you," he says.

"Don't you think that's wrong? Shouldn't you hate me?"

"It's not wrong and no matter how hard I try. I can't ever hate you." Cal lifts my chin, his touch making my entire being tingle. "We're meant to be."

Cal presses his lips against mine and all my fear and anxiousness disappears. He bites my bottom lip and I cling to him until he scoops me up and takes me to the bed. He takes off his shirt, and I take off mine. It's like I'm tripping off the berries and blood again. Everything about Cal makes me go crazy. The way his hair dangles down and tickles my face. The way his bronze skin glistens in the moon's eloquent glow, his muscles rippling underneath. The way he smiles—his scar making him the most beautiful man I've ever laid eyes upon. The way his gaze melts onto me at every glance. I'm captivated by his limitless affection.

I pull him toward me. We're a tangle of passion. Cal's lips brush against my neck and behind my ears. My chest. My stomach. He devours every piece of me until I can't take it anymore and squirm under him.

He stops, and it's like he reads my mind. "Are you sure?"

I nod.

"Then say it."

"I love you, Cal."

CHAPTER 46

MIA

January 1, 2146

Jade dashes forward, and Sannvi backpedals.

"No! Sannvi, don't retreat!" Cal yells, but it's too late.

Jade corners him, slashes at him, and he blocks, so Jade latches onto his energy spear and kicks him in the chest. Sannvi hits the ground, and Jade pounces on him, her dagger to his throat. "Surrender."

Sannvi holds up his hands, and Jade stands.

Cal raises her fist into the air. "And Jade wins! Again."

Daniel and a few others watching clap. The same person keeps winning, so fewer people come to the tournaments the children hold.

Seagull, a sunburnt man with a potbelly, turns toward his daughter, who stands back with the other children. "Sparrow, why can't ya be more like Jade?"

The eleven-year-old girl slumps.

"Seagull don't be mean. Sparrow will get there. If anything, her lacking is your fault," I say, rising from my chair.

Seagull spits toward my feet. "My fault?"

"Yes. Maybe you didn't train her en—"

Seagull lunges at me, but Daniel grabs him by his few brown and gray locs on his balding head. "Calm down. She has a point."

Seagull snatches his hair out of Daniel's fingers and storms off, commanding his daughter to follow him.

"Thank you," I tell Daniel.

He smiles, his eyes flashing with that familiar whimsical charm. Since we left the village in August, Daniel's changed quite a bit. He rocks a buzz cut, and a few more battle scars that he wears proudly over his lean but muscular torso.

"He'll get over it." Cal positions himself before the group of children on the sidelines. "Jade winning for the fifteenth time only means one thing. The rest of you are weak. Train harder!"

The children straighten up and wipe the frowns off their faces. "Yes, Chief!"

"Help Sannvi up," I tell Jade, who's walking away. She ignores me. Jade's twelve now, and Sannvi's eleven. Both have become more of a handful. I guess that's puberty. "Jade!"

She stops. "He's just going to swipe my hand!"

"Always be the bigger person."

Jade mopes over to Sannvi and reaches out her hand. He slaps it away, jumping up, fists balled. "Show off!"

"Loser!"

Sannvi spits at her feet, and Jade inspects her clothes to make sure it didn't land anywhere on her, then pulls out one of her daggers, grinning at him. "Wanna lose again?"

Sannvi readies his spear.

"Enough!" I walk between them. "Both of you, five laps around the junkyard."

They both complain, and I point, stern-faced, until they jog off, side by side, elbowing each other for first place.

Cal claps and whistles, pointing the way Jade and Sannvi are running. "The rest of you. Go! Mind the water dragons!"

The children sprint off, groaning, and Daniel trots after them. "I'll look out for them. I have to fish, anyway."

Cal wraps around me as we watch them leave out of the gate. "He sure does like fishing."

"We have enough fish."

"Better to have more than less," Cal says.

"Yeah."

That evening, Cal and I lean against the railing, watching a few of Calamity below. They sit around a trashcan fire, joking and eating. We live in a trash management building surrounded by a junkyard full of old cars, shipping containers, and, well… junk. Kirk showed me this place on the map. It's the piece of land farthest south on the east coast of the Territories. Most of it is under water and what's left has been conquered by the rising ocean and swamps teeming with man-eating water dragons. The proper name for them are alligators or crocodiles, but I've seen them, and they're too large to be considered kin to those reptiles of the past.

The animals, just like us humans, were affected by Anomaly Day. The rapid increase in temperature caused some species to grow larger, while others shrank. Because of the effects from the Scorpilionitis, I've seen plenty of mutant two-headed, multi-legged, and three-eyed creatures. Most of the deer we eat have multiple mutations, from stubby antlers to one ear, or an eye in the middle of their faces.

Cal sent Seagull here years ago to establish this place as a second Calamity Clan territory. I've eaten more water dragon than I care for, but at least it's been among people I now call my family. It took a while for me to get in the good graces with everyone again, but I seem to have the clan's trust. I received my Calamity marking in December, along with Jade, Sannvi, and Daniel. A sickle-shaped C with a sword through it is now burned into me and Daniel's right shoulders, while Jade and Sannvi went the less painful route of getting our clan's symbol tattooed.

I've been spending much of my time between Dana and Rhena. Dana's increased my breadth of knowledge on tech, and Rhena has shown me how to make several healing potions from plants. I've also been sparring with many of the clan members, learning how they fight. Marco and Phoenix prefer a standard sword or a bow and arrows. Lero is random—he switches weapons every time I spar him, and Tabatha always wields two machetes. The days have been long and sizzling, but we've made this building and junkyard our home.

"Mia? Mia?" Cal nudges me, and I blink a few times. "There you go. Daydreaming again."

"Sorry. What were you saying?"

"The Conclave. It's in April."

Yes. The Conclave. The annual gathering of the seven Savage clans in Damascus City, our headquarters.

"I want to meet the Wise One everyone speaks so highly of," I say. "She can read my palm."

Cal chuckles. "Stop. She really can see the pasts and futures of others, but she doesn't tell people their futures anymore."

"Why not?"

Cal shrugs. "You'll have to ask her. I'm sure you two will get along." He pauses, his eyes mirroring the flames below. "With you there, killing the Almighty will be easy."

"How?"

"Because you're my good luck charm."

I blush despite that being incredibly cheesy. "Are you sure you can do it? According to Seagull, he's a nine-foot-tall cannibal."

"I'll chop off his head. He bleeds like the rest of us." Cal squeezes my hand. "I need you to believe in me."

"Of course, she believes in ya, dumbass!" Seagull waddles our way, stabbing the air with his invisible sword. "Ya need to believe in yerself. The Almighty's skin is steel. Have ya been practicin' yer' thrust—can yer' thrust pierce him?" He squeezes between us, his glassy eyes finding mine. He's been using. "Mia! I wanted to say sorry bout earlier. This heat been messin' with my head."

"We know, Seagull. It's okay," I say with a grin.

He takes my hands. "I'd never harm a hair on yer gorgeous little head."

Cal pulls him away from me. "Yeah, because if you did, you'd be dead."

Seagull smothers Cal with affection, kissing him on the cheek. "It would be honorable to die by ya sword, Chief! But you should save it for the Almighty. You know, there's a rumor he's Gifted like Princess Raia. He eats people because it keeps his skin hard."

Cal pushes Seagull away, dragging him toward the steps. "He isn't Gifted. Let's get you to bed, crazy." He looks back at me. "I'll be back."

Cal and Seagull move down the stairs and leave the building as I listen to the clan party longer. Every time I'm alone, that ebb of worry comes to play with my heart. Is Leon okay? Did General Wilde manage to save him? I have no way of contacting her, but I wish there was some sign. I feel guilty for leaving the RFF when my brother was in trouble. Was there anything I could have done to help him? I shake my head. It's far too late to concern myself with things like that now. My next order of business will be to contact General Wilde somehow and ask for an update on my brother.

And what about Glare? Where is he now? I know he's out there skulking around, scheming for vengeance. That's why I've been training so hard these past few months. I'll never let someone else fight for me again. Next time, I'll take Glare down myself.

The fire below spikes, burning green, and the clan awes. I hear Daniel's voice. "Look at this one!"

Daniel tosses something into the fire, and it vaults into the air, turning blue. The Savages carry on, the noise becoming too much for me. I push into the room that Cal and I share. It used to be someone's office. It has a single large window that can only be seen through from the inside. After a few steps inside, bile rushes up from my stomach and onto the floor. I stare at the chunks of water dragon and vegetables, and panic screams through me as I clean it up with a towel.

What the hell just happened? Is the Scorpilionitis inside me deciding to rear its ugly head now? Dana's father died last month. A ceremony was held for several infants the other week. Then yesterday, a perfectly healthy Savage dropped while on patrol. The Sickness is a vicious disease, and I wonder as I scrub the floor if it's coming to take me next.

CHAPTER 47

JACE

January 15, 2146

The shivering doesn't stop, so Jace unfurls himself and sits up, inspecting the walls of snow around him. He's surprised this Quinzee shelter has held up for almost six months with all the fires he's started, but nothing melts in the Land of Ice. Not the snow. Not the ice. And not Jace's desire to kill Ivan. He hurt the first person that ever cared about Jace: Siggy.

Jace's stomach growls, which means it's time for him to eat his one meal a day. He positions himself upright, leans against the wall, and digs in his bag, pulling out a packet of food and a portable boiler. He tosses snow inside, boils it, and puts his packet in the hot water, reading the letters on it.

"Cheese Grits again," he says, laughing to himself, then frowning.

He rummages through his bag as the food cooks to check his provisions. He has enough food for a week. He wonders if Ivan intends to let him die out here. Jace always knew his uncle never approved of him because he was infected. Jace laughs to himself again as he crawls up his tunnel, thinking that since Ivan's prime minister, he'll send all the infected to the Land of Ice to die. He peeks out. It's snowing and windy as usual. Jace retreats into his snow shelter, putting on his top jacket, balaclava, and gloves.

"Time to stretch," he says, climbing out of his hole. Nothing but icy wind and a useless sun greet him.

Jace stretches and scans the barren, white land around him. He had to settle for this spot. Everywhere else had snow layered over with ice, and he didn't want to overexert himself digging.

He calls out, "Leon! Jenna! Liz! I'm here! I'm still alive!"

Jace waits several moments for a response, but like usual, one doesn't come. He goes back down into his home, strips off his cold weather gear, and makes a check on his to-do list next to the STRETCH AND SCREAM. Jace pulls his grits from the boiler, lets them cool, and spoons the mush into his mouth. Once his stomach is full and his body warm, he drifts back off to sleep.

Whistling wind wakes Jace. He yawns, stretching and cracking. He turns on his lamp and looks at his outdated map like he's done every evening. Jace sees all of North America. He can't pinpoint where he is because everywhere looks the same. Just snow and ice. Not a single tree in sight. The wind whistles again, and Jace freezes. Was that someone's voice?

He stops breathing and listens. Again, something resembling a voice comes, but the wind alters it, carrying it off somewhere. He scrambles, gathers his layers, and digs into his bag for a flare and a knife. He crawls out of his shelter.

"Hello? I'm here!" he shouts, squinting through the snowflakes and darkness. "Hello!"

Again. He hears it. A garbled voice through the howling wind. Jace warns himself that he might be hearing things. He knows being alone for excessive amounts of time can lead to hysteria, but tells himself this isn't the case. Someone is close by, and he must find them. Jace lights the flare and runs forward. "Hey, right here! This way! This way!"

As Jace gets closer to the sound, he thinks about turning back. The snow is dropping faster. He points the flare down behind him. His footsteps are already being covered. He will die if he gets lost out here at night. He berates himself and turns around, but the distorted voice calls out to him again.

It's close. Jace holds up his flare behind him. "Hello? I'm right here!"

The voice comes from Jace's two o'clock, and he trudges forth. That something cries out, and Jace's heart leaps into his throat when he points his flare at the source of the cry.

A polar bear cub.

"Shit." Jace spins away.

He can't stay near it. He can tell it hasn't eaten in days. If the mama is alive, then she's hungry too. He makes it back to his shelter and realizes two things. One, his home is being destroyed by the mama bear's digging. Two, he might die today.

Jace jumps into action. "Hey! Your baby is that way!"

The bear lifts its nose into the air, and Jace holds out his flare, his arm shaking. The polar bear turns its colossal head toward him, blinking five ocher-colored eyes. Jace retreats, careful not to make any sudden moves or turn his back to the beast. The polar bear hisses and chomps its teeth.

"Good, just follow—" Jace begins to say. Then his flare burns out.

The mama bear roars and hurtles toward him, swiping at Jace with a paw bigger than his head. Jace lunges to the side and reaches for his knife, but the bear barrels into him. Jace flips through the air and lands on his back.

The bear looms over Jace, and he rolls away before it can crush him. He tries to get up, but the bear seizes his ankle, shaking him as a dog would its toy. It stops for a moment, and Jace slashes across its nose. Mama bear cries out, veering back.

He gets up and shouts, "Go away!"

The polar bear protests with a mighty roar. It stands tall on its hind legs, then slams down into the snow, and charges again. Jace's ankle's busted, so there's no use in trying to run. He waits, and when the bear lunges at him, he sticks out his right arm to protect his face and neck. The bear clamps onto his arm, pinning him to the ground.

Jace yells in pain as the bear's teeth sink into his skin and crush through his bone. Mama bear shakes him, and Jace becomes dizzy. He can feel the bear's teeth ripping through his muscles and tendons.

Mama bear pauses, its five eyes become lightless as it senses death. Jace doesn't move. Maybe it will leave him alone. But when a spasm of pain crackles down his spine and a deep throb pulses throughout his head, Jace squirms. The bear snatches him off the ground by his arm and sends him tumbling through the snow.

Jace pushes himself up with his good arm as mama bear paces toward him. She knows she's won. He sits up on his knees, and another spasm racks through him. Every part of his body goes numb, and it feels as if time slows. Jace laughs, tilts his head back, and watches the snow float down from the blackness.

"Fuck you, Ivan." Jace clenches his teeth, and his body burns hot when he stands, holding his busted arm. Snow typhoons around the bear as it closes the distance. And to Jace, the bear transforms into Ivan, who gets closer and closer with that condescending scowl on his face.

"Die!" Jace screams, but Ivan pushes through the snow, and pulls out a pistol. "Die!"

Ivan places the pistol to Jace's forehead, smiling.

"DIE!" Jace yells.

The gun sings—the bear roars, and then there's nothing but black.

CHAPTER 48

GLARE

February 6, 2146

Eight tents made from animal pelts stand in a clearing under low-hanging clouds and a crescent moon. The fire in the middle rages as Glare leads three others into the camp. A skinny Savage with long, dirty blond hair sharpens a stick while he sits on a log, the brown freckles splashing over his cheeks illuminated by the flames.

"Anything interesting happen, Rollo?" Glare asks.

"Nah." Rollo jerks his thumb toward Glare's tent. "Piper's in there waitin' for ya."

Glare sighs, and the four men chuckle. A big man with a dark beard and a tattooed line splitting down the middle of his face slaps Glare on the back. "You should just kill her, boss, if you hate her so much."

"Bigfoot's right," Rollo adds. "She's annoying. Always fawning over ya."

Glare moves toward his tent. "Not yet."

Behind him, the Savages carry on. Bigfoot shoves Rollo. "Are you excited to be seeing your dad soon?"

Glare goes around his tent and urinates while he continues to listen. Rollo answers, "If we ever attack. I don't know what we're waiting for. We've been out here a while. I think that stab wound got him shakin' in his boots a bit."

Glare zips up his pants and lies a palm over the scar Cal gave him through the solar plexus. It's a dark scab, almost resembling Calamity Clan's symbol. A pain pulses from it, and Glare scratches into the surrounding skin, clenching and grinding his teeth with fury.

Glare enters through the back of the tent, taking off his vest and dropping it to the ground. He unsheathes his tomahawks and places them near where he'll sleep. Piper lies on top of his bed of furs. She's a petite woman with a bright pink birthmark on her left cheek.

Glare lowers himself, his bones crack, and she turns to him, her eyes lighting up.

"You're back," she says.

Glare pulls the blanket over himself. "I'm going to sleep."

Piper hits him. "You will not ignore me. You've been gone all day. I've waited long enough. I want to be satisfied."

Glare turns to her and places his fingers around her throat. "I told you. Not happening."

Piper inhales. She clutches his forearm. "Why'd you bring me along then?"

"I need to sleep."

"I think you're spending too much time watching Cal and that bitch. It's almost like you're in love with them or something."

"Shut up!"

She presses closer to Glare. "Choke me harder. Can't you at least do that?"

"Will you shut up?"

"I might die."

"Deal."

Glare gets on top of Piper and places both his hands around her neck. She moans out, her smiling face grows red. She blinks a few times, and her eyes stay closed. Glare pushes off Piper, hovers a hand over her mouth, and frowns when her breath hits his palm. He sighs, jumps up, and slips out of the tent, charging toward Rollo, who still sharpens his stick among Bigfoot and the others.

"Rollo!" Glare grabs Rollo's hair and pulls him close. "Do you doubt me?"

"N-n-no!" Rollo splutters.

Glare yanks the stick out of his hand and presses the sharp edge to his throat. "Never doubt me again, understand?"

"Yes!"

Glare throws Rollo to the ground. "Everyone, up!"

Soon fifteen other Savages stand around the fire, rubbing sleep from their eyes, brandishing their weapons.

"Do any of you doubt me?" Glare receives no answer, so he slaps his chest. "I challenge anyone who doubts me to a deathmatch!"

Bigfoot kneels first, then Rollo. Everyone else follows, and Glare grins. "Tomorrow, Cal falls by my hand. Blood will spill, and we'll have a feast beyond our wildest dreams!"

Glare and his band of Savages roar, beating their chests as the thrill of battle takes hold of their hearts.

CHAPTER 49

CAL

February 7, 2146

They slather themselves with mud in a solid clearing surrounded by frail pond cypresses draped in Spanish Moss. A mud-covered Cal sharpens his blade with a rock, and glances back at Daniel, who helps Sannvi cover himself.

"This sucks. And it stinks!" Sannvi complains as Daniel slaps a muddy palm on the boy's bare chest.

"You're the one that's been begging me to come on a hunt," Cal says. "Mia would have my ass if she knew I brought you along, so shut up."

Marco slings mud at Sannvi's face. "Time to be a man."

Phoenix points at the boy, his stomach rumbling with laughter. "Now you're looking like a real Savage."

Daniel rubs a grimy hand down Sannvi's face, smearing in the muck. "All done."

Cal curls an arm around Sannvi's. "You've been practicing your spear throw for months. The kill's yours. You can't go back home without it, or Jade will never let you live it down."

Sannvi's blue eyes burn with conviction, and Cal grins.

The group of five creep through shallow swamp water, stepping out of it onto mushy ground. Cal spots an animal's stool near a tree and put puts up a fist.

He kneels and rubs two fingers through the feces. "Still fresh. It's close."

They slink through the brush for another twenty minutes, stopping again, getting low, and lying still.

"Sannvi!" Cal whispers. "Did you see her?"

The boy nods and joins Cal, who low crawls forward, peeking through a bush. Forty meters ahead, across a small pond, is a doe with one ear. She laps the water, oblivious to the danger she's in.

"Drop her," Cal says. "Slow and steady."

Sannvi rises, his metallic spear elongates, and the end sharpens, crackling with blue energy.

¢

Cal pulls his bloody hands from the doe's belly. Intestines lie beside him, and flies swarm the guts. He wipes sweat from his brow, pointing at a section of the doe's body with his knife. "Cut there. You need to learn this. Me and Mia might not be around forever."

Sannvi tears into the doe's flesh.

"Hey, Cal!" Daniel calls.

"Yeah."

"I am going to check that pond to see if I can catch anything."

"All right. Make it quick. We're finishing soon."

"Gotcha." Daniel leaves the clearing.

An hour later, Cal, Sannvi, Marco, and Phoenix are divvying up the deer meat, each packing their bags with as much as they carry.

"We gotta hurry and get this back so it doesn't spoil in this heat," Marco says.

Cal lifts his head. "Where's Daniel? He should be back by now." Around them all is silent. Cal erects himself, scanning the greenery, then unsheathes his curved sword. "Boys."

Marco and Phoenix copy Cal. Sannvi looks up in confusion when he sees the others forming a triangle around him.

"Show yourselves!" Cal yells.

Glare steps out first, twirling one of his tomahawks in the air and catching it. Then, nineteen others.

Bigfoot tosses a bloodied and beaten Daniel to the ground. "We brought you back like we promised."

Daniel limps toward Cal and the others. Glare swaggers forward, wearing skull pauldrons and a fur cape on his shoulders. He pushes Daniel to the ground and Phoenix runs out to help him to his feet.

"I knew you'd come, eventually." Cal meets Glare in the middle of the clearing. "Let them go. If you want a deathmatch, I'll give you one."

"They stay. You die. I become chief."

"Calamity Clan won't surrender to you."

Glare nods toward Sannvi. "Mia will if I have that boy."

Cal's eyes darken. "You're exiled. You have no say in Savage affairs."

"I don't see an X anywhere on my body."

Cal distances himself and readies his blade. "Then allow me to give you one."

Glare cleaves through the air with his tomahawk—Cal sidesteps, thrusting his sword forward, but Glare parries into a vicious attack sequence. He swings his tomahawks relentlessly, forcing Cal back.

"Glare! Glare! Glare! Glare!" his Savages chant.

Cal evades Glare's last strike and gets out of his reach. The two circle each other.

"You could never lead a clan. That's why Scar chose Butterfly over you," Cal says.

Glare spits at Cal's feet. "You don't deserve to be the Almighty's son! You're a disgrace to his name!"

Cal slices at Glare's neck, but he dodges, and jumps into the air, smashing his tomahawks onto Cal's guard. Sparks fly, and then Glare kicks Cal in the chest, and he rolls, righting himself on all fours, looking back at Marco and Phoenix. "Go! Force through. Get out of here!"

"Don't let them!" Glare shouts, trying to clobber Cal.

Cal catches Glare's wrist and digs a fist into his gut, crumpling him. He tries to lop off Glare's head, but Glare tackles him, and punches him. Blood fills Cal's mouth. He spits it into Glare's face and kicks him away.

Cal looks back. Marco, Daniel, and Phoenix are fighting three of Glare's Savages. Sannvi watches their backs, poking with his spear at those who try to surround them.

"Don't run, coward!" Glare screams.

Cal gets up and sprints toward Sannvi. He thrust his sword through one of the Savage's back, then grabs the second one, slits his throat and slides behind him so he can take the tomahawk that's thrown by Glare in the chest. The third lashes out at Cal, but Sannvi slams the spear into the man's groin, and Cal decapitates him.

"Run!" Cal pushes Sannvi into the brush. "Warn the others!"

Cal rejoins the fray, taking the Savage attacking Daniel by his hair and shoving his sword into the man's side. "Daniel, go! Marco, Phoenix! Disengage!"

Cal sprints off after Daniel, and Marco and Phoenix follow him into the thicket.

"After them!" Glare hollers, snatching a bow and arrows from a Savage near him. "Don't let them escape!"

Arrows whiz past Cal's head. When he checks back, Glare and his band hurtle after them, leaping over fallen logs and swatting branches out of the way.

"Keep running. Don't stop!" Cal hollers.

Daniel trips ahead of him, and Cal stops. "Get it togeth—" An arrow stabs Cal in the back. He shoves Daniel forward. "Go!"

"I'm sorry!" Daniel sprints away.

Cal runs after him, yanking the arrow out, but another one punches into his left shoulder, and he topples to the ground.

"Hurry, get him!" Glare yells.

Marco and Phoenix each take one of Cal's arms, and he tries to push them off. "I said… go."

"We don't leave our chief behind!" Marco hoists Cal onto his shoulders. "Hang on tight."

"I'll cover," Phoenix says, readying his bow, and returning fire as arrows fly past them. "Run!"

Marco puts his head down and sprints as fast as he can.

CHAPTER 50

MIA

Rhena beams at me, and this nauseating feeling that's been far too common these past few months swells in my gut.

"What is it?" I ask.

"What are *they*?" Rhena places her wise hands on my belly.

No.

"Twins!"

I vomit.

Then, I'm out of Rhena's tent after apologizing one hundred times. What am I going to do? How did this happen? I can't be a mother! I can't raise children like this! Not with these Sava—No! I thought I had stopped thinking like that. I place my face in my hands.

"Mia?" When I lift my head, Jade stands before me, asking, "Are you okay? What did Rhena say?"

"Looks like you're going to have some siblings."

Her eyes light up. "Can I feel?"

"No. I've been keeping this secret. Only Rhena, Dana, and you know."

Jade's frown tugs at my heart, and I pull her to the side of Rhena's tent and let her feel my stomach under the clothes Rhena gave me days ago. I'm not showing yet, but Rhena said it could happen any moment.

"This is so cool!" Jade says.

I want to tell Jade this is a horrible situation. How can I raise children in a world like this? The land swelters. The seas to the east rise, and in the west, they recede. The plants and animals are dying or mutating, unable to keep up with the rapid increase in temperature. There are rumors among the clans of another Anomaly Day happening soon. What will the world be like then? What kind of selfish idiot am I?

"You gonna tell Cal?"

"Yes. Won't be able to hide this much longer. Where is he?" I pull my shirt down.

"He went out with Daniel, Marco, Phoenix, and Sannvi earlier this morning."

I sigh as we step from around Rhena's tent. I told Cal I didn't want Sannvi going out there with him on hunts. He's still just a kid. What if—

The Horn blares its dreadful tune. Rhena comes out of her tent. Calamity Clan spills from the building and their tents with their weapons, staring around in confusion.

Tabatha and Sannvi run from the gate. "Mia! Mia! Sannvi said Glare attacked them!"

The Horn bellows again as Seagull, Rhena, Jade, and I crowd around Sannvi.

Someone yells, "Attack!"

Another voice calls out, "Open the gate!"

"Jade, take Sannvi into the building," I say.

Jade takes Sannvi's hand, and I run toward the gate and onto the rampart to look out into a swampy field. Marco splashes through with Cal on his back. Daniel and Phoenix are behind them, and they both stop to fight the enemies pursuing them. It doesn't take me long to spot Glare. He aims a bow from the tree line.

"Marco, watch out!" I scream, but he doesn't hear me.

The arrow flies across the distance, ripping into Cal's back. Calamity Clan rages through the gate and war cries fill the sky as they stampede through the wet field to help Phoenix and Daniel. Marco keeps running, soon making it to safety behind Calamity Clan's ranks. I trample down the steps as he comes through the gate, lowering Cal onto his stomach.

Blood pours from three separate locations on his back, and two arrows poke out of him.

"Get him into my tent," Rhena says, and two others lift Cal away.

Metal scraping against metal rings in my ears. Glare. I whip out my sword and turn toward the gate.

"Stop her!" Rhena calls out, and Marco wraps around me.

"Let me go!"

"Mia, calm down. He'll retreat. He's outnumbered."

Marco holds onto me longer.

"Fine," I say. "Let me onto the rampart."

Marco follows me up the stairs. A large group of Calamity Clan Savages chase Glare and his band back into the forest.

Marco says, "I'm going to join them."

I head down with Marco, and Daniel limps through the gate with a busted lip, swollen left eye, and a gash on the side of his face. Marco pats him on the shoulder, then sprints after the rest of Calamity Clan. Daniel joins me as I rush toward Rhena's tent.

"What happened?" I ask.

"Glare ambushed us."

"But how? We patrol every day. We've seen no signs of him or anybody for miles."

Daniel shrugs, lifting Rhena's tent flap. "We'll figure it out."

I glance at Cal, the rise and fall of his chest slow. Blood drips onto the ground as Rhena and Stella work on him. I help, handing Rhena what she needs when she asks for it. Cal's face is slick with sweat and growing paler by the second.

"What's wrong with him?" I ask.

"He hasn't lost that much blood, but those arrows were laced with poison," Rhena says.

I clutch my chest. My breath catches in my throat.

"Mia, sit."

I do, with thoughts I don't want to think about storming through my mind. My journey with Cal has only just begun. I can't lose him yet.

We crowd around an unconscious Cal in Rhena's tent. His wounds are clean, and the bleeding has stopped, but the poison still runs through his bloodstream.

Rhena dabs Cal's forehead with a cloth. "He's stable for now, but the poison has already taken a major toll on his nervous system. I don't have a remedy for it. Whatever Glare used, it's from another region."

Silence. The forlorn expressions on Seagull, Dana, and Daniel's faces match mine.

"Mia. You need to take charge." Rhena moves to one of her drawers and digs inside, coming back out with Calamity Clan's emblem. "Cal never appointed another War Hand after Glare and gave me instructions that if something ever happened to him, you should lead the clan."

"Cal will wake soon, and there's Seagull."

Seagull shakes his head. "He chose you, plus, I don't want to the responsibility."

"This poison is malicious, Mia," Rhena says. "Even if he does wake, this is too much for his body to bear."

I stare into Rhena's red eyes, knowing what she means, but I can't accept it. Not like this. He needs to beat the Almighty. We're supposed to make everybody one, and I can't do that without Cal. We're Unified, and that's a promise of souls.

I clench the hems of my shirt. "Everyone except Rhena needs to leave."

Rhena rinses the cloth in a bucket of water and wrings it out as the others exit the tent.

"What about Null?" I ask.

"I told you that poison has a ninety-nine percent death rate. If I administer it to Cal, it will kill him."

"It saved the Great. Why can't it work for Cal?"

"The Great's situation was different. It would be impossible for us to keep him alive here." Rhena sets the cloth on Cal's forehead, turns to me, and grabs my face. "I understand how you feel. But right now, you must be strong. For the clan. For Jade and Sannvi. And for the children you carry. You are our leader."

"If you understood, then you wouldn't be trying to convince me to give up on him when there's a chance he could live."

Rhena drops her hands. "I've been healing since I was a girl. Null kills all. Everything. Cal will not survive."

"How did the Great survive then?"

"I am under oath. I cannot say. But the Second and Princess Raia may be able to help."

"Then we go to Damascus."

"Cal will not make the journey in this condition, Mia. If you wish to do this, then we do it soon, but you must address the clan first."

"What am I supposed to say?"

Rhena holds Calamity Clan's emblem out in her palm. "Tell them the truth."

A few hours pass. Calamity Clan has come back from chasing Glare. Marco reported they had to stop because someone fell into a claw trap. I stand in front of the entire clan, my soul filled with dread. They wait for my announcement as a cruel tension bears onto my shoulders. I take a deep breath, grounding myself. Everything within me shakes.

"Calamity! Cal… is going to die." I let my words settle over the clan, and then hold up the emblem. "He wanted me to lead if something ever happened to him, so if you all would accept me, I will gladly take the position of chieftess of Calamity Clan. I promise to uphold all his wishes and to do right by this clan." I place a hand on my stomach so everyone can see. "I carry Cal's children. His farewell gifts to us. I hope with everything in my heart that I have the support of you all for the trials to come. I hope that now, you guys trust me."

Jade, Sannvi, Dana, Daniel, and Seagull are the first to kneel. Then Marco and Phoenix and Tabatha. Then Lero. And one by one, until all of Calamity Clan in attendance approve my rise to chieftess.

Daniel throws a fist into the air, roaring, "Mia!"

The clan clamors my name. This should be a glorious moment. But I do not smile. There's someone down there I can't trust. That's the conclusion I've come to, so that's why I've lied about Cal dying. He may, but I'll cling to that one percent chance that he'll live. If he can just bear the Null here for a few weeks, then I can get him to Damascus, or better, the RFF.

Cal went on two patrols every day, so why did Glare wait until now to attack him? Someone must have tipped him off Sannvi would be on the hunting party. Marco, Phoenix, Daniel, and Sannvi told me the same story. The only part of all their stories that doesn't sit right with me is Daniel going to fish. Why would he need to fish when they were hunting deer? And now that I think about it, Daniel often would go fishing by himself. What if he was paying visits to Glare during that time? But then why would Glare attack him, and place him back here among us and risk losing his informant? Daniel has no reason to betray us, let alone me. But I can't dismiss his absences. I need answers, and soon.

"Thank you. Please stay vigilant, and rest assured, Glare will pay for his crimes. We have sent a message to all the clans and the Second of his actions." I turn away into my bedroom and close the door.

What is Glare's end goal? He doesn't have enough manpower to attack us. His plan failed when Cal and Sannvi escaped. I slide to the floor, too exhausted. I feel as if I'm backed into a corner all alone. Cal's not here to protect me, so if Glare or anyone comes, it's up to me to defend the clan. I stand and unsheathe my katana. There's no time for me to sulk. I must train. Fight. I slice through the air in a clean downward arc with a cry, then lift my sword again, and repeat, tear droplets raining to the floor.

Down. Up. Down. Up. Down. Up. Down. Up. Down. Up. Down. Up. Down. Up.

Kirk taught me to think ahead and try to control the situation, so I'll play this game with Glare. There is no losing. If I do, my life will become meaningless because the people I'm supposed to protect will be gone.

Down. Up.

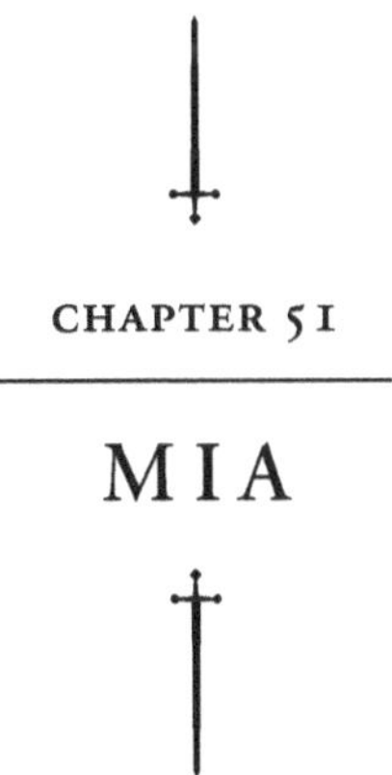

CHAPTER 51

MIA

I step into Rhena's tent, the last one to say my goodbyes to Cal. His face brightens. "There she is."

I grab his hand and place it on my stomach. "Here *we* are."

Cal's grip tightens around mine, and he tries to sit up, but I stop him. "No, no, no. Rest. It's going to be okay."

Tears surface in his eyes. "I can't leave you—"

"Don't worry. You'll be back before you know it. We're going to give you Null."

"I can fight this off myself!"

"Those arrows had a poison Rhena can't treat. Null is the only option," I whisper. "It'll put you in a state of comatose. I just need you to promise me you'll survive until we get to Damascus, or I get help from the RFF. You must trust me."

Cal takes a deep, labored breath. "I promise I won't leave you. Boy or girl?"

"Twins. Rhena says there'll be a boy and a girl. They'll be here in six or seven months."

"Six... late August."

"I say September. I'll name the boy after you."

"No! My father named me after him. Name the boy Ari."

The dichotomy of Cal's happiness and distress contorts his face. The emotions waver—tick changes. He hacks up blood, and I reach for the cloth, but he turns his head away, spitting red phlegm onto the ground.

"Next month at… the Conclave, make friends with Butterfly… Glare's older sister. She will… help you. Stay away from my father. Decline if he challenges… you."

"Why would he challenge me?"

"Glare!" Cal breaks into another fit of coughing.

"Rhena!"

Cal smiles. "Trying to get rid of me already? What… will you name the girl?"

"I don't know yet."

"Make it beautiful."

"I will," I say with a kiss.

"Take care of the clan while I'm gone."

"I will." My voice shakes.

Cal drudges up more blood, his fingers gripping around mine. He moans, with spit and blood foaming from his mouth.

Rhena bursts into the tent with Dana and Seagull. "We must administer Null now."

Cal's arms and legs flail. Dana and Seagull hold him down.

"He's in tremendous pain. Mia, get his head!" Rhena holds a small vial with an ink-colored liquid inside.

I nod and hold his head while Rhena pours the liquid into his mouth. He screams, his body tensing. My tears splash onto his chest as it deflates, and his head slumps to the side. I put two fingers on his neck, waiting for the dull thump of life to tell me he's still here with us, but it doesn't come. My heart splits. I think I might fall, but Rhena wraps her arms around me and holds me together. I bawl into her shoulder.

She whispers, "Give Cal the benefit of the doubt, child. Look."

I turn, placing a palm on Cal's chest. His heart thunders inside.

¢

A couple of hours later, deep into the night, I stand in front of Cal's coffin with a burning torch in my hand. Seagull found this somewhere in the landfill. I place Cal's headpiece inside, setting it on top of wood, dead rodents, animal bones, and disregarded food, a somber expression on my face.

"Let us mourn our chief," Rhena says, raising her hands in the air. The light from the fire illuminates half her face. "Let us not forget who caused this pain."

I drop the torch into the coffin, and the fire flashes, swallowing it, black smoke lifting into the sky. I move beside Rhena, and she chants.

"For our beloved chief, we bow our heads, close our eyes, and send him off like the warrior and kind spirit he was. Cal has perished in battle today at the hands of someone he called brother. We must not let this undeniable fact tinge our hearts with hatred, but with regret. We must honor our chief by remaining true to ourselves and to the version of Calamity Clan he built. We must protect each other, Chieftess Mia, and the children she carries, for Cal's spirit resides in them. We must live to fight another day and show Cal that everything he instilled into us will not be forgotten!"

Rhena beats her chest and screams into the night. The rest of Calamity follows her lead. I stop before everyone else. There's this emptiness inside me. Cal was always beside me, refusing to give up on me. Now, he's gone.

Seagull, Dana, and I lean on the railing of the bridge, watching some of our clan members mull around the trashcan fire.

"So, how'd it go?" Dana asks as she gnaws on a chicken leg.

Before I can say anything, Daniel slides in next to us, to my left. "How'd what go?"

Dana talks with her mouth full. "She's pregnant. What do you think?"

Daniel holds up his hands, smirking. "Sorry, sorry." He asks Dana, "Where were you? I didn't see you sending Cal off."

She says, "I was working on our barrier. Tightening the strings of energy. If an attack comes, they'll need to come from underground or have someone on the inside."

"We gonna have it up twenty-four-seven now?" Daniel asks.

"Mia thinks that's the best choice."

Daniel peers at me. "So, Chieftess. What's next?"

"What do you mean?" I ask.

"What are we going to do when we capture Glare? I think death is the best choice."

"I'm sure he will be slinking somewhere around Conclave. We will pin him there."

"Sounds like fun." I tighten my grip on the railing, and Daniel frowns down at the fire. "Mia, I'm so—"

I reach out, resting a hand over his, squeezing. "I know."

Daniel pulls his hand from under mine and hugs me like I'm made of fragile glass he doesn't want to shatter. He still smells of fish and blood.

"I'll protect you. No matter what," he says.

I push him away before I say something I might regret. I'm trying to value Kirk's lessons, so I move toward my bedroom door, speaking to everyone. "I've decided that Daniel will be Calamity Clan's new War Hand." I toss Daniel Calamity Clan's emblem. He fumbles to catch it, and I say, "Do right by us."

Daniel kneels, head down. "I give you and the clan my last breath!"

Dana gives me a "what the hell?" look.

"Good." I open the door, leaving them in the odd news when I close it.

Daniel will be by my side where I can watch him. I believe he's the traitor. He's the one that goes out alone the most. He's the one that went off by himself before Glare ambushed them. I sit on the bed. Alone. If Cal were here, he would wrap himself around me. I feel a faint thump in my gut.

"That's right," I say. "I'm not alone in this anymore."

I can do this. Kirk taught me many lessons about how to beat enemies in mental warfare. He made me read several old-world books. *The Art of War* by Sun Tzu is one of my favorites. All warfare is based on deception. I remember many things from that book. Glare has chosen war with me. He thinks I'm weak. He's probably picturing me lying in bed, sobbing. I will plan for his death instead.

There's a knock at my door, and I open it, sword in hand. A tray of food sits on the floor, a whole fish over a pile of rice. A fisheye stares up at me, and sickness curdles in my stomach. I kick the tray away and watch it flip over the railing, then slam the door shut. News of Cal's death will spread among the clans. I must prepare myself for scrutiny. Not everyone will trust me, and I shouldn't trust everyone. There could be other traitors within Calamity Clan. It could be anyone. Glare had a vast influence over the clan. I remember Lero hanging with him often. And Tabatha too. I sheathe my blade, but another knock comes at the door, and I unsheathe it. Glare could come at any moment. He could send assassins, and I must stay ready.

"Come in," I say.

Jade and Sannvi do, both their lips curled upwards. They grimace when they see me clenching the hilt of my katana. Jade reaches for my hand, easing the blade out of it.

She sheathes it for me. "You don't need this."

She wraps her arms around me. Sannvi joins her, adding, "Not when we're around."

CHAPTER 52

GLARE

Fog clings to the ground as they ascend the hillside, snaking between skinny trees, careful not to trip over the clay rocks that jut from the earth. Glare wipes sweat from his brow and looks back at his group. Most of them have their heads down in concentration.

"We're almost at the top!" Glare shouts.

No one acknowledges him but Rollo, with a scowl. Glare lets Bigfoot and Piper pass him and gets in Rollo's path. "Are you tired? Do you want to take a break?"

"No." Rollo tries to push past him, but Glare sticks his foot out and trips him.

Rollo falls, clawing for loose pebbles and dirt. "Enough of this!" He shoots to his feet and takes out his sword.

Everyone stops to watch the confrontation.

"So, you are tired." Glare smirks. "That's all you had to say."

"I am tired. Tired of following you!" Rollo looks around at the other Savages. "He almost got us killed. Because of him, we're exiled from Calamity Clan. We been walkin' for three days, and he still ain't told us where we goin'! He said we would have a feast, but we got no food and no water. If we keep following him, he's gonna burn us all down with him!"

"You're doubting me again."

"I'm not afraid of you." Rollo turns his back on Glare with his arms out. "If you follow me, we can go to the Savage King and beg for forgiveness. If we stay with Glare, he'll have us all dead."

"Now you suggest begging! You really are weak. There is no place for you where we're going."

Rollo turns, sword hungry for Glare, who evades, and cleaves into Rollo's left shoulder with his tomahawk. Rollo drops his sword and Glare chops into his other shoulder, then boots him in the chest, sending him tumbling down into a small clay boulder. Glare kicks Rollo's head into the rock and kneels over him, raising his tomahawk. "I'll tell Seagull how pathetic his son was in death. The Almighty doesn't need Savages like you, and I won't bring anybody unworthy with me to greet him!"

Glare plants his tomahawk in the middle of Rollo's skull. It splits, painting Glare red.

†

Rain dribbles down Glare's dirt-crusted cheeks as he stands outside of a walled area, the gates reading:

TECHNOLOGIC INC

HOME OF LINK TECHNOLOGY AND THE LINK SPACE

The only building he can see over the wall is a tall, white one with tinted windows. He presses the red button on the intercom system.

It rings a few times, and then a female's voice filters through. *Bold of you to show up on my doorstep, Glare.*

Glare stiffens when he feels the cool lick of metal against his throat. All around him and his group, Lost Clan Savages deCloak themselves. They're wrapped in bandages, their weapons ready to savor blood. Some of them have a single extremity missing, and there, they've replaced it with a blade. Other Lost Clan Savages' lost body parts are harder to find, but their mangled faces show evidence of Lost Soul's handiwork.

"We mean you no harm, Lost Soul. We've travelled for weeks to make it here. It would be a mistake to kill us," Glare says.

Lost Soul chuckles through the intercom. *"First you murder Cal, now you give me subtle threats. You wish for a brutal death, don't you?"*

"It's not what you think."

"Whatever stories you want to tell, you can save them for the Second. He's asked that you be brought in alive."

"No! I must speak with the Almighty. Tell me where he is."

"The Almighty will not save you. You killed his son."

Glare's fists ball. "With good reason. Our people are in danger. If you hand me over to the Second, we'll suffer. You must believe me!"

There is a long silence, then Lost Soul asks, *"What's in it for me?"*

"Piper, show her what's in the bag."

The Lost Clan Savage holding Piper backs away, and she reaches into a cloth sack, pulling out Rollo's head. The crevice in the middle of his skull is black with dried blood and infested with maggots.

"Hmm, Seagull's son. How long ago did you kill him?" Lost Soul asks.

"Two weeks ago. He didn't believe in the Almighty. He was weak," Glare says.

"I like that expression on his face. Bring Glare to me. Lock the others up until further notice."

Tendrils of green smoke drift back into Glare's face, coming from Lost Soul, a spindly, pale and bald woman with tattoos plastered over her face. She wears a holey and frayed white gown.

"Sorry about the electro cuffs," she says, glancing back at Glare. "I don't want to end up like Cal."

Glare follows Lost Soul down a wide hallway with granite floors. There are large, tinted windows on each side. He glowers at her. "It's not like I could, anyway. You probably have a few of your clan members right behind me."

Lost Soul turns, her blue irises glowing. "If you have something to say, say it."

"Modded eyes." Glare frowns with contempt. "Cloaks. I bet you have a link attached to your brain too?"

"I do. What of it?"

"Believe me when I say this, out of the current clan leaders, I respect you the most. But you use our enemies' technology. It makes you seem we—" Lost Soul places a knife to his throat. But Glare doesn't stop, and says, "We are Savage."

Lost Soul burst into laughter. "You are naïve. My use of technology only levels the playing field. The Republic for Freedom or Runesians could come by any Savage camp except for mine and Damascus City and wipe them off the map. Do you understand?"

"You should want to die better than those who taint their bodies with tech. They're the ones who ruined our world."

"One day, you will see technology as a tool that can help you progress. If you refuse to adapt, you'll die. My plan is for us to use it the right way, unlike those before us."

"Let's agree to disagree."

They continue in silence. The windows brighten and Glare can see what's on the other side. Down below, in a large, white room, are several Lost Clan Savages dressed in metal armor as they survey naked prisoners strapped to conveyor belts. Some prisoners cry, others beg, and more struggle in their restraints. The belt stops and a robotic arm comes down with a giant needle, stabbing into a man's stomach. He screams out, the arm rises, and the belt continues until the next person is under it.

Lost Soul stops and taps a window, revealing what's on the other side. A room full of hundreds of Lost Ones. Some scratch themselves, while others rock back and forth and dig up their noses. Glare watches a woman squat over a child and urinate, and the child giggles.

"You should count yourself blessed," Lost Soul says. "Few outside of Lost Clan get to see how we produce Lost Ones."

"Are they ready as is?"

"No. They must be disciplined. They must understand what happens when they do not obey their masters."

A door opens into the room and the Lost Ones screech and hoot, their ability to formulate coherent speech gone. A squad of seven Lost Clan Savages file inside, stomping one foot and dragging the other as they tap their swords against shields in perfect unison.

"Lost Ones are sensitive to noise," Lost Soul continues. "Their hearing and sense of smell have been heightened, so this intrigues them. I don't know what goes on in their brains, but sometimes their human pride lingers, and they want to retaliate against their oppressors."

Lost Soul motions toward the several Lost Ones who rise, screeching, beating themselves and each other. Then they charge the Savages. The first Lost Clan Savage in line pushes forward with his spiked shield, impaling a Lost One that leaps at him.

The lead Lost Clan Savage slings it to the floor. "Sit!"

More Lost Ones surround the seven Savages, clawing the floor and pulling their hair as drool pours out of their mouths.

"Sit!" the lead Savage commands again, but they do not listen.

The Lost Ones attack, and Lost Soul turns away. "Come."

Glare follows her, unable to tear himself away from the scene below. The lead Savage ducks under the wild swing from a Lost One, and the second in line lops off the Lost One's head, holding it up for the others to see.

"Sit!" she yells.

Glare catches up to Lost Soul. "How long does it take to train them?"

"Sometimes a few days. Sometimes a few hours. It's why I take so many prisoners. We have to kill so many because they don't want to listen. Death is a hard concept for them to learn, and the human trait of grieving doesn't exist for them anymore, but they get it. Eventually." Lost Soul turns, grabs Glare's chin. "You know, if you don't want to be executed, you could become my pet. I would take the best care of you. I wouldn't treat you like the others."

Glare jerks out of her grasp. "Pass. I am no one's pet."

Lost Soul leads them onto an elevator at the end of the hall. "You say that, yet you would lap water at the Almighty's feet."

"Any reasonable person would."

"What do you want with him?"

Glare grins Lost Soul's way. "I want him to lead the Savages. He is the only way we can move forward."

The doors open and Lost Soul steps out onto the roof, closing her eyes as the red sun beams onto her face. "Now, you've caught my attention. Go on."

"My sister. Mia. Raia. Ronan. People like them will ruin us. The Second is growing old and will die soon. Who will lead us after that? Raia? I've always thought she was pathetic. Even with her Gift, I don't think she'll steer us in the right direction. It should be the Almighty."

"And what if he wants to kill you?"

Glare steps up beside Lost Soul. "The Almighty will respect my strength. I killed Cal because Mia was poisoning his mind, turning Calamity Clan into something the Almighty would despise."

"Mia? Cal's partner, right?"

"Yes!" Glare's blue eyes burn cold with hate. "She's a liar. And an RFF spy. We must get rid of her the first chance we get."

Lost Soul watches Glare for a long moment, then his electro cuffs unlock and drop to the ground. "I will tell you where the Almighty is on the condition that you take me with you so I can confirm for myself your intentions."

Glare holds out his hand, palm up. "My heart is Savage."

"Mine as well," she says, slitting her palm, then Glare's, with a blade.

The two let their blood mix between them, the crimson sky matching their conviction.

LEON

November 11, 2129

A small, sun-kissed boy with dark curls peeks out his bedroom door, holding his favorite toy truck. Kirk, Lucia, and his father are at the front door.

A rotund man in a white lab coat stands in the entryway with a solemn expression. He polishes his tinted glasses with a handkerchief, then clears his throat. "Hello, Jacksons. I'm Roderic Ambleston, the pathologist assigned to Leonor's case. I'm sorry to inform you all that it was a suicide. It seems she got ahold of some Quantax and overdos—"

The boy pushes out of his bedroom, dropping his truck. "Dad, where's mommy? You said she was coming back."

His father covers his expression with one hand and points with the other. "Please, Leon. Go back to bed."

"What's Quantax?"

"Leon! Bed. Now!"

"I want mommy!" Leon stomps a foot. "You said—"

Lucia turns, wraps the boy up in her arms, and ushers him into his room. She closes the door behind them, and flicks on the light, kneeling in front of him. Tears stain her cheeks, and for some reason when she grasps Leon's face, he cries, too. She pulls him into a hug. "Oh, baby. Don't you worry about a thing."

"Grandma, is my mommy gone?"

Lucia shakes her head, wiping his tears away with her thumbs. "No, silly."

"Then where is she? She's supposed to read me a bedtime story. She always reads me a bedtime story."

"How about I do it?" Lucia pulls Leon toward the bed.

But the boy yanks out of her grasp, crossing his arms. "I want her to do it! She always does it! She's been gone for two days! Where is she, grandma?"

Lucia's smile wavers, and for a moment her body hollows out, and her knees weaken. She looks at her grandson, then smiles. "You're a smart boy, right Leon?"

The boy nods. "Yeah."

Lucia sits on Leon's bed and plucks a book from his shelf. On the cover, in the luminesce of a full moon, a feminine shadow figure stands. "Come sit. Let's read *Farewell To The Moon Lady*."

"But that's a sad story," Leon says as he sits beside his grandma.

"If you're a smart boy, by the time we get to the end, you'll understand what happened to your mother." Lucia grabs Leon's palm and places it over his heart. "And why she's right there. Always."

When Lucia exits Leon's bedroom, Kirk waits for her at the table. He motions toward a steaming mug. "Made you a cup of tea. How is he?"

"Cried himself to sleep, but I think he'll be fine as long as we show him that we'll be there for him." Lucia sits, pulling the mug toward her. "How's Danston?"

Kirk shakes his head. "He stormed out after the pathologist left. I tried to stop him, but he wouldn't listen. I'm worried."

Lucia places her palm over Kirk's balled fist. "All we can do is be there for the both of them. No one ever expects to lose their loved one to suicide."

"I just don't get it. She was so happy. Such a good mother to Leon. A great wife to our son."

"Everyone's fighting a war against themselves. Leonor must have been fighting for a long time. Unfortunately, she was already losing, and we never noticed."

¢

Leon enters the apartment with Lucia, hopping up and down with bags in his hand. "We're going to bake a cake! We're going to bake a cake!"

"Danston," Lucia calls while she sets the items on the counter. "Leon wants to bake a cake with you, remember? Come on out."

No answer.

"I'll get him." Leon skips toward his father's bedroom and knocks on the door. "Wake up, daddy. It's been four days since mommy's funeral. Let's be happy again and bake a cake! Come on!"

Leon glances back at Lucia, who comes to knock herself.

"Danston?" Still no answer, so Lucia opens the door. She gasps and pulls Leon back, covering his eyes.

Danston sits against the bed, still in the same baggy suit he wore to Leonor's funeral. Pills litter the floor, and a bottle of booze pools at his side. He lifts the gun in his right hand and presses the barrel against his temple as he looks at Leon and Lucia. "Hey, mom. You'll take good care of him, right?"

"He needs you, Dan."

"Kirk's a way better teacher than me. I can't do anything for him now. Not without Leo."

"Dan, please!"

Danston's glossy eyes shine with euphoria. "I feel good about this, mom. I'm not scared. Leo was the only good thing I had. Without her, nothing matters. I'd ruin Leon. I know that. So it's better for him if I just wasn't around." His finger tightens around the trigger. "I'm sorry, Leon."

Lucia pulls Leon out of the room and slams the door shut. They both flinch at the sound of the gun going off.

CHAPTER 53

LEON

March 10, 2146

Hot tears blister down his cheeks and freeze almost just as fast as they fall. Leon glances to his left at the silver-and-white heap of fur as he digs through hard snow. He flips the shovel over and stabs the ground again, hitting solid ice.

"Shit!" he pushes the shovel down, kneels, and grabs a stiff wolf. He drags it over to the hole that's quickly being covered and lies the animal inside. "Renji. Thanks for staying with me for so long. You were such a good girl, and I'll miss you and the rest of the pack. Please continue to watch over me."

Leon pulls his shovel free from the ice and fills the hole. When he finishes, he peers up at the full moon hanging in a purple sky. It reveals the other twelve mounds of snow in the clearing where Leon stands. He looks around, shakes his head, and clenches his teeth, then drags the shovel behind him up a slope.

Leon's almost to the mouth of a cave when he feels his nose bleeding. Then a wave of dizziness drowns him, and he trips over a rock. He shields his head as he crashes to the ground. Dimming stars and milky, thin clouds swirl above him as his spine tingles.

Danston towers over Leon, that wretched grin splitting across his face. "Everything keeps dying around you. I wonder why that is?"

The shadow manifests beside Danston and loops its arm through his. "Everyone leaves because you're not worth staying for. Even wild animals don't want to be stuck with you."

"Shut up!" Leon yells, the wind taking his voice away. Then a ripple of pain courses through him, and he moans out. The vertigo becomes numbness, and the howling wind becomes white noise. The purple sky cartwheels above Leon, and then it plummets toward him.

Fire warms his face, and Leon cracks open his eyes. A woman with rosy cheeks and platinum blond hair sits in front of him. She cradles a wooden bowl of stew in her lap, and with a free hand, she brings a spoonful out to Leon's face.

"Jenna." Leon's lips tremble. "No."

Jenna sighs. "I ate earlier. Come on."

"How much do we have left?"

"Enough. Eat." Jenna shoves the spoon closer, and he turns away, scooting up.

"You should head out by yourself before we get trapped in this cave. The snow and the temperature are getting worse."

Jenna sets the bowl down. "You've been telling me that for the past three months since we found each other. I'm not leaving you. If I go, you go."

"I won't make it. I'll die. You know I'm infected, and these episodes have become more frequent."

Jenna grabs Leon's hand and pulls him to his feet. She strips off her layers, and Leon puts his hands up to stop her, but she swats them down, and rolls up her sleeves. On each of her arms are scars, both horizontal and vertical. Too many to count.

"I'm sick of your pity party. Just shut up and listen," Jenna says. "Before Siggy adopted me when I was eleven, I was on the streets for five years. When I turned nine, I tried Quantax for the first time and got hooked. It was better than freezing in the slums with the rest of the homeless. A way to escape. But I didn't know about the repercussions. Hallucinations.

Suicidal ideation. Depression. Each of these cuts represents the number of times I tried to bleed myself to hell. Each of these cuts reminds me how many times I tried to give up. So I know what that feels like. I know what that looks like. But do you know what helps?"

Leon shakes his head and Jenna grabs his hands. A soft smile spreads across her face. "Love," she says. "Having people care about you. Siggy and Jace saved my life. If Siggy had never adopted me, I would be dead. If Jace had never accepted me as his little sister and came running after me every time I felt the urge to go find a dealer, I would be in some slum overdosed on the Q right now." Jenna pounds Leon in his chest. "You have people that care about you, man. Jace. Liz. Me. Your sister. So why are you trying to give up?"

"The people who were supposed to love me the most abandoned me. And everyone else in my life ends up leaving or dying. I couldn't help Jace or Liz. I couldn't do anything for Kirk. I couldn't save Mia. I got Julio killed. The kids I tried to save died. I'm worthless. So it's—"

Jenna slaps Leon in the face and pulls him close by the scruff of his jacket. "Stop it! You're worth more than you think. You're Liz's best friend. Jace's boyfriend. Mia's older brother. And the only Gifted Republic for Freedom soldier. You have saved so many lives, Leon. You're a good person, and a great leader. I need you to understand that." Jenna shakes Leon. "Look at me!" He does. "We can't stay here forever. Before I die, I want to give Siggy the world. I want to laugh with my brother again. I know you may hate yourself. But if you won't do it for you, at least do it for everyone that loves you. Please, Leon. Promise me, you'll try."

Leon stays silent for a long moment. He peers toward the cave entrance, and there, Danston and the shadow stand. A flurry of snow tornadoes around the two, carrying the apparitions away. Leon grips Jenna's shoulders and pulls her into a hug. "Thank you."

CHAPTER 54

M I A

March 23, 2146

To maintain appearances, I wrap rope around the wooden waist of my sculpture and bind the miniature version of Cal together. I take my stone dagger and slash a line into the right side of the figure's face. It looks nothing like Cal, but the scar makes it complete. I place it next to my sculpture of Basco, which is an even worse attempt. He would laugh at me if he were here. I was never an artistic person, but as I look around, I see that many of my clan members are naturals at sculpting. Wooden sculptures, full of expression, stand all around the junkyard—some life-size, others only a few inches tall like mine. Many are of the same people: Damascus the Great, Cal, and Basco.

"Took you long enough," Dana says, coming from behind me with two sculptures, one of her mother, and the other, her father. "The Weeping is in another hour."

I glance up at the pink sky as the orange sun sinks into the horizon. I pick up my figures. "Guess I should start the pile."

Dana follows me to the middle of the junkyard, and we both place our sculptures on the ground. Soon, others from Calamity Clan join us, and a mound of wooden sculptures form. Calamity Clan cries as they approach, gently placing their loved ones down and whispering prayers. Every year, a couple of weeks before the Conclave, each clan performs its own Weeping. A celebration of their deceased loved ones where they send gifts, prayers, promises, and ask for guidance.

Many in Calamity Clan have their faces painted black or wear masks. As the clan gathers behind me, the chorus of grief becomes louder. Phoenix plays his guitar. A soft melody emits from it that creates a claw of anguish in my heart. My life has been nothing but death. If I were to make sculptures for each person I loved, my fingers would cramp after days of labor. Rhena places a three-foot wooden statue of a smiling Basco next to the pile, then gets on her knees and clasps her hands together. A pang of guilt strikes me, and I look away.

"Hurts doesn't it, Blood Queen?" someone asks behind me.

I turn to see a tiny, dark woman wearing a silver bird's headpiece made from steel. It covers most of her face, but I can see the fury in the clench of her teeth and the tremble of her hands.

"Excuse me?" I ask.

If the woman's dark gaze could burn, I'd be nothing but ashes. "Me and my siblings are out on expeditions often, so you wouldn't know me, but after tonight, it doesn't really matter."

I step back and go for my sword, but the woman's faster, and draws a needle-thin blade. She lunges forth, and I sidestep her first strike, but then she pokes at me with a barrage of attacks I can't see. I backpedal, and she advances, slashing at me, missing, so I thrust my katana forward, and she leaps back, resets and jumps at me again.

"You don't deserve to be chieftess!" She nicks my shirt. "You're not one of us. You're a murderer. You murdered Basco!" She draws blood from my shoulder. "And Cal's death is on your hands. Everyone around you dies. You're a plague. Worse than the Sickness!" Her blade slices my cheek. "I don't care what happens, but I can't allow you to be here any longer!"

The bird woman jets forth. I slash at her, and she sends a roundhouse kick to my shin. My knee buckles, and then she slams a fist into my jaw. The world rattles and blood fills my mouth as I fall back.

"Please don't," I say, covering my stomach.

The bird woman points her blade at me. "You beg, Blood Queen? That's so unbefitting of a leader."

She thrusts forward and I close my eyes. The clang of metal rings in my ears. Marco shields me, his blade stopping the bird woman's. Daniel holds his sword to the woman's neck, and Jade has a dagger to the assailant's back.

"What's the call, Mia?" Daniel asks. "You want me to kill her?"

"Birdy!" Two others barge through the crowd. A woman around my stature with mocha skin and locs that are dyed red and blue, and a bearded, beefy dark-skinned man. They both wear bird headpieces like Birdy's and kneel.

The man speaks. "Forgive Birdy, Chieftess. I am Alba, her brother, and you may have my head in exchange for her life."

"I am Swallow," the woman says. "My sister is foolish and emotional. I will take lashings for her sake if I must. I beg you not—"

"Shut up!" Birdy screams. "Basco was our teacher. If you two won't do anything, I will. This is my decision."

Rhena comes and helps me up. "That's the Winged Trio. They're triplets. Cal had them out, and they return every so often for a break. The information they have is probably outdated."

"Leave her," I say.

Marco looks back at me. "Are you sure? She tried to kill you."

I nod, and he backs away with Jade and Daniel, and they gather around me. "Rise, Alba, Swallow. Explain to me what you've heard."

The two rise, stepping near their sister. Alba grips Birdy's shoulder, and the woman winces. "We met Glare while we were out several weeks ago. We had received messages of Basco's passing, but not Cal's. We knew of Glare's exile, but when he saw us, he wasn't violent, and invited us to have dinner with him. There, he shared with us the news of Cal's death, and how you were the cause. He said you were changing the clan and Cal. He said you were making him weak, and that it was up to him as Cal's best friend to save him. When he let us go, he left us with a choice: stay with him and meet the Almighty or come back here and make things right. We wanted to confirm for ourselves everything he said, and we agreed to not act rashly, but Birdy had other plans."

Of course. Glare. He's crafty, I'll give him that. "And where does this name Blood Queen come from?"

Swallow glances around at the clan. "It's what they call you. Through all seven clans. Has no one told you?"

I smile through the pain. "Thank you. Basco was my mentor as well. It is true that a lie I told is the reason for his death, but Glare is the one who killed him when he had no right. Glare was jealous of Cal, and that's why he killed him, too. If you three want to do something in redemption for their deaths, I suggest you pledge your allegiance to me because I carry Cal's children and wish to make Glare pay for his crimes before he can ruin their future and this clan any further."

"Is this true, Rhena?" Birdy asks. "I will only submit to her if you tell me it's alright."

Rhena rests a palm on my back. "Mia speaks the truth. She is Savage, and only wants what's best for the clan."

Birdy kneels. "If you would forgive me, Chieftess? My heart is yours. You may use me as you see fit."

Swallow and Alba follow, the latter saying, "Our hearts are yours. We will serve you as we did Cal until our dying breaths."

¢

I enter the building alone, going for the bathroom. Everyone should be at the Weeping. The fire has started, and the figures are burning. I lock myself in a stall and cry. The Blood Queen? That is an unsavory name. Savages only get names when their reputation proceeds them or if they've accomplished some great feat on the battlefield. The Great. The Almighty. The Scarlet Witch. The Wise One. Those are all names that reflect positives among the Savage peoples, but my name is derived from negativity. The bathroom door slides open and someone steps inside. I shut off the tears and hold my breath.

"Mia? I saw you come in here."

I fix my face and stand. "Just a moment." I flush the toilet and step out of the stall. "Oh, Tabatha. How are you? I haven't seen you all day."

Tabatha's skin is deathly white, her fingernails yellow, and pupils wide and bloodshot. She's been using. Tears roll over the dark bags under eyes and drip to the floor. She places her figure on the sink. "I came for your blessing."

I wash my hands under the flow of water as I take in Tabatha's handiwork. The figure is that of a little girl holding a balloon as she smiles.

"Why do you need my blessing? Are you Unifying with someone?"

"No." Tabatha sniffles, looking at her figure. "I can't go another year like this. A long time ago, I did the unthinkable. I haven't told anyone. When I joined the Savages, I did it to escape, but she always comes back. Always tells me how much of a horrible mother I was. I can't run anymore. I need to atone, and you're the only person who can help me."

"What happened to her?"

"She was infected, and I gave her too much medicine. On purpose. Then she died. I thought I was helping her, but what if she could have survived? What if she became Gifted like Princess Raia? What if the Sickness went away?" Tabatha clings to me. She's paper thin, nothing but skin and bones. "I want you to kill me. After I burn her."

"Tabatha, I—"

"You're chieftess. Please. I can already tell you'll be a great mother, and would never do something so selfish, so it's either you or I overdose."

"Fine." I can't kill Tabatha, but if I don't, she'll kill herself, so I'll give her something to hope for until I figure out something else. "But let's watch her burn together, and then you promise me, we'll wait until after the Conclave."

Tabatha sobs into my shoulder. "Thank you. Thank you. Thank you so much."

I take flame to Tabatha's daughter in the sink, and together we watch her whittle away.

Daniel stands out in the middle of the junkyard, watching the smoke rise from the ashes of everyone's sculptures.

"Dana said you asked for me," I say.

"Yeah." He turns to me. "Are you alright? That was crazy earlier."

"I'm okay. From now on, if anyone new enters the gate, I want to be notified." Daniel nods, and I sigh. "But I don't blame Birdy. There are many like her who hate me, I'm sure. I've been at the center of every tragedy within this clan."

"You should have been harder on her. What if more—"

"Daniel, don't." Silence boils between us, so I break it, asking, "Who did you burn?"

"My father."

"How'd he die?"

"He became infected while we were traveling between Compounds. Died right before we got to Marigold."

"Oh. I'm sor—"

"Don't be. He was a relic. I'm surprised he made as long as he did. He was seventy-four." Daniel grins sheepishly. "You know, you're the first person since him I've given a shit about, so I'll do whatever I need to do to make sure you're safe."

"I don't need your protection."

"Yes, you do. Glare's a monster. He's had it out for you since the beginning."

"And you helped him get rid of Cal, so what does that make you?" I grab the hilt of my sword. "You're not innocent, Daniel. You murdered two innocent women. You betrayed the clan. The only reason you are still around is so I can use you. When we get to the Conclave, you'll help me kill Glare."

"You knew!"

"Of course, I'm not stupid."

Daniel laughs. "So, you're not keeping me around because you love me?"

Classic Daniel. Making a joke out of everything. I walk away from him. "In your dreams. I'm going to bed."

"Mia!" I stop and Daniel continues. "That night you left the clan was one of the worst nights of my life. I felt… empty because I was scared I was never going to see you again. All I wanted to tell you was how much I loved you. How bad I wanted to come with you, but I couldn't. And I know I'm wrong for this, but I still love you, and I don't know when it happened, but it did, and I can't stop it. I helped Glare because he threatened you and the kids, and I didn't want to see you hurt. I'd do anything for you because you're a good person and deserve to have a good life. I'm sorry. I really am. I just want you to know that."

I don't turn around. I'm a good person? Hardly. I've done terrible things. I've gotten people killed and used others for my benefit. Despite Daniel's misplaced reverence, the way his eyes cling to me as I continue my journey away from him sends shivers down my spine. I don't know what I feel, but I know this needs to end, so I hurry into the building, cutting Daniel's gaze off, the sensation disappearing with it.

CHAPTER 55

GLARE

April 1, 2146

Distant explosions rock the ground Glare kneels on. He's thankful for the almost constant shudders from the warring in No Man's Land because they hide his trembling.

"How long are you two going to stay down there?" the Almighty asks. His voice seeps into Glare's bloodstream and spikes adrenaline through him. "Face me."

Perspiration drips from Glare's nose into the dirt, and he rises with Lost Soul, their heads held high, backs straight.

Calamity the Almighty sits in the obscurity of his tent on a throne made from the bones of his countless victims. The wolf headpiece he wears hides his face, but his long muscular arms and legs branch out, layered with thousands of kill dots.

"Lost Soul, why did you not bring more Lost Ones with you? I am running out."

"The new batch is still being trained. Apologies, War General."

"After the Conclave, I want the most ferocious ones. Get out."

"Yes, War General."

Lost Soul exits through the tent flap and out into the rain, leaving

Glare behind to take on the Almighty's presence alone. It crushes him. He swallows the lump in his throat.

"I never imagined that Scar's son would kill mine," the Almighty says. "You two were close. What happened?"

"Mia happened. As I'm sure you heard, Cal and Butterfly led a successful attack on Compound Marigold. He brought Mia back with him, and that's when everything changed. He chose her over the clan's well-being. I told him she was a spy, and he banished me for trying to kill her. I decided Cal had strayed too far from the Savage path, and I knew you would be ashamed, so I killed him hoping to take the title of chief, but Calamity Clan sided with Mia."

The Almighty stays silent for a long while. "How did you kill him?"

"We were in a deathmatch, but he ran away, so I shot him with—"

The Almighty holds up his hand, silencing Glare. "Enough. Cal was always weak. First his mother, now whoever this Mia is. Next week will she attend the Conclave?"

"Yes. We should get rid of her as soon as possible before her influence poisons more of our people."

"Come closer," the Almighty says, rising, towering over Glare.

He does, closing his eyes the moment the Almighty's palm rests on top of his head. "Ever since you were a boy, I've admired that look in your eyes." The Almighty's grip tightens. Glare thinks his skull might crack under the pressure. "Your father did you a great disservice by choosing Butterfly over you. I often wished you were my son instead of Cal. He was pathetic. No matter how hard I tried to mold him into what he was supposed to be, he rebelled. But thanks to you, he's been taken care of. He can no longer embarrass my legacy or our people."

"Thank you, War General. There is one more thing," Glare says, and the Almighty waits. "I believe you should be the one to lead the Savages. After the Second. Raia is too soft. It should be you."

The Almighty takes out his dagger. "I like that idea. Will you accept my will, boy?"

Glare crashes to his knees, head tilted back. "I am yours, War General."

The Almighty cuts across his palm and makes a fist. "Lost Soul, come bear witness!" She comes back inside, gasping as blood drips from the Almighty into Glare's open mouth. "Glare is mine! He is the son of Scar no longer!"

Glare relishes the flavor of the Almighty's blood. Every drop gets sweeter and sweeter.

CHAPTER 56

LIZ

April 4, 2146

Liz's white breath plumes out in front of her as she lifts one leg in front of the other, the thick snow impeding her movement. The sun bears down, bringing an abnormal heat, and a bead of sweat trickles from under her balaclava. She glances back, grinning. "Come on, slowpoke! We'll be there soon."

Jace keeps his head down. "I was fine in my hole!"

Liz waits for him. She pushes through the snow with him once he catches up. "I saved your ass from hypothermia and made sure your amputation didn't get infected, so please, grow a pair. If we stayed in your hole, we'd freeze to death." Liz pulls out a temperature reader. "See, it's already fifty degrees warmer."

"And that doesn't concern you? This is the Land of Ice."

Liz slaps Jace on the back. "You worry too much. Finding you was like finding a needle in a haystack. Can you just accept our luck and try to survive with me?"

Jace blows out a misty breath, and the two continue their arduous trek across the white wasteland. The blue suddenly drains from the sky, and is replaced by a dark, angry gray. Liz and Jace crane their heads back, stopping to inspect the knotted black clouds ganging up over their location.

"That doesn't look good," Jace says.

Liz checks her temperature reader. "Temperature's dropping." A baseball-sized piece of hail drops from the heavens and smashes into her shoulder. She covers her head. "Run!"

Jace takes off behind her as ice pelts them from above. The ground shakes, and dense snow swarms them.

"Grab my hand!" Liz screams, pulling Jace behind her.

They run onto an ice field, slipping and sliding across. The cry of ice shattering beneath them sends panic spiraling through Liz's heart. She looks back. Balls of ice blast holes into the snow. A screech sounds ahead, and Liz's eyes grow wide as a blizzard tumbles across the tundra toward them.

"We can't stay here!" Liz pulls Jace along.

The ground whines with separating ice, and then it bursts open behind the two. Jace slips, and Liz tries to help him up, but the ground rises and Jace goes flying into the blizzard ahead. Liz chases after him as the ice splits under her feet. Her boot plunges into water that sucks the warmth from her soul. She pulls it out and keeps running, but the ice splinters around her, giving way to water, and she falls under. The cold shocks her, so for a few seconds she doesn't realize she's drowning. By the time she does, her muscles are too tight for her to move. She opens her mouth to scream but only bubbles escape, and she sinks into darkness.

CHAPTER 57

JACE

He pounds at a wall of snow, scraping his knuckles bloody. "Shit!" He glances behind him at Liz, who still lies unconscious and pale next to a fire. He scoots closer to her and focuses on the ragged breath slipping from her chapped lips. Blood oozes from his left nostril. "LIZ, WAKE UP."

Liz groans and coughs. Jace compresses her chest until she throws up water. She sits up, gasping, emerald green eyes wide with fear. She looks around, then hugs Jace. "I'm not dead."

Jace wraps around her. "Not dead, not yet anyway."

The two break apart, and Liz looks around with a frown. "Where are we?"

"Underground. An old polar bear den. The good news is, we're in a forest. The bad news is, we're iced in. Unless the temperature rises again, we'll run out of air."

"Why don't we start a fire?"

Jace shakes his head. "I don't know how much snow and ice is over us. Plus, we'd probably die from smoke asphyxiation before we made it out."

"Well, shit."

"I wish my Gift was shooting fire from my hands instead of giving commands."

Liz laughs. "That would be badass. I wonder what my Gift would be if I had one?"

"Hmm. Probably something ginger-related."

Liz shoves Jace. "What's that supposed to mean?"

"Hey, you'd be like Jean Gray or something. That's a compliment."

"Jean Gray?"

Jace facepalms himself. "How have you spent so much time with Leon and not read any of the *X-Men* comics from the old-world?"

"Sorry, I'm not a nerd."

Jace laughs. "Screw you." He faces Liz, seriousness taking over his expression. "Do you think we'll ever see them again?"

"I mean, we are trapped under layers of snow and ice. But I'll be optimistic and say yes, we will."

"I hope Leon and Jenna are still alive."

"I'm sure they are." Liz stares into Jace's eyes, watching their misty breath mix in the middle. "You know I love him, right? I always have."

Jace smiles. "That's obvious. Leon's probably the only one who doesn't see it that way."

Liz's cheeks burn red. "I'm a tomboy, so it's understandable he'd see me like he does."

"You're cute. Listen, Leon loves you too. I'm sure if I never entered the picture, you two would be together. I was actually worried you hated me for a while."

"I could never hate you. You're amazing."

Jace reaches over and grabs Liz's hand. "I want you to promise me something. If we make it out of this alive, you'll tell Leon how you feel. And whatever happens, happens."

"I can't—"

"You will, Liz. You deserve to. Please."

"What if I ruin your relationship with him?"

"Then it wasn't meant to be. But personally, I'm hoping for something else entirely."

Liz's face turns red. "What is that?"

Jace grins, let's go of her hand, and winks at her. "Don't worry about it. We should get some sleep."

He flips over, and Liz burns so hot inside her cold-weather garments she sweats.

¢

Jace and Liz wake to water dripping onto them. They unfurl from around each other, and look up, confused.

"It's melting," Liz says.

It rains onto them and then muffled voices seep through from above. Liz and Jace share a glance and start clawing through the snow and ice. Soon a shovel stabs through between them.

"We're here!" Jace yells.

The shovel moves around, and sunlight pours into their icy grave. At first, Jace shields his eyes, and then the faces come into focus. Leon, Jenna, Zero, Barnes, and General Wilde stand around the hole, all smiling.

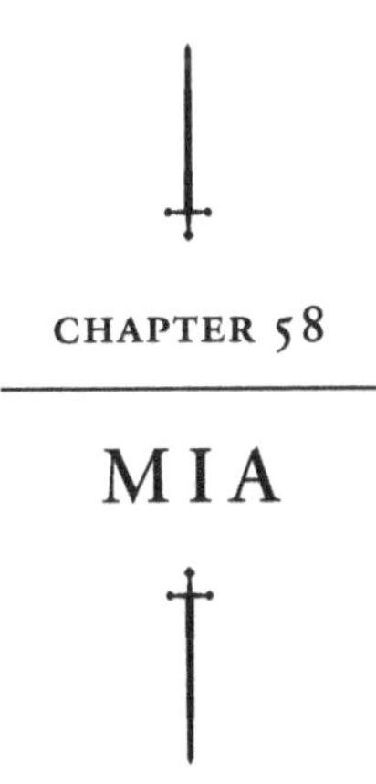

CHAPTER 58

MIA

April 8, 2146

Dried blood and paint mark the walls, dead bodies hang from old electrical wires, and random piles of trash and human remains burn. Savages dance on vehicles, fight in the middle of streets, and tweak in alleyways. There are deathmatches between Lost Ones. Deathmatches between slaves and Lost Ones. I cover Jade's and Sannvi's eyes. To our right, a Lost One tears into a man's throat, then digs into his eye socket, plucks the eyeball out, and slurps on it like a delicacy.

Back in Marigold, the soldiers were told to kill themselves if they thought they would be turned into a Lost One. Last year before my birthday, a few No Man's Land Savage veterans from Calamity Clan returned with three Runesians soldiers. All three committed suicide the night before Lost Soul was supposed to retrieve her shipment of prisoners.

I don't blame them.

The deeper we go, the more some of my old beliefs about Savages show themselves to be true. A group of slaves pull a car with no wheels down a street as four Savages ride on top, whips licking the slaves' backs when one of them falters.

This is Damascus City.

Daniel sucks his teeth and sighs, stopping as a group of Savages drag a man they've set on fire behind them. His agony-filled cries pierce my ears. What meaning does this senseless cruelty have? I reach for the door handle, but Rhena stops me.

"Don't. You can't infringe upon their freedoms," she says.

I settle in my seat and hold my stomach. Some freedom. Daniel reverses and turns down another street. "Where is this place?"

"It's in the middle of the city. Turn left. We're almost there," Rhena says.

This blood-stained city is where the Savage King, Damascus the Second, lives. It's outside the Territories, to the southwest. The weather here is hot and sticky, much like our junkyard camp. The Savages control the entire area and have a mass of warriors to the south defending against the Runesians in No Man's Land. As Rhena gives Daniel directions, I center myself.

I'm here now as chieftess of Calamity Clan. My feelings don't matter. What I must do now is prove my worth, protect my people, and find Glare so that I can clear my name. When I released my clan earlier, I saw how some Savages from the other clans were looking at us. So many of them spit on the ground in our direction. Whatever lies Glare has told have stained Calamity Clan's reputation. What's worse is there's been a rumor that he has won the Almighty's favor. If that's the case, then killing him here won't happen. I'll have to wait for another chance.

Damascus Hotel is the only area in this city that doesn't look like it's on the verge of collapse. The thirty-story building is D-shaped. Hundreds of balconies and windows peer down at us as we step out of the vehicle. The manicured grounds are lush with grass and sprinkled with fine-trimmed topiary of animals. Lights snake around poles and dress trees, flashing with an array of colors, and a large fountain in the front sprays water into the air. We cross a small street and pass under an awning where the doors slide open, a cool breeze hitting us.

As we step inside, a group of three burly Savages dressed in dark cloaks and white animal masks stops us.

"State your business!" one of them says, pointing a spear at us.

Rhena steps forward. "We're Calamity Clan. Here to introduce Chieftess Mia to the Savage King."

He pulls in his spear. "Apologies. Thirtieth floor."

They move aside. The hotel's interior is gloomy, but the light of the day and the many torches show us a path to the elevators.

"Why does he keep the lights off?" I ask.

"The Savage King is a peculiar man. He's done this for years to keep his eyes adapted to low levels of light," Rhena answers as we gather in the elevator. "He told me once it makes it easier to fight off those who use Cloaks."

We rise through the building, and then the elevator doors slide open. A dark hall with torches along the walls stretches out before us. I lead out, Jade and Sannvi a step behind me, weapons in hand.

We approach wide, dark-oak, double doors. I stop, take a deep breath, and push them open. A grand room made from stone swallows us. Light filters through carved-out windows near the high ceiling that's held up by four pillars in each corner of the room. Torches cast a surreal glow onto the various animal heads that watch us from the walls. Sixteen masked guards, eight on each side of a ripped red runner that leads to the Savage King and Princess Raia, stand motionless, holding dual-edged spears.

I move down the path but am halted by the Savage King's voice. It's like a firecracker. "Chimera Guard! You're dismissed."

The Chimera Guards turn and kneel toward the Savage King, then file out of the room. As I approach the Savage King, the first thing I notice is his nudity and his growing erection.

I make it a few feet from the giant stone thrones he and Princess Raia sit on and kneel. "Chieftess Mia of Calamity Clan, here to report, Your Eminence."

"Rise, and please call me Damascus," Damascus says. He looks past me and waves someone forth. "If it isn't the Scarlet Witch!"

Damascus rises from his seat—I divert my gaze from his swinging penis as he travels down the small flight of stairs to hug Rhena. The nudeness many Savages embrace still catches me off guard. They don't concern themselves with the puerility that comes with it in other cultures.

"I'm glad you're doing great, Damascus," Rhena says.

He jerks his thumb back toward his granddaughter. "Can't go until this one is ready."

Princess Raia watches one of the animal heads, the light from outside shining upon her narrow face, making her caramel skin glow. Unlike her grandfather, she's clothed, wearing a dark shawl that flows down her shoulders and merges with her gown. When she glances at me, the intensity of her scrutiny unnerves me. Something about the way she investigates me feels as if she's breaking me a part until she's gets down to the essence of who I am.

Damascus takes my hand after kissing Rhena's, helping me stand. His square-shaped face holds multiple piercings. He has dark gauges in his ears, and small, dark rods jut through the bridge of his nose. Four silver studs shine around his lips: two on the top and two on the bottom. Under each of his eyes is a row of tiny, glittery jewels, and then on his forehead is a large, see-through gauge, his brain pulsing behind the glass.

"Welcome to Damascus Hall. Nice to finally meet you, Blood Queen," he says.

"I am honored to be in your presence."

Damascus gives me a toothy grin. "Are you? I received your message, but from what I hear, you hate us."

"That's not true."

"Then why is Basco dead? What about the Almighty's boy? They were dear to my heart. Glare said you turned them against what our people stand for. Many are calling for your trial within the Hall of Judgement."

I step back, but Damascus's grip on my hand tightens.

"No, Glare is lying. He is the one who killed Basco and Cal. He's been banished for months." I place a palm on my chest. "I am not your enemy."

The Savage King says nothing, but his grasp cinches tighter and his gaze grows harder. I can't tell what he thinks. Having him as an enemy won't bring anything good. I won't make it out of this city alive.

"Grandfather, Mia speaks the truth. She is not who we should be concerned about," Princess Raia says. "And the fact that Rhena is here with her now means that there's no enmity over Basco."

Damascus drops my hand and turns to his granddaughter. "Are you saying she is trustworthy?"

"I am certain. I've seen these things."

"Then we should speak to the Almighty."

"No." Princess Raia rises from her throne, sauntering my way. She rests a hand upon my cheek, her pupils, like resplendent stars, shoot through me. "Whatever you say, it won't matter. The Almighty wants her head."

Damascus resigns, sighing. "If the Almighty wants to kill her, I cannot stop him. I won't."

"You don't have to stop him. She will." Raia's stars haven't stopped burning into my existence. "Nice to meet you. I'm Raia the Wise One, but just call me Raia."

"I'm...."

Raia touches my belly with her other hand. "I know who you are. Your children will be strong."

My heart's racing. What is this feeling? I try to tear away from her, but I can't, and she leans in, her lips brushing against my ear. "Your secret's safe with me."

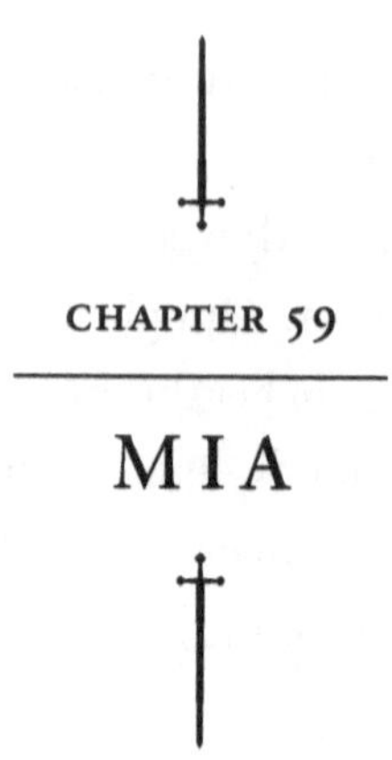

CHAPTER 59

MIA

The sound of water splashing against the porcelain sink calms my nerves. Raia knows. Of course, she does with her clairvoyance. She said my secret would be safe with her, but does she intend to hold it over my head? I turn out of the bathroom, entering the common area. Two queen-sized beds with floral pattern blankets on top of them are against the back wall. An old-world flatscreen television is mounted above a dresser and desk in front of the beds, and a couch sits along the wall on the right side of the room.

I sit on my bed and peer between the curtains at the starless sky. My entire plan is ruined if Raia says anything, and I'll be hated even more. I've lied to everyone except a select few to trick Glare. I must speak to her. I leave the bed and open the door.

Raia stands in the hall. She no longer wears the shawl, revealing her black and blond locs.

"What a coincidence. I was just getting ready to knock," she says, and steps inside, offering me a jar with yellow liquid inside. "You left dinner so quickly. I thought you were sick. This is honeyberry tea mixed with ginger and turmeric."

I close the door, lock it, and Raia moves down the short hall, sets the tea on the desk, and sits on the couch.

"Why are you here?" I ask.

"I want to be allies. Friends."

"I hardly know you."

"But I know you, Blood Queen." Raia pats beside her. "Come sit. I can explain everything."

I lower myself next to her.

"I will be the Savage Queen soon, once my grandfather passes. When that happens, I plan to change the direction of our people. I want peace. Like you and Cal," Raia says. "I'm sure you've heard about my Gift?"

"Clairvoyance."

Raia reads the look on my face, frowning. "Of course, an outsider like you would distrust such a thing. I'm the only Gifted one among the Savages."

"I'm sorry. This is—I just don't understand how somebody like you exists."

She stands and moves toward the window. "Nobody does. That's why it's called a Gift." She looks back at me. "Ever since I was seven, I've had these visions. The Healers told my parents and grandparents I was special. Blessed by our ancestors, but I think they've only cursed me."

"How is an ability like yours a curse?"

"Because I killed my parents with it when I was eleven." Raia moves back over to me and sits on the edge of Jade and Sannvi's bed, so she's in front of me. "One day before an upcoming battle, I dreamed my father would lose his arm. I told him, he told my mother, and they both went anyway, despite my warning. My mother stayed near my father to protect him and ended up dying, and then my father died soon after trying to avenge her. They would still be here if I had remained silent."

Before I can figure out what to say, Raia falls back onto the bed, sighing. "Apologies. I shouldn't have dumped that on you. Why should you believe me?"

I don't know what I believe, but I do know, the Wise One is someone Cal vouched for. He said she and I would get along. She may be my only chance at surviving the next few days here. I get up and fall beside her on the bed.

"It's fine. I believe you," I say.

"Do you still hate us?"

"Only some of you."

Raia chuckles. "Understandable. We need to keep you away from the Almighty tomorrow."

"Why can't you speak with him?"

"The Almighty's mind is set. He never approved of Cal, and he certainly doesn't approve of you or the children you carry."

"Then I won't attend."

"That's not a good look for a clan leader," Raia tells me. "You must attend. I won't let anything happen to you."

I sit up. "What if I tell everyone…." I trail off because Raia's already shaking her head.

"What remains unsaid must stay that way, so the future doesn't change. Besides, with Glare in his ear, nothing but your death matters."

I clench my fists. Everything is working against me. I can't take out Glare if he's under the strongest Savage's protection. Raia sits up and cups a hand under her nose as it bleeds.

"Raia?" I ask.

She stands, catching the blood in her palm. "I told you this Gift is also a curse. Migraines. Nose bleeds. Seizures. Nausea. Fainting. It slowly kills me. And… something's changed."

"What?"

Raia's eyes flutter, and I jump up, holding her when she loses her balance. She comes to in my arms, stands on her own, and wipes her hand off on her gown. "I must go."

I grab her. "What did you see? Was it about me?"

She opens the door. I place my hand on it, slamming it shut, and she whirls.

"You must trust me," Raia says. "I don't want to cause you any misfortune."

"Whatever it was, maybe we can stop it."

Raia shakes her head. "We shouldn't."

"Please!"

She takes a deep breath. "I think by now you know why you have your title."

The twins wriggle in my gut.

Blood trails from Raia's left nostril. "You are not a formidable fighter among us Savages, Mia, but the people you cross with die, anyway. The people who love you."

"Who?" I ask, losing the strength in my arm. Raia opens the door. "Who dies?"

She looks back at me. "I'll see you tomorrow. Steel yourself and be ready."

CHAPTER 60

MIA

I f I had a gun, I'd shoot that smirk off Glare's face. His tan skin is darker, blond hair filthier. I can't believe he dares to still wear Calamity Clan's emblem over his eyebrow. One day, I'll slice the skin there off. When he sees me watching him, Glare's blue eyes flash with malice.

I divert my gaze to the six flags flapping in the hot wind along with Calamity Clan's around the rectangular-shaped arena. Roach Clan's flag is light blue with a flying roach emblem. Moon Keeper Clan's flag is black, with an emblem of hands holding a moon. Lost Clan's flag is just a blank, holey piece of white fabric. Sun Walker Clan's flag is white with a bright orange sun emblem. Perish Clan's flag is purple with a burning smile emblem. For All Clan's flag is dark with a blueish-white symbol that resembles a gust of air.

A wired fence separates me from Rhena, the predetermined overseer of the future battles. The heat squashes me and I pull my shirt away from clammy neck to let in some air. Everyone is yelling and drooling, ready for blood. Damascus sits on the opposite end of the arena just outside the wire, picking his nose on a high wooden throne above a mix of his Chimera Guards and the Almighty's battle-hardened Savages, wearing a golden loincloth skirt with white fur at the hem and sandals. His hairy, bulging belly protrudes, slick with sweat.

I notice members of my clan moving out of the way, kneeling. Raia approaches me, flanked by two Chimera Guards, with a trail of seven more following her. She waves at me. "Hello, Mia. I've come to enjoy the fights with you."

The Chimera Guards make a semi-circle around us. Jade and Sannvi inch closer to me, their hands going for their weapons.

"Be easy," I whisper, looking around for Daniel.

Where is he? My War Hand should be beside me. If he betrays me again, I'll have his head. Today is an important day for all the clans. Today the tournament begins. Each clan gets to prove who is the best in individual deathmatches, and if they win, they get one feasible wish from the Savage King.

Rhena lifts her arms as the day rises higher over the city. Silence swoops down upon us as the stench of dead things passes with the wind—the crow feathers hanging from Rhena's ear lobes spin.

"The one hundred and first annual Savage Conclave begins now! Let us wish our sisters and brothers who have died the best of things in the next world. Let us respect Savage tradition and celebrate our freedoms, their freedoms, and more freedoms to come. Let us rejoice in the blood of our people in the Savage King's name, Damascus the Second! Son of our founder, Damascus the Great. Let us praise them and show them we are grateful for their service to our people! I, Rhena the Scarlet Witch, will oversee these battles. I wish you all courage in the face of death!"

The Savages cheer, but their noise cuts when Damascus lifts his hand in the air. Rhena looks toward him. The Savage King rests his head on his fist, an indifferent expression on his face. "Let's get started."

Rhena turns our way, red eyes scanning the crowd of Calamity Clan until they stick to someone dear to my heart. Sickness ferments in my gut.

"Jade of Calamity Clan versus Viper of Roach Clan. Fighters, please enter the arena," Rhena announces.

I grip Jade's arm. "When did you sign up for this?"

"The Savage King asked me last night after you left the dinner table!"

"Why did you say yes? Are you stupid?"

"He heard that I was exceptional for my age. He wants to see what I'm capable of. I'm sorry," Jade says.

I look out into the arena. A thin woman with green hair enters bare-knuckled. I grimace. "If you cannot win, beg for mercy, or run. Nobody here will blame you."

Jade looks away, and I shake her.

Raia intervenes. "Mia, she will be fine."

I glower at Raia. How am I supposed to keep calm after what she said last night? My hand tightens around the hilt of my blade. If that woman tries to kill Jade, I will interfere. I don't care about the consequences. Jade climbs through the fence after I kiss her on the forehead. Murmurs of doubt ripple around the arena when Jade makes her debut, but she doesn't seem concerned about her predicament. Calamity Clan cheers for Jade when she unsheathes her daggers. She's a talented child. She spars with adults all the time. She'll be fine. But the things I tell myself don't negate the facts.

This is not sparring. It's a deathmatch. Jade nods at me, then faces her opponent.

I grip the wires. "If anything happens to her, I swear—"

Raia places a hand on my shoulder and nods toward the arena. "You need to have faith. Watch."

Jade jets forth, slashing at Viper, who sidesteps, and strikes back with a series of punches. Jade weaves under and around the barrage, darting past Viper, and cuts her in the side.

They both move to attack, but Jade's faster.

She slips to the side, scrambles up Viper's back, and holds a dagger to her throat, whispering something in the woman's ear. Viper growls something, and Jade draws blood.

"Jade, don't!" I scream. "Mercy!"

She stops, and unlatches from Viper, who twists around. "I said I don't want your mercy, girl!"

Jade grins, raising her daggers, but before the two can clash, someone interrupts.

An angelic woman with rosy olive skin and dusty blond hair styled down into a long, thick braid points her blade into the arena. Her eyes are piercing but centered and calm, like a blue sky before a harsh storm.

Butterfly. The chieftess of Roach Clan. How is someone so gorgeous Glare's sister?

"Viper!" Butterfly says. "Accept the girl's mercy, or I will end you myself!"

Viper bares her teeth, then storms out of the arena. Calamity Clan cheers for Jade as she exits, sheathing her daggers. Butterfly finds me with her gaze and gives me a single nod, and Rhena calls out the next fighters. "Chieftess Smile of Perish Clan versus Argo of the Chimera Guard."

The Chimera Guards raise their spears, saluting their comrade-in-arms as he enters the arena.

Smile receives a raging applause from her clan. She's a short, virile, dark-skinned woman with untamed hair and wild, green eyes. She wears a thin muslin cloth over her private area and breasts. On her back, I see the large tattoo of her clan's symbol, a burning smile.

"Submit or die." Smile holds two axes across one another, making an X. Her toes wiggle in anticipation.

Argo points his spear at her, and that's it. It happens so fast I can barely register it in my brain. Smile throws one of her axes at him, and he dodges to the side—right into the trajectory of her other axe, which slices his head clean off. It rolls across the ground and his body crumples. Smile picks up Argo's head, and the Savages praise her. She lets the blood from the decapitation cascade onto her face, then she smears it over her chest, whispering something I can't hear.

I search for Jade, but she hasn't come back over. Where did she go? I can't let her fight that mad woman. I turn to Raia. "Jade will not fight her."

I'm ignored, and the Savage King cries out. "Argo is free from this world's pain! Let us not grieve, but rage for his ascension among our fallen! He can now rest with our ancestors!"

The Savages go wild, and then the next fight starts. Butterfly versus a Savage from For All Clan.

Butterfly is slender, but ample in all the right places. I'm mesmerized by her beauty more than her fighting style, which is graceful and measured. It's like she's dancing. She uses one arm, keeping the other behind her back as she jabs and slices at her opponent with a series of quick strikes. By the time her fourth attack comes, the Savage is on his back.

She pokes him in the shoulder with her blade. "Submit."

The Savage nods, and Butterfly helps him out. I continue searching for Jade as another fight begins. Moments later, it has ended, and Chief Nico of Sun Walker Clan, a sinewy, light-skinned man with an afro of ginger hair, raises his spiked whip into the air.

Sorrow, Moon Keeper Clan's War Hand, a tall, beefy, brown-blond haired woman with blue eyes and two vertical lines tattooed down her face from her forehead to chin, and a third splitting horizontally across her face from ear to ear, limps out of the arena holding her shoulder.

Rhena announces the next fight, and the surrounding noise becomes muffled. No. Why would he do this? I climb onto the fence, but someone pulls me down.

"Mia!" Sannvi cries.

I look back, and the Chimera Guards force Sannvi outside of their perimeter. I turn and try to reach him, but a Chimera Guard blocks my path, and another takes hold of me.

"You knew this would happen!" I scream at Raia.

"And it must," she says.

Then I hear it.

CHAPTER 61

MIA

The chant. Droves of Savages kneel together. "Almighty. Almighty. Almighty. Almighty."

Anxiety scorches over my skin. Chains rattle. Heavy footfalls. And then I see the man whose name means death in No Man's Land. The man who caused Cal so much grief.

Calamity the Almighty.

He's enormous, wearing a hooded wolf headpiece. He really might be nine feet tall, but I can't tell from here. When he shoves his dual-edged spear into the ground, the chains around his waist clink together. The spearhead is three-pronged, with sharp, golden tips reflecting the sunlight. The Almighty's muscles writhe under his brown skin covered in scores of kill dots. He might have an endless amount on his god-like body.

Everything inside of me tingles. Adrenaline pumps into my legs. I need to get far away from here. *Stop staring. Stop staring, Mia before he—*

The Almighty catches my eyes with his, and I squirm in the Chimera Guard's grasp. Is this man a demon?

Rhena raises her hands into the air. "We welcome our best warrior! Killer of thousands! Rival of gods! More beast than man! War General Calamity the Almighty!"

The Savages spring up, louder than ever, pounding their chests and howling into the sky. "ALMIGHTY! ALMIGHTY! ALMIGHTY! ALMIGHTY!"

The Savage King dances atop his seat, and then the cheers and applause cut.

Daniel enters the arena, bombarded by meteors of spit. He keeps his head down to avoid my gaze. Why is he sacrificing himself? I find Glare across the arena, and he's dying from laughter. If my gaze could make his head explode, it would.

Daniel bows toward the Almighty. "I'm Daniel, Calamity Clan's War Hand. It's an honor to meet you."

"I've heard about you from Glare. Under other circumstances, I would want someone like you following me."

"I only have loyalty to Mia," Daniel says.

The Almighty pulls back his headpiece, revealing a bald head with rows and rows of more kill dots. He unclips it and throws it aside, then grips his spear, aiming it at Daniel. "Then get ready to die for her, boy."

Daniel readies his sword with a shaky grasp. Birdy and Raia were right about me. I get others killed. They die because they value my life more than their own. They protect me because I'm weak.

"Daniel!" I yell. "It's not your fault. I understand why. Cal's—"

The Chimera Guard holding me covers my mouth.

Daniel leaps away from the Almighty's slash and thrust forward. The Almighty stops Daniel's blade with his bare hand. He doesn't bleed. Is his skin really made of steel? Is he Gifted like Raia? He yanks the sword away from Daniel and tosses it aside.

There's a commotion behind me.

"Mia!" Jade comes flying over the Chimera Guards, who've formed a tighter formation around me and Raia. Jade crashes into the one that holds me. She claws into his face, and he lets me go, trying to pull her off—just enough time for me to escape.

Calamity Clan breaks the Chimera Guards' formation, and I climb over the fence. I must save Daniel. He shouldn't die by the Almighty's hands, but it's too late. Carnage unfolds before me. I reach out anyway, knowing I will grasp nothing.

The Almighty swings his spear and Daniel ducks, unable to dodge the kick the War General sends next. Daniel topples through the dirt, then the Almighty punches his spear through Daniel's gut, pinning him to the ground. I take out my sword, but someone snatches my wrist from behind.

"Don't!" Raia pulls me back.

"Let go of me!"

"If you interfere with this fight, you will be considered a participant. The Almighty will kill you, make no mistake," Raia says. "Think about the ones that depend upon you. Daniel betrayed you, so why do you try to save him?"

The Almighty taunts me. "Blood Queen, look at your pathetic War Hand!" Daniel squirms. His blood darkens the dirt. "Don't you want to save him, girl? Come closer."

The Almighty's big, white teeth gleam at me, and I jerk forward, but Raia is relentless. "He's baiting you. Stop!"

The Almighty rips his spear out of Daniel and stomps on his head, then picks him up and squeezes his neck. Daniel claws at the Almighty's hands.

I speak through bared teeth. "Glare is the reason Cal's dead! I did not kill him!"

"And?" The Almighty flips his spear around and eases the rear end of it through Daniel's chest. "In another life, serve the strong, boy."

Daniel coughs up blood, and then the Almighty rips his spear out. Blood flies, and Daniel goes limp.

"Daniel!" I crash to my knees.

The Almighty drops Daniel, then shoves his spear into the dirt, and kneels over him. He slices off Daniel's left ear in one clean motion with a knife. He tilts his head back and opens his mouth, dropping Daniel's ear onto his tongue. He chews. "This man was weak. Like you. Like Cal. He could have been strong, but you tainted him."

The Almighty looms over me and Raia. He crunches on the cartilage of Daniel's ear as his red-brown eyes ravage my entire being. I can't move. If I do, I think he'll kill me. Raia tries to help me up, but the Almighty lifts me by my neck.

"She's pregnant!" Raia tugs at my shirt. "Let her go!"

The Almighty brings me eye level with him, grinning as he crushes my windpipes.

"Grandfather!" Raia yells but Damascus does not help.

The Almighty's cackles. The world grows darker and darker. I can feel the twins thrashing around inside me, and then I'm on the ground.

"I will rip those abominations out of you, girl," the Almighty says. "My son deserves no offspring."

"Cal's… a better man than you'll ever be."

The Almighty crouches near me. "Look at my clan! It's weaker than ever, and now it's led by you, a woman from the outside! I should have killed Cal's mother as soon as he was born!"

"You're… despicable."

"I am the Almighty," he says with his knife pressed against my stomach. "I will rid this world of people like you and my son."

I feel the steel lick my flesh. He'll kill me, my children, and everything Cal worked so hard to achieve. A man like this isn't how we move forward. He murders progression.

"Are you ready?" The Almighty presses harder, and I feel blood ooze from my stomach.

No, my children!

"Almighty! Watch out!" someone screams.

The Almighty has no time to defend. Tabatha jams a knife into his back. "Keep your filthy hands off my chieftess!"

I can't save her. She gives me a toothy grin and then the Almighty turns and slashes her throat. Blood spills out of her, and she collapses to the ground, smile permanent. He turns back toward me and pulls Tabatha's knife out like it's nothing but a common splinter.

He spits on me. "You've made my clan nothing but weaklings and hopeless idiots. It's time to end you."

Raia shields me. "You will not touch her."

"Move," the Almighty says.

Raia holds her arms out wide. The Almighty growls, and goes to grab his spear, the knife wound bleeding on his right side. I am saved, but after what this monster has said and done, I have no choice. If I leave here like this, he will hunt me. He will kill all those he deems weak. This is for Cal and our future.

I push myself up with a hand on Raia's shoulder for stability. "I challenge you, Calamity the Almighty, to a deathmatch!"

I reach for my stone dagger and cut my palm. The Almighty's shoulders rumble with laughter as he faces me. "I will indulge you. Do you want to die now or later?"

"October. Right here. It would be unfair if I fought you pregnant."

He slits his palm. "You can have your children, but after you, I will kill them. Hide them all you want. I will find them and put their heads on sticks."

I hold out my fist, letting my blood drip into the dirt with his, and then the Almighty raises his bloody fist into the air. "Bear witness, Savages! The Blood Queen and I have made a blood oath to fight to the death in October. It is people like her making us weak. Her death will be the beginning of a reformed era for our peoples. I should also let it be known that Glare is my kin. My new son. A dead man's banishment means nothing! Any assassination attempts against him are a direct challenge to me. My wish for our people is for us to be strong. For us to rule! But there are those among us who go against our nature. In October, I will put an end to all of that. The Blood Queen and those loyal to her will be martyrs for what's coming. If you are beside me in this… Kneel!"

Rhena, Jade, and Sannvi crowd around me, checking my stomach as Savages around the arena lower themselves.

"What do you think you're doing?" Raia asks.

The Almighty glares back at her. "The Savage King's fight is almost over. I've taken it upon myself to redeem what he and his father started. You will ruin our people."

"I will lead them to salvation! You don't have the right."

The Almighty gestures around the arena with smugness. "The right is given by the people, Wise One."

Moon Keeper Clan, Sun Walker Clan, Perish Clan, and Lost Clan kneel. Only my clan, Roach Clan, and For All Clan, stay on their feet.

The Almighty turns toward Damascus. "Savage King, I apologize. You've done so much for me, and here I am, trying to sweep the rug from under you. I hope you understand where I'm coming from. I wish you no ill will."

"I appreciate your ambitions, Calamity, and you're free to them. All I ask is that you never harm my granddaughter," Damascus says.

The Almighty places a hand upon his heart and bows. "You have my heart, Your Eminence. I will always respect and honor your wishes."

Damascus nods and rises. "Very well. I think for today, this is enough. I am exhausted. My old bones need rest."

Damascus disappears down the steps, and the Almighty rests his spear over his shoulder, looking back at me. "In October, you'll get to see Cal again."

"Burn in hell!"

"I will relish in the flames," the Almighty says, turning away from me.

"Give Daniel my condolences!" Glare shouts from the sidelines.

I lurch forward, but Jade and Sannvi grab me.

Rhena says, "Calm down. Please."

Everyone disperses but me and my clan. We crowd around Daniel and Tabatha. I won't grieve for Tabatha because she wanted to die. Instead, I will celebrate. Maybe she knew I was lying when I said I would kill her. I won't forget her loyalty. What she did was honorable, and now I know the Almighty isn't invincible. He bleeds, just like Cal said.

But Daniel. He's still as a dead person ought to be.

Raia steps into our gathering behind me. "Mia, I'm sorry. This had to happen."

"You need to leave."

"Mia—"

"Go!"

Raia takes one last glance at Daniel, then excuses herself. I cradle him and close his eyes. My tears drench his face. Now, he can rest. He was always my friend, even before I knew it. Everything he did, he did it for my sake. Daniel loved me, and I am sorry I could not love him back the way he must have wanted.

CHAPTER 62

RAIA

"Grandfather! What is the meaning of this? I thought I was to be the third ruler of our people?" Raia demands, storming into Damascus Hall.

Damascus the Second snoozes on his throne, head bobbing up and down.

"Grandfather!"

He jumps awake. "Raia. Why are you so angry? And loud? You're like a banshee."

"You make a fool out of me!"

"Have you eaten?" Damascus asks while he scratches his groin.

"The Almighty cannot lead the Savages. He's a monster!"

Damascus sighs. "Should you rule simply because you're my granddaughter and Gifted? No. We Savages are about freedom. And the Almighty or any Savage is free to claim my place when I'm gone. You know this."

"The Almighty kills freedom. He takes lives and doesn't show any remorse. How could you betray me like this?"

The Savage King stands and pulls a cloak around his naked body. "I betrayed no one. With your clairvoyance, you should be able to see a way forward."

"Why do you not care?" Raia asks as Damascus brushes past her.

"We should have roasted duck tonight."

Raia chases after him, out of Damascus Hall, and down the dark corridor. She clutches onto his arm. "He will kill me."

"I forbade him."

"You asked him not to. That doesn't mean he will keep his promise once you're gone."

Damascus shrugs. "You have the Chimera Guard, the Blood Queen, Butterfly, and your boy toy from For All. Surely, you can figure something out if he goes against my wishes."

"You shouldn't have given him the right!"

Damascus snatches his arm away from her. "Rights? You know nothing about rights, child! The Almighty already had the right long before you took your first steps! If he wanted to, he could kill me and take the throne now or could have years ago. Be smarter, my dear. You are the Wise One, after all. Your parents nor I raised you to cry about something when it wasn't going in your favor. You will figure it out or suffer."

Silence drips between the two as they enter the elevator together.

"Grandfather?" Raia's starry pupils glow in the darkness. "Do you want to know when you'll die?"

"Won't that mess it up? I do love a surprise."

Raia's nose bleeds. "I think you've had enough of those in your lifetime."

Damascus smirks. "And what will you do once I'm dead?"

"I'll use my influence to get rid of the Almighty. I'll start building bridges instead of burning them down."

"Naïve of you, child," Damascus says. "This war will continue until one side wins and the others lose, or this blasted planet kills you all. Only the soft think of alliances."

"I am tired of the fighting. When does it stop?"

"The day you take your last breath. I love you, child, but with your foolish notion, you will incite a civil war. The Almighty has four of the seven clans on his side. You saw. You will not win if you pick a fight against him."

Raia peers deep into her grandfather's eyes. "How can I be foolish when I see what lies ahead?"

"Then why are you before me whining?" Damascus asks.

"In front of our people, I want to be respected. You made me seem insignificant."

"You will never be insignificant with your clairvoyance."

The elevator stops, and the doors open. "I will become the Queen of Savages tonight."

Damascus smiles and wraps an arm around Raia's waist as they exit into a hall. "You ruined the surprise."

"No, your death date is three weeks away. This is a preemptive move on my part. I see the way the forward."

"Are you sure you're ready?"

Raia hugs her grandfather. "I have to be."

CHAPTER 63

LEON

April 10, 2146, 17:45

Blood drips into the sink, and Leon throws water into his face. A dull pain throbs in his temples, and that familiar grip of coldness cinches his spine. A voice speaks through the airship's intercom system. *"ETA to drop zone ten minutes. All parties under General Wilde's command please be ready in the hangar."*

Leon turns away, but his father sneers at him through the mirror. "Do you think you're going to be some sort of hero?"

"I'm just doing what's right. One and Ivan need to go down."

Iciness slithers around his neck as the shadow wraps around Leon, its face near his ear. "You can't change who you are. Doing one good thing doesn't outweigh all the bad. It's easy to see how much you can't stand yourself."

"I'm doing this for—"

"For Mia, right?" Danston asks, appearing in front of Leon. "It's a shame. You probably won't get to see her again."

"Why won't I? I'm going to talk some sense into her once I get back."

The shadow snickers and joins Danston. "Oh, dear. That's your problem. You think she needs saving. You're the one that's dying, sweetie. You might as well take that gun and put yourself out of misery."

293

Blood falls out of Leon's nose, and he backs away from the two, gripping the edge of the sink. "Shut up!"

"Don't let that doctor get your hopes up," his father says. "You'll die and join us. You can let go, son. It's okay to give up."

"I'll never be like you. Like mom."

Danston laughs. "It's funny because you think we had a choice. Death chooses who it wants. There's no fighting it, so...."

His father raises the pistol. It kicks. A light flashes, and then the sweet and spicy aroma of honey and cinnamon curl around him.

"What the hell are you doing, boy?" Kirk forces Leon's gun away from his head. "You're better than that."

Lucia embraces him. "You are loved. You must stay here. This world, and the next, needs you, Leon."

Leon's pistol clatters to the floor. Then he looks between his grandparents. "I can't control them."

Kirk places a palm over Leon's heart. "Find the courage within to forgive."

And then his grandparents are gone.

ONE

October 4, 2133

Katherine strides up a hill toward the moon that peeks over the summit, gripping a skinny tree for support, tailed by a scrawny eleven-year-old Zeke, who drags his rifle through dead leaves. His brown hair tumbles over his sweat-drenched face as he tries to keep pace with his aunt.

A ten-year-old Liz trails twenty feet behind them, freckled cheeks flushed. "Aunt Kathie, I'm tired. Can we stop, please?"

Her voice echoes, and Katherine glares back at the two children, then downs her pack and pulls out a packet meal. "We'll take a break. Ten minutes. Hurry and eat something."

Liz collapses, and Zeke rushes to her. "Are you okay?"

"No." Liz pulls out her meal with a frown. "My legs feel like logs. The heat is killing me, and now I have to eat this nasty paste again."

Zeke sits next to her, grabs her meal, and opens it. "Well, we gotta eat it. We need our strength."

Zeke tears open his packet and tilts his head back, squeezing noodles congealed with red sauce into his mouth. Liz closes her eyes and copies her brother. Katherine watches them as she drinks from her canteen.

"Zeke, what are you doing?" Katherine asks. He holds up his meal and

Katherine charges toward him, snatches his rifle, and shakes it in his face. "This! Why is it lying here like a toy? Why does it look as if you've thrown it through the mud instead of carrying it like I taught you? Clean it. Now."

Katherine shoves the gun into Zeke's trembling hands, and he drops his food.

"I'm sorry."

"Sorry gets you and your sister killed. You'll never be able to protect her acting like this."

Liz glowers at her. "He's just tired because you're going too fast. We're just kids!"

Katherine seizes Liz by her shirt. "Keep your voice down. Do you know where we are?"

"You're hurting me!"

She lets the girl go. "We're in No Man's Land. A place where the only thing that matters is strength. I promised Katrina I'd keep you both safe, so get it together and do what's expected of you. Zeke, clean your weapon and stay vigilant. I'm going to the bathroom. When I come back, we'll step off again."

Katherine grabs her pack and backtracks downhill until she reaches an area with shrubberies crowding the trees. She squats in between two bushes near a tree with her pistol in her free hand. When she's done, she retrieves a black sphere from her bag and presses the top of it.

The slim-faced headshot of a dark-haired, brown-skinned man with wide, hazel eyes appears. Above his head, words fade in, then dissolve.

Name: Refi Chun

Age: 34

Status: Deserter

Plan of Action: Terminate

Katherine smiles and takes out a burner. She sucks in the nicotine, coughing, when a high-pitch scream cuts through her moment of bliss. Katherine jumps up and sprints back toward the children.

"Hurry!" Refi shakes Liz by the hair.

Zeke shovels his and his sister's remaining meals into a black bag.

Katherine slinks out of the brush behind Refi, shoots him in the ankle, and he crumples. Liz runs for Zeke, clinging to him.

"Lieutenant Chun reduced to a petty raider." Katherine stands over Refi, who clutches his ankle, teeth bared. "I knew you would show, eventually."

"You used children as bait. What if I had killed them?"

"That's not in your nature. Your people gave me everything I needed to know about you. That's how bad they want you dead, coward."

Refi reaches behind him, but Katherine shoots him again, this time in the shoulder.

"Did you think trying to flee into the Territories would save you?" Katherine says. "I can offer you asylum if you give me the coordinates to every Runesian base and stronghold."

Refi groans, gaze full of contempt.

"Why do you protect them? You deserted." Katherine checks Refi's bag, then his pockets. "Here we are." She kneels in front of him, showing him a picture of a woman and two girls. "Cute. You know what Runesians do to deserters and their families, right? Your wife and daughters are dead or worse, concubines and servants to one of your generals. They'll be abused and treated like those in your lowest class every day. I'll give you one last chance to redeem yourself for messing with my nephew and niece. Tell me something worth more than your life, and maybe I get the RFF to protect you."

"Screw you!" Refi says. "My family is safe. I am done with this war, and horrible people like you and my superiors. All of you are just as corrupt as the next. Nothing's changed over the past century. You instigate war, use one another, and kill the other side under the guise of freedom. But we'll never be free because of sick individuals like yourself! You're immoral, and human life means nothing to you. You're disgusting and empty and hopeless!"

"Fine." Katherine sighs, and takes Refi's pistol, turning to Zeke, who's consoles Liz. "Come shoot him."

"W-w-what?" the boy stammers.

"Kill this man. He's a Runesian. Our enemy." Zeke steps back, but Katherine approaches him, pulling him close. "He could have killed Liz. What if this happens again and I'm not around? What are you going to do? How are you going to protect Liz? Didn't you tell me you wanted to get stronger to do that?"

Zeke's fists curl and he takes the gun.

Katherine slides behind him, whispering, "Aim for the head."

"You are a repulsive person." Refi spits at Katherine. "I pity the boy."

Zeke's hands quake and Katherine holds his trembling shoulders. "Out here, it's us or them. You do this now, and no one will ever be able to hurt you or your sister ever again."

Zeke eases the trigger back and blood explodes from Refi's skull.

CHAPTER 64

ONE

April 10, 2146, 18:00

It rains. Thunder booms as One steps into Penelope Hall with a smile. Ivan sits at one end of the table sipping wine. One takes her seat and gestures toward the food. "Impressive spread. What's the occasion?"

Ivan raises his glass. "To our new beginning as partners. Soon we will crush the Republic for Freedom generals, and then we can end this war our way."

One clinks her glass against his and the two drink. She says, "They should be attacking soon. Are you ready?"

"Of course. Are you? After this, we take over."

One shovels green beans and slices of pork roast onto her plate. "I've been ready for years. The generals have put off winning this war long enough."

Ivan watches One saw through her meat. "Are you sure nuking the west coast is the best option against the Runesians? The people enslaved there will be wiped out as well. The land will be inhospitable for years."

"Collateral. The land will heal. I rather save the majority than worry about everyone over there who was unlucky in 2055. Don't tell me you're having second thoughts?"

Ivan snorts in dismissal, and the two eat in silence for a while, forks and spoons scraping against glassware.

Then he asks, "Do you think you did a good job raising Zero and Liz?"

One pauses and looks at him before clearing her throat. "I taught them how to take care of themselves and did the best I could, considering how they were just thrown on me once my sister and their worthless father died."

"I wish I got the chance to raise a child, but Siggy took that away from me when she sent Isabelle to space."

One's throat itches, and she drinks some water. She reaches for the gun strapped to her thigh. "Was she pregnant?"

Ivan shakes his head. "No, but we talked about it a lot. I know she's up there. I just hope she's waiting for me."

"Iv—" One's throat swells, her eyes bulging. She wheezes. "Iv-Iv-an… you—"

He smirks. "You don't look so hot. I could give you the antidote, but if I allow a sociopath like you alongside me too much longer, who knows what will happen. Did you think I wouldn't find out it was you who tried to kill me during the speech?"

Spit foams in the corner of One's lips and dark veins bulge in her forehead.

"You know Zero hates your guts. Poor kid was just following your lead to protect his sister." Ivan stuffs a cloth inside his shirt. "We're both ambitious, One, but my ambitions are more important than yours. Mine is for Isabelle. Yours are decadent."

One keels over, out of her seat. She chokes and spasms on the ground. She utters one last word. A name. "Katrina."

Ivan cuts into his steak, red flowing from the meat. He sticks a cube of beef into his mouth and chews.

CHAPTER 65

LEON

Leon rappels into the room behind Liz and joins General Wilde and Zero in the darkness.

General Wilde moves toward the door. "General Flower's distraction on the ground level is working. Many of the soldiers here are being sent to stop his advance. Jace and Jenna just confirmed that they secured Siggy. We're right on time and should have a straight shot to Penelope Hall."

Zero presses the button, and the door slides open. General Wilde leads out with Leon in the rear. They move down the hall and enter the stairwell, climbing to level thirty-eight.

General Wilde pushes the door open and throws out an EMP grenade. *Let's move. Cloaks on.*

She leads out into the hall, gun leveled and ready. They clear a corner and approach the wooden doors of Penelope Hall. Liz and Zero stack on each side of the entryway, and then their Cloaks deactivate.

What's happening? General Wilde asks.

Zero shrugs. *Maybe they have the room under an EMP barrier.*

Leon, try sending a drone under the door.

Leon reaches into one of his pouches and sets a six-legged drone on the floor, but it doesn't move.

Jammed, he says, approaching the door, his Cloak deactivating. *Looks like we do this loud.*

General Wilde nods, and Leon boots the door. The four flow into the room, aiming their rifles at Ivan and One, who sit on opposite ends of a long dinner table. One slouches forward, her face in a plate of mashed potatoes.

Ivan raises his wineglass. "Welcome."

"Hands up!" General Wilde shouts.

One's heart isn't beating, Liz links.

"I said hands up, Ivan!" General Wilde repeats, and Ivan dabs at his face with a cloth, then sticks his hands into the air. She presses toward him, then links, *Leon, check One. Liz, Zero, on me.*

Leon splits from the group toward One's end of the table. The red heat inside of her body dissipates, leaving her thermal image a yellowish-green.

"She had a bit too much to drink," Ivan calls from the other end of the table as Liz detains him in electro-cuffs.

Leon places two fingers on One's neck and confirms her death. He grins, then his spine tingles, and Kirk's voice is in his ear. "Above."

Leon glances up. A dozen of Cloaked CAF soldiers hover near the ceiling silently with jetpacks.

Attac—

The soldiers send a volley of energy beams his way, and he sprints for cover behind a statue in the room's corner. He peeks around the statue, seeing General Wilde and Liz on the ground near Ivan and Zero.

"Drop your weapons and come out," Zero calls.

"This is low." Leon switches his gun to lethal. "Teaming up with the man who killed your aunt."

"Killing her was my idea."

"Yeah, sure. One owner to another. You just love being a good boy, don't you?"

Ivan points his gun at General Wilde. "Enough stalling, Jackson."

Leon tosses his rifle, pistol, and knife onto the floor and comes from behind the statue with his hands in the air. He scowls at Zero. "Why go through all the trouble of saving us from the Land of Ice if you were just going to betray us anyway?"

"Everything I do, I do for Liz," Zero says.

Leon shakes his head. "She'll never forgive you."

"As long as she's safe, I don't care if she hates me." Zero gets in Leon's face. "I don't know what she sees in you. Get on your knees."

"She sees someone dependable. Unlike you, who stabs her in the back every chance he gets. You're just a dog, Zero. First One, and now Iv—"

Zero buttstrokes Leon in the head, and his legs give out from under him. Stars explode in his vision. Leon hears his heart thump. Feels the blood snaking down his face, and then nothing at all.

CHAPTER 66

MIA

April 11, 2146

I kneel in the front between Butterfly and Nico, the other four clan leaders behind us.

"Thank you all for coming," Raia says from her throne. "You may rise. I called you all here to discuss the future of our people."

We rise, and Lost Soul steps forward, saying, "You do the Almighty a dishonor. Why is he not here?"

Nico nods beside me in agreement.

"I am queen now," Raia says. "Things will be changing. You all must understand this. Besides, the Almighty has left already for No Man's Land. What he stands for is not unison. It is not peace, and I don't want us to end up killing each other because of his beliefs."

Nico scratches his neck. "His beliefs? I believe what the Almighty believes." He shrugs, looking back at Chief Kaiser of Moon Keeper Clan and Lost Soul. "They do too. It is you, Wise One, who will aggravate civil war by allowing Mia to be among us!"

"She has every right to be here. She earned her title and is Savage. I don't see your reason," Raia says.

"Cal's death is her fault. And should we forget that she was and maybe still is an RFF spy?" Kaiser, a gremlin-like, bearded man with brown-gray hair, and four black lines tattooed down his pink face asks.

"Cal's death is Glare's fault, and I don't spy for the RFF," I say.

"You lie!" Lost Soul hisses.

"You accuse her without evidence and believe ridiculous rumors. How naïve of you all." Raia rises from her throne and moves before us. "We need to grow together and find peace instead of wanting to always war."

"We live to fight. It is who we are," Lost Soul says.

Raia grimaces, then pulls a cloth from under her robes, and places it to her nose.

"Are you sick, Raia?" Nico asks, grinning. "Are you even fit to lead us?"

Chief Ronan of For All Clan steps out of line, and shoves Nico. "You disrespect our queen, Sun Walker. All of you. She is our leader, and you should address her as such!"

Ronan is handsome and muscular, with a magnificent beard. He has braids on top of his head with the sides shaven. He wears maroon cargo pants, dark combat boots, and an open, dark Hawaiian shirt with blooming roses all over it.

Nico turns on him. "Why don't you crawl deeper into her—"

Ronan punches Nico in the jaw, knocking him to the ground. Kaiser and Lost Soul unsheathe their blades and lunge forward, but Ronan whips out one of his two swords, halting their advance. He pins Nico to the floor with his foot and points his second blade at his throat. "Show our queen some respect!"

Kaiser stomps the ground. "She doesn't deserve it! She becomes queen in the middle of the night and announces it in the morning once the Almighty leaves. He had a legitimate right to the throne. The Second said so!"

"And the Second is dead," Raia says. "I am the only one here who can rule us."

"Get the fuck off me!" Nico squirms under Ronan's weight, and he lifts his foot. Nico jumps up, unfurling his whip. "I'll make you my slave!"

"Enough!" Raia steps between the two men. "From now on, any

fighting or killing among Savages is prohibited unless sanctioned in a deathmatch by me."

"I could kill him if the Second were still alive!" Nico spits on the ground near Ronan's feet. "Kiss ass."

Ronan smirks. "You couldn't kill me if you tried one million times."

Raia pushes Ronan away from Nico. "It seems the Almighty's words have divided us. This is not what my grandfather wanted. You all tarnish his name. You should be ashamed."

"Because we disagree with your ideologies?" Lost Soul asks. "It seems you are the one tarnishing his name."

"I am trying to do what's best for our people!" Raia produces a knife from her garments and slits her palm. Her blood drips onto the stone floor. "That is why we will do a blood oath on the Second's soul."

"Blood oath to what?"

"To not fighting amongst ourselves. No Savage-on-Savage bloodshed. And Mia is off limits."

"And what if we refuse?"

"As queen, I'll do what's necessary for the future of the majority. Our people's freedom and peace will come with or without you."

Raia makes a fist and more of her blood rains down. She unclenches it, her hand steady as it floats there, waiting for others to join it.

No one moves.

There's a clear divide. Me, Raia, Butterfly, and Ronan are on one side. Nico, Lost Soul, and Kaiser are on the other. Smile stands alone, ivy green eyes radiant, flicking between us and them.

Butterfly grabs the hilt of her sword, and I do the same. Ronan steps in front of Raia.

Lost Soul's eyes narrow. "All of you disgust me. The Almighty will hear of this."

"You're either with me, or dead, Lost Soul," Raia says. "I will scream for the Chimera Guard. None of you will leave this room alive if choose to go against me."

"This doesn't earn you loyalty, girl!" Kaiser shouts.

"Who says I'm yearning for it? I'm making you obey for peace. Come. Do the oath, live, and address me with respect!"

Kaiser's lips curl with fury. "Peace? Your years show. Peace is a fairytale, Your Eminence!"

"Chimera Guard!" Raia yells, and sixteen of them enter, surrounding us.

Lost Soul holds up her hand. "Wait! We will agree to the oath on one condition."

"Which is?" Raia asks.

"In October, when the Blood Queen loses her head, you will step down from your position and let Calamity the Almighty be king."

Raia nods. "I accept."

"Very well, Your Eminence," Lost Soul says and cuts her palm, looking at Kaiser and Nico.

Soon we all stand in a circle over a dark red puddle.

"Any deviation from this oath agreed upon by all individuals here will result in execution, so I advise everyone to keep their clans in line. You are free to leave," Raia announces.

Lost Soul, Nico, and Kaiser leave. Smile leans against a pillar with her arms crossed.

"Claus," Raia says, and a Chimera Guard wearing a vulture mask steps forward and kneels. "I want Lost Clan, Sun Walker Clan, and Moon Keeper Clan watched while in the city. Report any suspicious activity to me."

"Yes, Your Eminence." He rises, and the Chimera Guard exit Damascus Hall.

"Why would you agree to that? It's the Almighty!" Ronan asks. "Mia cannot beat him."

"She can," Raia says.

"You've seen it?" Butterfly asks.

"I cannot say. It is uncertain. But what I know is that Mia has allies she can trust and depend on," Raia says.

I follow her gaze toward Smile, whose shoulders rumble with crazed laughter.

CHAPTER 67

LIZ

April 14, 2146

A gray sky swirls over the dark city of Toronto. Sleek black, red, and white hovering vehicles zip below on a sky highway identified by glowing rails over the ground streets. Fat droplets of rain patter against a large window, and Liz sighs, turning away as her door opens. The pale green in her pupils drains out to match the color of the gloom outside.

Zero smiles and sets a covered dish on a nightstand near her bed. "I brought you some food."

"I thought I told you not to come in here."

"Figured you'd be hungry. I'm just trying to help."

Liz scoffs, grabs her wrist and squeezes. "If you want to help, let me go. You know this is wrong, Zeke."

"Zeke died a long time ago."

"It's the name our parents gave you. You're not what One raised you to be." Liz moves closer and relaxes her hands, letting them rest at her sides. She reaches for him. "Please. I don't want to be here."

Zero smacks her hand away. "It's my job to protect you."

"Don't you want to do one right thing?"

"I am doing the right thing. I'm saving your life."

Liz throws her hands up and whirls away from her brother. "Please enlighten me on how keeping me locked in a room for the past four days is saving my life."

Zero rushes behind Liz and makes her face him. "Earth is dying. The scientists here in Canada confirmed that, and the fact that Anomaly Day never ended. I saw the data myself. The random weather and climate changes will get worse. The natural disasters will come again and wreak more havoc. And you know what we've been doing? Fighting an unwinnable war instead of figuring out a way off this planet. That's why I'm following Ivan. He's taking us to space where we'll be safe."

Liz rips out of Zero's grasp. "The Optimus missions failed, remember? No one knows what happened to the people who tried to make it to space. That data could be fake. Ivan's using you just like One. He'll get us killed."

"I'd rather take my chances with him than dying here for the RFF."

Liz moves back over to the window. "Get out."

Behind her, the door the slides open, but it doesn't close. Zero says, "You may hate me now, but in the future, you'll be thankful for what I'm doing. If you stay here, Leon's going to get you killed, and for what? He's never going to love you, Liz. Quit being delusional."

The door hisses shut, and Liz hugs herself, holding her tears at bay as she watches the grim world grow darker and darker.

☽

A soldier brings Liz her next meal. "The chef said you should really like this one. I'll come back for the cart."

Liz approaches the dish, and lifts the silver cover, closing it when she spots a single, baseball-sized, spherical object. The entire tray vibrates, and Liz lifts the top again. A voice comes from the device. *"There's a Jammer built in, and Barnes is actively running a loop for the next three minutes, so hurry up and dig in."*

"Jace! You guys got away, thank god." Liz pulls the cart deeper into the room, takes the cover off, picks up the sphere, and clicks the button.

Jace's holographic head appears with a smile. "Listen, tomorrow we're coming to rescue you guys. Be ready."

"You know I'm always ready. You did all this to tell me that?"

"No. We can't locate General Wilde or Leon. We were hoping you could pull some info out of Zero somehow and get back to us, so we're not wasting time clearing all the cells tomorrow."

Liz shakes her head. "He won't tell me. We got into a fight earlier. But he did mention Ivan wanting to go to space, and Anomaly Day never ending."

"Zero didn't mention anything about a ship, did he?"

"No."

"Good. Sit tight, Liz. We're coming."

CHAPTER 68

LEON

April 15, 2146

Useless!

Kill yourself....
We left because of you....
They died because of you!
Join us!
What is your worth?
It's all your fault.
Worthless!
You're dying....
Kill yourself....
You shouldn't be here.
You'll be trapped here forever.
Join us!
You're worthless!

Leon clutches his head and headbutts the rough pillow, screaming into it. His body shudders, and seconds later, he drenches the pillow with tears.

"I'm sorry. I'm sorry. I'm sorry."

A cold hand touches his back. The shadow stands over him. "Don't be sorry. Do something about it."

Danston appears beside him, sitting on the bed. "We're waiting, Leon."

Leon shakes his head. "I can't."

"You can. All that's left here is chaos and death and more misery. We're trying to help you." Danston holds out his palm, and in it is a shank made from a toothbrush handle. "It'll slip right in, and it'll all be over. Me and your mother miss you."

Leon stares up at the shadow. Tears roll down his face. "Mom?"

The tendrils of black unfurl, revealing brown skin, a heart-shaped face, forest-like pupils, and dark, wavy hair traveling to the woman's shoulders. "You finally remember what I look like," Leonor says, smiling.

Leon rushes his mother and embraces her. Kirk's voice sings through his head. *Find the courage within to forgive.*

Leon's eyes widen, a sudden realization washing over him. He asks, "Why do you want me to die?"

She buries her head into his shoulder. "I miss you."

"Do you remember reading stories about superheroes to me?" Leon asks, squeezing his mother tighter when she nods. "They never gave up. No matter how hard it got. You would always tell me to be like them, so I can't just go."

"You'll d—"

Leon shakes his mother. "I love you. I miss you. And I forgive you. I'm not mad. I'm not worthless. I'm your son, and I belong here."

Leonor's mouth falls open, but no words come out. She's frozen, unable to move.

Danston pushes Leon away. "Leo? What did you do to her?"

Leon repeats himself. "I love you. I miss you. And I forgive you. I'm not mad. I'm not worthless. I'm your son, and I belong here."

Danston freezes just like Leonor, and Leon repeats the mantra. "I love you. I miss you. And I forgive you. I'm not mad. I'm not worthless. I'm your son, and I belong here."

He gets closer to them, arms spread out. "I love you. I miss you. And I forgive you. I'm not mad. I'm not worthless. I'm your son, and I belong here."

Leon pulls his parents into a hug. "I know it was hard. I still can't understand why you both left me, but I'm not going to be angry about it anymore. I'm not going to blame you or myself. I'm moving past this, and I'm not giving up. I want to live. I want to save Mia. If you really love me, then help me, please."

Leon's parents' hands cling to the back of his shirt.

Danston says, "You didn't deserve what we put you through."

"I'm so sorry, Leon. I shouldn't have left you," Leonor says, crying.

"It's okay. You're here now." Leon wipes his mother's tears.

"We're going to get you out of here." Leonor breaks away from them and steps through the wall. She returns moments later with a smile. "Seems the calvary's already here."

Leon's door slides open, and Jace stands in the entryway in a CAF uniform. "Why are you crying?"

Leon looks around for his parents, but they're gone. He feels a slight pressure on his shoulder and then hears his father's voice inside his head. *Call us whenever you need us. We'll always be here to protect you.*

Leon smiles. "I'm just really happy to see you."

"Well, be happy later." Jace holds out a spare pistol for Leon. "We gotta capture Ivan before he escapes. Liz is with him."

Leon and Jace join Jenna, Siggy, General Wilde, General Flower, and a mixed squad of Foundation members and RFF soldiers on the thirty-eighth floor, who are tucked behind an energy shield, blocking a barrage of bullets and energy shots.

"We're pinned down!" Jenna yells. "They're covering the service elevator to the roof. We'll only catch Ivan if we take the secret passageway in Siggy's room. Now would be a really great time for one of you to use your Gift to clear a path for us."

"Mine only works if they can hear me," Jace says.

Everyone looks to Leon. He nods and closes his eyes. "I'll try. Give me a second."

He concentrates and thinks of Kirk, Lucia, and his parents all together. Blood trickles from his nose, and then his entire body tingles.

"You called?" Kirk manifests beside Leon.

"Can you guys help us get into Siggy's room?"

"Sure. Just give us some guns. We'll show you where you got all your skills from," Leon's father says from his other side.

Leon hands Kirk his pistol and takes a rifle from a nearby soldier, handing it to Danston. The two ghosts step around the barrier and walk down the hall through the bullets and energy blasts. To the CAF soldiers, two guns are simply floating through the air.

General Wilde looks at Leon. "They're still our allies."

"Don't kill them!" Leon yells.

"We'll try not to!" Danston raises the rifle and runs forward, shooting.

Leon's legs go numb, and he crashes to a knee when a sharp migraine crackles through his skull.

Jace crouches near him. "You're overusing your Gift."

The CAF soldiers flee as a few of their allies are shot down by Kirk and Danston. Leon leads the group around the corner, but he stumbles, and Jace catches him. His vision blurs just as the doors to Siggy's room burst open, and a human-sized mecha steps out with raised arms. It's a coil of dark wires, metal, and alloy with glaring red eyes. Behind it, four CAF soldiers set their sights on Leon's group but are quickly mowed down by Kirk and Danston.

General Flower throws a shield down just as lasers spit from the mecha's arm, needling into the blue energy wall. He unstraps a grenade launcher from his back. "Shield won't last long."

"I got it." Leon winces as a streak of pain ripples from the base of his skull to his tailbone.

"We better hurry before the boy dies," Kirk says, and runs toward the mecha, Danston following.

The two shoot at the mecha, and it melts the guns they're carrying. Kirk looks at Danston. "How do we kill it?"

Danston shrugs. "You're the war hero."

"I'm not into the fancy tech these days."

Danston approaches the mecha, who continues chipping away at the energy shield of Leon's group. He sticks his hand through the mecha's gut. "It's core should be somewhere around here. There… got it!"

Danston rips out a baseball-sized sphere of metal and wires surrounding a white source of energy. Electricity crackles through the air as the mecha's gut smokes. Danston waits for the mecha to crumple, but it doesn't. He looks back at Kirk. "I don't know what's happening!"

Kirk fades, his voice echoing in and out. "Well, we're running out of time. The boy's straining to keep us on this side. Maybe there's a second one."

Danston reaches into the mecha's skull. He grabs another sphere, then his fingers slip through. Kirk vanishes behind him, and Danston yells back, "Leon, just a bit longer!"

"I'm trying!" Blood streams from Leon's nose. "Do it!"

Danston grips the sphere and yanks it out. Like a can exploding, the mecha's head splinters open, and then it's nothing but a pile of metal and wires.

The core falls through Danston's hand as he grins at Leon, then fades. "The rest is up to you."

On the roof, the helicopter blades create a harsh wind that pushes against them. Ivan steps onto the bird, and Zero with three soldiers, who surround Liz, wait their turn.

"Ivan!" Siggy screams.

He turns and smiles. "Sigs!"

"You rat shit bastard! How dare you?"

"Now, is that any way for an elegant woman like yourself to speak?"

Siggy glances back. "Disable the helicopter."

"Mom, we can't," Jenna says. "It'll crash below and kill civilians."

Siggy sucks her teeth as the helicopter rises, and then a smirk pulls at the corners of her lips. "Where will you go without a spaceship? I know you never found the one I hid away."

"I'm resourceful. You of all people should know," Ivan says.

"Ivan!" Zero grabs Liz and reaches up.

Ivan laughs and salutes as he goes higher and higher. "Sorry, kid." The helicopter swings around and faces the building. Ivan's voice booms out of speakers. *I'll leave you all with a parting gift.*

Two soldiers aim guns out of the helicopter and fire two capsules onto the roof. They tumble over the concrete and stop between Leon's group and Zero and Liz. Nobody has time to react.

Liz's and Zero's eyes widen. They're near the edge.

"Blowback!" General Flower yells.

Leon reaches out. "Liz!"

The capsules split, a coalescence of white noise, air, and flashes erupts. First, Leon goes blind. Then, he's thrown across the roof into a wall. When he comes to, it's like a million whistles are going off inside his head. The dark, blurry world distorts. He tries to look around, but even that slight movement makes him dizzy. Someone kneels next to him. He can't make out the face, but he reads their lips.

Don't worry, crow.

Leon grins, and then everything slips away, and he plunges into a spiraling abyss.

CHAPTER 69

MIA

April 18, 2146

Rhena and I travel down a dark corridor in the basement of Damascus Hotel. The air is stale and cool, and the blaze from Rhena's torch illuminates the giant cobwebs dominating the corners. Why would Raia want to meet here at this hour? We turn a corner and stop.

A cloaked person stands in front of a steel door. Was this a trap? I go for my sword, but the person pulls back their hood.

"Come," Raia says, and punches the passcode into a keypad. She pulls open the door, and leads us down a spiral, stone staircase. Blue torches burn along the walls as we curve downward until we reach the bottom, where a realistic statue of Damascus the Great in his prime stands guard.

The founder of Savages holds a sword high in the air, a triumphant war cry on his face that's surrounded by shoulder-length dreadlocks with golden rings around them. A black rod juts through the bridge of his nose, and he wears golden armbands around his forearms. One of his legs is forward, as if he's ready to pounce into battle.

The room has whirlpool patterns carved into the stone floor, and the ceiling makes me believe we've somehow traveled into a cave deep under the earth. Stalactites stab toward us.

Raia gestures toward a rectangular-shaped pool in the back of the area.

"The Great built this place. It is one of many from his time before Anomaly Day. It's called The Tears of Felicity." A surreal blue glow rises with the steam from the vibrant waters. "It's a healing pool. It's how the Great stayed alive for so long. I think this may help Cal like it did my great grandfather."

Raia brings a knife from under her cloak and slits her left palm, then kneels near the water and sticks her hand in. "Come."

Rhena and I gather around her, and the water pulses and swirls around Raia's hand, washing the blood away.

"The healing properties of these waters are beyond comprehension. My grandfather said it was an advance version of hydrotherapy." She pulls her hand out. The cut no longer exists. Her skin is smooth, as if she never slashed herself.

"So, Mia, what do you think?" she asks.

"It's amazing. I've never seen anything like it."

"Will you bring Cal here?"

"We must return to our camp tomorrow. How will I know if he's okay?"

Raia smiles. "You can leave guards of your choosing here if you wish. I promise, no harm shall come to him. He will die otherwise."

I look at the water, then at Raia. It's true what she says. Cal's clinging to life. Dana, Rhena, and I have been taking turns caring for him, and every day, I'm worried his breath will stop. It's a miracle he's lasted this long under these conditions, but I can't help but feel wary of Raia's offer. She knew Daniel would die and said nothing. How long did she know what would happen to Cal before everyone else did? Raia sees things no one else can, so to me, it's always like she's playing some game, and she's a step ahead of everyone else.

"Let me show you something." Raia grabs my hand. We go to the bottom of the stairs, and Raia points to the wall. Stretching down toward the pool is a row of drawings resembling hieroglyphics. Some pictures are scratched onto the wall with rock, others slathered on with paint. "When I was a girl, I recorded some of my visions."

She trails her finger along the row and stops after a vertical line that indicates the ending of one segment and the beginning of another. The first drawing is one of a stick man and woman facing away from one another, and the second shows a painting of a merging sun and moon hovering over the man and woman as they hold hands. The third portrays the woman holding a knife toward a sneering woman who also has a knife. In the next sketch, the man lies on the ground with arrows sticking out of him, and the woman cries over him. The last recording in this story shows the man floating above water with a powerful aura bursting around him.

"I've seen fragments of you and Cal since I was a child. That's why I believe you can beat the Almighty. That's why I want you to trust me. It's no coincidence that everything that's happened until now has happened. You're supposed to be here. You're one of the keys to stopping this endless bloodshed. The future is in your hands, Mia."

CHAPTER 70

LEON

May 27, 2146

Leon keeps hearing that same cry. That same hoarse voice. He appears in an alleyway, and that voice screams, "Every day is Anomaly Day! Every day is Anomaly Day. It's upon us! Bet they ain't tell you that, boy! But I see it! And it'll ruin us all! Do you have some points to spare?"

A man with a cold-burnt, red face and snow-dusted beard comes from the shadows, clinging to him. Leon shoves the guy away, then he's back in darkness, drowned in the smell of honey. His grandmother's voice echoes through the black.

This world, and the next, needs you, Leon.

And then Leon wakes. He clutches his head. It feels like someone's taken a hammer to his brain. He sighs and flips his pillow over to the cool side.

Leon pulls open the door to a dark room. A blue holo-screen covers the entire back wall showing North America. Around a glowing white table sits Siggy, General Wilde, General Flower, Liz, Jace, Jenna, Barnes, the Foundation leader, Desmond Worrell, and the holographic versions of General Freed, General Asaju, and General Campos.

Leon sits in between Jace and General Wilde.

General Wilde leans toward Leon, asking, *Were you up all night searching for Mia on the drones? I told you, she's safe.*

How do you know she's safe? You guys marked her as a criminal. How did she even leave Talon with all the security?

We'll talk about this later, Jackson. General Wilde sits back in her seat and nods at Siggy.

Siggy clears her throat. "Thank you everyone for attending this meeting. Has everybody reviewed the data from my scientists regarding Anomaly Day?"

Nods around the room.

"So, what are your thoughts?"

"I agree with the data mostly due to the weird occurrences. We know that throughout the Territories, the heatwaves have become more severe. We've been keeping a steady eye on the Atlantic Ocean and the Gulf of Mexico," General Campos says. "The Atlantic is rising again. Many of our sea posts since the last flood in 2045 have been evacuated. But in the Gulf, the sea is disappearing."

"Is there drone footage?" Desmond asks.

"Yes," General Campos answers, and on the holo-screen she shares a video of a giant whirlpool in the middle of the ocean with multiple smaller ones surrounding it. Blue-and-white seawater churns, funneling down. The video changes to pictures of the Gulf. Wreckage, trash, and dead marine life litter the soggy ground where the sea hasn't yet returned.

"That's unnatural," Barnes says. "The water should return. I've heard from Nomads that in the Pacific, the sea is receding, and the Runesians are preparing for a massive tsunami by building a wall along the west coast."

Siggy shakes her head. "A wall won't help them. Nothing humanity does can stop nature itself. The weather and climate are too unpredictable. Liz and Jace can attest to that from their experience in the Land of Ice. I think we should prepare to leave this planet."

Silence takes over the room. Leon thinks of his odd dream of the homeless man and his strange words. *Every day is Anomaly Day! Every day is Anomaly Day. It's upon us!*

"I think so, too," Leon says, and everyone focuses on him. "We're running out of food. The edible plants and animals everywhere are dying. I watched an entire pack of wolves die in the Land of Ice because they couldn't find any prey to eat."

"We can all agree." General Freed's image cuts in and out for a split-second. "But what is the plan? We don't have spaceships. We don't know what space is like. Are there enemies up there? What happened to your Optimus crews, Siggy? Simply knowing what we must do and doing it are two different things. There are too many unknown variables with the departure for space idea. We should hunker down here and do as the Runesians and prepare for the worse."

"We can't prepare for the death of a planet, general," Siggy says. "I believe there are people in space. I believe they took my people on the Optimus missions."

"What proof do you have?"

"Nothing concrete," Siggy says. "But six years ago, I sent Ivan's fiancé, Isabelle, on our last mission to space. Optimus VII. She was our head scientist and one of the smartest people I've ever known. Isabelle believed, too, that there were people in space, and wanted to confirm for herself. So, I let her go, and she met the same fate as the others, and never returned. Isabelle thought it was strange that through all the disappearances, not a single audio file or video log ever returned here, especially when we stayed online with the crews throughout their journeys. One moment they were there, and the next, they were gone."

General Asaju places a hand under his chin. "It's a possibility that the people up there in 2045 survived after Anomaly Day. The Republic for Freedom in the past has sent signals and drones up in attempts to contact potential life, and nothing's ever come of it. We all know that once Anomaly Day began, the natural disasters that ensued broke all contact with the space stations, hotels, and biodomes. My only counter to that is resources. How would they survive without the constant shipments from Earth?"

"You just said it," Barnes says. "The biodomes. They could grow food and create water. Granted, in 2044, when the first successful terraforming operations were completed on the moon and Mars, many reports claimed they were having trouble being self-sufficient, but that could have been propaganda. Personally, I don't believe it."

Siggy raises her hand. "So, let's put it to a vote now. We can start building more spaceships based on the model I have in hiding. We can figure out the statistics later, but I think we should at least start. All in favor of preparing to leave, please raise your hands." Leon, Liz, Jace, Jenna, General Wilde, General Asaju, and General Campos raise their hands. "Nine to three. Then it's settled. I'll have my engineers send blueprints to the RFF. Does anyone have any updates on my brother's whereabouts? It's pertinent we capture him."

"We found the helicopter wreckage near our northern border," General Wilde says. "So it's safe to assume he's now moving on foot. We've had units tracking him, but his trail disappeared in No Man's Land."

"He's heading for the Runesians." Siggy rests her elbows on the table and massages her temples. "This is bad. He knows too much."

"Why do you think he'd do that?" General Flower asks. "They're loose cannons. They could just kill him."

"Ivan's crafty. Smart. The Runesians are the only ones he can turn to now to get to space. He's not the type to do something if he doesn't think it'll work."

"It's been a month," Desmond says, looking around the room. "He may already be with them as we speak."

"A very high chance of that." Barnes stands. "I fear that two of our most powerful assets may be in jeopardy, and we should make it a priority to protect them. Ivan will certainly use that information to his advantage, and it could be a long-term weakness for the alliance and the health of humanity."

Silence. Leon and Jace share a glance.

"Me and Jace can protect ourselves," Leon says. "We don't need to be babysat."

"Your Gifts are valuable. Powerful. But more than that, your blood, your DNA, your very existence." Barnes's dark brown pupils enlarge. "We can't let either of you fall into the wrong hands. You both are keys to ending the Sickness and this war. I suggest a lockdown for the time being, if the generals and the Prime Minister will agree? You both can live on a Compound where you'll be surveilled 24/7. I'll run my tests, do experiments, and together we'll work on a cure. Only until things have calmed down, and I've deemed you both field ready."

Leon rises from his seat. "I don't need your permission to be in the field. I need to find my sister."

"Generals?" Barnes peers around the room and raises his hand. "Siggy?"

Leon watches distraught as all the generals and Siggy raise their hands in support of Barnes.

"Mom!" Jace shoots out of his chair.

Siggy shakes her head. "It's not safe here for you. Ivan has spies, and I know he'll target you. I also want to get rid of the Sickness. Your Gifts are volatile, and neither of you can control your abilities fully yet. Leon was out of for a week after using his Gift to help us and save Liz. You'll both be safer inside the Territories, and Barnes can help you learn more about your powers."

Jace, let's go. Now. Leon grabs Jace's hand and turns for the door, but when he reaches them, they don't open.

General Wilde rises behind them. "I'm sorry, Leon. We can't just let you do what you want. I hereby appoint Elizabeth Rodgers in temporary commandership of the Wolves platoon. When Barnes has deemed you stable and field ready, I'll let you off the Compound. I give you my word."

Leon pounds at the door, and Barnes approaches him like a kid eyeing candy. "I apologize but think about the pros. I'll help you further master your Gift, and I'll figure out everything there is to know about the Scorpilionitis. You'll be a savior of humanity."

Leon steps closer, getting in Barnes's face. "I knew I couldn't trust you. You just see me as an experiment."

"I see you as a potential cure, Leon." A smile widens on Barnes's face. "Cooperate and help me answer all my questions. I want to know where the Scorpilionitis bacteria originated and how?"

LANDI

January 14, 2041

My parents call me a miracle because I was born three months early. The doctors told them I was going to die. My older sister Mirza calls me a gem, but she's prettier than me. I don't know why she ignores all the boys at our school. My older brother, Basil, just calls me a brat, but Father calls him an asshole, which makes me giggle, so I let it slide.

Already, vehicle horns blare and Mumbians yell slurs to each other out of their windows. Usually, this annoys me, but today, I smile as I slip from under my covers and pull back the curtains to let the sunlight bless me. I dare not open my windows because the stench of exhaust from vehicles panting in traffic and spices from local market stands will invade the house, and Mum will be angry. Basil always opens his window, though. He likes the pong of this city and said to me once that he'd never leave. I can't relate. But I think he only said that because he has a girlfriend here.

A knock comes at my door. I grin as it creaks open. Mum comes in with Father's tall, rotund body failing to hide behind her petite frame—their pecan faces beaming, illuminated by a candle that protrudes from a large blueberry muffin.

"Happy birthday, Landi!" they both cheer.

I run to the muffin and grab the plate it sits on. I blow out the candle. "What did the twelve-year-old wish for?" Father asks.

I see Mirza behind them, sneaking by toward the bathroom. "For Mirza to get a boyfriend!"

They both burst into laughter, and Mirza pops her head into my room, sticking her tongue out at me. "You first!"

She wraps a long arm around our father. She's the same height as him. The guys like her athletic legs. She could be a model. I hope I'm as gorgeous as her when I'm fifteen. The tee shirt she wears says: Go Bengals! Our school's mascot. Mirza is the star volleyball player and the school's top math student.

"Thank you, guys," I say, lifting the muffin to my mouth. I bite into it, and the sweetness and slight tang of fresh blueberries melt on my tongue. I take another bite.

"Well, hurry up. Today's your day," Mirza says, half turning away.

I look up. "Is school and work canceled?"

Mum and Father smile, and he pulls her closer to him. "No. Mirza is excelling, and you're doing well. Today, we spend as a family."

"What about Basil?"

Mirza puts her face between our parents' heads, teeth bright as she cheeses my way. "You're too young to be worrying. He'll join us later after work! Let's go! Let's go!"

And the day is alive. I'm alive. I will admit, for the past year, I was feeling like I was dying. I think this city was killing me. The constant noise. The people. The trash. The poverty. Mirza and I usually can't walk down the streets without a beggar haggling us. I wish I could give them something, but my family isn't rich. My parents work hard to keep a roof over me and my siblings' heads. This might be their only day off this year besides certain religious holidays. I will be the happiest kid ever.

We walk through the markets, a rainbow of colors swirling and swimming through my vision from the sarees thousands of Indian women wear. I eat so many Gulab jamun doughnuts within our first two hours that I could fly off into the sky. We have a picnic in a green park where people meditate, pray, jog, and children play. At the rail station, Mirza goes off to buy some ice cream for me, while Mum and Father chat with a friend of theirs as we wait for the train. I glance up at a holo-screen. There's a world meeting today. The headline is in Marathi and then English under that.

It says: Will We Make It?

Now, that's strange. I step closer. Of course, I can't hear what all the world's politicians are saying, but I can read. My excitement wanes. They're just talking about the climate and natural state of the world again. We've had debates in class about this, and I'm sick of it. Is it getting too hot or too cold? Is the Indian Ocean lowering or rising? Where are the fish swimming to? I've concluded that nobody knows. So, why do we worry about it? By the time the world ends, we'll all be dead.

We go to places where tourists visit. Mirza knows they're my favorite. I love watching tourists. They fascinate me because they come from all over, and seeing them enjoying their time here reminds me that there's more than Mumbai.

A lady in a hijab excuses herself past me as my parents walk a little ahead, searching for a clear spot for us to gather as a family. Marine Drive is bustling with tourists and commoners alike. It's packed, but that's to be expected. Tonight, if someone pushes too hard, a person might tumble down the rocky edge. But no one wants to miss the shooting stars that will fly over the city. They're all I want to see for my birthday.

I'll wish to travel the world when I'm older. I'll go to every major city, write a forum or book or something about their similarities and differences, and rate them. Me and Mirza make fun of Americans near us as they point up at the constellations. I think American voices are so bland. There's no texture there.

A British man squeezes in beside us with a camera. "Excuse me."

Now, that's texture. The British man is sunburnt with curly, brown hair. He wears a purple collared shirt and above-the-knee khaki shorts. He aims his camera at the sky, and I glance around, again realizing how big this event must be. Netaji Subhash Chandra Bose Road is closed. Behind us, thousands of people are gathered.

Mirza elbows me, whispering over the background chatter. So many languages and accents. "These comets better make us all rich."

We laugh together. Someone grabs my shoulder, and Mirza tenses beside me, prepared to fight. We both turn, but it's Basil, his spiky, black hair glistening with sweat as he peers at me with affection. He has two jobs. I think he's saving up so he and his girlfriend can get their own place.

"There she is!" My older brother spreads his arms out.

I wrap around him. "Basil!"

"Happy birthday!" he says, picking me up and spinning me around.

I sniff him. "You stink."

He drops me. "You try working in a slaughterhouse." He grabs my hand and looks around. "Damned tourists."

Somehow, Mum hears that, and Basil flinches away from her glare. He slaps Father's sweaty back as we move toward the edge. "Old man, are you going to survive? You're dripping!"

Father grins at Basil. "Asshole. You smell like pig shit."

We all laugh as Mum lays into both of them. About thirty minutes pass, and then people begin to whisper. Basil watches his phone, waiting for the news.

The British man grins over at me. "Look up! They're coming!"

How does he know, though? He must have a link. They came out last year, but my family cannot afford such technology. I stand on the ledge, Basil clinging to the back of my shirt, so I don't fall. Mirza stands next to me. Everyone's head tilts back. My breath catches in my chest, and then I see the first one bust through a thin cloud. The release of oxygen fills me with exhilaration as the streaking star swims over the night sky, its fiery tail drumming and wiggling behind it, waving at me.

The comet is golden with bits of dark orange and red. I close my eyes and make my wish. Mirza laces her fingers through mine and squeezes. I make several more wishes, then Basil tugs at my shirt.

"Look! Landi! Mirza!"

My mouth drops. It's like hundreds of flaming eyes are blinking down at us. Everyone's in awe. They seem to be paused in the heavens, inspecting us. But then they get bigger, and my entire body tingles. My heart swings like a pendulum. Everything in me is telling me I must run. I slip off the ledge, but Basil and Mirza grab hold of me.

The awe switches off and is replaced by frenzied panic.

"Run!"

"Oh my god!"

Voices. Praying. Feet stomp the pavement and people shriek. Basil and Mirza drag me after them, and we join our parents, fleeing.

The British guy runs beside us, screaming. "It's a meteor shower! It's a meteor shower! Run! Run!"

The air shakes and the ground rumbles as the meteors crash into it. Smoke. Wails of terror. Babies cry. The meteors don't care. They rain on us, spitting flames. They smash us like the insignificant ants we are. People shove, and my grip on Basil and Mirza loosens. A mother with an infant shoulders into me, and I trip. People trample me, and I curl into a ball to protect my head.

"Landi!" Mirza and Basil try to come back for me, but the tide of people rages against them.

I unfurl myself when all the people have passed and pick myself up.

"Landi! Run!"

Basil and Mirza beckon me forth, and I scramble up, but the cry of a child stops me. I turn back, sprinting for a crying boy.

"Come, come!" I heft him into my arms, and a meteor the size of a basketball crashes near us.

Debris explodes out of it, and it batters me as I shield the kid. I ignore the pain digging into the back of my arm and run until I'm with my family. We take shelter in the nearest building and find the child's mother right away at the entrance. She thanks me relentlessly.

"You are a hero," she says, hugging me, and I grin.

I slip away to the bathroom before Mum has time to check me. Two meteorite shards are embedded into the back of my right arm like splinters. I try to get them out myself but can't.

The bathroom door opens. "Landi?" I open the stall, and Mirza's there. "Mum sent me. The paramedics are here. Are you okay?"

I turn my back to her. "Take these splinters out of my arm. I don't want mum to freak out."

Mirza does, and I turn around with my hand out.

"You want to keep them?" she asks.

"Yes. Promise me you won't tell our parents."

Mirza squints. "What are you up to, Landi?"

"Just souvenirs from the best birthday ever!"

We exit back out into the lobby and a paramedic inspects my arm, cleans it, wraps it, and clears us to go home once it's safe to go outside.

We sit together as a family, with me in the middle, watching the news of tonight's events. Mirza is on the left end, and Father has an arm wrapped around her. Basil is on the right end, his arm around Mum. We've all been silent, processing what happened. And what could have happened. We could have died, but a part of me is still excited by it all. Already, the entire world is talking about what happened. Other countries are coming over to investigate the meteors.

I yawn, and Father asks, "Are you tired, Landi?"

"I think so. I'm going to go to bed." I get up, and Father follows me.

"I can take myself to bed."

"Let me tuck you in," he says, placing a hand on my back. "I know you think you're too old now. Just one last time."

I nod, letting Father scoop me up in his strong arms.

Once I'm all snug in my bed, Father kisses me on the forehead. "Sleep tight, hero."

"Thank you for an awesome birthday. Don't ever forget this moment." I grin. "You'll never tuck me in again."

Father smiles, the furry mustache on his lips wriggling. "Of course, and you're welcome. I love you, Landi."

"I love you too," I say back, and Father steps out of the room.

My hands burn.

I throw the covers off me and stare at them in the moonlight. There's this constant stinging rippling through them as if fire ants are biting me. I don't want my parents to worry, so I creep out of my room and into the bathroom. I run cold water over my hands, grimacing. They throb now. The pain streaks up my arms, and I look at the agony crinkling across my face in the mirror, noticing something else.

There is blood streaming from both my nostrils.

I grab tissues to stop the bleeding. What is this? Is this because of the meteorite shards? Do I have a disease from space? The bathroom door flies open, and Basil rushes inside.

"What's going on?" he asks.

"I don't know!" I cry. "My hands are on fire!"

"What? Here, give me the tissue...." his voice fades away.

All the strength leaves my body, and my legs give out as something far worse than a migraine racks my skull. My brain feels like it's being mashed into a paste. I shriek out as my fingers blaze and itch. Basil presses the tissue to my nose, but the bleeding doesn't stop, and the pressure in my hands builds. The pain in my head crackles, and I can only whimper in Basil's arms.

"It's going to be okay!" Basil tells me.

I think my parents and Mirza come. They take me out into the common area.

"Call emergency services!" someone says.

"Her nose won't stop bleeding!"

What's this pressure in my hands? My head's going to explode. Something's coming. Something horrible. I curl into a ball.

"Landi!" It's Mirza's voice.

"Get—away!" I manage.

I clasp my hands together and put them between my legs. It hurts. Why won't this stop?

"Get some water for her hands!"

I must let it go. Whatever this is, I must release it, and then I won't be in pain. Basil comes back over with a bucket and places my hands in the water. The water bubbles as the pressure in my hands builds. I scream out, and the water glows green and erupts out of the bucket onto my face. When I open my eyes, my hands shimmer green. They hum with power.

"Guys, look!" I say and turn to my family.

All the sound drains from the world. I scramble back, and my gut flips over as I retch onto the floor.

My family is strewn about, skin welted and red as if something has burned them. Half of Basil's face is swollen and his left eye twitches. Vomit and blood dribble from Father's lip as he shivers on his side. I don't see Mum, but Mirza lies a few feet away, so I crawl to her first.

"Mirza! What happened?" I grab her arm and watch her skin sizzle from my green touch. I jerk away.

She looks terrified, the veins around her eyes swollen and dark. I rise, dizzy, my lit hands fighting the darkness shrouding our apartment.

"Landi…." I hear.

Mum rushes toward me, but I back away from her. "Don't touch me! There's something wrong with me!"

Half her face sags to one side, wrinkled and pruned.

"This is not your fault…." Mum says. She stumbles, holding her chest. "Run… Get far away from here… I love…." Mum vomits blood and falls. The last thing she does is reach out and grab my ankle as her body goes limp.

"Mum!"

The front door crashes open, and paramedics charge in with flashlights.

"Her hands are glowing," one of them says.

"Call the government."

I fall to my knees beside Mum. Now, I get it. My family is dead because I killed them with this strange power in my hands. Something hits me in the back, and the light in my palms shuts off. I fall over my mum. When I was younger, I would sit and listen to her heart pulse in her chest. Now, there is nothing.

Because she's dead. I murdered her.

I cry as my body stiffens. I don't feel anything, but I can see around me. I am lifted from the ground and put on a stretcher. I want to stay with my family, but maybe this is for the best. I'm a monster. There are people in suits here now—the kind of suits they wear when they don't want to catch a plague. I watch the night sky and pray.

Please take me away. Take me to where my family is so I can apologize and tell them how much I love and miss them already. But the stars don't answer. The people in suits crowd around me, tinted glass reflecting someone I don't recognize. Her eyebrows and hair are frosted over a silverish white. My hair was dark before. What is happening to me?

A suit turns to her partner, saying, "She's infected."

I wish my lips would move. I'd ask these suits to kill me.

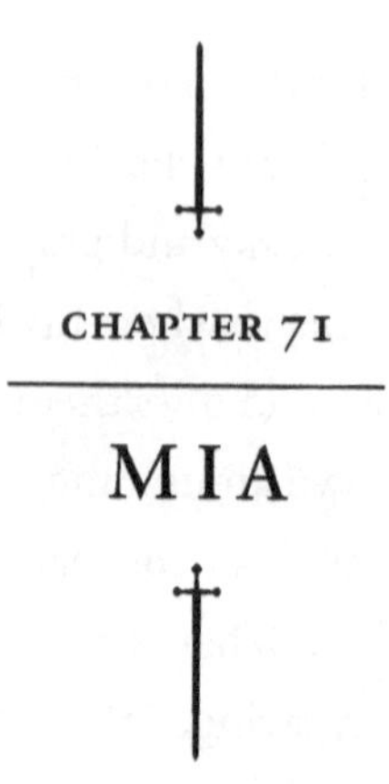

CHAPTER 71

MIA

August 29, 2146

Butterfly and Sannvi practice their sword swings in the middle of the junkyard. Butterfly's been around for the past month. She insisted on assisting in delivering the twins when they come and helping me train. I rub my belly as I rest in a beach chair. It looks like it's about to burst, and I wish it would, but I need to prove Cal wrong. The heat has been driving me crazy, and carrying this extra weight isn't ideal.

Jade comes up behind me with a cold towel and places it on the back of my neck. "Rhena says you're due any moment."

"I have to win the bet I made with Cal," I say, patting my stomach. "You brats stay put for a few more days."

Jade chuckles. Her birthday was August tenth, and again she's sprouted. No longer is she the little eleven-year-old girl I found in the pit field, but a teenager. After what happened at the Conclave, I made her promise never to keep secrets from me again. I don't want her in harm's way just because she thinks I'm heaven sent. The late Damascus the Second told her if she won, she'd be invited to join his Chimera Guard when she was fifteen, and I would be under his full protection.

"I think I agree with Rhena," Jade says as Butterfly and Sannvi come over.

"It's hot!" Sannvi cries as he wipes sweat from his brow.

"Go get some water," Jade says.

"What are you, my mom?" Sannvi scowls, shoulder bumping her as he walks away.

Jade smirks and doesn't let Sannvi's immaturity get the best of her. Or at least that's what she wants me to think. I see how her hand twitches near one of her daggers.

Butterfly says, "He reminds me of Glare when he was younger."

I shift uncomfortably. I find it so hard to believe that Butterfly and Glare are siblings. They're complete opposites.

Butterfly undoes her braid and shakes her hair free. The dark tangles of her sweat-drenched blond hair sticks to her rosy cheeks. She takes off her shirt, and I swear everyone in the clearing gawks her way. It's hard not to stare, but I tear my gaze away from her as she puts on another shirt.

"Mia, I need to talk to you. Care for a walk?" Butterfly asks.

"Yeah, sure," I say, and Butterfly helps me out of the chair.

We walk through the junkyard to a less-traveled area. Cars, trash, and furniture tower around us on both sides. Butterfly stops and kneels before me.

"What are—"

"I want to apologize for my brother's actions. Everything. I know it doesn't mean much now, but we can't choose our family." She looks up at me, blue eyes fierce with solemnity. "Can I request something of you?"

I nod.

"Allow me to handle Glare. I know you want his head, but he's my responsibility."

"Glare's dangerous. Letting him live could ruin what we're trying to achieve."

Butterfly rises, takes my hands, and squeezes. "I will make sure he never hurts you again. If death should come to him, it should be by my hand. I'm asking this of you as a friend."

Who am I to deny Butterfly her brother? I want Glare dead, but if she says she'll take care of him, I trust she will.

"Fine," I say with a smile, pulling away. We continue walking side by side. "But I want to see his face after I take the Almighty's head."

Butterfly nudges me with her elbow. "Somebody's confident."

"I rather be confident than scared. If the Almighty wins, can I trust that you'll take Jade, Sannvi, and the twins to the RFF?"

"He won't win," Butterfly says. "Not against us."

"That won't be allowed. It's a deathmatch."

"He'll allow it. His pride will be his downfall."

"Why would he put himself at a disadvantage?"

Butterfly grins. "The Almighty's an old-world misogynist. His beliefs are outdated, and he doesn't take you seriously. We can use that against him."

I stop, placing a palm on my stomach. "We could both die."

The twins could grow up without a mother. Without me here to protect them, what will happen to them? The Almighty would never stop hunting them. The thought of my kids living a life on the run brings tears. I don't have a choice. The Almighty must fall, or my children will suffer.

"Mia?" Butterfly rests a palm on my shoulder.

"I'm fine. Just pregnant. Emotio—" Water streams down my legs. I clutch my stomach, moaning as a deep contraction pains me.

"Let's get you to Rhena." Butterfly helps me forth. "Come on, just breathe, and walk. Take it easy."

But I can't. The twins want out. I scream, my pain being drowned out by the ominous bellow of the Horn.

"Attack!" someone yells in the distance.

Pain ripples across my gut, and Butterfly lowers me to the ground. The Horn sounds again. Weapons clang against each other. Who's attacking? How did they get inside with our barrier up?

"Go," I say through gritted teeth. "I'll be okay!"

Butterfly whips out her sword. "I'm not leaving you."

Another contraction. I groan, and then old metal dents somewhere above us. Three masked Savages hop down the mound of junk.

"Mia. You must stand!" Butterfly drags me back.

I force myself up just as a Savage slashes at me with his sword. I kick out at him, and Butterfly pushes me behind her and plunges her blade through his gut.

The other two Savages circle Butterfly. She clashes with one of the Savages, and kicks back at the other, spins, and aims for the Savage's throat. The Savage ducks and shoots in, stabbing Butterfly in the side as she tackles her to the ground. No! I pull out my dagger—

I crash to a knee in pain. I think my stomach might split open.

"Mia!" I look back. Rhena and Jade are running toward us.

Butterfly wrestles for dominance with the female Savage. The male Savage sneaks into Butterfly's blind spot, sword ready to strike.

"Butterfly!" I scream.

Metals whirrs past my head, and then I see throwing knives sticking out of the male Savage's neck and chest. He falls to the side.

"Mia." Jade crouches next to me with Rhena.

I hear a crack, and then the sounds of struggle die out. Butterfly makes sure the three Savages are dead, poking each of them in the throat with her blade. She comes over, holding her side, nodding at Jade. "Thanks for the help."

Rhena looks between my legs. "Jade, go get Stella, some towels, and hot water. They're coming now!"

ϙ

The twins are born three minutes apart. Rhena forces me to rest. Seagull and Butterfly assure me they have everything under control. I don't think about who died when I stare into my children's eyes.

Ari is the oldest. He's a bundle of cuteness, with dark curls and light skin like mine. He has Cal's hard brown eyes.

Arria has Cal's bronze skin, and dark, curly hair like her brother's. Her smile is full of dimples that melt every horrible thing inside me, and her eyes are pools of honey like mine.

These lives came out of me. These lives are the future, and Glare, the Almighty, or some other clan, just tried to rip that future away.

I look up at Dana and Rhena. "Hold them."

"Mia, you should rest. It's only been a few hours. We've captured a few of the attackers, and the rest are dead. Everything is fine now."

"I am chieftess here. Take them. Please."

Rhena and Dana each take one of the twins. Sorely, I rise.

"They killed Marco," Rhena tells me as I hobble toward the tent flap.

I grimace as I push out into the sun. Seagull, Butterfly, Phoenix, Jade, and Sannvi are in the middle of the junkyard. They look at me with concern as I approach.

"You shouldn't be walking!" Jade ducks under my arm, helping me forth.

"I'm fine," I say. "Has word been sent to Raia?" Everyone nods. "Which clan? Raia forbid—"

Lero interrupts us. His larger eye is puffy and bloodshot. He's been using. He crashes to the ground at my feet. "Chieftess, I'm so sorry! This is all my fault. Marco was murdered because of me!"

"Rise," I say.

Lero hangs his head lower. "You can have my heart!"

"I said rise, Lero. It's fine. They took us by surprise."

Lero rises and digs into his pocket. "I have one of their eyeballs as a gift. Please accept it?"

"Lero, we have—"

"Please!"

I hold out my palm. This is gross, but it's my job to ease my clan's pain. This isn't Lero's fault. He drops the eyeball into my palm. It's soft and squishy.

—a shot of pain zaps down my spine as metal slides into my gut. I drop the eyeball and look down at Lero, who tears a blade out of my flesh. He shanks me again and twists the blade into my side. "Glare wants you to know that you'll never be safe!"

Jade tries to stab him, but he smacks her to the ground. I stumble forward and latch onto him as he yanks the blade out again. Seagull and Butterfly pull him away before he can stab me a third time and disarm him. Butterfly snaps one of his arms and throws him down.

Lero cackles, and Seagull kicks him in the face. "Ya piece of shit!"

I crash to my knees, holding both my wounds as blood spills through my fingers. Then I fall to the side. Jade and Sannvi rush over to me, placing their hands over mine.

"Mia!" they both cry.

"Why?" I say as the world grows darker and darker.

"Rhena!" Phoenix screams.

Lero yells, "For the Almigh—"

Someone kicks his teeth out.

I've been far too complacent. That's why this happened. I didn't do my due diligence as the chieftess of Calamity Clan. I should have rooted out all of the traitors. Of course, there were more, and of course, Glare would use them to spite me. He'll never leave me at peace. He doesn't care about my deathmatch with the Almighty, he wants to make me suffer.

Coldness blisters over my skin, and I blink as the sky flees, drifting farther and farther away. I sink into the earth. This is what death feels like.

Like falling.

"Mia, don't di—"

Jade's and Sannvi's voices fade, and I plummet, like a bird with broken wings. I plunge through reality into an unknown land where nothing exists.

CHAPTER 72

MIA

I hang in an abyss of nothingness. Numbness crawls over my being until the sounds of glass shattering somewhere overhead pull my attention. Panels of my existence burst into oblivion. The day Kirk first praised me for me shooting a perfect on my marksmanship test explodes into crystal fragments that rain upon me. My being becomes colder, and my memory of Kirk fades. His voice. His sweaty back on our runs around Compound Marigold. His glasses, and how he always smelled of cinnamon. Who was Kirk?

A panel of a sword skewering a man I think I should know, but can't place the name shatters, and some primal instinct kicks me into action. I swim up through the blackness as another panel floats above.

The day Leon and I snuck out of the Compound Marigold and played in the surrounding forest. The way his hand felt. The way his smile spread warmth through my veins. The panel erupts into a bunch of shards as I try to grasp it. I kick up, but my memories fly higher, breaking, bursting, and vanishing. People. Places. Feelings. Gone forever.

The day Jade and Sannvi clung to me after I survived my deathmatch against the Ogor. Gone. Who were those two children? Why did I try to save them? The night I Unified with Cal explodes into this space, joining its emptiness. All the kisses he and I shared. All the times his breath tickled my soul. All the times his arms felt like the most secure place in the world. Why did I grow to love this man? How did he get that gruesome scar? Cal's face splinters and everything about him gets sucked into this hollow Hell.

One final panel floats by before me. No! Not them. I hug the panel that shows Ari and Arria in my arms. I can't lose them. It's my responsibility as their mother to protect them, and if I'm dead, that's impossible. If I lose everything that makes me who I am, I'll become a shell, and one with this black void where souls come to die.

The panel tries to break, but I squeeze it and hold the pieces together. I won't let my existence sink here. I refuse to let myself be erased and lose everyone I love! I kick up and up and up until a light shines down upon me. Cracks snake through the darkness, and as I rise closer, the fractures web out. I push my hand up, and this purgatory disintegrates....

¢

Air flows into my lungs, and I sit up, coughing. A hand touches my back and another puts water to my lips.

"Thank you, ancestors," someone says.

The blurry faces around me come into focus.

"She's back! Sannvi, come on!" Jade squeals.

"Mia, can you hear me, child?" Rhena asks. I nod and go to feel my stomach, but Rhena stops me. "You will be fine. The wounds had poison, but it was a manageable one. I imagine Glare only wanted to antagonize you. He can't kill you before your deathmatch with the Almighty."

"How long has it been?" I ask.

"Four days."

"Ari and Arria?"

"They're safe. Sleeping," Jade says.

I take in the surrounding faces. Rhena. Jade. Sannvi. Dana. Stella. Seagull. Phoenix. Butterfly. None of them are safe here.

"Rhena, send word to Raia," I say. "Tell her we're coming to Damascus. All of us."

"Yes, Chieftess. Please don't push yourself too hard while I'm gone." Rhena leaves the tent.

"Where is he?"

"We strapped him to the roof of a car so he can melt," Seagull says with a smile. "I think he's still kickin'."

"Take him off, and someone bring me my sword."

Near the gate of our junkyard, the clan gathers behind me as I limp toward Lero, who stands between Seagull and Phoenix, a toothless grin on his face. His one big eye is black, swollen, and closed.

"Knew that wouldn't kill you!" Lero spits blood at my feet.

I place my sword to his throat. "Your heart is mine, remember?"

"My heart belongs to Gla—"

I slice off Lero's ear and he shrieks out, clutching it. Seagull kicks the back of his knees, and he wallows in the dirt. I place my foot on Lero's chest. "Your heart is mine. Mine to take whenever I please! But for today, you will run back to Glare and tell him…." I kneel, pull Lero up by the scruff of his shirt, and whisper, "Cal is alive."

I grin at the disbelief on his face.

"You lie!" he yells.

I shove him back down and rise. "I have no need. Tell Glare to watch his back. We'll be hunting him from here on out. Go, the gate is open. Get as far as you can before I let the hounds loose."

Seagull and Phoenix pull Lero to his feet and push him toward the gate. He stumbles and turns back toward us. I sheathe my blade and hold my palms up. Three of my clanspeople place leashes in my hands, and the dogs on the other end yank toward Lero as they bark and snarl.

Phoenix tosses Lero a dagger. "Better hurry. They're hungry."

"Sit!" I command, and the dogs do. Drool stretches from their mouths as they whine.

Lero sprints out of the gate and through the swampy field. When he's halfway across, I undo the dogs' leashes.

"Go!"

They kick up dust as they bound off in pursuit, and I hurry onto the rampart. The orange sun hangs over the trees that Lero finds cover within. Rhena, Seagull, Dana, Phoenix, and Butterfly join me.

"What now?" Dana asks.

"We pack up. Phoenix, you'll lead a search party for Glare into No Man's Land."

"What kind of search party, Chieftess?" he asks.

"A search and destroy. You leave tomorrow afternoon. Do whatever it takes to bring me his head."

He pounds a fist against his chest. "My heart is yours. I won't fail you."

"What about the blood oath we made with Raia?" Butterfly asks. "We all agreed to not fight amongst each other."

"Glare didn't. Nor did the Almighty. They're excluded. I'm sorry, Butterfly, I take back what I said."

"The queen will never allow it. She'll ord—"

"I don't care! Glare has tried to kill me several times now. I am done playing these games with him. I'll accept whatever consequences may come my way, and I know he's your brother, but he is ours to kill. He's hurt this clan too many times."

"He has." Rhena rests a palm on my shoulder. "But Butterfly has a point. And I think acting like this makes you more like him."

I shrug her off and turn away from them. "Then so be it." Lero's wails are music to my ears, and my smile matches many of my clanspeople below as they cheer. "Calamity! I vow here and now to end all our enemies. No one will ever hurt us again without facing the most severe repercussions. This I swear to you!"

I take out my stone dagger, slit my palm, and raise my fist out in the air toward them. "My heart is yours! Now and always!"

Calamity Clan roars as my blood rains upon them.

THE END

Prepare for book two of the
Anomaly Rising series: *No Man's Land*

ACKNOWLEDGEMENTS

There are so many people to thank for this book's completion, but I will try to keep it brief. First and foremost, I want to thank all my writing peers and co-authors for working with me to develop this novel to what it is now. Without your feedback, my characters' lives would not be able to be experienced by so many readers. Next, I'd like to thank Garrett Bruen, one of my old Savannah College of Art and Design professors. He read my book, certain excerpts, query letters, and synopses. He responded to questions and emails. He was there for me when I needed him, and to this day I still don't quite understand why, but I appreciate the help. Garrett, I appreciate you. Thank you so much. You are truly someone that touched my heart.

Next are the beta readers who read a premature version of the novel and gave me much needed feedback. Thank you, Matthew Montalvan, my dear brother. Thank you, Melvin Umana, my ride or die. Thank you, Max Sweet, my fellow groomsman. We're friends for life now. Thank you, Val Zeigler, my Bee-In-Arms. Thank you, Luis Calleros, my fellow C Block Inmate. (That's an inside joke only a few will understand). Thank you, Tiara Crown, my fellow creative and hustler. My editor, Chad Rhoad, also deserves a mention. He guided me to further develop my novel and helped me realize that I apparently love overusing gerunds. Thank you for your expertise and knowledge of the craft. Thank you to my cover designer, Rafal

Kucharczuk, who listened to my requests and made my vision a reality. I appreciate your hard work and your thoughts about my book.

I'd like to give thanks to the family and friends that supported and believed in me. Thank you for listening to me babble on about my book. Thank you for always asking how it was coming. Thank you for giving me encouragement. All those small moments added up and helped make this possible.

And lastly, my characters. Many think I'm crazy when I say I can go to some other place deep within me and talk to you guys. That I've met you guys. That we've sat and talked over tea, walked the streets of your world, and been on crazy adventures. It brings tears to my eyes that you guys choose me to tell your stories. That you trusted me. Forever, we are bonded, and I love you guys and thank you the most.

This mission is not over. My heart is yours.